READER COMMENTS

"Your book is compelling to read. I could identify with so many aspects of growing up in a small rural community. You have referred to our German-Russian background throughout the book." (MW)

"Congratulations! It's a very accessible and sweet story. And I found it so interesting to hear about the history of the German Russians. A piece of history I knew nothing about. Thanks so much for opening it up!" (NT)

"I thoroughly enjoyed it, every page. Your story of the main character's problems of growing up, resolving feelings of her ancestry and untimely deaths, kept things flowing. You worked in all the details of the language and the customs. Even though it is your fictionalized ethnic story, it is still a story many of us felt growing up. In other words your story speaks to all, in a far wider audience that just German Russians. A job well done." (MF)

"The first chapter put me back in South Dakota. My grandparents were children of German immigrants, so I smiled at the same German words used by them and my mother from time to time. It's a moving piece of work. I found that I connected with it on many levels. I can see parallels in the story with my years growing up. It brought back many memories of my own family, my experiences, and the small town cast of characters. And yes, I even have to admit to shedding a tear. I guess a Renaissance man such as myself doesn't find any shame in that. You packed a lot of things that stir ones emotions into that one novel." (GM)

"What a delightful book to read. I enjoyed it for its location, its familiar landscape, customs, and people. The characters were believable--those I liked and those I couldn't like. When I finished the book, my thoughts were, I'd like to know about their lives after this book ends." (JB)

"A story about forgiveness. How parents do the best they can to raise a child under adverse conditions." (DF)

"It brought me to tears. I could relate to the things German Russian because that is my culture. I hadn't thought of those things in years." (SS)

"You have a gift. I was taken back in time with all your wonderful easy to read descriptions of a time and a place in the past." (RC)

"After reading your book, I was 16 years old again living in the small town. You took me back in time. So many memories." (BE)

"I grew up in Minnesota and your book brought back many memories of living on a farm in a small rural community. I enjoyed it very much." (AB)

"It brought back memories of being raised in South Dakota on a sugar beet farm - all the work, the food, the gardens, the fair, the factory in Belle Fourche." (DB)

A Stranger to Myself

Also by this author: Stories

Justice and Anna's Quilts

Published in the anthology:
We Remember
Stories of the Germans from Russia
Copyright 2006
Compiled and Edited by
Timothy J. Kloberdanz and Rosalinda Kloberdanz

Grandpa's Violin

Published in the anthology:
Treasured Tales
of Germans From Russia
Copyright 2008
Compiled and Edited by
Velma Jesser, Ph.D.

They Called It Noah's Ark

Upcoming publication:

These stories have also been published in:

The Journal of the
American Historical Society
of Germans from Russia.

A STRANGER TO MYSELF

Judy Frothinger

To my niece, Vicky

Love,

Aunt Judy

A Stranger to Myself is a work of fiction; however, the places in this story are real towns in South Dakota. The author has given some locations fictitious names. The characters and their actions are products of the author's imagination. The historical events are accurate.

Cover design by Mike Frothinger

Printed in the United States of America

ISBN 978-1-450-56968-2

Second Printing: March 2010

Printed by:
CreateSpace
An Amazon.com Company

To order additional copies
Visit the website at:
www.judyfrothinger.com

To the memory of my parents

Mollie (Hoffman) Elenberger

1907 - 1974

Alexander Elenberger

1907 - 1984

ACKNOWLEDGEMENTS

Thank you to the staff at the Belle Fourche Library for providing research materials, and microfilm from the *Belle Fourche Post* for the years 1957-1958.

Thank you to those who did editing for me: Joan Steiger, Margaret Freeman, and my husband, Mike.

Thank you to my husband, Mike, for all of his encouragement and counsel. I love you, Mike.

CHAPTER 1

March 16, 1957

The moment she knocked on Anna's door, her twisted emotions unraveled like a braid. Marka watched Bodie drive away in his pickup and giggled at how the inside of it smelled like aftershave. He was trying to cover the smell of his unwashed hair. She placed her suitcase on the freshly swept concrete porch and then knocked on Anna's door again. The cold air stung her lungs as she took in a deep breath and let it out in small white puffs. Marka peered through a slit in the curtain on the inside of the storm door. Where was Anna? She studied her reflection in the polished glass. She looked haggard after the long trip from Denver.

Anna's house had always been her safe haven. The thought of this made her cry. The raw March wind blew across her face and stung her tear-filled eyes. She wiped the icy droplets away with the wool scarf Anna had sent for her twenty-fifth birthday.

Finally, the door swung open, and there stood Anna with outstretched arms. She clasped Marka's hands in hers and pulled her into the front room. Marka leaned down to kiss Anna's soft, warm cheek. "It's so good to see you. It's good to be home."

The afternoon sun drifted into the room though lace curtains and Venetian blinds, making random designs on the cream-colored walls. Marka set her suitcase beside a chair, unbuttoned her heavy winter coat, then took off her gloves, and stuffed them into the deep pockets. The house smelled of freshly baked bread.

"Take your coat off and sit down," Anna said, slowly lowering her body into a green and gold brocade armchair. Her feet settled into the worn spots on the carpet. "Let me look at you. It's been so long." Anna repositioned the round, steel-rimmed glasses resting on the bridge of her nose. "I saw you drive up in Bodie's pickup. I had to take my *kuchen,* cake out of the oven. I thought I better do it while I remembered, you know, before we started yakking. Well, anyways, I made it just for you. Ach, I'm talking too much. How was your trip?"

"The plane ride was —"

Anna interrupted. "We had a thaw yesterday, and then last night, a quick freeze. Makes such nasty ruts in the roads. It's been a cold winter. *Ach, Ja*, Oh, yes, what did you say about the plane ride?"

Marka couldn't help chuckling over her aunt's excitement. "The ride was bumpy—" Marka waited to see whether Anna was going to interrupt again, "and being the first time I flew, well, I was a little nervous. A woman in the seat next to me tried to make me feel better telling me everything would be okay."

"That's something I never was crazy about doing. Flying in an airplane," Anna said. "You'd never get me up in one of those things. So, anyhow, about the roads. Were they icy?"

"The highway was clear from Rapid City to Clayton so the bus made it through fine. Bodie had to drive slowly in town because, yes, the roads are icy."

"That's one thing I hate about this time of year. It warms up, and you think spring is on its way, and then the weather turns cold. Well, anyways, I'm glad you're here safe and sound."

"Me too, Anna."

"You know, ever since you called and said you was coming, well, I don't know what to make of it." Anna cocked her head and raised an eyebrow. "I've been kind of worried. You wouldn't come back just out of the blue, especially this time of year. It's usually something serious that brings on a move like this. Are you sick?"

"No, Anna."

"Money problems?" Anna probed. "Did you lose your job because they found out you're German Russian? I hear that's happening to people all over the country because of what that Senator McCarthy is doing." Anna fidgeted in her chair. "It makes our people afraid to tell anyone they came from Russia. During the war, we was all worried about being German, and now this. They call us dirty Rooshians. We are so afraid they will think we're communists."

"Gosh, Anna, I don't know what you're talking about. What do you mean we came from Russia? Mom always told me we are German."

"Ach, never mind what I just said. Forget it. I'm *fericht,* crazy. Just a crazy old woman." Anna sat quiet for a moment and then blurted, "A man. You're having man problems."

"No! I just wanted to come home," Marka fibbed. There was no way she was going to tell her aunt the truth. Anna had never married; never even had a boyfriend. How was she to understand? Besides, this was different from when she was a child and had scuffed a knee. Anna would put a band-aid on her wound. This wound was too deep.

It would be difficult to keep this secret from Anna. She knew how to pry things out of her. When she was a little girl, her aunt's inquisitions prompted her to tell lies. She'd stand before Anna with her hands held behind her back, fingers crossed, and she'd tell wild tales.

"*Madchen*, girl. You look far away." Anna sat quietly studying Marka's face. "How about some *kuchen*? It should be cool now. It's your favorite. Cherry. First thing I'm going to do is fatten you up." Anna's eyes sparkled. "You're so skinny."

Anna unfolded her hands and pressed them against the arms of the chair. She stiffened her legs, gave herself a boost, and then pointed herself in the direction of the kitchen. "Put your suitcase in your bedroom and hang up that stylish coat of yours. Last month, I sewed one just like that for Frieda Wieizel."

Marka glanced at the dining room table piled high with fabric and paper patterns. A dress dummy was tucked back into the corner of the room. Marka remembered how Anna had always been aware of fashion when she sewed for others, because those patterns were what her clients brought her. "I see you're still a seamstress."

"Yah, I still do sewing. Not like I used to. My eyes water a lot and the arthritis in my hands is giving me fits." Anna shuffled into the kitchen, the floorboards squeaking beneath her small feet.

Marka walked down the hall to the bedroom. She set her suitcase next to the chest of drawers and sat on the bed. The room was decorated with the same humble things: a crocheted dresser scarf, Dotted-Swiss curtains, and a latch hook rug with a floral border that protected the hardwood floor. She moved her fingers across the familiar, blue, chenille bedspread and thought about the many nights she slept on this lovely soft mattress. How no one but her used this sturdy bed with its wide footboard and finial posts. It

3

made her warm inside to remember those nights she and Anna spent making fudge and popcorn balls. And Anna had shown her how to embroider dishtowels too.

Marka opened the closet door and looked for hangers so she could start to unpack. She noticed marks on the door jam and touched the grooves made by a hard lead pencil. Squinting her eyes, she made out the numbers: 10-4/1, 12-4/6, 14-5/6. She remembered Anna bragging, "You're going to be tall like your *Grossmutter,* Grandmother Katherina. Only fourteen years old and you are already well over five foot."

Anna stooped to pour cream into a small dish sitting by the refrigerator.

"Oh, Anna. You still have Sasha?"

"Yah, she'll be coming to the door. She always has her cream this time of day. Sit," Anna touched the back of the kitchen chair. "I was so happy when you called and said you was coming. What's it been now, five years or so, yah?" Anna filled the percolator with water, spooned coffee into its basket, and placed it on the hottest spot of the cook stove. She held the coffee cups to her eyes to make sure they were clean, then sat across from Marka at the square Formica table.

"It has been seven years, Anna."

"*Gott im Himmel.* God in Heaven. Seven years. When you left Ridley you had big plans. Well, I think city life would be like living in a zoo. So, what are you going to do now? And what are you going to do with your folks' house? Why don't you sell it and live here with me."

"I was thinking of moving back in," Marka said, reaching across the table to touch Anna's small soft hands. "I've missed you, my *Vasia*, my Aunt."

Anna thrust her shoulders back and tilted her head. "So, you do remember some German words," she laughed and scooped a large slice of *kuchen* onto a plate and placed it in front of Marka.

Marka sniffed the sweet cake, and then took a bite. "Um, this tastes good. As good as I remember." She licked her fingers. "Anna, I realize how I abandoned the house, and—you. And I'm sorry for that, but after the folks were killed, well, I had to leave everything as it was. Having them gone was hard enough. Some

4

people sell everything, every reminder of the person. I couldn't do that."

"*Ach*, Oh, that accident was uncalled for. The hay truck must have been going down the wrong side of the road. Let's not talk about that right now," Anna took a deep breath. "As a rule I never stick my nose in other people's business, but I do want to know what you are going to do with that house. You should have rented it out. You could have made a little money."

"Bodie told me there are things that need to be fixed. He said the roof is leaking, and the house needs paint. The water heater is completely rusted out," Marka sighed.

"To be truthful with you I never go over there. I just can't get used to your folks being gone."

"Anna, I have a confession. It's something Mom said right before she died."

The water in the percolator began to boil. Anna got up from the table and pulled the pot to a cooler spot on the stove.

"I never told you this, but there is another reason for keeping the house. Mom told me there was something valuable hidden in it. She was in so much pain. I didn't want to ask her a lot of questions. So, I'm not sure what she meant."

"*Ach, du lieber,* Oh, my gosh, she never told me anything like that. It had to be those pain medicines they were giving her. She was out of her head."

"Every time I think of her—Oh, I hated seeing her like that. I tried to put the whole thing out of my mind."

"Why didn't you come back and look?" Anna filled their cups with coffee. "It would have drove me nuts."

"Bodie said he's interested in buying the house if I decide to sell."

Anna's eyes widened. "Ach, Bodie buying a house! Carl would never stand for Bodie being on his own. Ever since he came back from Korea with that bum hip he's lived with his dad above the store." Anna wiped a spoon with her thumb then stirred cream into her coffee. "Anyways, Bodie is kind of slow and as lazy as a dog who sits down to bark. How could he take care of a house?"

"He's been taking care of it all these years." Marka took a sip of her coffee. "It's still standing, right?"

5

"Well, not such good care. A couple months ago a water pipe broke under the kitchen sink. Bodie forgot to shut the water off outside and we had a freeze. I heard about it from Sophie who happened to be in the store when he was telling Carl. I called him right away and told him he better get it fixed and clean up the mess." Anna chewed the inside of her cheek. "And, I didn't tell you. I didn't want you to worry."

"Anna, it's all right. Bodie told me about it."

"Hope you didn't pay him too much. That sure sounds strange to me, him wanting your house. On the one hand if you sold, you could get out from under it. You can live with me."

Marka scraped cake crumbs off to the side of her plate with her fork. Thoughts whirled inside her head like eddies in a river. She was going to have to make so many decisions.

"So, *kindchen*, child, you have come back to stay, yah? You know you'll never make the kind of money around here you made in Denver. You'll have to work in Clayton.

"I'll be fine, Anna."

"I hope you'll make out all right. To think that when you graduated high school you couldn't wait to get away from here, and now you're back."

"I know. I've learned a lot since then, Anna. Life doesn't always go the way you want it to."

"Something in your house? I can't believe it. Ach, your mom had to be full of those medicines." Anna raised her eyebrows and squinted. "You better not tell anyone what you just told me. In Ridley, you tell one person and the whole town knows."

"You're too suspicious," Marka laughed. "All German Russians are going to lose their jobs because the government thinks they are communists, and Bodie's going to cheat me out of something. I just had a funny thought. Dad robbed a bank and the walls are stuffed with money?"

"*Ach, Gott*, Oh, God." Anna burst into laughter.

"Let's go over to the house. Come on, Anna. I can't wait until tomorrow."

"It won't be light out much longer and the power is off over there. Let's go over tomorrow after church." Anna reached into her apron pocket, took out a photo, and held it out for Marka to see. "This is a picture of you when you was a little girl. Ever since you called and said you was coming, I've carried it with me." Anna laid her hand on Marka's shoulder. "When you was little, well, you was like my own daughter. *Glina madchen*, little girl." The lines in Anna's face deepened. "Your mother always sent you over to me when she was busy. She was always so busy."

Marka's throat tightened. A tear welled up in her eye; she quickly blinked it away. She rested her elbow on the table and cupped her chin in her hand. Yes, she had spent much of her childhood with Anna who had been more like a mother than an aunt. And she always felt guilty because she wanted to be Anna's little girl and stay at her house forever. Marka loved being with her aunt. And Anna was the one who was always there when Marka needed her.

Sasha meowed at the door. Anna let her in. The cat paced back and forth between the two of them, then went over to the bowl and drank her cream.

"Tell me what you want out of life," Anna patted Marka's cheek.

"I want to be happy. I want to belong in this town again."

"There isn't any reason you can't. You'll be glad you came back. People in a small town stick together; help each other out. The neighbors will be happy to see the house alive again." Anna's face grew serious. "Some people say they have seen flickers of light at night. Ghosts! They call it the haunted house. Ach, I tell them 'It's just some kids snooping around with flashlights. You know how kids are.' Talking about this does remind me of a story about a couple who thought they had a ghost in their house. Well, anyways, they would leave food on the table at night and in the morning, it would be gone."

Marka's eyes blinked hard. "You're kidding, right?"

"No, that's the truth," Anna laughed.

Marka knew she could no longer let the house sit vacant. She needed to move in, and if there really was something valuable in the house, she wanted to be the one to find it.

CHAPTER 2

The next morning, the smell of coffee and fried bacon drifted into the bedroom where Marka lay wiggling her toes against flannel sheets. She pulled the patchwork quilt up around her shoulders and reminisced about her aunt. Every morning Anna smeared cold cream on her face after scrubbing it with soap. She'd slick her gray hair back with water, then form it into a bun at the back of her neck. Anna would put on her brown cotton stockings, and black, Red Cross lace-up shoes. She always wore a cotton flower-print housedress and two gingham aprons that she wore until she went to bed at night. One apron was worn over another so if someone came over to visit she could shed the dirty one. Anna always rose before sunrise. She'd light a fire in the cook stove, snuggle under a lap quilt and read her Bible while she waited for the stove to heat up the kitchen.

Marka sat up in bed and propped the soft, down-filled pillows against the sturdy headboard. She mused over her plane ride from Denver to Rapid City. Would life have turned out differently had she become an airline stewardess instead of going to secretarial school? Her parents insisted it would be a much better job in the working world. But if she had been a stewardess, she would have flown all over the world and met her ideal man. Things didn't work out in Denver. She was supposed to meet a handsome budding executive and end up marrying him so she wouldn't be stuck behind a typewriter for the rest of her life. Only, the man she met turned out to be all wrong.

She liked the plane ride, she decided. Especially the white puffy clouds and how the ground below turned into smooth flatlands that spread out to the edges of a blue sky. On the other hand, the sudden unexpected bumps made her stomach feel light, made her feel like she would be sick. She hated how the plane bounced around like a kite in the wind. The young woman sitting next to her said, "Close your eyes." The plane tipped its wings and dropped elevation preparing to land. Her ears hurt, her palms were moist. She thought her heart would beat right out of her chest.

The woman was friendly and assured her that the plane had landed safely. Funny, she never told Marka her name. They talked all the way from Denver. Marka told the stranger secrets she promised she'd never tell anyone, things about the man in Denver. Why is it you can do that with a stranger? Tell them so much about yourself. Maybe it was because you knew you'd never see them again.

Bursts of laughter from the kitchen prompted Marka out of bed. A visitor so early in the morning? A man's voice? She put a robe on over her flannel pajamas, and quietly slipped into the bathroom. She splashed water over her face and brushed her hair back into a ponytail. Marka studied her face in the mirror. Her blue eyes had regained their sparkle. She didn't consider herself beautiful, but she knew she turned a few heads. Perhaps it's my warm smile, she grinned. She tightened the belt of her robe and crept down the hall to the kitchen.

"Marka." Anna got up from her chair. "I was just telling Jonny how you quit your job as executive secretary. How you are moving back to Ridley just to be by me." Anna gave Marka a little pat on her arm. "You're such a good girl."

Marka pulled a chair out from under the table and sat across from Jonny. "Hello," she said softly, wrapping her robe tighter around her waist.

Jonny swallowed the last bite of his *kuchen*, reached across the table and shook her hand. "Glad to meet you. How was your trip? Anna said you flew into Rapid and then took a bus to Clayton. I didn't know there was a bus that ran this far north."

"Yes, the Jackrabbit Line. It leaves from the Hotel Alex Johnson," Marka said.

"How'd you get to Ridley? Anna, don't tell me you drove on these icy roads."

"Ach, no. Bodie picked her up." Anna stooped to get wood from the well-used apple basket. She lifted the handle of the cast iron lid with a potholder and stuffed the wood into the cook stove.

Jonny raised a flirting eyebrow. "Why didn't you ask me? I would have been happy to—pick up Marka." He laughed. "Get it—pick up?"

Marka blushed. Jonny was a good-looking man. He had dark brown hair that stood high on his head, a mass of waves. His eyes were the color of chocolate, and he had a broad smile.

"Bodie said he had to get a haircut so I took him up on it," Anna said. "I never turn down an offer of help."

"I don't think he got a haircut," Marka chuckled, "because when he took off his hat to say hello the first thing I noticed was his unruly hair. All I could think about were those big ears of his, and how the kids always called him Dumbo."

"So, that's why he wears that goofy hunting cap," Jonny said.

"*Ach, du lieber*, I just wish he'd take a bath once in a while."

Marka roared with laughter.

"I wasn't being funny," Anna said. "He needs a wife to take care of him."

"I was laughing at something else," Marka said. "On the way home after Bodie picked me up at the bus, he filled his mouth with sunflower seeds. He rolled his cheeks around like a washing machine and then shells came shooting out the side of his mouth." Marka laughed so hard tears ran down her cheeks. Jonny joined in, but Anna remained serious not seeing the humor in it except to inform them that sunflower seeds were called Russian peanuts or *knuppern kern*.

They sat quietly drinking their coffee. Marka noticed that Anna and Jonny would smile at each other then shrug their shoulders, as people do when they know something you don't. You wonder whether or not they will share.

"I had a wonderful sleep last night. I didn't hear a sound," Marka said setting down her coffee cup. "Guess that's the difference between the city and a small town."

"Quiet, but not boring." Jonny grinned and leaned across the table to get closer to Marka. He whispered loud enough for Anna to hear. "You'd be amazed at what goes on in this town. Ridley has the appearance of angelic solitude, but it's filled with shocking secrets."

"Ach, not much shocks me anymore." Anna poured bacon grease into a coffee can and put the can under the sink next to the rest of her stash of grease for soap making. "In this town you never know what's going to happen next. There's Millie and all her fooling around. The floozy. And, Ruby and her queer ways."

10

"A regular *Peyton Place*," Jonny laughed. "Marka, have you read it? It's a spicy new novel."

"No. I didn't have time to read. I worked overtime almost every night. Hope I'll have time for reading now."

"I'll bring you some books. I'm the English teacher and the school library is adequate. Also, I have a good collection of my own, so please don't hesitate to ask."

"I always thought I'd like to be a teacher," Marka said.

"Okay. Long enough," Anna interrupted. "Marka don't you know who this is? Ach, you don't. We had a bet. I said you would remember and he said you wouldn't. Marka, you and Jonny went to grade school together."

Marka tilted her head and chewed on her lip.

"I sat behind you in Mrs.Wyder's class. I pulled your braids. Jonny Sanders. Fifth grade." His face brightened.

"Oh, my gosh." Marka's eyes widened. "I thought you two were keeping something from me. Jonny! In fifth grade you moved away, right? Your father died. You were so shy. I don't remember you pulling my braids."

"I'm still shy, can't you tell?" Jonny gave a boyish grin.

"You're a teacher...gosh...that's really something."

"Yah. A *schulmeister*, a school teacher," Anna piped in.

"I also coach football, basketball, and track."

"I remember the time we got sent to the principal's office for smoking cigarettes out behind the school," Marka said. "He lined us against the wall, told us to hold out our hands, then slapped them with a ruler." Marka took a sip of her coffee and wished she could have a cigarette. She hadn't had one since she stepped off the bus at Clayton. Her tongue rummaged around the inside of her mouth. She had four cigarettes in her suitcase and when she got a chance, she'd sneak out of the house and smoke. Maybe tonight after Anna went to bed.

"That really taught me a lesson. I haven't smoked a cigarette since," Jonny said. "Of course, being a coach, I have to set a good example for the boys. I can't indulge in anything that would be considered harmful to the body. Like smoking or drinking."

"That's one thing I never wanted to do. Smoke cigarettes." Anna swirled the spoon around in her coffee cup and looked Marka straight in the eye. "You don't smoke do you, Marka?"

"No, Anna," Marka fibbed, and then chided herself for acting like a child. Why not just tell her, yes, I smoke and I drink and I'm not a good little girl. "Any more surprises? Any old classmates still live around here? Has anyone new moved to town?"

"Well, let me think," Anna said. "George Hanson. He lives across the street where Florence Beaumer lived before she died. She died, you know."

"I didn't know. We use to call her Frightful Florry," Marka laughed. "We never went to her house on Halloween trick or treating, because she'd throw hot water on us. Do you remember that Jonny?"

"Oh, yes, I remember her."

"Who is George Hanson?" Marka asked Anna.

"He moved here from Chicago. He was a depot agent for Chicago Northwestern Railroad. Ridley was his last assignment, and then he retired. "Yah. He liked it so much here he stayed."

"We're fishing buddies, fishing and cribbage. George is quite the cribbage player," Jonny added. "Anna, did you tell Marka about Ruby?"

"*Gott in himmel*, yah, Ruby. She moved here a couple of years ago from a ranch up north, a big cattle ranch. Well, anyways, that's what she tells everyone. Her husband was thrown from a horse and killed. She sold the ranch and moved to Ridley. She's a *Zigeuner*, a Gypsy." Anna took off her glasses and held them up to the light. "She won't have nothing to do with the womenfolk. She likes the men who hang out in her pool hall," Anna said rubbing specks off her glasses with the corner of her apron.

"Sounds like she adds some flavor to the town," Marka said. "Can't wait to meet her."

"Stay away from Ruby. She's not one of us," Anna said.

"Did Bodie tell you about his sister-in-law, Stella?" Jonny raised an eyebrow. "She's fairly new in town. Buddy Erlich rode the train to St.Louis, with a load of wool and came back with a wife. Poor guy didn't know what was in store for him. There's a woman that will make your hair curl."

Anna slapped his hand. "Didn't know you could be so ornery."

"I sat next to a woman on the plane who said she was born and raised in St. Louis. She lives in a small farm town. Wouldn't it be weird if it were the same person? No, she would have told me if she was coming to the same place I was. No! It couldn't be her."

"Stella can be as charming as a hungry cat when she wants something," Jonny said. "If she decides against you, watch out. Bodie can tell you horror stories about his sister-in-law."

"Jonny." Anna said. "That's not like you. I've never heard you say a bad thing about a soul. There's nothing wrong with Stella. Don't listen to him."

"Speaking of Bodie, he didn't talk much on the way here, and when he did, all he wanted to talk about was my house. I felt a little uncomfortable around him. He acted like he didn't even remember me."

"There's an old saying that goes like this. A fool eventually opens his mouth and gives himself away. Jonny, he wants to buy Marka's house. Can you believe it?"

"I might be interested too. I don't want to live in the dormitory forever. I've been saving up for a house. But there's talk about closing the high school, so I'm kind of unsure about things."

"She might sell for the right price," Anna laughed. "I want her to live right here with me. We haven't seen much of each other over the years, but we're going to make up for lost time, aren't we, Marka? I'm going to teach you to cook and sew. You will go to church with me. And to Ladies' Aid. It will be so wonderful. Maybe even find a husband."

"Anna!" Marka's cheeks flushed. "Sounds like you have my whole life planned!"

"Think you will be able to squeeze in some time for a movie once in a while?" Jonny asked. "Don't forget what I said about the books. Say, why don't you drop by the school and sit in on one of my classes. See what a teacher really has to do."

"Marka better be hunting for a job. Money doesn't just drop from the air you know."

"Anna, don't worry about me. I have a nest egg, and I won't have to pay rent because I have a house to live in."

"You still have to pay taxes," Anna said.

Jonny fiddled with his fork. "Won't you miss city life?"

"No. I'll love the peace and quiet."

Jonny stood and pushed his chair under the table. He took his plate and silverware to the sink. "Well, I better get going," he said looking at his watch.

"Yah, okay then, we'll be seeing you in church," Anna said.

"Not this morning. George told me the walleyed pike are biting. I'm going to spend the day with him."

"Just a minute. Let me get your shirts," Anna said, walking across the kitchen towards her bedroom. "Let me know if I put too much starch in them."

"You do them just the way I like." Jonny took out his wallet and fumbled through the bills. "I'm glad you decided to move back to Ridley, Marka. You'll be a nice addition to the town."

Anna returned to the kitchen with the shirts and handed them to Jonny. He slung them over his shoulder and placed a five-dollar bill in her hand. "Thanks. You ladies have a nice day. Oh, Marka, there's a sock hop after the basketball game Friday night. We always need chaperones; so, if you think it sounds fun, give me a call."

"I'll be busy with the house, but I'll keep it in mind." She stayed seated at the table and smiled as Jonny backed his way out of the kitchen. Yes, she was glad she came back, and she was excited knowing there was one attractive, eligible bachelor in Ridley.

CHAPTER 3

"Marka, get dressed for church. It's getting late. I better get some meat out so it thaws in time for supper."

"I want to go over to the house, Anna."

"Yah, after we go to church." Anna poked her head into the freezer compartment of the refrigerator.

"Jonny's nice." Marka nibbled on a piece of bacon. "I had a little crush on him. He was shy back then. Doesn't seem shy now."

Anna stood close to Marka, eyes serious. "I think you make him a little nervous. He's the catch of the town and he's interested in you. I could tell."

"How could you tell?"

"The way he looked at you. He goes to our church even though he's not German Russian. There's more marrying outside of our people, you know. How about I invite him for Easter dinner? I'm trying to be a *freier*, a matchmaker. Like they did in the old country," Anna laughed.

"I don't want Jonny to think I'm chasing him, but you could invite him to dinner."

"Yah, okay. I'm going to invite him."

Marka opened her suitcase and started to unpack. Before she left Denver, she crammed in clothing she would need right away: Capri pants, dungarees, blouses, skirts and a couple sweater sets. She stuffed her penny loafers and a pair of flat-heeled shoes around the sides of the case. Her other belongings she packed in two large boxes and mailed to Ridley.

Gently spreading a pink mohair sweater across her chest, she thought about Rex. He had given it to her for a birthday gift, along with a string of real pearls. She flung the sweater across the room. Men. How could she even consider becoming involved with another man? And, marriage! She didn't like what Anna said about finding a husband. She could end up like her mother. No, not that!

It was far better to follow in Anna's footsteps, stay single and take care of yourself just like her aunt had done all these years.

Marka pulled a slip up under her wool skirt, and tucked in the white blouse with the Peter-Pan collar. She brushed her hair with long, sweeping strokes, and pulled it back into a ponytail. She tied a red scarf around her neck and rubbed on pink lipstick. Church! Anna better not ask if she had been attending. It had been a long time since she prayed. None of her prayers were ever answered, so what was the use? She blotted her lips leaving only a twinge of color. She slipped her feet into black flats. She was going to church just to please Anna.

"Radio said it was going to warm up," Anna said shifting the car into reverse. She let the clutch out too fast; the car lunged back, and then rolled forward stalling the engine. She started it again; only this time let the clutch out slowly. The car shook a little then smoothed out. Anna grasped the steering wheel and pulled herself closer to the edge of the seat. The car sputtered down the alley, tires kicking up mud and loose gravel. She turned right at the corner, then made another right onto Main Street.

"I bought this Studebaker a year ago," Anna said. "The paint's a little faded, but the inside's like new. It's been a good car except for the clutch. I already had it at Jake's Garage two times. Jake said, 'You ride the clutch.' I told him, 'I do not, and I've been driving for twenty-five years.' Well, anyways, other than the clutch it's been good. You can drive it any time you want."

They pulled into the church parking lot. The bell was still ringing.

"I'm sorry I made us late. I just couldn't decide what to wear," Marka said.

They climbed the steps of the white frame building and walked into the vestibule. "Let's sit in the back. Here, hold my pocketbook," Anna said stopping to catch her breath. She reached down the front of her dress for the hanky tucked neatly between her bosoms. "My nose runs when I hurry."

A tall, slim man handed them a bulletin and pointed to the front of the church. Anna took hold of Marka's elbow and guided her to the fourth row from the back, nodding at the people to slide down to make room. "Let's sit here, I'm not about to have everyone seeing

16

us coming in late." She opened a hymnal and stood close to Marka so they could share. She belted out the words to *Onward Christian Soldiers*. "Marka," she raised an eyebrow and whispered, "why aren't you singing?"

"Because I sing like a frog."

"Sing. The birds outside are trying to outdo each other. If only the ones with the best voices sang, it would be kind of dull."

So, Marka's heart sang along with the birds.

After the hymn and opening prayer, the pastor read the Announcements and welcomed everyone to church. "We have a visitor," Reverend Rugart's voice boomed. "Way in the back. Would you please stand for us?" He pointed at Marka.

Anna nudged her. "Go on. He means you."

"Do I have to?" Her face and neck flushed. She stood, forced a smile, and nodded, but she felt violated and fretted through the rest of the service. Now, everyone in town would know that Marka Becker was back in Ridley. She felt relieved when the service was over even though she had spent most of the time staring off into space, her mind drifting. After they sang the last hymn and had the Benediction, everyone exited the building. In the vestibule, people jammed together. Anna took hold of Marka's hand, pulling her through the crowd. Marka smiled and nodded to those near, wondering if they did remember her.

Suddenly, she found herself standing face to face with a woman who glared at her. Marka's stomach tightened, her legs went numb. She gritted her teeth and smiled, but she really wanted to cry. The woman returned her smile with a cunning smirk. It was the woman on the plane! She was wearing a wide-brimmed hat, stylish two-piece suit, and kidskin gloves.

Marka felt like a dowdy schoolgirl in her bobby socks and flats, with her hair pulled back into a ponytail. She wanted to say something, but the woman looked away and sauntered out the door. Marka's heart raced and her hands turned to ice. She recognized the man with her. It was Buddy Erlich, and that meant the woman was his wife, Stella. Marka wanted to run to Anna's car, but people crowded around her, welcoming her back to Ridley.

"It was just awful about your parents being hit by that hay truck," a buxom woman in a fur coat said, her pill box hat teetering on the top of her head. "No one could figure out how it happened, and right in the middle of the afternoon. Some say that the sun must have gotten in your father's eyes," the woman went on. "It was a terrible thing."

"Yes, it was," the woman's husband said putting his hand out for Marka to shake. "Don't know if you remember, we're the Weissons, Herb and Katie."

"Yes, of course, I remember you," Marka said, knowing somewhere in her memory the Weissons existed, but now all she could think about was Stella. Not once had Stella mentioned she lived in Ridley. She let Marka talk on and on without saying a word. How could she be that cruel? So much for secrets shared with a stranger.

"Your mother was a saint, a regular saint." Katie Weisson said in a crisp voice.

"And your father was a hard working man. How long you plan on staying? What are you going to do with your house? I said... what will you do with the house," Herb waved his hand in front of Marka's face.

"I'm sorry." Marka watched Stella and Buddy get into their car and drive away. "What did you say?"

"Poor dear." Katie touched Marka's arm. "Forget all our questions. Herb, leave her alone."

"The house, yes, I plan to live in the house. I've moved back."

"That's wonderful, dear," Katie said. "It has been sad to see the house just sit there empty all these years."

"We're glad to have you back in Ridley and you came at the right time," Herb said. "This is the pastor's last sermon. Going to have a new pastor for Easter service. Hope to see you then too."

On the way home Marka told Anna about Stella. "She's the woman who sat next to me on the plane. We visited all the way to Rapid. I told her who I was, where I was going, and—I told her—" Marka clenched her teeth. "Oh—Christ!"

"Marka, *Gott im Himmel,* we just got out of church. *Pfui,* Shame."

"I'm sorry, Anna."

"Ach, it wasn't her. Are you sure it was her?"

"Yes!" Marka felt a gnawing in her stomach recalling that they talked about her relationship with Rex and what she had gone through the last year. Would Stella double cross her? Would she gossip about her until the whole town knew? A look of pain crossed Marka's face.

"Ach, you're being too sensitive. She comes over to the house a lot. I do sewing for her. She's a good customer and pays me well. You go to Ladies' Aid with me Wednesday night. She'll be there, then you can talk to her."

"I don't want to go, Anna," Marka shouted then felt ashamed. She hated it when she lost her temper, but she felt the old familiar feelings coming over her. She was being discounted; her feelings dismissed. She was tired of people telling her how to think and feel.

"You'll remember a lot of the women once you go to Ladies' Aid. If you're going to be living here, you need to make friends with the womenfolk," Anna insisted. "Soon you'll feel right at home."

Marka tried to convince her aunt it would be best if she didn't go to Ladies' Aid, that she should avoid Stella for a while, but Anna persisted.

"Oh, I'll go then." Marka closed her eyes and shook her head in defeat. "Drive by my house, Anna."

"No. After we eat lunch and have a nap, we'll go over," Anna said.

In the middle of the afternoon, Marka woke feeling scared the whole town would find out about her past. They would condemn her and convince Anna she was worthless. Things weren't working the way she wanted.

She got out of bed and dug a pack of cigarettes out of her suitcase. She opened the window a crack and lit one and blew smoke out into the cold air. Will I ever be able to quit these? Yes, I will when things settle out, she whispered to herself.

19

CHAPTER 4

"Anna, are you ready to go over to the house?" Marka called as she made her way down the hall from the bedroom. Anna was asleep in her armchair; her small hands resting on top of the quilt sprawled across her legs. Anna is exhausted from all the work she has been doing to make me feel at home, Marka thought.

Anna, now seventy-four, had always lived in this small house. She supported herself as a cook at the local school preparing the noon lunch, and she cooked at the dormitory for teachers and students who lived in the country and stayed in town during the week. After Anna turned sixty-two and retired, she took in ironing and sewing to supplement her pension.

Marka leaned down and kissed the top of Anna's head. She had survived all these years without a man. At twenty-five, Marka still had not managed to get a husband. By Ridley standards, she was considered a spinster. Once, when Marka asked Anna why she never married, Anna replied, "I have to live the life I've been given. I guess if God wanted me to have a husband He would have plunked one in my lap." Marka's mother, Rachel, had felt sorry for her sister, yet envied her freedom and independence. "My sister, Anna, is made out of strong stuff."

"Aunt," Marka whispered in Anna's ear. "Oh, it's okay, you sleep. I'll take a walk around town and come back for you, then we'll go over to the house." Marka tiptoed across the living room and closed the door behind her.

Marka breathed in crisp, cold air. She smelled the smoke coming from chimneys. The town hadn't changed in seven years. Huge cottonwood trees towered over the streets, standing nude against the sky. Soon spring would force buds and change their bareness into a beautiful hue of green.

Marka couldn't wait to move back into her house. Anna will probably try to convince me to sell. Why not live with me? Think of the money we'll both save, she'll say. Yes, it would help Anna. Maybe she could even stop taking in ironing and sewing, but it won't work for me, Marka thought. I've been on my own for years.

She reached into her coat pocket for the crumpled pack of cigarettes. She lit one, and drew the smoke deep into her lungs. She had taken to cigarettes after she graduated from Business College and moved to Denver. Lately, she found that she liked the taste of liquor and the way it made her feel. Anna disliked both, and as long as she lived under Anna's roof, she'd have to show respect. And that's why it just wouldn't work!

Birds flew across the pale blue sky, a sky that seemed to go on forever. Marka followed the birds with her eyes until they disappeared. The town of Ridley was no more than a speck on a map with a population of only two hundred, twenty-one. It rested in a valley between a steep hill and a river that meandered across the prairie, all flatland except for Bear Butte to the southeast. Highway 212 passed at the top of the hill. A gravel road turned from the highway and made its way to Main Street. From there, orderly streets were dotted with small frame houses; houses with no numbers, streets with no names. Anna once told Marka that in 1924, a map of the town had been drawn up, and it had street names and lot dimensions. "There's never enough money in the town budget to blacktop or put up street signs," Anna said. "We're lucky to have street lights," she laughed. "At one time Main Street had walks made out of planks. They finally replaced them with concrete sidewalks."

A black, 1949 Hudson, moved down the street slow, like a cat crawling along on its belly. The woman driving waved to Marka. Marka waved back and tried to get a closer look to see if she recognized her. In Ridley, you wave at everyone. Marka laughed and admitted, it felt good compared to Denver where you hardly knew your next-door neighbor.

Marka walked down Main Street, past the Legion Hall, stopping at People's Grocery. The first floor of the store was merchandise, the second floor, the proprietor's living quarters. "So, Bodie lives up there with his father and he's interested in my house," she whispered to herself. "Maybe he wants to live on his own like me. I love Anna, but sometimes we don't see things the same way. Bodie can take care of himself. He's always been a little slow but he's not stupid for cripes sake." Marka continued the conversation with herself. "I understand his interest in my house because there's never been much turnover in housing in Ridley. Someone has to move or die."

She walked past the post office, a tiny square building. Next to it was the cafe with the words "Millie's Café" written across the large plate glass window in black letters trimmed in red. She crossed the street and walked by the Jake's filling station and garage. Next to it sat the saloon, which had rooms for rent upstairs. Heading back in the direction she had come from on the other side of the street was a weedy lot where years ago a building had burned to the ground. Finally, at the end of the street was the pool hall.

Yes, leaving Denver was the right thing to do. Ridley is where her roots could grow deep. It's where life is predictable and nothing changes. She would make a life for herself in this town. A town so quiet, even the trees whisper.

"Hello," a middle-aged woman said. She stood in the stairway that led up to the apartment above the pool hall. Marka recognized her as the woman who waved from the slow moving car.

"Please, join me for a cup of tea. Sundays are too quiet, no one around to talk to. Oh, my name is Ruby Swain," she held out her hand, her black eyes dancing.

"I'm headed home. My aunt is waiting for me," Marka stammered. "I mean, I really should get back to my aunt."

"I know who you are." Ruby cocked her head and raised her thick black eyebrows.

"You do?"

"Nothing stays a secret in Ridley. You're Anna's niece. Come upstairs to my home. You can spare a few minutes, can't you? I'll brew us some tea."

Marka changed her mind and followed Ruby up the enclosed stairway. "I guess it would be all right."

They reached the top of the stairs and Ruby opened the door and waved Marka inside. The room was large with a ten-foot ceiling. To the left was a kitchen and eating area. To the right, there was a teakwood table and four cane-back chairs situated on a red and black oriental rug. In one corner, hung a birdcage with a cockatiel inside. It ruffled its feathers and startled Marka.

"I can't bare to keep Fedora in her cage all the time, so I leave the door open. She may decide to fly around, but she won't hurt you. You aren't afraid of birds are you? You don't have to be afraid of my Fedora."

Two overstuffed chairs covered with bright fabric sat in the part of the room that was the sitting area. Chintz drapes covered a large window that made the room feel dark and gloomy. The drapes, a mixture of red, yellow and black, made Marka dizzy. This was not typical decor for a Ridley home, and Marka wondered how many people in town had ever seen it.

Ruby flitted about like a butterfly. A blue silk sash tied loosely around her waist divided the black satin skirt from the gold, long-sleeved blouse. She moved about the room, and then settled in one of the chairs. She motioned Marka to sit in the chair beside her.

"I saw you earlier. I waved and you waved back." Ruby played with the pink plastic pop-it beads around her neck. "That meant a lot to me. I saw you walking around town. I've been watching from my window. Oh, I just had to meet you." Ruby took a cigarette out of a mother of pearl case, and stuck it into a black plastic holder. She lit the end with her lighter, drew in the smoke then blew smoke rings into the air. "I knew you were coming because Bodie was in the pool hall and mentioned he was going to Clayton to pick you up."

Marka felt her body relax. She liked the smell of Ruby's tobacco. "Could I bum a cigarette?"

"Why are you whispering? There's no one here but us."

"I feel like a kid sneaking cigarettes. I've never smoked in front of Anna. She doesn't approve."

"You're no kid; you should do whatever you want." Ruby took a cigarette out of the case, handed it to Marka, and lit it for her. "Has anyone ever told you, you are a beautiful woman? Your eyes are so blue. Why don't you wear your hair loose around your shoulders? The red in it would make your face glow." Ruby leaned forward in her chair. "You will be the talk of the town. Some women will fear you, but if they don't know how to hold onto their men that's their problem." Ruby exploded in laughter, the light reflected off her mischievous eyes. "Oh, to be your age again. How old do you think I am?"

"I don't know."

"I'm almost fifty. Can you believe it? I don't look it, do I?" Ruby took a long drag off her cigarette, pinched it loose from the holder, and crushed it into the side of an ashtray. "I'll put water on for tea. You sit here and have your cigarette. I'll be right back."

Marka looked around the room and noticed oil paintings stacked against one wall. There was an easel standing near the large window that looked onto Main Street. "Do you mind if I look at your paintings?"

"Go ahead," Ruby shouted from the kitchen.

Marka went to the corner of the room and looked at the paintings starting with the one closest to the wall. It was a still life of apples, oranges, and a teapot on a table. In front of it was a painting of Main Street, the view from the window: People's Grocery, the post office, and Millie's Cafe. There were two paintings of Fedora, and one of a deck of cards spread across a table.

Ruby returned from the kitchen and joined Marka at the paintings. "I hear many interesting things when I'm in the pool hall, but I have no one to share these bits with. I miss my friends from the ranch, such freedom I had there. My husband and I rode horses. My mother-in-law, God rest her soul, taught me how to paint. What do you think of my paintings?"

"I like them. The one of the deck of cards is different."

Ruby pulled the painting out of the stack.

"These are Tarot cards. See, this is the Fool, like the Joker in a regular set of cards." Ruby lightly touched the painting. "This is the King, and the Queen, the Knight, and the Page. I keep my cards wrapped in a dark-blue velvet cloth. I haven't used them since Henry was killed. One month before he died, I spread them out and the death card …" Ruby quickly set the painting down.

"I'm sorry." Marka felt embarrassed.

"Look, I'm painting a portrait of him," Ruby removed a cloth from the canvas perched on the easel. "I've been working on it for a year, but I just can't get the eyes right. The eyes, they don't speak to me." Ruby pulled the curtain back from the window to let in more light, then picked up a dry paintbrush. She dabbed at Henry's unfinished eyes. "I did a magnificent job on the horse though, don't you think?" She placed the cloth back over the canvas.

"Yes, I think it's very good."

"I haven't done much painting this winter because the oils smell awful," Ruby pinched her nostrils shut. "Besides, I need the warmth of the sun coming in." She put the brush back with the rest of her paint supplies, walked over to her chair and flopped down.

"Why didn't you stay on the ranch after your husband died?"

"I had to sell." Ruby lit another cigarette. "I can't read. Not a word." The cigarette holder wobbled up and down between her teeth. "I was afraid someone would take advantage of me. I might sign something I shouldn't. My brother-in-law wanted to buy the ranch and I trusted him. He helped me with the legal matters."

"You can't read?" Marka tilted her head. "Didn't you go to school?"

"Gypsies don't go to school. A waste of time. I know things that can't be found in books. One learns from life's experiences. It never hurt me not to go to school. I know how to survive, anything! Some of it is Gypsy luck, but most of it is knowing what you have to do. I have not suffered because of it."

"You can't have what you want. You can't have your ranch because you can't read. Isn't that hurting you?" Marka put her hand over her mouth and pressed her fingers to her lips. "I'm sorry; it's none of my business."

"No, I want you to say what you think. I have no problem saying what's on my mind," Ruby laughed and planted her hands on her broad hips. "Anyway, I would never go back to the ranch. If I made any change in my life it would be to look for my people."

Marka watched the ashes from Ruby's cigarette grow longer and longer. She wondered if they were going to fall on the floor before Ruby got them to the ashtray.

"Where are your people?"

"We came from the east, but my family is in this state somewhere. They'll show up some day, I know they will."

"I lived in Ridley most of my life. I was born and raised in the same house. My family is German."

"I know all about your people. They stick together. They are good, humble folk, but most of them treat me like an outsider. The people in this town say I'm taking business away from the saloon, and the money that comes from the saloon goes to run the town. I'm not asking for a license to sell liquor. All I want is to have pop and candy bars for my customers. Phooey! It's a piddling little

25

amount. I don't really need the money. I just like running the pool hall so I have men to talk to. Guess on the ranch I got use to being around men." Ruby got up from her chair and motioned for Marka to join her at the kitchen table. "I hear the teakettle whistling. Do you use milk and sugar in your tea?"

"No, just plain."

"Sometimes, I like to talk to another woman. That's why I'm talking your ear off," Ruby laughed.

"I'm glad you asked me up. I won't treat you like an outsider," Marka said.

"Good. People talk behind my back, they call me Madame Zola. Sure, I read tea leaves and I read palms. If only they knew I do have special powers to see things about people," her voice was soft and hypnotic.

Marka's eyes widened. "Really?"

"Oh, yes. My grandmother had the gift, and my mother, and then she passed it on to me. Would you like me to tell your fortune? Here, let me have a look at your palm. Let me look for your hidden fate." Ruby slid her chair close to Marka. She took Marka's hand and laid it on the table. Her dark eyes sparked like a piece of flint struck against steel. She took Marka's hand and turned it palm up.

Fedora swooped down from the top of her cage and flew around the room. She circled around three times, then landed on Ruby's shoulder and fluttered her wings. "Oh, Fedora, don't start that. She's jealous. It's okay, Fedora."

The bird stared at Marka, its black eyes intent.

Marka found the whole thing amusing and smiled. It was charming that the bird looked so much like Ruby with its yellow plumes and orange cheek patches. Ruby was wearing a yellow bandanna that covered most of her black hair; her high cheekbones smudged with orange rouge.

"I like your bird's name," Marka said.

"I named her Fedora, because she likes to sit on my head just like a hat," Ruby laughed.

"I feel kind of funny about this. I've never had my fortune told," Marka felt nervous.

Ruby shoved her clunky, bangle bracelets up the middle of her arm. "Your hand is like ice. You are worried about something aren't you?"

Marka's shoulders tightened. She raised them and pulled in her neck to relieve the tension.

First, Ruby examined her thumb. "You are a loyal friend, but you let others influence you too much." Ruby pressed her thumb into the palm of Marka's hand. "You try hard to please everyone. It's hard for you to say "No". This keeps you from your destiny. Ruby's face twisted and she stiffened her body. "You are haunted by something. Ghosts from the past."

Marka pulled her hand away.

"I can only tell you what I see. But wait—" Ruby raised an eyebrow. "Wait! We aren't through!"

Marka looked frightened. She reluctantly laid her hand back on the table. "I'm not sure whether you are serious or teasing."

Ruby caressed Marka's hand. "Let's continue." She uncurled Marka's fingers and flattened her hand onto the table. "You have a long palm and long fingers. This is your lifeline—it's strong. Oh, your heart line goes way across your palm. There will be many men in your life."

Marka laughed and slipped her hand away. "Thank you for the tea. I really have to go, it's three o'clock. I have to go to my house and I feel a little eerie about it. I haven't been there since my parents died."

"See! Ghosts from the past, but no need to feel scared if you've made peace with them," Ruby said.

"What do you mean?"

"If the deceased leave the world on good terms with the living, they will not come back and cause trouble. But, if there has been something unresolved, then they will not leave you alone until it is settled."

Marka left Ruby's apartment and headed towards Anna's. Ruby was bizarre. Yet, there was something, something mysterious about her. Marka was in awe and didn't know why.

Marka, determined to see her house before dark, decided not to stop for Anna. She'll just say, "Let's wait and go over in the morning." But, she couldn't wait another day. Marka walked briskly past Anna's. If she hurried she'd have time to walk through the house before supper. Only one more block and she'd be there.

She livened her step as she turned the corner and caught sight of the house. It was a single-story structure with a slightly peaked roof and low hanging eaves. When she reached the edge of the front lawn, she stood firm. A cold chill came over her, as if she were standing in front of an unattended grave. The house looked dreary under the gray March sky. Harsh Dakota winters had eaten away at it. The siding was dingy, and the windows were caked with dirt. The house looked shabby like a piece of worn out cloth. It wasn't the house she remembered; the one with the sparkling windows, and cozy rooms. And it looked so much smaller. Seeing the house in this run down condition disturbed her, but she had no one to blame but herself.

Marka bent down and touched a yellow crocus pushing up through the debris of fallen leaves. The sight of it lifted her spirits. Her mother had always gotten excited when they bloomed. "It's a sign that winter is coming to an end," she would say. Marka turned the knob on the kitchen door, gave a push, and when it opened, it surprised her. She trusted Bodie with the safety of her house. He had been careless and left it unlocked. No one in Ridley bothered much with locking their doors, but under these circumstances, well, it didn't seem right. The house contained all her parents' belongings.

She felt reluctant, but she stepped into the kitchen and the cold linoleum floor crackled beneath her feet. The house felt damp and it smelled like mice. She surveyed the kitchen and felt comforted that nothing had been disturbed. A tea towel folded in thirds still hung on the drying rack behind the stove. She looked through the cupboards and found the dishes neatly stacked. She opened the silverware drawer and spoons, knives, and forks were neatly piled between the wooden slats. And then a memory, one that had carved itself in her mind, grabbed hold of her. Her mother was at the kitchen sink looking out the window at the vegetable garden. Her dad came through the door, his hair a mess, his eyes wild. He had a blackened eye and a cut on his lip. "Don't say a word, Rachel. Put supper on the table." He looked at Marka. "What you gawking at?" She remembered feeling frightened, but she never let him see her cry.

There were cobwebs hanging from the ceiling in the living room and everything was covered with dust. She should have covered the furniture with bed sheets before she left for Denver. A pungent odor filled the room. What is that strange smell? She pulled the drapes open uncovering the large picture window and found it covered with flyspecks. In one corner there was a small hole from a bee-bee gun. On one side of the room the wall was stained from a leak in the roof. It would take so much work just to make the house livable.

Scratch. Scratch. A noise came from behind the oil stove. Mice! She hated mice. It stuck out its head and ran across the room. Marka cringed. Mice always seemed to delight in frightening a person half to death. There's that smell again. What could it be?

Marka went into her bedroom and pulled the lace curtains back from the window. The sun was setting and it would soon be getting dark. She better hurry her tour of the house.

Her bedroom, a converted sun porch, contained a wrought-iron bed, and mahogany mirrored-dresser with matching armoire. Cobwebs hung from orange and black felt high school pennants. She rummaged through dresser drawers, through all the things she had left behind. Each time she visited, her mother asked her to either take her things back with her, or dispose of them. But something kept her from it. Maybe she wanted to leave a part of herself in the house.

In the bottom of her dresser drawer Marka came across a special tin box that she treasured as a child. She opened it and found report cards, awards from spelling bees, and a bronze medal, a Citizenship Award. There were pictures clipped from magazines. One was of the Statue of Liberty in New York. She found three one-dollar bills folded in half. She smiled and chuckled and remembered that this was the money she had started to save so she could leave home when she grew up.

So, why had she come back? Was it because she felt like such a failure, botching things in Denver? What made her think coming back would make everything all right? All those years away had left her with a feeling of guilt for leaving her mother. She worried something terrible might happen, and it had! Maybe if she had been here the terrible accident wouldn't have happened. They were probably arguing. Dad took his eyes off the road to scowl and shake his fist. Or, more likely, he was drunk and lost control of the car.

Marka thought of the war between her parents. Most of their fights were over her father's drinking. "Stop your drinking, Philip. Don't spend so much time in the saloon," her mother would plead. "That's how you get into trouble." All the angry words they hurled at each other. Yet, Marka was never allowed to express *her* anger. Her father's harsh words were stuck in her memories. "I am the father!" he would say pounding his fist on the supper table. Marka felt a twinge in her stomach and resentment boiled up like black clouds in a thunderstorm. Her parents would argue, then go to bed. Sometimes, she heard murmurs, heard them comfort each other. She lay shivering in her bed looking out the window at the dark sky and the alabaster moon that glowed pure and unblemished, unlike her childhood where innocence was lost forever.

Marka put the lid on the tin box and put it back in the dresser. She picked up a small cardboard box covered with faded purple crepe paper. She and her mother always made a May Day basket for Anna, a custom carried over "from the old country," her mother said. They filled the basket with homemade cookies then they waited until dusk and snuck to Anna's house. They placed the basket beside the door, knocked, and ran home. She made this basket when she was twelve, but never delivered it because she was too grown up for childish games. It was during the time she became interested in boys.   Marka picked up a small white book with the word "Diary" etched into white leather. Boys had replaced making paper baskets. She tucked the book under her arm and pinched the handle of the May basket between her fingers. She would take these back to Anna's and they would reminisce over fun times.

A white sweater lay folded on the bed. It was the one she wore to the funeral. Another memory pierced her heart; her mother's face before she died, as she lay in the hospital bed. And her mother's words, "Something hidden in the house." What could it be? She wrapped the sweater around the diary and basket and walked towards her parents' bedroom. The light in the house had faded and it was almost dark.

Could she trust her mother's words or should she just put the whole thing out of her mind? Was it, whatever it was, hidden or in plain sight? After the accident, they were going to do surgery on her mother the following morning, but she died that evening. Marka wanted to take one peek into the room and then she'd go to Anna's.

She stepped into her parents' bedroom. A noise startled her. She stood still and listened. She heard breathing. There was an inhale, then a murmur after the exhale. Yes, it definitely was breathing. The bed springs squeaked. Marka screamed and ran out of the room, into the dining room, past the table and chairs. In her haste, she bumped a chair and it fell to the floor. Her knees felt like they would buckle beneath her. She hurried through the living room and as she ran out of the house, she heard a voice. Her fingers gripped the bundle as she hurried across the lawn onto the street. She ran all the way to Anna's.

Marka burst through the kitchen door. "There's someone in my house!"

"*Gott im Himmel.* What's the matter? You look like you've seen a ghost." Anna's eyes widened and she stepped back out of the way as Marka pushed past her and headed for the telephone. "Who in hell do I call for help?" her jaw trembled.

"Solly. He's the town deputy, but—what's the matter?"

Marka held up her hand. "I'll tell you later." She felt the blood draining from her face.

Anna nervously shuffled over to the telephone. "Let me think now. The number is 4322." She dialed and handed the phone to Marka.

"Hello. My name is Marka Becker. Is Solly there? Yes. I am enjoying my visit with Anna, but I need to speak with Solly right now! There's someone in my house."

Anna took the phone from Marka. "Edna, get Solly. We need him." She tried to calm Marka by assuring her there had to be a good explanation for what she'd seen. "Why didn't you come and get me before you went to the house?"

"I should have. What if they run away? No one will believe me. Just a frantic female, that's what they'll say."

Half an hour passed before Solly drove up. He got out of his station wagon and walked up to Anna's house. He knocked hard on the kitchen door.

"Everything's okay. It was just an Indian sleeping it off. He got drunk last night and wandered around town looking for a place to sleep. He told me he remembered back to when he was a kid and

31

how a nice man took him and his sister to the house and gave them food. That's why he ended up at your house. I told him to be on his way." Solly stood with his hands on his hips, feet spread wide apart. "He told me he didn't mean any harm. Guess he and his woman were drinking down at the saloon, and she drove off and left him."

"What makes him think he can just go into someone's house any time he wants? What if he decides to come back?" Marka fumed.

"He promised he won't ever do it again, but if you want me to I'll haul him to jail. Do you want to press charges?"

"No, but he better not ever come back."

"That's good. Just leave it go," Anna said. "I feel sorry for the Indian people. Living in shacks on the reservation."

"His Indian name is Deer Ears," Solly said. "He lives on the reservation east of Mud Butte. Doesn't work, gets his government check at the beginning of the month and spends it all on liquor. He wouldn't hurt a soul. Well, I'll be going now. Are you sure you're okay? You still look a little ragged around the edges."

"I'm okay."

Anna put her hand to her chin and rubbed her fingers across it several times. "Yah. Your dad used to do things like that, you know. He always felt kind of sorry for the little Indian kids that sat in the cars while their parents were in the saloon. He'd bring them home and ask your mom to fix them something to eat. Sometimes even a woman with her kids. But, your mom, she used to get so angry with him. Not because of the food. It was because of the saloon."

"Yes. I remember." Marka slumped in the kitchen chair. "He could be a kind man when he wanted."

"Look, your hands are still shaking," Anna said.

"What a day." Marka spread her hands across her chest and tossed her head back. "First, I run into Stella."

"Ach, it will be okay," Anna insisted. "You're being too sensitive."

"Then I meet Ruby and she reads my palms."

"What? That Gypsy woman?"

"Yes, she invited me for tea and read my palms."

"Ach, Gott. You let that *Zigeuner* do that too you. It goes against God's commands. You must never do that again! The Bible says we are not to have anything to do with such things." Anna shook her finger at Marka. "*Pfui.* Sometimes, it's best if we don't know what lies in the future."

"Anna, she's nice. She didn't do anything wrong. It was all in fun. I didn't take her seriously."

"You can't trust them. They have weird ideas. You didn't tell her about the money in the house did you?"

"No! I don't agree with you about Ruby, and that's not what you taught me as a child. You said that we should love everyone. That we were all God's children."

Anna pursed her lips and shook her finger again. "In Russia there were Gypsies that came around and entertained us with their music. Sometimes, they even had a dancing bear. But, our parents told us that we were to stay away from them because they would kidnap us. You didn't tell Ruby our people came from Russia, did you? As far as other people are concerned we are German."

"I'm sorry I upset you." Marka got up from her chair, went over to Anna, leaned down, and hugged her. "You said money in the house."

"I don't know why I said money. A hunch I guess."

"So how does that differ from what Ruby said? You call it a hunch, she says she's telling my future," Marka laughed.

"I don't want to argue with you, Marka. Just be careful. Watch what you are doing. Come, now. Let's fix supper."

"Anna, I want to go over and lock the house."

"He won't come back if that's what you're worried about. He's more scared then you are," Anna chuckled.

"Anna, did you ever think about the house being haunted?"

"*Gott.* No! Why would you think such a thing? Oh, yah, don't tell me, that Ruby woman. Come, help me peel potatoes," Anna stoked the fire in the cook stove. "We have more serious things to worry about, like what that Senator McCarthy is going to do next. They say we are having a Cold War with Russia. I'm worried they will send us all back."

CHAPTER 5

Saturday afternoon, one week after she arrived and already Marka felt restless. She wanted a pack of cigarettes, so she walked the few blocks to town. She hated being sneaky, but Anna wouldn't like her smoking. She had an insatiable hunger ever since she had tea with Ruby. The night before she left Denver she swore off them, but the need for just one nagged her.

Marka walked along Main Street and noticed more cars in town than usual. Monday through Friday only a few cars nosed into the curb along the street. On Sundays, the street was bare, but on Saturday nights cars and pickups packed both sides. Farmers and ranchers started showing up shortly after supper.

The women did their shopping at People's Grocery, then sat in their cars or stood around the sidewalks, visiting. They drank soda pop and chewed sunflower seeds. The children spent nickels and dimes at the store and played hopscotch on the sidewalk. Some played hide-and-seek behind store buildings and in alleys. Others played King of the Mountain and Captain May I. Some boys got into fist fights, others got into trouble for using sling shots to fire dried beans at the girls' behinds. The men shot the bull, standing around on sidewalks or leaning against storefronts. Others went to the pool hall; most went to the saloon.

Before she realized it, Marka found herself in front of the saloon.

Many times her mother sent her there to get her father. "You tell him to come home for supper," she'd say. Marka was that skinny girl with long, stringy hair opening the saloon door, cautiously peeking in at the men sitting at the long wooden bar. She never said a word. Someone would notice her and they'd yell, "Hey, Philip, your kid's here." The big room was always dark. She barely made out the faces. Her father came to the door with a disgusted look. "Tell your mother I'll be right home." Then he'd wave her away.

The saloon was the cause of many disagreements between her parents. It seemed ridiculous to Marka that her parents fought over it. "It's just a place where men tell tall tales," her father would say.

"And vulgar jokes! You men go to the saloon to brag," her mother would say. "We discuss the weather and talk about the market for sugar beets. And we talk politics." Then she'd say, "Most of all, you just go there to get drunk. It's an evil place that is ruining our lives."

It was still early enough to beat the Saturday saloon crowd. What would be the harm if she just bought a pack of cigarettes? She felt exhilarated and somewhat naughty about what she was about to do. She opened the door and stepped inside. The room smelled of stale smoke, beer, and body odor.

Marka climbed onto a barstool and looked around. There was a pot-bellied, wood burning stove in the middle of the room. Overhead fans on long metal bars hung down from a high ceiling made of ornate tin plates. Roller shades darkened one side of the room, the side for the serious drinkers who didn't want to be seen. The large plate glass window facing the street glowed with colorful Grain Belt Beer signs.

Someone at the far end of the room yelled, "You big lummox."

A guy with a deep voice rumbled, "Shut your damn mouth. You're nothing but a dirty, rotten, little son of a bitch."

Marka looked around the room to see if she recognized anyone. Someone told a joke, then they all shook their heads and laughed loudly and banged their fists on the top of the bar.

"Awe, come on now. It was just a little joke."

"You damn bastard," the deep voice rumbled again.

Marka watched one man nudge the fellow next to him giving a slight nod toward her. The men poked each other down the row of bar stools. There was a low murmur, eyes momentarily fixed on Marka, then they ignored her and went back to their joking around.

"It gets a little rowdy in here. They're not used to a woman in the saloon." The bartender was drying glasses and ashtrays and stacking them under the counter. "Once in a while someone will bring in an Indian squaw. Really this isn't a place for a woman." He flung the white towel over his shoulder and put a clean ashtray on the bar. "You don't look like a woman that hangs out in saloons. He held out his hand. "I'm Elton. Who might you be? You look a little familiar."

Marka took her last cigarette out of a crumpled pack. "I was born and raised here. Just came in for a pack of cigarettes. Wasn't planning on staying. I lived in Denver for seven years and women *are* welcome in the bars there." Marka tapped the end of her cigarette against the counter.

Elton reached into his shirt pocket, pulled out his Zippo, and lit it for her. "They sell cigarettes at the grocery store too, you know," he said, picking up another tray of wet glasses. "This isn't Denver. Don't want to offend, just want you to know how it is here."

A young man with flirty eyes and a wide teasing smile walked over to the bar and sat down. "Who do we have here?" He focused hard on Marka. "And, I forgot to shave today. Damn it all."

Marka's heart raced and she felt breathless. Buddy Erlich. Would he recognize her?

"What'll you have, Buddy?" Elton's brow knitted together.

"Pack a Camels and a draft," he slapped a dollar bill down on the bar.

Buddy hadn't changed much since high school. When Marka saw him in church he was with his wife, Stella. My God, she probably told him every word I said on the flight from Denver to Rapid.

"I just want a pack of Viceroys and a couple of Hershey bars. Oh, and a bag of sunflower seeds," Marka said to Elton ignoring Buddy.

Elton reached into the cigarette rack on the wall next to the neon sign advertising Old Crow. Buddy got down from the bar stool and walked to the middle of the room. He put one hand in the pocket of his jeans, and rocked back on the heels of his cowboy boots. He was short, but solid and muscular. Marka stared into the mirror that ran the length of the bar and watched him size her up. He walked back to the bar where she was sitting. "Marka Becker. You're still as pretty as ever." He looked her over again, and walked away.

A hot flush burned up her neck to her face. "I don't suppose I can have a drink in here?" she asked Elton. "If that's a problem for you I'll understand."

Elton wrinkled his nose and scratched his head. "I don't think there's a city ordinance against serving women in the saloon."

"How about selling liquor to a woman? I suppose there's a law against that. Suppose I said it was for my aging aunt, for medicinal reasons?"

"You are drinking age, aren't you? I do bend the rules now and then if I know the person," he smiled and winked behind thick glasses. "Oh shucks, one drink can't hurt."

"I'll have a Vodka Collins and a pint of vodka to go."

"Most of the men take their whiskey straight. I'm not used to this cocktail stuff, but I'll give it a try," Elton said.

Again, Marka glanced in the mirror and her eyes connected with Buddy who gazed intently at her. She could hardly wait for Elton to get the drink fixed. She had to calm her nerves.

Elton wiped down the counter with a dry rag, set the drink on a napkin, and pushed it towards Marka. "Vodka, huh? Anna usually has someone pick her up a bottle of peppermint Schnapps."

Marka chuckled. Finally, she had something on Anna. It was nice to know Anna had vices too.

"So, you know my aunt, so you do know who I am?" Marka sipped her drink.

Elton tilted his head. "Of course I do. I just wanted to give you a hard time. I remember you most as a little girl in pigtails riding your bicycle all over the place. When you got older you'd speed around town in your dad's yellow Chevy. How's the drink?"

"It's good." She flinched as someone tickled her arm. Buddy had walked back up behind her while she and Elton were talking.

"Elton. I'll have another draft and something for Marka, whatever she's drinking." Buddy put a cigarette in his mouth and struck a match on the underside of his boot.

"I put everything in the bag for you," Elton said, handing Marka a small brown paper sack.

"Thanks." She gathered her hair into one long strand and pulled it over her shoulder. Her neck felt hot. Ruby had told her she should wear it loose to make her face glow. Now, all of her burned like an inferno. Why did Buddy make her feel this way, all nervous and self-conscious?

"I work for Peter Kewit, and make damn good money." Buddy puffed on a cigarette to get it going. "We're putting in missile sites. Can't let the Russians get the best of us. We are living under the threat of nuclear war. If they attack, we'll be ready for them."

"I say someone will push the wrong button and blow up the whole state," Elton said. "The center of the nation, all right. That's the first place the Russians will attack. We'll be the first to go."

"Never going to happen. They got all that figured out in Washington," Buddy said. He turned to Marka. "Say, saw you in church last Sunday."

Marka spun sideways on the barstool, and then slid off. She dug deep into her pocket for a $5.00 bill. No way did she want to get into a serious conversation.

"Aren't you even going to shake my hand or—something?" Buddy grinned.

Marka held out her hand.

"You can do better than that, can't you?" He put his arms around her and gave her a hug.

"So, so—you're as rich as Rockefeller," she said, pulling away. How was it that she was embarrassed yet excited at the same time?

"Bodie told me he was going to Clayton to pick you up. I had to drive to Rapid to pick up my wife. Thinks she's too good to ride the bus. Oh, I forgot she had shopping to do," Buddy laughed. "She said you flew together from Denver. Are you staying with Anna?"

"Yes. Until I get my house fixed up."

Elton placed fresh drinks on the counter. Marka finished her first drink and took a sip from the fresh one. What was coming next? Wives tell their husbands everything. Would the whole story spill out across the bar top like oozing slime? The saloon, the perfect place for juicy gossip.

"Let's go over and say hello to your dad's old drinking buddies." Buddy took Marka by the hand and led her over to a table where a group of men were playing cards. "This here's Fred Wiserman. Over there, Harry Paddock, and this guy here is Joe Stobner. Remember these old beet farmers?"

"Sure." She kind of did.

"This is Philip Becker's daughter, Marka," Buddy said. The men rose from their chairs, nodded, sat back down and returned to their game.

"We miss your dad," Joe Stobner said. "That was a terrible accident."

"Fred, got your beets planted yet?" Buddy asked.

"Not yet. The factory field man was out and checked my soil. Said the field was ready for planting and he would bring seed next week."

"You wanna join us?" Harry asked Buddy. "We're playing Shoot The Moon. Ace, King, Queen, and Duce all five points. Have to warn you though; we don't take a card game serious unless we put some money on it."

"Naw, got to get home," Buddy said. "It's getting close to suppertime. I don't want to miss one of Stella's deluxe meals. She's been trying out more of them recipes from *McCall's* magazines."

"We need rain," Fred said. "Sure hope we don't get a late frost."

"You got to get your seed in first week of April," Buddy said. "Have you signed your contracts with the sugar company yet?"

"Yes. I'm putting in fifty acres. Hope I do better this year. Last year, had a shitty yield and the sugar content was too low. If I don't make a profit this year, I'm gonna put more acreage into alfalfa. Or, I may decide to raise sheep. It's too much to worry about—it's either frost, hail, or drought."

"Damn I wish we hadn't sold the farm," Buddy complained. "I still miss it. Someday, I'm gonna buy it back, or one just like it. I've been putting money aside. If Stella would just stop wanting every new appliance and car that comes out."

"Got to almost be a weatherman to be a farmer," Joe laughed. "Need to know how to read the clouds, watch for sundogs, and count rings around the moon."

Marka folded her arms across her chest. She needed to get going. What was the point of staying? They excluded her from their conversation. Why had Buddy brought her back to talk with the men? They weren't interested in her. It was probably just so he could show off. First, the job with Kewit, and now this. She wasn't impressed with his knowledge of farming.

Just as she was about to leave, a large burly man walked up to the table. "What's she doing in here? Women don't belong in no bar," his square jaw moved back and forth as he talked.

"Calm yourself Red," Buddy wrapped his arms around Red's huge shoulders. "Don't worry. She didn't see you sitting back there looking at those girlie magazines. You know, the ones you keep hidden in your overalls next to your heart," Buddy laughed.

Red pushed Buddy aside. The purple veins stood out on his large red nose. He jerked his head back and gulped down a shot of whiskey. He rubbed his hands across his whiskered face, and then tapped the empty glass on the table to get Elton's attention.

"Be right there," Elton hollered.

Red held the two-ounce jigger above his head motioning with his other hand. Elton brought a bottle back to the table and filled the glass to the brim. Red emptied the glass and asked for another.

"Red, you drink like a real man," Buddy laughed. "You remember Phillip Becker? This is his daughter, Marka. She's a looker, huh?"

"Women all look alike in the dark," Red answered, moving the wad of chewing tobacco around his bottom lip and teeth. He walked over to get the spittoon next to the stove.

The door to the saloon opened. A rancher walked in and announced that he was looking for a wrangler to help move some ewes into pens for shearing.

"There's a job for you, Red," Buddy said.

"I've got to get going," Marka said, thinking this was a good time to make her exit.

"Don't let this big lummox scare you off."

The men at the other table roared with laughter.

"Anna's expecting me," Marka said, tucking the brown paper sack under her arm. Elton was right. The saloon was no place for a woman. Red gave her the creeps. She wouldn't be back again. She headed for the door, her long hair swinging across her shoulders.

"See you soon," Buddy hollered as Marka opened the door and stepped out onto the sidewalk.

"Maybe so, Rockefeller," Marka smiled. She let the door swing wide, and then slam shut.

CHAPTER 6

After Marka left the saloon, she walked across the street to the cafe. She wanted to stop for a cup of coffee so she could smoke another cigarette before heading back to Anna's. She needed time to clear her mind. The Vodka Collins made her lightheaded. Should I tell Anna I went to the saloon? I don't think Anna will believe me if I say I was trying to be sociable, like going to Ladies' Aid. Word could get back to Anna. What was I thinking? I wasn't thinking, that's the problem. This isn't Denver, Marka. And I shouldn't be drinking. All it does is get me into trouble.

It was 3:30 p.m. and Main Street had filled with cars. The cafe was still open; the yellowed cardboard sign hanging in the window read: Open 7 AM to 4 PM - Mon. thru Sat — Breakfast and Lunch. Marka tucked the brown paper bag under her arm and went inside. Two young girls sat at the Formica counter licking ice cream cones. They moved side-to-side on swivel stools. Ceiling fans circulated the air. Overhead lights brightened the room and made the old waxed floor glisten. The jukebox blared Elvis Presley's, *Heartbreak Hotel.*

There were only a few people in the cafe. The tables up front by the window were full of dirty dishes, so Marka selected a clean booth at the back of the room. She took the sunflower seeds and Hershey bars out of the brown paper bag and stuffed them into her coat pocket; then tucked the bag with the vodka back into the corner of the booth. A waitress walked towards her. As the woman got closer, Marka decided it was Millie. They never had much to do with each other in school because Millie was three grades ahead. Marka wondered if Millie would remember her.

"What can I get you?" Millie had a large nose and small beady eyes. She wore her hair pulled back behind her ears and covered it with a coarse black hairnet.

"I'll have coffee with cream. Oh, do you have any matches?" Millie walked over to the cash register, took a matchbook out of a glass dish, and then walked back to Marka's booth.

"I just had these made. Nifty, huh?" Millie cracked her chewing gum. The bright yellow matchbook with gold lettering read: **Four Season's Cafe, Ridley, South Dakota**.

"I want to rename my café. Oh—one coffee, coming right up," she said.

Marka lit a cigarette and inhaled deeply. She watched Millie walk back to the counter, her pink nylon uniform so tight against her body it clung to her like cellophane.

"You look so familiar." Millie set the coffee and cream down on the table. "I can't place you though."

"I've been gone quite a few years. I lived in Denver." Marka sipped the hot coffee and flicked her ashes into an aluminum ashtray.

Millie paused then looked pleased she remembered.

"Marka Becker, right? I was a senior when you were a freshman." Millie sat down in the booth across from Marka. "Millie Walker. Do you remember me?"

"Of course. You were one of those stuck up seniors. I hated all of you for putting us through such a grueling freshman initiation," Marka laughed. "So, you stayed in Ridley, huh?"

"That wasn't what I wanted. After graduation, I stayed here and helped Mother with the cafe. Two years ago, she had a stroke; so now I run it by myself. I remember waiting on you and your friends when you came in."

"Yes. I remember," Marka said.

"It was a rough year when Mother had her stroke. It was awful for Ida Mae too. That's her up there clearing the tables." Millie pointed to a short, plump girl with heavy legs. "My little sister—course, not so little any more—she's fifteen. She works here after school and on Saturdays." Millie chewed on her fingernail. "She spends all her tips on that jukebox. I guess kids her age are really into rock and roll. So, you lived in Denver? I wish I could get out of here and go somewhere like Denver. But, I gotta keep the cafe going, at least as long as Mother is alive."

Marka leaned across the table closer to Millie and lowered her voice. "I've moved back to Ridley."

"Eee, gads. What for? If I ever get the chance to get out of here, I'm going to take it and run." Millie slid out of the booth. "Excuse me. I gotta ring up Charlie," she said, heading towards the cash register.

The strength and hardy aroma of the coffee helped Marka clear her head from the drinks she had in the saloon. Millie seems kind of fun. Marka closed her eyes and remembered back when she and Millie were on the girl's basketball team. Buddy had been a senior too and he was their coach. She had tried to get his attention with her special jump shot, but he treated her like a kid. She smiled and thought how he flirted with her in the saloon.

Millie returned to the booth. "See that guy I just rang up? Too bad he's married and has three kids. There aren't many unattached men in Ridley."

Marka crushed her cigarette out in the ashtray and laid a dime on the table for the coffee. "I've got to go. It's good to see you again, Millie."

"You're going to be bored out of your mind living here after Denver. Nothing exciting ever happens. Say, there's a dance over in Deerfield tonight. Wanna go?"

"Maybe some other time." Marka's stomach growled.

"Anna is fixing a special meal for me. Since I've been back, all she does is cook."

She stepped out into the street. The town was noisy with cars and people hollering across the street to each other. She turned away from the cafe and headed towards Anna's house. She lit another cigarette with the matches Millie gave her. Anna made Millie sound so awful. She didn't seem so bad to her. Anna was blowing things way out of proportion.

Marka reached deep into her coat pocket for the Hershey bars and sunflower seeds she bought Anna. Damn it. She had left the vodka behind. Just as well. What the hell was she thinking anyway? She'd have to hide it from Anna. Cripes. That would make her no better than her dad always hiding his bottles around the garage and house. He'd come home from the saloon with candy and seeds for she and her mother. She was doing the same thing. No, it's not the same. She was just trying to do something nice for Anna. But, she bought booze, and then lied to Elton about Anna wanting it. All this had to stop—the lying, the smoking, and the drinking. They were bad habits she picked up in Denver.

The smell of sweet dough filled the kitchen. The counter of the Hoosier cabinet was covered with flour and baking pans.

Marka hugged Anna and wiped flour off Anna's chin with the tips of her fingers. "Here." Marka held out the Hershey bar and sunflower seeds. "I brought these for you."

"Been to the store, huh? You smell like you've been in a fire." Anna wiped her hands on a dishtowel and put the candy and seeds in her apron pocket.

"I stopped at the cafe for a cup of coffee. It was smoky in there."

"Ach, I have a whole pot of coffee. What? You don't like my coffee?" Anna frowned.

Marka poured herself coffee and sat at the kitchen table. She watched Anna sprinkle flour on the counter and knead a hunk of dough.

"Jonny stopped by and left some books for you. I put them in on the buffet. He wanted to know how you were getting along."

"He did? That was nice of him." She felt butterflies in her stomach thinking maybe he was interested in her. "Anna, I've been giving it a lot of thought. I definitely want to keep the house; fix it up, and move in."

Anna spread the dough in a greased pan and flattened it so she could make it into a *kuchen*. "Bodie told you it needed a lot of work. Have you got money for that? Why not stay here with me? I have the extra bedroom. You don't have to go back into that house. Besides, I'd like the company." Anna arranged apple slices on the dough and then sprinkled the crumbled mixture of butter, flour and sugar on top of it. She sat down at the table and took the Hershey bar out of her apron and unwrapped it.

"I need a place of my own," Marka said. "Besides, you've lived alone all these years. You'd get tired of having me under foot."

Anna put a piece of chocolate in her mouth and smoothed the foil wrapper over the rest of the candy bar to save for later. "So, you want to move into an old worn out house and live by yourself." Anna gave Marka a long, thoughtful look. "What's going on *madchen*?"

Marka braced her elbows on the table. Her stomach twisted into a knot. How could she tell her aunt that she wanted to live by herself? She wanted to be independent and in charge of her own life. Anna seemed to want things her own way. I can't go back to being her little girl again! Besides, if Anna ever found out the truth about what happened in Denver, well, things wouldn't be the same between us.

"You're in the middle of baking, and it's a long story. Maybe we should talk about it later."

"Bake, shmake. Tell me now."

Marka's cheeks burned and her mouth felt dry. How can I tell Anna that I had an affair with my boss? Marka sat quietly a few minutes thinking, trying to concoct a story that would satisfy her aunt.

"The company I worked for is going broke," she said, feeling like such a liar. "People are being laid off." Marka took a deep breath. "My boss fired me. You can't trust men. I mean—you can't trust them—big companies. One day you got a job and the next day—"

Anna got up from the table and kindled the fire in the cook stove. She shoved in two pieces of wood. "The dough is raising. I better get the oven hot. I saved some dough out; so we could have fried bread with our *schnitz suppe,* dried fruit soup. Sounds good. Yah? Your company wasn't a socialist one was it? Because the government thinks these people are being disloyal."

Marka got up from her chair and joined Anna at the stove. "No, nothing like that. You are happy I've moved back aren't you?"

Anna wiped flour off her hands with a dishtowel. "Yah, I'm happy you're back. I just wish you'd live with me. It would be good for both of us. But I guess you don't think so."

"Please try to understand why I want my own place." Marka looked into Anna's disappointed eyes. "It's not that I don't like being here with you. It's just that I'm twenty-five. I'm not a kid anymore. I need to get on with my life. And, what if we didn't get along? I've gotten used to being by myself and you've lived alone all these years."

"Well, I guess you already decided," Anna said, looking away. "If you're going to live in the house you better get busy and look around for someone to work on it. And then you have to get yourself a job," she said matter of fact. "But, at least wait until after Easter." Anna dropped slices of dough into the pan of hot oil. The oil crackled and the bread dough hissed. "It's only a few weeks away."

"Anna, I really don't want to wait. I want to get started right away."

"But it's still so cold. I would think it would be better to wait."

The telephone rang; one long, one short.

"Is that your ring, Anna?"

"Yah. Get it; I'm busy with the frying."

"Oh, hello, Millie. No. I didn't forget anything."

Anna turned from the stove and gave Marka a confused stare.

Marka felt her face flush. "I mean—I won't be needing it. Hang onto it for me okay?"

Marka watched Anna as she put the *kuchen* into the oven, and then she slammed the door shut.

The evening was quiet with only the sound of the clock ticking, and the periodic purr of the refrigerator. Marka watched Anna crochet. Her fingers moved steadily, pulling and looping yarn through the hook. She unwound some yarn, and then settled the ball on her lap. She uncrossed her ankles and the ball of yarn tumbled to the floor and rolled across the room. Sasha eyed it through narrowed eyelids, but was too tired for the chase.

"*Wie grell is der Dag rumgegange.* How quickly the day passed," Anna said.

Marka turned to the first page of the book Jonny left, *The Scarlet Letter* by Nathaniel Hawthorne. She remembered it was one of the books on her high school reading list, but she had chosen to read Dickens instead. After a half hour reading, Marka couldn't remember a word. There were too many thoughts whirling around in her head. She wondered if Anna believed what she told her about being fired from her job. Anna would be ashamed of me if she knew the truth.

Anna doesn't want me to move back into my house. But I have to. I have to stand my ground with her. Anna wants—what about what I want? There was no way she could tell her aunt about going to the saloon. Anna was already angry with her. But what if she

46

finds out? Well, I guess I will just have to deal with that when the time comes.

Marka closed her eyes and laid her head back on the chair. Could it be that Jonny was really interested in her? He brought the books. Oh, that's impossible. How could someone as perfect as Jonny possibly be interested in her?

Marka bent the corner of the page to mark where she stopped reading. "I'm going to bed," she said. Anna was already asleep. Her shallow breathing turned into a light snore.

CHAPTER 7

Monday was washday. Marka and Anna went down to the basement and filled the old wringer washing machine and rinse tubs with water from the faucet, one bucket at a time. Anna added bluing to the rinse tubs to make the whites look sterile and bright.

Anna said, "First, we wash the sheets and pillowcases, then the underwear. Next, the blouses, then skirts and dresses, and last, we do the rugs."

After the washing was done, they sorted everything into wooden bushel baskets and carried them up the stairs and out to the clotheslines. The day was warm. The sun glared through the tall cottonwood trees. Marka liked how a light breeze blew across her bare arms as she hung the clothes.

"The sheets can't sag, and the underpants and bras have to be hung between the towels so they are out of sight," Anna said. "No, no, Marka. The socks have to be hung by the toes." Anna unpinned a sock and redid it. "The skirts and aprons hang by the waistband, and dresses, upside down."

Marka sniffed the air and tried not to be irritated with Anna's bossiness. "Smell the fragrance coming from the locust tree," Marka said. The clusters of white flowers bobbed about in the breeze. "And look at the way the elm tree at the corner of the yard stands so graceful against the sky."

Anna was too busy hanging clothes to notice.

Marka said, "I need to go to the post office to check on my boxes and I will rent a mailbox."

"Yah, okay. You better do it right away this morning," Anna said, shaking out washcloths and placing them around the rim of the basket. She handed Marka some clothespins. "Let's hurry and get done here. I have a hunch a storm's going to move in some time today."

Marka pinned the tails of a blouse to the line. A hunch. There she goes again making predictions. It's a beautiful day. The

Chinook winds are melting all the ice. "I think you're wrong about a storm, Anna."

"My bones aren't aching for nothing. We're going to get a storm, you wait and see." Anna shook a towel, and then pinned it to the line. "You'll get a chance to visit with Stella. She's the postmistress, you know. I told you that. Yah?"

"No! You didn't!" The last thing Marka wanted was a nice chat with Stella. She hadn't seen her since that Sunday in church. Facing her wouldn't be easy. What would they say to each other? But she *had* to get the boxes. They contained all of her belongings. She desperately needed to move out of the small bedroom at Anna's. Oh, how she wanted to be settled in her own house.

After they ate lunch and washed the dishes Marka walked to the post office. It was a small building with mailboxes and a gated teller's window on one side. On the opposite wall there was a small writing counter and window that looked out on the street. Marka waited patiently at the teller's window. She heard voices coming from the back of the room. "Excuse me," she said. No one answered.

She read the handwritten note taped to the metal counter. Post card-2 cents, Letter-8 cents, and Air Mail-10 cents.

"You're so damn stupid." A woman's voice boomed from the rear of the building. "Can't you do anything right? Bodie, you'd be a bum on the street if it weren't for your family looking out for you."

Marka felt a twinge in her stomach. Stella! She was not ready to face her especially with Bodie around. She'd have to leave and come later in the day. Besides, she wasn't about to let Stella humiliate Bodie in front of her.

She stepped out onto the sidewalk, and lit a cigarette. Just as she passed People's Grocery, she saw Anna's car racing down the street towards her. A cloud of dust followed the faded green Studebaker. Anna parked diagonally, resting the car's bullet-nose and bumper against the cement sidewalk.

"Oh, cripes." Marka threw the cigarette down and ground it into the sidewalk. It was too late to turn back. She tore open a pack of Sen-Sen and poured half of it in her mouth to sweeten her breath.

Anna opened her car door and walked up the steps to the store.

Marka ran toward the store calling out to Anna.

"Ach, Gott. I didn't even see you. I need a few things." She opened the door and stepped into the store. "Come and say hello to Carl. You remember old man Erlich, don't you?" Anna sniffed Marka and waved her hand back and forth. "You been in that smoky cafe again?"

Carl was at the cash register counting money. Yes, she remembered Mr. Erlich with his black hair and big bushy eyebrows.

"So, Carl, *ve gates*, how goes it?" Anna was cheerful.

"*Allis gutt*, all is good, Anna." Carl smiled and closed the register drawer. "Marka, you look just like your mother," he said tipping his head to one side and raising his brow over the top of his dark-rimmed glasses.

"She doesn't. She's much taller than my sister and her hair is reddish brown, not dark like Rachel's. She looks more like me."

"*So wie die Alte sunge, so zwitschern die Junge?*" Carl asked.

Marka gave him a puzzled look.

"So, what then did I just say to you?"

"I don't know."

He pursed his lips and shook his head. He tucked his thumbs under the flap of his white-bibbed apron. "I said that children take after their parents." He turned towards Anna. "So, why do you come in today?"

"To shop." Anna clutched her pocketbook to her chest. She turned to Marka. "I got to get me a box of that Oxydol soap. Hope I get another cup this time. I'll probably get another saucer. Got so many saucers already."

Carl asked. "Want me to add this to your bill or you paying cash today?"

"Add it to my bill. I know my bill aint' too high. I keep close track of it."

Carl reached under the counter and took out a shoebox filled with receipt books.

"You got any of that Sala Padika?"

"I never heard of it."

"Don't you ever listen to Paul Harvey? I listen to him every day," Anna said. "Sala Padika's suppose to be good for colds."

"You got a cold, Anna? Too bad," Carl said.

"No, I don't have a cold, but someday I may get one. So, anyways, I need some Butternut coffee and you got some of that Ralston cereal?"

"You'll have to settle for Quaker oatmeal. Butternut coffee, yah."

"And yeast, too."

"Ran out yesterday."

"I got to have yeast." Anna raised her voice. "Every time I come in here you're always out of something. Don't know why I even bother to shop here. I ought to take *all* my business to Clayton."

"If everyone had your attitude, Anna, well, I would have to close the store. And if I end up doing that, what will you do then? You'll be sunk."

Why were Anna and Carl being nasty to one another, Marka wondered? Anna always enjoyed the company of her fellow Germans. It made Marka uncomfortable. "Anna, I'm going to look around the store. Call me when you've finished shopping."

Marka walked to the back of the store, the plank floorboards creaked beneath her feet. The floor, recently oiled, smelled of linseed. She walked around inspecting shelves neatly stacked with cans. One shelf was stocked with bags of U & I sugar and flour in cloth sacks. There were bags of oatmeal, and three red and white checkerboard boxes of Ralston shredded wheat. Carl told Anna he was out. And, there next to the flour was the yeast, small cakes wrapped in foil and paper. Why did Carl fib to Anna? Was Anna not paying her grocery bill?

Marka inspected more shelves. Carl had a well-stocked store with the latest products: Rinso for dishes, Lifeboy and Lava soap, Wildroot Cream oil, and Arrid deodorant. There were even packages of colorless oleomargarine. It had a drop of red dye inside; so you could squeeze the package and make it yellow. The meat counter was filled with ground beef, smoked hams, wieners, wheels of cheese, and of course, Carl's famous German garlic sausage. When she was a child she liked to watch Carl rip the pink wrapping paper off the huge roll, and then he would tie it with the string attached to the butcher-block counter.

At the back of the store there were stairs that led up to an apartment. She noticed a tall, slim figure come down the stairs then walk towards her. It was Bodie. He walked with an awkward gait because of his bad hip.

"Bodie. I want to talk to you. A while ago I was in the post office to check whether or not my boxes had arrived. I didn't stay because, well, I—"

"You heard me and Stella? Well, she gets upset with me when, when I don't do things right." Bodie blinked his eyes and scratched the back of his neck.

"I didn't like the way she talked to you."

"Stella, well, she—" Bodie blinked his eyes faster.

"You don't have to explain."

"I do work for Stella. I run errands." Bodie ran his fingers through his long, greasy hair pulling it back behind his ears. "You'll have to talk to her about your boxes."

Marka walked over to the potbellied wood stove and held her hands over the warm drift of air. Her intention had been that the next time she saw Bodie she would lecture him for leaving the door to her house unlocked. Now, she didn't have the heart to. He looked like a beaten dog. He stood with his hands in the pockets of dirty overalls, the cuffs stuffed into the tops of black engineer boots. His shirt was wrinkled and stained.

Bodie joined her at the stove.

"Thank you for taking such good care of my house." Marka said. "I'll bring the money I owe you next time I come to town."

"Okey-doke." Bodie wiped his hand on his overalls, and then held it out for Marka to shake. He smiled, the corners of his mouth curling. "You decided yet what you gonna do with the house?"

"Clean it up and move in. I can hardly wait," Marka said. "Anna wants me to wait until after Easter, but I don't want to. I'm going to start on it right away. I can't wait to make it my home."

"You gonna live in it with the leaky roof and bad plumbing?"

"I'm going to get those things fixed. Say, would you be interested in earning some extra money? The house is full of mice. If I get the traps, will you set and empty them?"

"Why not just take Anna's cat over and lock her in for a few days," Bodie laughed. "She'd get them mice for you."

Anna called to Marka saying she was finished with her shopping. Carl spotted Bodie. He shook his fist and yelled for him to get busy with his chores. Bodie pulled in his shoulders and limped to the back of the store.

"We got to go now." Anna picked up her sack of groceries.

Carl handed her the carbon copy from the charge book. She studied the slip, signed her name, and handed it back to Carl.

"Ich wollen nicht uber die vergangenheit reden." No more talking about the past," Anna said to Carl.

"Yah, yah," Carl frowned. "The past is over."

Marka asked Carl if he had mousetraps. "I need a dozen."

Carl put them in a paper bag. "Do you want to start an account?"

"Yes. Thank you, Mr. Erlick."

Carl wrote her name at the top of a new charge book and had her sign for the mousetraps.

After they left the store and reached the car, Anna calmly got into the car, and smoothed out her dress.

Marka got into the passenger side and slammed her door shut. "Is everything okay, Ann?"

"Yes, Carl thought he didn't have the Ralston and yeast; so I made him look again, and he had it after all." Anna had the look of victory.

"Anna, while I was at the post office I heard Stella saying some horrible things to Bodie."

"Don't get yourself in the middle of something between Bodie and Stella. Anyways, Bodie probably had it coming."

"Since you have your car, it would be a good time for me to check on my boxes."

"*Na*, No, we have to go home. Look at those dark clouds rolling in. My hunch was right," Anna said. "There's a storm brewing. While I'm fixing us supper you can get the clothes off the lines. I'll fix one of your favorites, *kartofal and glace*, potatoes and hard dumplings. Maybe I can fatten you up. You don't eat enough. That's why you're so skinny."

Anna slammed her car door and situated herself on the seat. She turned on the ignition and backed away from the curb. The engine whined like a sick calf.

The next morning, Marka walked to the post office. A driving wind pressed against her. She pulled the hood of her parka over her head to keep the cold off her ears. Anna was right. A storm came during the night and now the sky was a dull gray, and the air was cold. A bird flew overhead and made a chilling sound. Dark clouds had accumulated and hovered above the town. The wind stirred dust in the street.

Marka walked past the Legion Hall and grocery store to the post office. She felt a gnawing in the pit of her stomach. She had worried herself to sleep about how the encounter with Stella would go. How stupid, to tell a stranger so much about your life! Stella had the power to ruin everything for her. It was a bitter twist of fate. Marka certainly was not going to mention a word about it. She would not bring it up.

"Good morning," Marka said as Stella approached the window.

Stella stretched her short body to reach the window shelf. She tipped her head back and pointed her nose like a gun, at Marka's face.

Marka gave Stella a wide smile despite her apprehension. "I'm expecting two large boxes."

"The boxes came in on the train. The depot agent called yesterday. I'll tell Bodie to go over and pick them up."

"Would you tell him to take them to Anna's?"

Stella raised an eyebrow and nodded, yes.

"And, I need to rent a mailbox."

Stella placed a green form on the shelf and handed Marka the pen attached to a chain. "Write your name here. Phone number and address right here on this line." Stella was curt.

"That's funny," Marka choked on a nervous giggle. "An address in Ridley?"

"Well, phone number then. I still can't get used to the way things are done around here," Stella said. "In St. Louis, things were professional."

"Did you work for the post office back there?"

"Yes. That's one of the reasons I got this job. Good jobs aren't that easy to find around here. You'll find that out *if* you decide to stay."

Marka took Stella's emphasis on the word "if" as a threat. "Stella, please don't say anything to anyone about what I told you on the plane."

"I can't make a promise like that." Her face was stern, eyes glaring.

"Why not? Can't we just say we met on the plane and leave it at that?"

"What would Anna think if she knew you'd been so naughty?" Stella smirked.

"I did some foolish things. It would only hurt Anna if she found out."

Stella rolled her eyes with contempt. "Oh, a letter came for you. You should have come in sooner, or had Anna rent a box for you before you got here. The Postal Department cannot hold letters without a return address. I had to send it to the dead letter office in Washington."

"Why?"

"You didn't have a box." Stella stuck out her chin.

"Couldn't you have just held the letter for me or given it to Anna?"

"Absolutely not! Government regulations say all undeliverable mail must be sent to the dead letter office. There was no return address."

Stella's small pudgy hand slid a piece of paper under the grate. "This is your combination for box number 144. Most people pay rent by the year. You can pay by the month, if you're not sure how long you will be staying."

"I'll pay for the year." Marka's heart raced. Her face flushed. She stood silent and waited for Stella to finish filling out the form. A spider descended from the ceiling hanging off its web like a man on a rope. Marka watched it slide down and land on top of Stella's head. Let the spider have its fun, she said to herself. I'm so mad I could knock her head off.

After Stella finished, she said, "I did notice that the letter was postmarked Denver, Colorado. That's the best I can do."

For the rest of the day, the encounter with Stella hovered over Marka like a veil of gloom. If Stella told anyone it would eventually get back to Anna. She'd have to leave town. This would be juicy gossip. Oh, what could she do to convince Stella not to tell?

"Let's sit down and eat supper," Anna folded her hands. "I made some chicken noodle soup and butter balls. Let's pray now." Anna said a prayer: *Komm Herr Jesu, sei Du unser Gast, Segne uns, und alles was Du uns bescheret hast. Amen.* Come Lord Jesus, be our guest and let these gifts to us be blessed. Amen.

They ate in silence talking only about how to make butterballs. Marka told Anna how she missed all the good German meals. It seemed nice to sit and eat with Anna at the table. In Denver, she ate standing over the kitchen sink.

"I will teach you how to cook. You have to cook for your husband when you get one."

Marka said, "I'm angry at Stella. She said the letter was from Denver, but because it had no return address, she had to send it to the dead letter office. You know what that means don't you? The letter is as good as dead."

"What you talking about, *madchen?*"

"A letter came for me before I had a chance to rent a box. Stella wouldn't hold it. She said the letter…" Marka's jaw tightened. "How could she do that? Why didn't she just give the letter to you?"

"She was just doing her job, Marka. Why are you so against her? You are too sensitive. You take everything so serious."

"I think Stella is mean." Marka got up from the table and slammed her dish in the sink. "I'm going over to the house."

"The days are kind of short yet. It will be getting dark soon," Anna said. "That's why I think it's a good idea to wait until after Easter."

"I can't wait. I want to go over now. I need to take a better look to see what needs fixing."

"I don't understand why you just can't wait. Well, I guess you've made up your mind, right? I can't go over with you. I have to get to work on that dress Stella wants for Easter Sunday."

"I'll go alone. I won't be gone long." Marka fumed inside. I don't want Anna going to the house with me. Why didn't Anna stick up for me? I guess there's a side to Anna I don't know. Her eyes swam with tears. Maybe Anna doesn't really want me here.

CHAPTER 8

Marka felt frightened as she approached the house. She shuddered at the memory of Danny Deer Ears, and hoped nothing awful would happen this time. She thought about what Ruby said about ghosts—how silly. She pushed the thought out of her mind and focused on the brick planter that ran along the front of the house and the huge garden plot off to the right, full of weeds. She would have plenty to keep her busy in the weeks ahead.

Marka dug deep into her pocket for the house key. She did feel a bit safer now that she kept the house locked. She opened the door and stepped into the kitchen. She still felt like an intruder even though the house and everything in it belonged to her. Even the mysterious something her mother desperately wanted her to know about. At the hospital her mother had said, "Ask your Dad." I guess that meant she didn't know he had died.

Marka thought how often she got angry with her father. There were times when she hated him. That was because he was always teasing and heckling, always making things difficult. That's the way he was. He was not a protective father, but mean. "This will make you strong; so you can survive in the world," he would say. How would gutting a chicken, chopping baskets of wood, and working in the garden in the hot sun help her survive? Survive what? He'd say, "A woman has to learn to work hard, not be afraid of anything. You may marry a farmer and you'll need to know all of this."

Marka went from room to room, looking for a hiding place, for something—large or small? Was it in a drawer, a closet, or cupboard? No, that was too obvious. If her father stashed it, it would be in a dark dreary place. A place, like the cellar! That would be just like him, to hide something where it was dark, and cold, and full of creeping things.

Marka went outside and walked around to the side of the house. She lifted the cellar door and leaned it against the wall, and then

57

walked down the concrete steps kicking at spider webs. The steps were caked with dirt and still had icy corners. When she reached the bottom of the steps there was another door that led into the underground room. The room rested under a small portion of the house and had an earthen floor.

Marka opened the door. There was only a small amount of light coming down the stairway. She couldn't see; so she dug a book of matches out of her jeans, and lit one. It gave off a bright glow.

The room was filled with wooden shelves that held mason jars. Some were streaked with dried food seeping out of leaking lids. There was an empty vegetable bin in one corner and several large crocks sitting around. In another corner, there were wooden cases of empty bottles, her father used to make homemade beer.

Marka lit another match before the one burned down, and stepped into the middle of the small room. The match went out. She reached for the pull chain attached to the dangling light socket, then remembered there was no electricity. Just then the outside cellar door slammed shut. She was terrified remembering huge crawling spiders she had seen during her childhood. She had more matches, and if she could manage to strike one in the dark, she would have enough light to find her way up the stairs.

Marka lit a match and slowly crept up the stairs holding her breath. She pushed on the heavy wooden door, but it wouldn't give. Don't panic, she told herself. Try again. She used her shoulder and pushed harder. Her heart beat fast. She began to tremble.

The cellar was so cold. Anna will wonder where I am, and she'll come looking for me. It will be okay. She pushed hard against the door with her arms. She pushed again and again until finally, the door lifted. She climbed out of the cellar, and tumbled onto the ground. She caught her breath, but her heart wouldn't stop pounding. She brushed dirt from her jeans and got to her feet.

Bodie came around the corner of the house.

"Bodie. Did you see someone running away from the house?"

"Uh, no."

Marka stomped the cellar door tight against its frame. She wouldn't tell Bodie a word about what just happened. She wouldn't tell Anna either.

"I came to set the mouse traps for you," Bodie said. "I see cat tracks. Anna's cat must have been over here."

"Sasha is a lazy cat," Marka laughed. "Anna feeds her too good."

Before she returned to Anna's, Marka went to visit Ruby. She told her what happened at the house, and about her encounter with Stella. "I wouldn't be surprised if she read people's mail," Ruby said.

"I'm going to try to be nice to her, if I have the stomach for it. Oh, I don't know Ruby. I hope I'm doing the right thing. Seems like I had good reasons for everything I did. I thought keeping the house was the right thing to do. Oh, I don't know what to do. I feel like I'm going crazy."

Ruby raised an eyebrow. "It's like I said before. You'll never be free until you understand it all. If strange things are happening in the house, perhaps it's the ghosts of your past trying to get your attention."

"You mean my father is trying to scare me; so I don't find what's in the house? But, my mother wants me to find it."

"What do you think you'll find?" Ruby asked in a hushed voice.

Marka stopped short and remembered what Anna said about not telling anyone what her mother told her. Ruby was different. She could be trusted.

"Right before my mother died, she told me there was something hidden in the house. Maybe I'm wasting my time looking for it."

"So, what are you looking for?"

"I don't know. And every time I start to look, something strange happens."

"First time I met you I had a feeling you would come into something big. Some night we'll read tea leaves. I feel sure there's a treasure in that house. And, you will find it. But, first, you must make peace with the past.   Just because your parents are dead doesn't mean their ghosts aren't trying to tell you something. Have you thought about the things I said to you the first time we met? How you can't say "No", and you are always trying to please everyone."

Marka said, "I haven't had time to think about much of anything. But I will, Ruby. I will."

CHAPTER 9

The next day, Anna and Marka went to visit Anna's friend, Sophie, who lived across the street. Sophie bustled around her kitchen getting a party together for Anna.

"Happy birthday! This is for you," Sophie said, placing a brightly colored crocheted shawl around Anna's small shoulders.

"*Vergels Gott fer alles*, Praise God for everything. You are good to me." Anna kissed Sophie on the cheek. "Marka gave me a beautiful card with a fifty dollar bill inside. I told her this is way too much."

"I want you to buy something nice. Something you've been wanting for a long time," Marka said.

Sophie cut large pieces of lemon chiffon cake and placed them on plates. She poured them coffee. They sat talking about planting gardens. Sophie said she wanted to set pansies in the earth as soon as it was warm enough.

"How old are you now, Anna?" Sophie asked.

"Seventy-five. I thank the good Lord I've lived all these years and hope to live more, at least long enough to see Marka married." Anna laughed. "I keep telling her Jonny is a good catch even though he's not German Russian. He does go to church though."

"Anna, what makes you think he doesn't have a girlfriend?" Marka felt irritated that her aunt assumed she would be interested in him. "If he likes me so much why hasn't he been over to the house?"

"Jonny doesn't have a lady friend. I would know," Anna said. "And he does come over, but you're always gone. He brought books for you. He said he'd come more if he wasn't so busy. He wants the basketball team to go to State this year." Anna pressed her fork against the spongy cake, and tore a chunk off with her fingers. "I don't want you to end up like me. Single women lead lonely lives."

"I never thought of you as lonely, Anna," Marka said. "You've always had so much going on in your life."

"I've missed having a partner. Someone to talk things over with."

"Guess I was blessed to get a husband," Sophie said.

Anna turned sharply in her chair and announced to Sophie, "Well, it isn't that I didn't have a marriage proposal. Carl Erlich asked me to marry him and Lydia wasn't even dead a year."

Marka recalled Carl's behavior from the previous day. She felt a little confused and wondered if Anna was making this up just to save face with Sophie. "But you and Carl act like you hate each other," Marka said.

"Yah, sometimes I am put out with him."

"She's always put out with him about something," Sophie said.

"Ach, not even to wait at least a year after Lydia died. She was a good woman."

"Too good for him," Sophie piped in. "I think he worked her to death."

"Sophie, we women was raised to work hard. I don't think you are right. Well, anyways, I told him I was too set in my ways to be getting married. I'd never marry Carl. Well, let's not talk about it anymore. Can I have some more coffee, Sophie?"

Sophie filled Anna's cup.

"I do think that Lydia was a good woman. She was kind of homely looking though. Bodie looks a lot like her," Anna said, pouring cream in her coffee.

"What did he do when you turned down his marriage proposal?" Marka asked. Anna's angry with him, but when Sophie knocks him, she comes to his defense?

"He was disappointed. He said since we was both German Russian it would be good because we wouldn't have to guess at things. Ach, who cares anyways. He's nothing but a stubborn old *dummkopf,* dumbhead."

"If only Dan wouldn't have had to give up the store," Sophie's eyes were downcast. "Dan never pressured anyone to pay their bill. He trusted you for it."

"And, he always gave you a sack of hard candy when you paid up," Anna added.

"Dan was always nice when you came in the store. When we was still on the farm, I used to bring in eggs and he'd credit my account."

Marka realized she was bored with the conversation when she noticed she was counting the hairs on Sophie's chin. "When did Carl buy the store?" Marka asked. "A lot has happened in Ridley since I've been gone."

"Let me think now," Anna counted on her fingers. "The fall of 1950, Bodie went off to Korea. Marka, you graduated high school that year. Anyways, Buddy stayed home and worked the farm with Carl. Lydia died in '52. The reason I remember it, Marka, is it was six months after your folks were killed. Then, right before the war ended, Bodie got shot in the hip and came home."

Sophie refilled their coffee cups. "Buddy went to St. Louis to a Wool Growers Convention and that's where he met Stella," Anna said.

"Did they know each other long?" Marka asked trying not to sound too interested.

"Heavens no!" Sophie said. "She tells everyone how Buddy swept her off her feet, how they were married by the Justice of the Peace. She says someday she wants a diamond set instead of her cheap wedding band, and she wants a church wedding."

Marka tightened her lips, but the words wouldn't stay in her mouth. "Who could say such a thing about the man they loved?"

"Stella hates living in Ridley," Sophie added. She's always talking about how great things were back in St. Louis. I say, well, why did she marry him and come here then?"

"Does Stella get along with Carl and Bodie?" Marka asked.

"Carl was glad when Buddy married Stella because he thought he had a woman to do the chores," Sophie laughed. "Only the old man got fooled because Stella nagged him until he finally sold the farm and moved to town."

"Men can't make a go of it on a farm without a woman to work daylight to dark." Anna said. "*Gela*, isn't that so, Sophie? Well, he got a good price for his place. It had good sandy soil, not the gumbo like some of the other farms around here."

"Carl bought a house for Buddy and Stella and the store for himself." Sophie shook her head and looked disgusted. "Bodie didn't get much out of the whole thing. Stella must have thought she hooked a guy with money. Poor unsuspecting man, that Buddy."

"Well, no one forced him to marry her," Anna said.

Marka thought about Stella and how she didn't mention her husband the entire plane ride.

"Bill and I worked beets for Carl for a while. I saw how Stella buttered him up. She knew what his weak spots were. He loves it when someone makes him feel important. What a pair. He's the pot and she's the matching lid," Sophie giggled.

Now, Marka was totally immersed in what they were talking about.

"Ach, now, you're being cruel. Stella has to put up with those three men. Carl is always fussing about how he is losing business to the big stores in Clayton. That's cause his prices are too high and he doesn't give trading stamps. Smiley's gives Red Stamps. A person can save up for dishes. And he could be a little more understanding when people can't pay their bill right at the end of the month."

Anna shifted her body in the chair. "Carl and I had a real blow out yesterday, Sophie. I told him to let you charge again." Anna's face tightened and she pressed her lips together.

"He still thinks of me as a beet worker," Sophie said.

"*Na, Ja*, his own wife and kids worked out there in the fields. Crawling around on the ground thinning sugar beets. I worked beets when we lived in Greeley, Colorado. I know how hard it is. No more working beets for Sophie," Anna slapped the table. "I'm glad to give you some of my sewing jobs. It takes the load off me. Some of these women love all the new styles. I can barely keep up."

Sophie rested her hand on Anna's arm. "Yes, you give me your extra work, not sewing for Stella though, oh no, she's too particular. The jobs are enough to get me by since Bill passed away. I still think we made the right decision to stay on at Fred Wiserman's working as hired help. That's when I stopped working in the fields and did cleaning and cooking for them. Fred helped us get our citizenship papers."

"Carl's bitter since Lydia died," Anna said, fixing the pins in her bun at the back of her neck.

63

Marka changed the subject. She wanted the conversation to center around Stella. "I still don't understand why Stella sent my letter to the dead letter office."

"What? But she knew you were coming. Why didn't she hold it for you?" Sophie's eyes widened. "She heard us talking plenty of times about your coming back."

"She has to be professional about her job. Just because this is a small town doesn't mean she can break the rules," Anna said.

"Phooey," Sophie protested. "I think she's jealous of Marka because you always brag about her and her good job in Denver. Ach, I don't like her. I'll tell you something. She sure likes money and what it will buy. She dresses stylish, wears the finest. Buddy makes good money and she sure spends it."

"She was probably just worried she'd lose her job if she didn't do it right. It isn't the kind of job that's easy to come by," Anna said. "Anyways, the letter didn't even have a return address on it."

There she goes again defending Stella. "I'll never know who that letter was from or what it said." Marka was irked at Anna. Why not make sure Sophie knew everything. It can't hurt. "And she rode all the way from Denver with me, and never even said she lived in Ridley."

"She's kind of a devil." Sophie shook her head.

"I just wish you'd forget the whole thing!" Anna's voice was loud and angry.

"Why are you defending her, and why do you do all that sewing for her?"

"I need the money, Marka. My social security check doesn't go far enough. She can afford to pay good."

"Bodie's the peculiar one," Sophie sensed the tension and quickly changed the subject. "But, I feel kind of sorry for him."

"I heard Stella belittle him. It makes me mad. I just want to..." Marka couldn't resist taking one more swipe at Stella.

"Ach, Gott, don't say anything more." Anna shook her finger at Marka. "She's coming over today with a pattern and some material. I want you to be nice to her."

Marka felt like a child being reprimanded. She got up from the table and went to the living room. Should she tell Anna why she was upset? Anna didn't realize the power Stella had over her. Anna had such fear of authority. Does she think being a postmistress is such an important job? Oh, why had she let the conversation go so far? She ruined the party. Marka turned around and went back to the table where Anna was sitting. "I'm sorry I made you angry. I'll be nice to Stella. Happy birthday." She leaned down and kissed Anna on the forehead.

She said her good-byes and went to the front room to get her coat. She heard Sophie say, "I think Marka is having a hard time getting used to living in Ridley. Try to be more understanding, Anna."

Marka said under her breath, "I hope Stella gets a varicose vein on her nose and all her hair falls out.

White smoke floated above the grill; the aroma of sizzling food filled the air. Millie took a piece of pie out of the glass case next to a white menu board. Scribbled on the board were the words: **Today's Special - Mutton Chops, fried potatoes, and vegetable soup - $1.50.**

Marka sat down at the counter.

"You look so serious," Millie said. "What can I get for you?"

"Coffee, hope it's strong, I need a jolt." Marka tapped a cigarette out of the crumpled pack she kept stuffed in the pocket of her parka. "It's Anna. She always sticks up for Stella."

Three farmers walked into the cafe and sat at the table up front.

"How you fellas doin?" Millie chirped and waved hello. She unbuttoned her uniform, three buttons down, and straightened her apron. "Let me get these orders, then we'll talk."

Marka watched Millie waltz across the room over to their table. Millie tilted her head, smiled, and fluttered her eyelashes. "The special. That's what you want? Okay." She chewed on the eraser of the pencil she usually had stuck through her hairnet. She leaned close to the men and whispered something. Marka couldn't hear what she said, but they roared with laughter. Millie walked back behind the counter over to the sizzling grill. She scraped fried potatoes off to one side, and then tossed on three chops.

Buddy meandered into the cafe and sat on the stool next to Marka. "Bodie tells me you want to get the work done on your house. Can't think of a nicer thing than having you back in Ridley," his eyes teased.

"What can I get you, Buddy?" Millie set down a cup and filled it with coffee.

"I'll have the special."

Millie tossed on another mutton chop.

"Looks like the farmers are going to be getting a little help from the government this year," Buddy said. "It's about time."

"How's that?" Marka asked.

Buddy dumped two teaspoons of sugar into his coffee and spread the *Clayton Post* across the counter. "Says here that emergency loans will be made through June, to farmers and ranchers for this year's crop. They're making loans up to $15,000 at three percent interest."

"Good for the farmers," Marka acted interested.

"The loans are for seed, feed, and fuel. The money has to be repaid out of the first income received in the fall when the crop is harvested. God, I wish, I was still on the farm. I know I could grow the biggest beet in the state."

"Why'd you sell?" Marka wanted Buddy's side of the story. Sophie said it was because of Stella.

"Bodie went off to Korea, then Mom died. We weren't making it. Each year, the beet crop was less. I think Dad was just tired of farming."

"Hope the farmers have a good year. Tips are always better when they do," Millie winked at Marka. "They'll be happy to hear the news about the loans. All I ever hear around here is complaining. It's either too windy to plant, there's insect infestations, or hail has destroyed everything. Eee gads."

"Sometimes you gotta wait for next year to be better, but farming is what I like to do," Buddy said.

Millie skipped across the room to answer the telephone on the wall next to the restroom. "Buddy, it's for you," she hollered.

"Who is it?"

"Your wife."

Buddy stood up, spun his stool hard, and walked over to the phone.

Millie reached under the counter and brought up a brown paper bag.

Marka said, "I don't want it now."

66

"What about the dance in Deerfield? Bobbie V's playing, and we can bring this with us. Something for intermission." Millie's eyes twinkled.

Marka watched Buddy out of the corner of her eye. He shuffled his feet and then leaned against the wall. Marka thought how she never noticed before that Buddy was slightly pigeon toed, but his blonde crew cut made him look so cute. Marka listened to Millie with one ear and to Buddy with the other.

"Stella, damn it, I told you before not to take it off when you did dishes. You want a new one—a red sapphire? What the hell's a sapphire?" He slammed down the receiver and stomped back to the counter.

"That woman can be a pain in the—"

The words, "I'll go to the dance with you," slipped out of Marka's mouth.

"Hooey," Millie yelped. "Buddy, Marka's going with me to the Deerfield dance."

"Ach, Gott, it's almost suppertime, and I haven't any idea what to fix." Anna walked back and forth from the refrigerator to the pantry. "How about some potato soup? First, I'll put coffee on."

She peeled potatoes and onions, put them in a kettle of salted water, and placed the kettle on the cook stove. "After you left Sophie's, we got to talking about that Senator McCarthy. There's so much going on now with our government and Russia." Anna put the peelings in the bucket under the sink. "Our people can't afford to draw attention to themselves, you know. A person's got to be so careful nowadays about everything they do and say, or else they'll be called a communist. That McCarthy just may be out to turn the country against our people. We have many German Russians in Ridley, you know."

Anna sat down at the table.

"We're German? Why would the government be interested in us?" Marka asked.

"Yah, we're Germans, but we are also five generations in Russia; so really, that makes us Russian. But, we are the lucky ones who left. We still have relatives there, you know. They went through hard times. Many of them starved to death because Stalin was so ruthless. Sophie tells me what her cousin reads in the *Die Welt*

67

Post, the German newspaper. Our people work so hard. Work, work, work. That's all we know. Earn respect. Be good American citizens and church goers." Anna started to cry. She took a hanky out of her apron pocket and dabbed the corners of her eyes. "During the war it was not good to be German. People actually spit on us. And now because of the Cold War with Russia it's even worse to be Russian. People call us stupid Rooshians, but that don't mean we're communists."

"Anna, please try not to get so upset. I doubt the government will be interested in a little town like Ridley."

Anna thought about what Marka said. "Yah, yah, I guess you're right." Anna picked up a bundle from one corner of the table. "I must get the buttons sewed on this dress and then, I am through for the day." She wet the end of a thread with her tongue, and then rolled it around between her thumb and middle finger. She jabbed at the small hole, but her hands were shaking, she was so upset. She couldn't thread the needle.

Marka took the thread and needle out of Anna's hands. "Here, let me do it for you. I notice you hold everything so close to your eyes, Anna. I think you need new glasses." Marka threaded the needle and twirled the end of the thread into a knot, then handed it back to Anna. "Make an appointment with the eye doctor in Clayton and I'll drive you."

"We are hard working people. We don't ever expect to get something for nothing." Anna put the thimble on her middle finger and made stitches. "When we came to this country, we left a lot behind. Even with this scare, don't forget your heritage, Marka. Always remember our traditions and language."

"I will remember," Marka comforted Anna.

"I'm grateful I learned to do so many things, like how to cook and sew. I have no education. How else would I have supported myself? Yah, yah, my eyes are getting a little bad. They water so much. But, I really need to get this dress done for Stella. I promised her I'd have it done so she could wear it Easter Sunday to church."

"You work too hard; you were up late last night. I wish you would quit these sewing jobs, or try and give more of them to Sophie."

"Yah, I know." She blew her nose in her hanky, wadded it up, and put it in her apron pocket.

"There's something I want to talk to you about, Anna. Millie asked me to go to a dance in Deerfield Saturday night. The band is supposed to be good. Now, I know what you think of her, but—"

Anna leaned over and adjusted the elastic bands that held up her cloth stockings. She smoothed the stocking over her leg from her ankle up to her knee, adjusted the top, then rolled the stocking back over the elastic. "You better stay away from that Millie," Anna shook her finger at Marka.

"I need to be around people my own age."

"That Millie is crazy for the men. I've heard wild stories about her," Anna said. *Gleiche Bruder, gleiche Kappe.*"

"What's that mean?"

"It means, kind of like you say, birds of a feather flock together. If you hang around with her, what will the people think? They'll say you're a whore like her. This is a small town and people talk. Everyone knows when you so much as sneeze. The women gossip and Millie gives them plenty to talk about. Besides, you can't be going to dances during Lent. It's only one week before Easter, and we're suppose to think about Jesus on the cross not be going out and having fun. When I was growing up we weren't allowed to play cards or go to dances."

I'm not a child, Anna, Marka thought to herself. And don't use that motherly tone of voice. I am an adult. "I respect that it's Lent. I'm going to Ladies' Aid with you on Wednesday night. Doesn't that count? I'm sorry Anna, but I really want to go."

Anna took off her glasses and wiped her watery eyes with the corner of her apron. "I won't argue. It's a waste of time to try and change someone's mind. I know that. Besides you're grown now." Anna tucked her hands under her armpits and sat quietly, thinking. "Instead of going to the dance with Millie, why not ask Jonny to come and have supper with us?"

"I can't ask a man for a date."

"Well, then, I'll ask him. He's coming over tomorrow to pick up his shirts. Every time he asks about you."

"No, don't say anything to him. If he asks me out, I want it to be because he wants to. Not to please you. Promise you won't say anything. I told Millie I would go with her to the dance and I can't go back on my word."

"I can't understand what that Millie's doing going to dances, anyways. I thought she was a Methodist."

Anna stood at the back door in her flannel nightgown and slippers looking at the soggy snow that fell during the night. "A spring snowstorm. The farmers and ranchers are going to think this is an answer to prayer. Looks like we got about four inches."

Marka stepped down the steps into the small porch off the kitchen. "Maybe the farmers will be happy, but I'm not. I want winter to be over. I'm looking forward to warm weather; so I can start work on my house."

"You got spring fever?" Anna said.

They sat at the kitchen table eating oatmeal and cinnamon toast. Marka took a couple of bites then pushed her plate away.

"I made a couple loaves of *roggenbrot*, rye bread this morning," Anna said opening the oven door to check on her bread.   She thumped the loaves with her thumb. "Done."

"Anna, look the little witch is out of her house." Marka pointed to the colorful chalet with the thermometer attached. It hung on the wall next to Anna's newly embroidered dishtowels. "It really is a weather predictor," Marka gazed up at the miniature wooden house. "I remember when I was little and you told me that if the witch stays inside that means it is going to be a nice day. Look. She came out and it snowed last night."

"Ach, that's just superstitious stuff I told you when you were too young to know better."

"Look at it!"

Anna stared intently at the little house. "Well, I do see what you mean. The witch sure is out, and all the way."

"You're so funny," Marka laughed. "This is superstitious and yet you say things like, knock on wood, and you throw salt over your shoulder. I remember you saying once that you had a lucky dress you wore."

"Leave the dishes for now," Anna scowled. "Let's go into the living room and listen to the news about the storm."

She sat in her chair and turned on the radio.

"Residents of the County can now breathe a sigh of relief," the announcer said. "The spring storm has brought good moisture to the area. Farmers and ranchers have suffered through five seasons of drought."

"Good. It's awful to see the crops wither and die in the fields. The soil turns to dust," Anna said. "Back in the thirties we had such terrible dust storms."

By Saturday, Chinook winds had blown in and melted the snow. The temperature was in the fifties. It was a typical spring day with huge clouds floating around a pale blue sky. Rain was forecast for Sunday, but that didn't dampen Marka's enthusiasm for the upcoming dance. She spent the entire day getting ready. She took a long bath, plucked her eyebrows, and wound her hair on rollers.

Millie picked her up at 7:30 p.m. She shifted into gear and backed out of Anna's driveway. They drove along Main Street, then turned left onto the steep hill. The car bumped along the washboard road; the black and white dice hanging from the rear-view mirror swayed back and forth. Millie spun the tires as they left the gravel road and pulled onto Highway 212, the two-lane blacktop. They sped past barbed-wire fences separating the grassy plains from the highway. The landscape was treeless and flat with the exception of an occasional butte.

"I don't think your aunt likes me. I phoned you this afternoon and when she answered, she pretended like we had a bad connection. She kept saying, 'I can't hear you. I can't hear you'."

"There's nothing wrong with the telephone or Anna's hearing," Marka laughed. "Don't pay any attention to her. I don't know what to think. Guess when I was a kid I ignored a lot of things about her. I feel like she's mothering me with her constant, 'What will people think? Don't make waves; don't have any fun during Lent'. I can't wait to move into my own house."

"You've been on your own a long time. I never left home, I had to take care of Mother and the cafe." Millie turned on the car radio and when it warmed up, Bill Haley and the Comets blasted *Rock Around the Clock*. "We're going to have ourselves one good time tonight. I'm in the mood for dancing. Maybe tonight we'll meet our Prince Charming," Millie giggled and adjusted the blue neck scarf off to the side of her throat. "If you wait around expecting a Ridley man to notice you, you may as well give up. You'll end up an old maid like Anna."

They pulled up in front of the dance hall.

"The music doesn't start until nine o'clock." Millie reached under the front seat and dragged out the brown paper bag. She pulled out the pint of vodka and unscrewed the lid. "I didn't forget it—one good thing vodka has over rum or whiskey is that you can't smell it on your breath. I brought some pop to mix with it."

"Give me the bottle. I'll have it straight." Marka tipped the bottle, filled her mouth, and swallowed. "Ugh. On second thought, I'll have mine in pop too. I haven't been to a dance for so long. In Denver, the only place we danced was in lounges." Marka swallowed the orange liquid in full gulps, and then filled the pop bottle with vodka. "This helps me loosen up."

"These dances are a real blast," Millie said. "The flyboys from the Air Base in Rapid are cool. I'm tired of the hayseeds around Ridley."

"Do you ever bring Ida with you?"

"Ida hasn't discovered what boys are all about. She's still content to stay at home with Mother. Besides, I couldn't leave Mother alone at night. I bought a television set. She watches until it goes off the air at eleven; she even watches the test pattern," Millie laughed. "I don't want Ida to turn out like me, working at the cafe, waiting for someone to come along and marry her. She's real smart in school, gets all A's. I want her to go to college."

"It's nice the way you care about Ida and your mother."

Millie tapped the steering wheel with her fingernails. "Never really had a choice in the matter. When Ida was three, our old man took off. We haven't heard from him since. He could be dead for all we know. That's when Mother started the bakery and cafe, that's how she supported us."

Marka opened another bottle of Nesbitt's orange, chugged it half way down, and then filled it to the brim with vodka. "Are we freaks because we aren't married?"

Millie said, "Probably. Benjamin Spock says that women were made to be concerned first and foremost with husbands, children, and home. You don't have to worry."

"What's that supposed to mean?"

"You're pretty; you'll find someone."

"Someday you'll meet a man Millie, either at a dance or he'll walk right into the cafe."

"I'll drink to that," Millie said, pouring more vodka into her pop bottle.

"Gee, your father ran out on you. Guess I never paid much attention to what was going on in Ridley. After I graduated high school, all I wanted to do was split. I thought I was too big for this little place. So, what am I doing back here you probably want to know?" Marka shook her head. "I'll tell you a secret, but you have to promise you'll never tell anyone. In Denver, well, I was involved with a married man. I'll tell you all about it some day."

"Some day. Tell me. Your life is so exciting."

"I don't want to talk about it tonight, Millie."

"They say you can never go back," Millie said. "Bet it seems strange to be in your house, your folks gone and everything."

"I haven't been over to the house much. Ever since I found that Indian asleep, I'm scared he'll come back."

"What Indian?"

"The first time I went to the house, there was an Indian sleeping it off in my folks' bed."

Millie laughed until tears came to her eyes. "Welcome to Ridley, kiddo."

"There's so much work to do on the house," Marka said.

"What are you doing for money? If you need to make a few bucks, I could use some help at the cafe."

"I have some saved up. It should last me for a while."

"I could really use you at the cafe, especially in the mornings. Breakfast is hectic. Farmers come in at eight and sit around drinking coffee until ten waiting for the mail to get sorted. Summer is the busiest. They have their crops in; so they come to town a little more often." Millie turned on the dome light and looked at her wristwatch. "Let's go in now. We have to time this just right. We arrive early and dance a couple of dances together; so the guys can get a good look at us and see that we're—cool. Guys want you to make them look good on the dance floor."

They went inside the large pavilion. Millie sauntered onto the dance floor, her tight skirt and angora sweater hugged her body. Marka joined her and they jitterbugged. She felt pretty in her red A-line skirt and black Orlon sweater. She wore a headband to hold her hair back from her face.

They clasped hands and moved to the music. Bobby V and his band hadn't yet appeared on stage, but a stack of popular forty-fives played loudly. Millie stuck her rear out and wiggled it. She jerked her arms back to show off her ample breasts.

Marka felt frisky. If a wind came along she would let it blow her where it wanted. She felt free. It was the alcohol. It was the most she had to drink since she left Denver.

Millie was right about getting out on the dance floor and strutting your stuff. Marka never danced so much in her life. She would finish a dance and there would be someone standing with his hand out asking her for another. She and Millie occasionally bumped into one another. Millie usually winked and waved.

During a slow dance, Marka felt a touch on her shoulder. The lights were low; it was difficult to see his face, but when he spoke she recognized Buddy.

"Excuse me." He tapped her dance partner on the arm.

Marka placed one arm around Buddy's neck and the other on his shoulder. She smiled shyly and asked, "Where's your wife?"

"She doesn't care to come along, says her ankles are too weak for dancing."

"What a shame," Marka smiled again.

They whirled around the dance floor. Buddy told her she was a good dancer. To think when she was a kid in high school she felt so clumsy and speechless around him and here she was feeling like the cat that got the canary.

They danced until intermission, and then Marka told Buddy she needed to find Millie. "She's probably outside waiting for me."

"She's out in a car with someone, bet on it," Buddy said.

Marka looked surprised. "We were to meet at her car at intermission."

"Come on, I'll help you look for her." Buddy squeezed Marka's hand and they walked out of the dance hall.

They found Millie and her new friend making out in the back seat of Millie's car. Buddy rapped on the window and when Millie finally came up for air, she opened the door, jumped out of the back seat, and ran over to Marka. "I met this guy and I really want to go with him after the dance. He's a telephone crewman staying at the

Don Pratt Hotel in Clayton. Buddy can drive you home," she whispered in Marka's ear.

"Millie—I don't—think—"

"Please, Marka! He really likes me. I have a chance with this guy. Buddy, you don't mind giving Marka a lift home do you?"

"Sure, I'll give her a ride." Buddy smiled wide.

"Have a snort," Millie handed Marka a bottle of Four Roses whiskey. Marka drank straight from the bottle. The whiskey burned her throat, and warmed her insides.

Marka danced several more dances with Buddy, and then he drove her back to Ridley. When they reached Anna's house, he parked in the alley. He turned off the headlights and ignition.

Marka felt dizzy and giddy from all she drank at the dance, plus she and Buddy downed warm beers on the way home. Buddy helped Marka out of the car, and just as she got both feet planted on the ground, he pulled her close and kissed her. She felt limp in his arms. The kiss seemed to go on forever and then he said, "I had a fun time tonight. When can we do it again?"

She pulled away, said goodnight, and walked to the house.

Marka pulled the covers over her and closed her eyes. The room was spinning. She opened her eyes to make it stop. She felt like she was going to be sick. She thought of Buddy, and what had happened. She was getting herself into another big mess. This is the last time anything like this will happen. You're drunk, Marka. Go to sleep.

Wednesday night was Ladies' Aid. Marka put effort into what to wear. She decided on a light-blue shirtwaist dress. She turned the collar up on the dress and pulled her hair into a ponytail tying it back with a green scarf. It's so important to Anna that the women of this town accept me, she reminded herself. And she wanted it too. She wanted to be accepted and feel part of Ridley again.

Anna sat in the car honking for Marka to hurry. They picked up Sophie, and then drove to Katie Wiesson's house.

The women were sitting on folding chairs set in one big circle. The warm room was saturated with perfume. Anna proudly introduced Marka, then placed her pocketbook on an empty chair and went into the kitchen. Marka found a chair and sat down. All she could think to do was, smile. She smiled so much the corners of her lips hurt. She tuned her ears in to bits of conversation trying to appear confident, but she felt like a fish out of water. Why do I always feel underdressed? Everyone else is wearing floral print dresses and rhinestone earrings.

A woman, slight in build, medium brown hair, and small eyes, sat next to her. "My name is Emma. You may not remember me." She wiped beads of perspiration from her lips and chin. "When you were a little girl, your mother used to bring you to meetings." She tucked the hanky under the sleeve of her dress.

"Yes, I remember you," Marka said thinking how she never did like Emma much as a kid.

"Your mother would put those cute little braids in your hair and dress you up so cute," Emma said.

Marka remembered back to when she was a child, sitting on a cold medal chair, hands folded together, tucked between her knees. She would swing her legs and click her heels loudly watching the ladies and listening to their conversations. Emma was always gossiping about someone.

"Don't you think it's hot in here?" Emma asked.

"No. I think it's just right."

"Could be me I guess? I'm going through the change."

Marka heard a voice calling the meeting to order. "It's almost time for opening prayer." The ladies ignored Katie and continued their conversations.

Charlene came over to Marka and introduced herself. She had a beehive hairdo and wore black cat-eye glasses. "I'm so glad you came with Anna. I've wanted to get over to say hello and welcome you back to Ridley. See that heavy-set woman over there. That's Edith. Watch, she won't say a word all evening. Her dentist gave her ill-fitted false teeth." Charlene blinked and giggled.

"Where's Stella?" Nettie asked. "We can't start without *her*." Nettie was a skinny woman with light-brown hair done up in a bun on the top of her head like a little loaf of bread. Her bushy eyebrows met in the middle of her nose.

"She knows we start promptly at seven thirty," Charlene's voice boomed across the room and everyone quieted down.

"She's here. She's in the kitchen fancying-up a dessert she brought," Emma said aloud then turned and whispered to Marka,

"Nettie is Stella's friend and the town gossip. Don't ever tell her a thing."

When Stella walked into the room and sat down, all eyes were on her.

"She's always such a fashion statement," Emma whispered to Marka. "When you get a chance, go into the bedroom and look where the coats are. The leopard skin is hers. It goes good with her blonde hair."

Stella stuffed white gloves into her handbag. She was wearing a pompadour hat, and stiletto heels. She smiled at Marka. "So glad you came. I always seem to miss you when I come over to Anna's for fittings. You seem to be keeping yourself so—occupied!"

Marka thought to herself how Stella had walked into the room like a movie star, all gussied up.

Katie started the meeting with an opening prayer. "Eastertide, the Glory of the Resurrection," she bowed her head low and folded her hands in her lap. "Dear Lord, we are gathered together here tonight in your presence. We come to do your work and your will, whatever that may be. We thank you for all the blessings you bring to us. This we pray in the name of Jesus Christ our Lord. Amen."

They sat in silence for a while then read from the Bible, each member giving a Bible verse for roll call. They discussed who would clean the church for Easter service, and they took up a special collection for flowers for the altar.

"Marka, because you're a visitor, you don't have to give any money," Stella said from across the room.

"I hope you'll decide to become an active member of our Guild," Charlene said. "There's no doubt in my mind that you'll be graciously welcomed into the fold."

They sang an Easter hymn and continued the meeting.

"Many of us belong to sewing circles, and we work on quilts at our meetings," Emma said to Marka. "We make quilts for the Indian missions."

Katie reminded the group that they had to discuss the purchase of ten Luther's Catechism for the confirmation class.

"What about the new flatware for the church kitchen?" Charlene asked. "Didn't we talk about each of us bringing a book of Gold Bond Stamps to a meeting, then trading them in for flatware?"

"And what about raising money for a new organ for the church?" Anna said. "And I think we should make a quilt and raffle it. I have boxes of scraps left from sewing jobs and I have a pattern that Ma Perkins sent me."

"Really? However did you come by that? " Stella asked.

"Yah. All I had to do was send a dime and an Oxydol box top. She sent me a pattern. It's a dogwood blossom in a woven basket. If we make twenty blocks, we can have a pretty good sized quilt, don't you think?"

"Speaking of dogwood, my little doggie is missing," Stella whined. She's been gone for two days now. Has anyone seen her around town?"

"Which dog is yours? I forget. There's so many running around town," Sophie said.

Nettie wrinkled her nose. "Yesterday there was a dog sniffing around my garage."

"My dog is a Pekinese! She wouldn't do that!"

A pompous Pekinese, Marka thought to herself. They say dogs resemble their owners.

"Marka is going to move back into her house," Sophie said.

"That's wonderful," Katie clapped her hands. "If you need any work done, remember my Herb. He's a good carpenter."

"I was thinking of Bodie, but I'll certainly keep Herb in mind."

"Pay him good," Stella moaned. "He still owes us money. We loaned him some to fix up that old pickup of his. Bodie would be nothing but a bum if it weren't for us looking out for him."

"I would certainly pay him well."

"I think it's wonderful that you've moved back," Katie interrupted. "How nice for you, Anna."

"Yah. I'm glad to have my Marka back." Anna's eyes lit with pride.

"So tell us, Marka," Nettie said, "why you decided to come back. Seems strange that in a city as big as Denver you couldn't find a man, settle down, and get married."

"It's none of our business," Katie said. "Just leave her alone."

Marka blushed. "Guess I just haven't found the right one."

"Oh, phooey. There's plenty of men out there looking for a good wife," Nettie objected, "but she's got to be settled down. I read an article in *Ladies' Home Journal* that said homemaking is more important to women then competing with men. A woman's place is in the home being supportive of her husband. A man wants someone who will keep a well organized home. Maybe you just haven't been willing to settle down."

Stella spoke up. "Are you sure you don't have a man in Denver?"

Marka's heart sank. Stella is going to tell.

"My niece is no shrinking violet. She's pretty, smart, and besides there's already someone interested in her."

"Who?" Stella leaned forward on her chair. "That brother-in-law of mine? If he's got a crush on you, you'll never get rid of him."

"Ach, no, not Bodie, it's Jonny Sanders."

"I wouldn't count on that," Stella sniggered. "He receives perfumed letters from Texas."

"His mother lives in Texas," Sophie blurted out.

"These aren't from his mother. Would a mother perfume her letters?" Stella stuck her pointed nose in the air. "Anyway, I can't imagine anyone leaving a big exciting city to come to a little one-horse town like Ridley."

"Isn't that what you did?" Sophie asked.

Stella wrinkled her nose and pursed her lips.

"I decided I didn't like the city," Marka said. "Too much confusion. Besides, I missed Anna."

"Wanting to settle for a quiet life. I have a hard time believing that." Stella would not relent. "You won't tell us the real reason will you?"

Marka's inside's heated up like a boiling pot. There was a part of her that felt afraid and a part of her that was furious. Is Stella going to tell in front of everyone? This will be the end for me. Anna will feel humiliated, and she will never forgive me for lying to her.

Charlene asked, "When are we going to have dessert?" Marka breathed a sigh of relief. Thank you, Charlene. If Stella keeps it up, maybe I'll just have to tell everyone about Friday night. What would Stella think if she knew her husband had been out dancing with me, and that he drove me home and kissed me, and the kiss was not solicited. Is Stella going to tell, or just play with me—like a cat plays with a mouse?

"I hear there's an opening at the Court House in Clayton for an office clerk in the coroner's office," Stella said. She passed out plates of frozen icebox dessert. She handed Emma a plate, skipping Marka.

Marka lowered her eyes and fumbled with her fingers. Why was it Stella made her feel as small as a gnat? She skipped me on purpose.

"Ach, no. Marka was an executive secretary. She wouldn't want no office clerk's job," Anna said.

"How did you get your government job as postmistress?" Marka asked Stella, trying to fit in and not appear nervous. "That's a civil service job."

"Carl knew the right people and pulled some strings. Of course, I worked for the postal department in St. Louis; so, I was pretty sure I would get it."

Sophie got up from her chair and handed Marka her plate of dessert. "You forgot Marka, Stella." Stella went back to the kitchen, brought out another plate for Sophie, and sat down. "They may cut out Saturday mail delivery starting the thirteenth," she said. "That would make it nice for me."

The evening ended with closing prayer.

"I have a prayer request." Stella crossed her legs and straightened her skirt. "Pray I find my little dog. I just can't believe she's gone."

"Yah, okay," Anna said. "Now, let's bow our heads and pray."

After they prayed, Marka got the group's attention by raising her hand. "Stella, I remember I saw something that may interest you. Yesterday, I saw a little dog jump into a car, and then the car drove away."

"My God! Why didn't you say something? What did the car look like?"

"It was a pink and black 1955 Ford. There was a bunch of kids in the back seat. That's what I remember the most."

"Oh my God, somebody stole my dog, I just know it. They just took her. I've got to go now. I have to tell Buddy." She went into the bedroom and came out wearing the leopard skin. "See you all at church. Anna, I'll be over soon for my last fitting."

The door slammed behind her. Anna looked at Marka. Marka rolled her eyes and looked the other way.

On the way home, Marka told Anna that she wasn't going to go to Ladies' Aid again. "I just don't fit in, I feel like an outsider. No one was interested in talking to me; they left me out of their conversations. Everyone knew each other. When I did speak up, I felt like I always said the wrong thing." Really, she was worried about Stella. This time, she kept quiet, but maybe next meeting she'd tell everything.

"You've been away for a long time, Marka. Be patient. Just like you have to wait for the pot to heat up after you put it on the stove. Stella, well, I can tell she's jealous of you. She wants all the attention. She's afraid she won't be queen bee any more."

"Thanks for being on my side. I feel like you're always defending her."

"Maybe when she comes for the dress fitting you can try and get to know her a little better. Maybe she isn't as bad as you think."

"Did you hear what she said about Jonny? See, I told you he probably had someone."

"I don't believe it, Marka. He always asks about you. I have to ask you something though. Did you really see someone take Stella's dog?"

"No. I made it up. I couldn't help myself. I'm sorry."

"Ach, Gott, you stinker," Anna giggled.

"Anna, thanks for saying, I'm not a shrinking violet."

CHAPTER 10

It was another one of those glorious spring days; bright, clear and fresh. Robins, purple finches, and chickadees greeted the morning. They sounded like the warming-up of an orchestra. After breakfast, Marka headed for the river south of town. She took the familiar shortcut down Dead Man's Hill, and then walked along the well-worn path that led to the bridge.

She leaned against the bridge and gazed at the water below. The steel frame felt cold against her shoulder. She watched the water flow, and she heard sounds and felt the pulse of life in the river. This had been one of her favorite places. She'd stand on the bridge and throw rocks in the water or climb down under, and hide from the cars that crossed overhead. She had to be careful, for under the bridge, the water was deep and the river wide.

Was it a mistake, coming back to Ridley? Things weren't going the way she'd planned. She loved Anna; yet she felt anger towards her. She thought Anna would be there for her no matter what. She hated the way Anna always discounted her feelings. She hated all the lies, but she couldn't tell Anna the truth. She wasn't really sure what she wanted, and she certainly didn't know who she was. One minute, she was trying to please everyone and the next, she was furious at them.

Most of all, Marka was worried about Stella. After last night, she knew Stella had her future in her hands. Will Stella tell the whole story at once or let it out, piece by piece? It seemed to Marka that she had come to Ridley and found herself in another ugly mess.

Marka lingered on the bridge a long while letting the quietness of the morning and the flow of the water soothe her troubled mind. The glow of the sun cast light on the fast moving water. She walked to the end of the bridge and made her way down the hill to the water's edge.

Spring rains and melted snow had filled the river so full it flowed with force. The green water sped along, grabbing at loose grass and low hanging tree branches. Marka walked a long ways until she reached a shallow spot in the river with an outcrop of rocks running from one side of the shore to the other. She stepped on the stones crossing over to the middle until she reached a huge boulder. Then she sat down and watched the clear, cool water and thought how she hoped she wasn't like the river, never content being where it was, always moving elsewhere.

The last six months had been the unhappiest of her life. She couldn't sleep or eat. It had become impossible to concentrate at work. She had taken dictation, then not been able to transcribe it. She made mistake after mistake while typing. The nights were the worst. After work she would go to the tavern, drink and smoke cigarettes, and listen to sad songs on the jukebox.

She'd been such a fool. Rex filled her with promises. He had no intention of divorcing Geraldine. Give up all that money? Rex wasn't a man; he was more like Geraldine's possession. And he needed someone to make him feel big; so he went for me, someone ten years his junior. Sure, he was good looking and had power. After all, his father-in-law owned the company. And sure, he could give promotions and raises to anyone he wanted. Geraldine would loosen her reins on him; he would run to me. Then, she'd rein him in, and he would ignore me.

She didn't make executive secretary because of Rex. She was capable and competent. It wasn't his influence that got her to the top of the secretarial pool and then his private secretary. Tears rolled down Marka's cheeks, thinking how Geraldine screamed at her the night before she left, "Don't you know why he gave you all those promotions?"

She had to leave Denver. She had no choice. Marka rubbed the tightened muscles in the back of her neck.

The eastern sky was gorgeous, filled with puffs of clouds close to the horizon. A flock of geese honked overhead as they moved across the sky. Marka heard someone hollering up the river. As the figure got closer, she saw it was an older man. He was clad in khaki pants and shirt. He laid a string of fish on the grassy riverbank.

She climbed off the boulder and stepped across the rocks to the edge of the shore. She stepped down on the soft ground.

"Look at that," he pointed his finger at the sky. "The geese are going home for the summer." He took off his fishing hat and wiped sweat from his forehead with a handkerchief. "George Hanson. Who might you be?"

"Marka Becker."

"Anna's niece. Yes, she told me you were coming. For the last month, that's all she's talked about. I live a few houses down from her. Welcome home."

"You're the one who keeps her freezer stocked with fish. She thinks a lot of you."

"Well, I like her too."

"You were with the railroad then stayed after you retired. Right?"

"Sounds like Anna filled you in. I worked for them for forty years, ten as a depot agent, my last couple years here in Ridley. I like the town."

"I met Jonny Sanders. He said the two of you go fishing and play cribbage."

"Yes, Jonny. He reads a lot. Keeps me supplied with books. I mostly read the newspaper though. I like to keep up on things."

"My dad liked to read the newspaper too. He used to get huffy when the paperboy forgot to deliver it."

"Guess I'm a little like your dad. I get miffed about that too."

George opened a pouch of tobacco and stuffed a pinch into the bowl of his pipe.

"I like the sweet smell of your tobacco. I like to smoke a cigarette once in a while."

"I mostly smoke a pipe. This one's an oldie. I like my oldest pipes the best."

"It's very nice."

"Sometimes, I roll my own cigarettes. I don't like the tailor-made kind. I use Bull Durham." George chewed on the stem of his pipe. "So, what you doing down here by the river?"

"It's always been a favorite spot of mine," Marka said.

"I like it too. I come down here to think. Helps clear my mind. Course, I catch fish too," he laughed. "Do you like to fish?"

"I tried it a few times when I was a kid, but I really never had anyone to show me how."

"You mean your father never took you fishing?"

"No. He'd take some of the neighbor boys but never me."

"You ever decide you want to go, let me know."

84

A second flock of geese flew over, so high they were only a faint line across the sky.

"They're coming back from their vacation down south," George said, putting a lit match to the bowl of his pipe. "Now they'll mate and raise their young. Remarkable the way they always return to the same place they left the season before. Geese live by instinct, you know. Now we humans don't. We make choices, and sometimes we make mistakes. Guess that's what makes us human."

Marka felt a breeze brush lightly across her face. The river seemed to whisper as it swirled along the banks. Another group of geese honked overhead, their perfect V shape pushing north. She stood with her hands on her hips looking up at them.

There was a rustle in the weeds; a jackrabbit hopped out in front them. It stopped for a moment, gave them a timid look, then darted away across the high grass of the riverbank. The warmth of the sun, the sound of the river, the geese, the rabbit, and George made her feel at ease.

CHAPTER 11

Saturday, the day before Easter, Marka spent most of the day cleaning Anna's house. She mopped the floors, washed windows, and polished furniture. Anna wanted everything perfect because Jonny was coming for dinner.

"You clean the house good, and I'll do the cooking. I'm going to fix a ham. I have a new recipe for a glaze," Anna said.

As Marka worked, she thought about the previous week and how Stella bothered Anna every day about her suit. "Isn't it finished yet? I hope it looks like a Christian Dior. I love the S-Line and the way the skirt is pegged at the back."

Yes, Stella would certainly be the best-dressed woman in church, but it was Anna who stayed up late every night struggling to match the difficult plaid.

When Stella came over for fittings, Marka stayed in her bedroom with the door ajar so she could listen to their conversations. She feared if given the opportunity or right reason, Stella would tell Anna everything—everything about Rex, but the week went by and Stella didn't say a word.

One day, Stella said, "According to the weight charts, I shouldn't weigh any more than one hundred thirty-two pounds. That's what it says for women twenty-three and five feet four. I've been on a reducing plan, all I can eat is Melba toast, grapefruit, and celery. Buddy is having a fit. I tell him to go to the cafe and eat."

All week long, Anna persisted, "Marka, let's sew something for you to wear on Sunday."

"You don't have time, Anna. Stella keeps hounding you and making changes to the pattern. I have something to wear."

"Yah, I do feel a little rushed. On Saturdays, I got to do the baking, and I can't sew on Sundays. You know what they say: everything you sew on Sunday, you'll end up tearing apart and redoing on Monday." Anna said, still concerned, "What about wearing one of those nice suits you wore to work in Denver? Look through your boxes; you must have something you could wear."

"Maybe I could order something from the Montgomery Ward Catalog," Marka said.

"No. It wouldn't get here on time. Come on. Let's make something together. I have lots of yardage. Here, you look through these patterns. Maybe you'll find one you like."

It was Marka's first sewing project, and Anna was patient and encouraging. They spread the lavender cotton out across the dining room table. They pinned the onionskin paper pattern pieces to it. Anna showed Marka how to line up the arrows with the weave of the fabric, and how to pin.

The dress would have been beautiful with its scooped neck and large white buttons down the front. But, she wouldn't be wearing it to church because they only got part of the skirt finished. Marka wasn't that upset. What's all the fuss over what to wear Easter Sunday? Who cares? Thinking about it only upset her. What she needed to do was walk downtown and stop in and say hello to Millie.

When she arrived at the cafe, she noticed Herb Weisson going into the saloon, and she wanted to talk to him about doing some carpenter work. Against her better judgment, she followed him in. They sat at the bar, and Herb bought her a Vodka Collins.

"Yes, Katie told me you were going to fix up the house. I won't charge you much seeings you're a single woman and I liked your dad." Herb dabbed his tongue along the edge of a cigarette paper. "Your father was the best damn cement mason there was, and when he built a house, he did it right. He knew that plumb lines made all the difference. Yes, your dad and I were pretty good friends. He was the kind of guy who would do anything for you." Herb filled the paper with tobacco, wet the edge again, and rolled a cigarette.

"I don't feel the same fondness towards my father as you do." Marka took a sip of her cocktail and lit a cigarette. "When I think of him, all I seem to remember is that he mostly ignored me."

"Awe, come on now."

"When I wanted to do something with him he'd say, 'Go to the house and stay with your mother.' He never took me fishing or taught me how to pound a nail. 'Girls belong in the house with their mother,' he'd say. 'Doing the cooking, baking, washing, and sewing'."

"What's the frown for?" Herb picked a sliver of tobacco off the end of his tongue."

"I'm asking for trouble coming in the saloon like this, aren't I?"

"You aren't the first woman to come in here," Herb said. "I remember this pretty thing who used to come in with her father. They lived north of Garrison. Her name was Tillie, and she'd sit right here with him while he drank. Then, she'd drive all the way home. Thing is, she had a club foot, but that never stopped her."

"That was my cousin, Tillie. I haven't seen her in years. Anna told me she and her father were close. It was her mother she didn't get along with."

"I heard he ended up leaving that big ranch to her. He had another daughter and a son."

"Yes. I can't remember their names. Anna only talked about Tillie."

Herb scratched his head. "There's a woman lives here in town—she used to live up north. She comes in once in a while but not that often. She runs the pool hall, her name's Ruby."

"Already met her," Marka said.

"Ruby says she feels like a pheasant in a chicken coop living here in Ridley. She told me at least on the ranch she was free to ride the range. You know, when she was fifteen she was bought by a rich cattleman up north. The sheriff took her father away because they said he knifed a guy. Her mother sold her to Henry because she needed the money."

"How do you know so much about her?"

"I hang out at the pool hall. I like Ruby. People are suspicious of Gypsies; say they'll steal anything that ain't nailed down. Ruby's not like that."

"I happen to like her even though Anna doesn't." Marka's eyes twinkled.

Herb drank the rest of his beer and set the empty glass down on the bar. He ran his hand over his unshaven cheeks. "Ruby mostly keeps to herself."

"Kind of what I feel like doing sometimes," Marka had a strange, painful look on her face.

Herb doubled his fist and lightly hit her on the shoulder. "I don't think Anna will let you keep to yourself," he laughed.

Marka finished her Vodka Collins and crushed out her cigarette. "I'm going to walk over to the pool hall and visit Ruby. I feel like we've been talking about her behind her back."

"I'll walk over with you. I want to see if Bodie's there. I promised him a few games of pool for some work he did for me."

The pool hall reeked of stale smoke. It took a while for Marka's eyes to adjust to the dimly lit room. There were card tables and chairs scattered around. The walls of the large room were smudged with chalk dust and grime, and the paint had been scraped off the walls from chairs rubbing up against them. A Coke machine sat in one corner, a rack of pool sticks in another. Marka pushed a dime through the coin slot and heard it clink. She opened the narrow glass door and pulled out a bottle.

"I'm racking up the balls. Let's have a little action, before Bodie comes," Herb yelled from a pool table at the far end of the room. "Marka, women who go to the saloon ought to play pool too. Oh, I forgot, women can't shoot pool worth a darn," he egged her on.

"I'd clear the table before you even got a shot," Marka teased. "But not right now. I'm going upstairs to visit Ruby."

"I bet you're a regular Willie Misconi," Herb yelled at her.

"No. Minnesota Fats," Marka yelled back.

Marka walked out onto the sidewalk, and then climbed the stairs to the apartment. She knocked on the heavy wooden door. Ruby pushed aside a dark green curtain covering a window to see who it was.

"Marka, come in, quick! Fedora is out of her cage. She might fly out the door. I should keep her caged up more, but she enjoys the freedom."

They sat down on the sofa in the little parlor area of the large room. Fedora flew over to Ruby, landed on her shoulder, and then dropped down on her arm. Ruby stroked the bird about the head. "We both live half-caged lives. She can leave this cage, but not this room. Same with me, I can leave this room, but not this town. Freedom. Sometimes I think I should just open my door and let the poor thing fly free." Ruby seemed frazzled.

Fedora looked up at Ruby and performed some amusing antics. This made Ruby laugh. She lifted the bird to her mouth and gave it a kiss. The bird flew back to its cage.

"Should I come back some other time?"

"No, I'm pleased you came back to see me. I've been watching you for days, walking to the grocery store and post office. And I heard you've been to the saloon too. You're a bit of a rebel, aren't you?"

"Where did you hear that?"

Ruby lit a cigarette and dangled it from the corner of her mouth. "Word gets around this town. Does Anna know about it?"

"No, and she wouldn't like it if she found out."

"She will find out," Ruby said, tapping the ash off her cigarette into her hand. "Let me tell you something about this town. Everyone knows your business!" She tossed her head back and laughed. "The women of this town find me horrifying. One time I baked an angel food cake for one of their church bake sales. I put red food coloring in it to make it pretty pink. They snubbed their noses at it." Ruby shook her head. The large silver earrings tapped the side of her neck. "I use to go to the church on the hill and when people found out I read palms and tea leaves, they said I was doing the devil's work. They are the same people who say we must love everyone. I'll tell you a secret. I don't even know the devil." She roared with laughter.

"They don't really know you," Marka said. "I feel like I've known you all my life. When you haven't seen a friend in years, you start up a conversation, and it's like you saw each other yesterday. That's how I feel about you."

"God has given me a gift. My mother had it too. She could see things no one else saw. Let's go sit at the table. Let me pour you some tea."

She filled their cups. "Drink and then I'll read the leaves for you."

Fedora flew down from her cage and landed on Marka's hand. She pinched the skin with her beak.

"Ouch!"

"Fedora! I think it's time to clip your wings." Ruby cupped the bird in her hands and placed her inside the cage. "Are you all right, Marka? Did she break the skin?"

"I'm okay, just a little scared. I never knew anyone who had a bird that flew around free." What a nasty little creature, Marka thought.

Fedora beat her wings against the cage door and chattered loudly.

"Ruby shook her fist. "I'll clip your wings, Fedora. Then there will be no more freedom for you."

"I'm fine," Marka said feeling a little sorry for the bird.

"I rarely have company. She doesn't know how to act. She can be easily frightened."

"Ruby, I was wondering about something. You spend most of your time around men. Well—do you think you know more about men than other women? I mean, because you have the pool hall and ..." Marka took a big sip of her tea.

"Yes, I think I do know about men," Ruby answered. "What do you want to know about them?"

"Everything."

"Well, first thing is you have to sacrifice some of your feminine charms or they will not trust you. Like some men don't trust their wives. They won't talk freely with you. One thing you learn about men is that they have feelings too, but they think it is weak to reveal themselves; so, they keep it all inside. They don't want the other men to make fun of them. They have to act big and strong. When a man is more interested in love than power, he is a real man."

"I'm a fool when it comes to men," Marka said. "I came back to Ridley because—oh, I don't know where to start."

"Start at the ending and work towards the beginning," Ruby said.

Marka laughed. "Isn't it the other way around?"

"Not if I am going to understand. Get on with it."

"I was involved with a man in Denver. He was my boss, and he said he would divorce his wife."

"Get to the good part."

"His wife called me, and said to meet her in a restaurant. She told me she was on to us, and she said I had only one option, to take the money and leave. She told me this wasn't the first time Rex had a little fling."

Ruby said. "Maybe that wasn't true. She just wanted to get rid of you."

"I feel so stupid and ashamed."

"I can see you are naive, easy prey for a man like that. Drink your tea. Leave a little at the bottom. I'll read your leaves."

Marka lifted the cup to her lips and drank leaving a small amount of leaves in the cup, just like Ruby said. Ruby took the cup and swirled the tea leaves three times to the right, and three times to the left. She sat the cup down on the table and waited for the leaves to settle to the bottom; then she studied them. "There's something more going on in your life than what you've just told me. I see another man coming into your life."

Marka didn't believe Ruby could really see things. The reading of tea leaves was just some sort of game. But, how did she know about Buddy? She must have heard gossip. Yes, that must be it.

"Do you think I should tell Anna about this man in Denver?"

"Secrets only make things worse. You have too many unsettled things in your life. Have you been back to your house to look for your treasure?"

"I hear strange sounds and feel spooky when I'm there."

"You will be haunted until everything is settled. If a person dies with unfinished business or anger towards someone, they will return from the other side. Remember, I warned you about that before."

"Are you talking about my parents?"

"Did you make peace with them before they died? Did you forgive them for everything?"

"No. They were terribly angry because I left Ridley, especially my father."

Ruby got up from the table and went into her bedroom. After a couple of minutes, she came out of the room and handed something to Marka. "This will protect you from any angry spirits. It's a scapular. My Catholic mother-in-law gave it to me." Ruby lifted Marka's long hair and slipped the cloth over her neck. "You've got to take care of yourself if you're going to survive."

"I can't take this," Marka said. "Anna would have a fit. She doesn't like Catholics."

"Aren't you free to make choices, Marka?"

"No one has complete freedom, Ruby."

"We do. Yes, we do. Do you always do what Anna wants?"

"What about you? You aren't free to leave Ridley and go where you want," Marka said.

"Oh, you are a tough one." Ruby grabbed Marka and hugged her. "You are right. We choose our lot in life then we have to live with it. Freedom! I should let Fedora out of the cage, out of my house, and just let her fly free."

CHAPTER 12

Peace Church stood atop the hill like a watchman, stern against the pale blue sky. The town of Ridley sprawled below. Silence reined in Ridley except for tractors in the fields and an occasional car driving down Main Street. Ridley was a pretty little town of dirt roads, modest houses and streets lined with elm, birch, and cottonwoods. The railroad station was at the bottom of the hill. Chicago Northwestern Railway put in a line that ran through Ridley where it picked up sugar beets at the dumpsite and hauled them to the factory in Clayton. Across from the station stood the galvanized steel grain elevator with the words "Trisco Flour" painted on one side. The town had a small business district and houses with grassy lawns and garden plots ready to be tilled for spring planting.

That morning at breakfast, Anna told Marka about the church, how it was built in the thirties and was designed after the Lutheran churches in Russia. Important were the Gothic windows, five on each side, and a tall steeple that reached up to the sky. Inside the church, a red carpet runner led to the most striking part of the church, its ornate altar mounted in front of a Prussian-blue wall. It was intricately carved wood, painted white, with lustrous gold trim. The altar table was covered with crocheted linens, the pattern of a cross worked into its design.

That morning, the small church filled with people. Everyone for miles around went to Easter Sunday service. Marka took off her gloves and put them in her handbag. Anna, Marka, and Jonny squished together as the pew filled. Marka felt her leg touch Jonny's.

The opening hymn was *Holy, Holy, Holy*.

It was Reverend Thurber's first Sunday of preaching. He instructed the congregation to call him by his first name, Jordan. "This is my wife, Louise, and our three sons: John, eleven; Adam, eight; and Jacob, three."

The congregation clapped.

"I attended Seminary in Boston, and thus far have pastored three churches; one in Nebraska, one in Missouri, and another in Kansas. My wife and I are delighted with our assignment to this small, picturesque community. I'm sure I will be glad I accepted the call to pastor your church."

After the Offertory, Jordan's voice shifted to a serious tone. "Today is Easter Sunday. Two thousand years ago Jesus was crucified." Jordan grasped the podium and steadied himself. "The Bible says that the risen Lord appeared so they might understand the scriptures. It was only after they understood the significance of his life, his ministry, and his death and resurrection, that they were able to proclaim victory. And it transformed the world." His voice boomed.

Marka couldn't concentrate on the service with Jonny sitting so close. They weren't a couple like Stella and Buddy who sat only a couple pews ahead of them. What was Buddy thinking, glancing back as if he were looking for someone? He'd scan the room and then, stop to stare at her. She didn't smile even though she wanted to. He did look handsome in his light blue leisure suit.

It was the same blue as the taffeta dress she had worn for her confirmation. That Sunday, there were eight of them; six boys and two girls. They had to learn the ten commandments, the beatitudes, and the names of the books of the Bible. The pastor questioned them in front of the congregation. "Name the books of the New Testament." She was nervous and afterwards, wondered if her confirmation even took. She thought something mystical was supposed to happen, but it didn't. After confirmation, she lost interest in God and hadn't been to church since.

Her mother bought her the blue dress, high-heeled shoes, and nylon stockings. She was a shy fourteen year old. She walked with her shoulders slumped and her head down. She and her mother had an argument that morning before church. Her mother cried when she confessed she shaved her legs and underarms.

"Mother, why are you so upset with me?"

"Only bad ladies shave," her mother said. "Be careful around the boys. If something happens and you end up—well you know— well, just remember, make sure it's someone whose face you want to look at every morning at the breakfast table."

Buddy looked back again. Marka turned her head and closed her eyes.

"So, we must ask ourselves what would Jesus do in a given situation. If we model his behavior, we must meet the real needs of people," Pastor Thurber continued his sermon. "Feed them when they are hungry; comfort them when they mourn."

The sermon ended with the closing hymn, *He has Risen.*

Jonny left immediately after church. Marka and Anna stayed and welcomed the new pastor, and visited with a few people. Anna didn't want to linger. "We better get home and finish getting dinner ready."

They got in the car and drove down the bumpy, gravel hill.

"Jonny said he would be over after he changed out of his church clothes." Anna hugged the steering wheel. "Didn't he look good?"

"I think you're more excited about him coming to dinner than I am," Marka laughed.

"Ach, that's not true."

"Anna, do you really believe God hears prayers and answers them?"

"Well, I use to think if I prayed hard enough God surely had to answer—especially if I was perfectly good all the time. Now, I believe if God thinks something is right for me he will provide. I don't always know what's good for me, so I put things in His hands."

"I can't remember ever having a prayer answered," Marka said. "Guess I'm not as fortunate as some people. Like—Stella."

"What's that supposed to mean?" Anna's voice was stern.

"Bodie told me her dog finally showed up. Sounds like maybe someone really did kidnap it. If it's true what they say about an animal taking on the likeness of their owner, then the kidnapper probably couldn't wait to bring the little darling back," Marka sniggered.

"Marka, you just got out of church. You're letting a seed of hate grow in your heart. This is not good. You are glad Jonny's coming to dinner, aren't you?"

"Yes, Anna, but please don't push. I don't want him to think he's being chased."

At 1:00 p.m., a dark green Ford Woody pulled up in front of Anna's house.

"That car is Jonny's pride and joy. He drove it all the way from Houston, loaded with all his personal things," Anna said. "He told me this car is the most expensive Ford made that year. Brand new it cost him two thousand dollars."

There was a knock at the door. Marka took off her apron and straightened her dress. She opened the door and invited Jonny inside. "Hope you're hungry. Anna has enough food for the whole town."

Anna sliced the ham and covered the plate with a dishtowel. She told Marka, "Put the mashed potatoes in this bowl and put the lid on so they stay warm. I'll finish this relish dish. Jonny, you love my pickled beets, yah?"

Jonny smiled and nodded.

"So, do I." Marka gave Anna a hug.

"I got to know Jonny real well when I cooked at the dormitory. We hit it off right away. Right Jonny? I gave him some rugs and a couple of pictures to make it more like a home. You paid me to make curtains for your windows. Remember? I still think what you need is a wife."

"Anna. Leave Jonny alone."

They sat down at the dining room table. Anna informed them she used her best-crocheted tablecloth. They folded their hands. Anna said the prayer, "Come Lord Jesus..." They dished up their plates.

"I think Reverend Thurber is going to fit right in," Anna said.

"A few more boys and he'll have a basketball team," Jonny laughed.

"I heard something interesting this morning, after church," Marka joined in. "Years ago, the women sat on one side of the church and the men on the other?"

"Yah, sure. That's the way it was. And the services used to be in German. Now, this goes way back. When I was little, the folks used to have meetings at our house. They would read out of the Bible, and sing songs. They called them *fershumlum,* prayer meetings, and the meetings were held by the *bruthershuft,* brotherhood," Anna said. "Some of the old people still have them. They don't like things to change much."

"And they don't like to mix with other people," Jonny added.

"Yah, we keep to ourselves, but now with someone like you, well, how can we help ourselves?" Anna looked pleased.

After dinner, Anna took a nap in her chair, while Marka and Jonny sat in the front room and visited. Jonny wanted to know how she was coming along with her house and if she'd been looking for a job.

"Why don't you try to get a job as school secretary? You have experience. At least put in an application with the school board."

"I think what I really always wanted to be was a teacher."

"Why didn't you do it then?"

"Because it would have taken me four years of college and secretarial school was only a year. I was anxious to get away from Ridley and to be on my own."

"You have to like to read to get through four years of college. Do you like to read?"

"Of course, I just never seem to have the time."

"Did you read the book I brought over?"

"Oh, yes," she fibbed. *The Scarlet Letter.*"

If he quizzed her, she'd flunk. So much for making a good impression. She only got as far as the forward and preface. The one night she did try to read, she couldn't concentrate because she had too many things on her mind. She couldn't remember a single word she had read.

"What I find interesting about *The Scarlet Letter* is that the sin of adultery was the scarlet sin, meaning it glared for all to see," Jonny said. "But what about man's other sins: jealousy, anger and bad thoughts? Not actually murdering someone, but wishing they were dead? In God's sight those are just as heinous," he added. "Guess I am getting pretty deep here, aren't I?"

"Oh no, I think you've summed it up quite well," Marka swallowed hard and wished Stella were dead. That would certainly solve her problems. My God, what was she thinking? Marka coughed hard and had to go to the kitchen for a glass or water.

"Are you all right?"

"Yes, just a little tickle in my throat." She sipped the water thinking how easily she could lie.

"I love literature. My favorites are Dickens, Kipling, and Steinbeck. Right now my students are finishing up Stevenson's *Kidnapped*. I'll bring you more books if you like. I have some in my car that I could bring in before I leave. Or, I can check them out of the school library for you."

"Anna always likes to get books from the Bookmobile," Marka said. "I'll get some for me. I don't want to bother you. Besides, I have so much to do on my house I doubt if I'll have time to read."

"May tenth, I'm chaperoning the school prom. Would you be interested in going with me? Actually, you'd be my date. The kids would see it that way. You may get some teasing," Jonny smiled. "So, will you be my date for the prom?"

"Yes, I think that would be fun." Marka blushed and felt excited, him asking her for a date all on his own, no prompting from Anna. She could hardly wait to see the look on Stella's face. A girlfriend in Texas! Stella probably made the whole thing up just to upset her.

"The Junior-Senior Banquet is the ninth. The kids have been working on a sea scene for decorations. They will be crowning Queen Neptune and Old King Fish."

"I can't wait." Marka said. She thought she just might have a chance with Jonny after all.

CHAPTER 13

The day after Easter it poured, but Marka went over to her house anyway. Anna wanted to finish the dress they had started. She insisted Marka wait to start cleaning and fixing. Are Anna's wishes influencing the weather? First, the unexpected snowstorm, now this rain.

Marka sat in the kitchen listening to the rain beat on the roof. She watched drops cling to the window screen, trickled down the dusty window, and then disappear. The spring rain seemed to settle her; quiet her soul. She could see the big, old cottonwood at the edge of the yard. The leaves were budding fast now that spring had arrived. She liked this time of year; it was like the world was giving birth. Rivers and creeks were running full; the countryside was deepening into an emerald green. She felt the urge to run through the streets of Ridley and soak up the rain like the spring grass.

Finally, the rain stopped and sun streamed in through the streaked windows. Marka thought about Ruby believing in ghosts. "When a person dies, if they're angry, they will haunt you," Ruby had said. It was the certainty in Ruby's voice that bothered Marka, but then Ruby liked to be dramatic. Marka had hidden the scapular Ruby gave her in the dresser drawer so Anna wouldn't find it. Anna didn't share Ruby's opinions about such things. When Marka tried to tell her what Ruby said about ghosts in the house, Anna said "Ach, every time you go near that woman she tells you things that make you worry. I wish you'd just stay away from her."

Marka couldn't bring herself to tell Anna that every time she went to the house memories came back. Memories that sucked the breath out of her, and made her heart ache. She couldn't talk to Anna about it; tell her about all those times her parent's waged war against each other. One time she tried to discuss it, but Anna argued saying, "You aren't remembering it right." Anna didn't want to hear that her sister was unhappy because her husband drank too much. Anna didn't want to hear about the hollering, pushing, and shoving. How Phillip would hit Rachel. Didn't Anna ever wonder why Marka would run to her house, crawl into bed, and pull the covers over her head?

Where should she start? Marka shook dust from the drapes. She coughed and sneezed. She thought she would sort through things and what she didn't want; she'd donate to Ladies' Aid for their next rummage sale. She'd make this house sparkle; make it her own. She walked around the living room taking note of all the bric-a-brac. Like the ceramic leopard and the poodle dogs on top of the radio; her mother's cup and saucer collection in the pine cabinet. She shook the drapes again and the dust sifted through the air.

The plastic covers on the lampshades were there to keep the satin from turning yellow. She'd buy a floor lamp. Something modern. She'd definitely replace the slipcovers on the couch. The living room carpet was gray with maroon leaves. It was her mother's most prized possession. She bought it from the Olson Rug Company in Chicago. "It will last longer than our lifetime," she said. Yes, it did last—her lifetime. Marka swallowed hard. "I saved old wool clothes for years, then turned them in for credit towards the rug," her mother had said.

In the corner stood her mother's treadle sewing machine. Anna could teach her to sew on it. What happened to the radio? The one they sat next to listening to *Fibber McGee and Molly, Life of Riley*, and *The Shadow*. What evil lurks in the hearts of men? Marka laughed and then noticed that this old radio looked like a piece of junk. It was not the one she remembered.

Marka went into her parents' bedroom and sat down at the dressing table. I'll fix the house, but what about the memories? Will they go away? She picked up her mother's silver dresser set—a hand mirror, comb and brush. She ran her fingers across the engraving of roses and vines. When she was little, she'd hold the mirror in front of her face and brush her hair. She opened a drawer and found neatly folded, white linen hankies with embroidered floral patterns. She took one, ran her finger across the tiny hem, and then tucked it into the pocket of her dungarees.

Thoughts wove in and out of Marka's mind. She recalled how her mother always wore her hair held back with combs. On the dresser sat a little blue bottle with a gold tassel, Evening in Paris. Marka unscrewed the lid and sniffed the sweet fragrance. Why hadn't there ever been affection between her parents? What happened to cause the bitter arguments? She hated the sound of her father's angry voice. It always made her feel out of touch with the world.

And why was she always afraid and confused? Why couldn't she feel close to anyone? Not even Anna. Nothing made sense. Nothing made sense when she was a little girl. She would run off to her secret place to try and figure things out.

"I wonder?" Marka whispered, "my place, my own special place." She tightened the lid on the perfume bottle, and set it back on the dressing table. She wanted to go to that place where in summer the ground felt warm on her bare feet. She would sit and listen to the songs of crickets and to the leaves clatter in the breeze.

The weeds had grown tall behind the garage. Marka rolled down her dungarees to cover her bare legs. She walked over to the big cottonwood, to the little spot of ground under it that had once been her sanctuary. The wooden bench had rotted away and lay in a heap. The lilac bush was overgrown. Her special place; she hadn't been there in years.

Marka tromped the weeds down and sat under the cottonwood tree. It was under this tree now shading her from the sun that she would think things over. Her parents would be in the middle of one of their battles and Anna wasn't available because she'd be cooking at the school or busy sewing.

Who was that little girl who sat under this tree? Did she want to remember? She hated thinking about it. Tears streamed down her cheeks and fell like rain watering the soil. She took the handkerchief from her pocket and wiped her face. She missed her mother. She hugged her legs close to her body and rested her head on her knees. She couldn't understand what happened. Why did things have to turn out like this? Marka wept in short gasping breaths.

Anna called. "Marka. Marka."

Marka rose to her feet, the muscles tightening in her legs. She had been here for a long time. She made her way around the side of the garage and headed toward the house.

"What were you doing back there?" Anna said.

Marka rushed to Anna and threw her arms around her neck. "Oh, Anna, I hurt." Tears squeezed out of her eyes and ran down her smudged face.

"*Madchen. You* should see yourself." Anna smoothed Marka's bangs to one side. "You look just like you did when you was a little girl and you would come to my house all upset about something. You'd be crying and feeling so blue." Anna tilted her head to one side, then the other. There was gentleness in her voice and softness in her eyes.

"I feel like a little girl. I feel like I haven't grown up," Marka wiped the tears from her cheeks.

Anna said, "Growing is painful."

"Life seems so cruel. Why does God let bad things happen?"

"We're like little plants. Ever notice how they push the dirt and pebbles out of their way so they can grow to full size? Their soft, tender stems push upward past jagged edges hoping not to get too many scars. They become strong, repairing themselves as they grow. We are like that, Marka. Give life a chance. Come, let's go inside the house," Anna said, lightly squeezing Marka's hand.

"I never got to tell her how much I loved her," Marka sobbed, her blue eyes filled with tears. "I want to touch her, hold her hand like I'm holding yours, feel her close to me. I don't want to admit how much I miss her. I tell myself she didn't love me just so I won't miss her so much."

"I know. I know," Anna said comforting words. "Your mother loved you."

"Guess I feel guilty because I always wanted you to be my mother because she was never there for me. When I come to this house, I remember—things."

"You need to forget. Let your heart soften. I can tell you are bitter against your parents. You need to forgive and forget."

"They were angry when I left Ridley. Guess I was only thinking of myself. I did want to get away from here. I couldn't stand all the fighting and bickering."

"Marka, just forget about it, okay?"

"The last time I came home for a visit, we had a terrible fight. When I left, I didn't even tell them good-bye. Do you think they're angry with me?"

"Marka, they're dead!"

103

"Did Mom ever say anything to you about that day? Please, Anna, I have to know. Was she hurt and angry with me?"

"Your mother always kept everything to herself. She never shared her thoughts with me."

"Anna, I want to make a life here, but I don't know how to make the bad memories go away." Marka put her arms around her aunt and held her close.

"Ach, let's forget about it then. You have to live your life. I was thinking that there are no jobs here in Ridley. You'll have to drive to Clayton, and you don't even have a car so you use mine."

"I'm not worried about money." Marka wanted to tell Anna about the money from Geraldine, but how could she? She'd have to tell her the whole story.

"Millie offered me a job at the cafe."

"How much can you make waiting tables?"

"She's going to pay me fifty cents an hour. She says tips are good."

"Maybe she makes good tips from the men." Anna frowned. "Anyways, would it be enough to live on?"

"The truth is, I'm not worried about money. I have plenty. Before I left Denver, I took money," Marka blurted.

"My Gott. Are you in trouble with the law?"

"Nothing like that," Marka laughed, "but, I did take money from a man. Well, sort of from a man, but I earned every cent of it."

"*Ach, du Lieber.*" Anna's eyes widened.

"For heaven sake, nothing like that. I did do a stupid thing. I let myself become involved with a married man. There. Now I've said it."

"*Gott, im Himmel!*"

"His wife paid me to leave Denver. Maybe I shouldn't have taken the money, but at the time …"

"How much money?"

"Is that all you can say? Aren't you going to tell me you're ashamed of me?"

"How much?"

"A lot of money, enough to live in Ridley for a long, long time. Anna, I'm sorry. I feel terrible. I was afraid to tell you, because I thought you'd be angry with me. Maybe I shouldn't have taken the money, but I had to give up my job and leave town. I couldn't face

104

the people at work. The man I was involved with was my boss. A woman in the office wrote a letter to his wife and told her we were having a love affair. She was jealous, because I got promoted to executive secretary, his secretary. His wife paid me to leave town. And, there's more. Stella knows about all of this. I couldn't tell you before. Remember, I told you I sat beside her on the plane?"

"Yah?"

"Well, I told her the whole story. I didn't know who she was, and she didn't tell me she was from Ridley. She's holding this secret over my head. Anna, are you angry with me? I'm sorry. I'm sorry."

Anna stood quiet. "I'm not angry with you. I don't have to know your secrets."

"The truth is Rex and I weren't good for each other. We would have eventually called it quits."

Anna pressed her cheek to Marka's, and then stepped away. "What you did has nothing to do with whether or not I love you." She sniffed Marka's hair. "You smell good today. Not like a smokestack."

"And I've been lying about that too, the cigarettes."

"Yah. I know you smoke."

"No more lies," Marka shook her head. "Was it a mistake to come back?"

"No, everything will work out. Soon the weather will warm up, then you can work on your house."

"Do you think Stella will blab?"

"I don't know, Marka. Come, let's go home and make supper."

CHAPTER 14

As spring marched forward, the weather warmed. For three Sundays in a row, Marka called George and asked him to take her fishing. She told Anna, "No church," because she didn't want to run into Stella. Anna was gracious about it and seemed to understand now that she knew the reason.

At the crack of dawn, just as the first rays of sun peeked over the eastern horizon, George and Marka walked to the river south of town. They walked down the steep hill through tall prairie grass, and then crossed the gravel road that led to the bridge.

"When spring comes, the river runs fast and full," George said adjusting the brim of his straw hat. "It's not the best fishing. Summer's usually better cause the river slows down and the water clears so the fish can see the bait—kind of like people—when they slow down, they can see better."

Sometimes, when George spoke, Marka just nodded her head like she understood. George was deep, like the middle of the river. She liked how they spent their time talking about important matters. George was a good-natured, no-nonsense kind of guy, and Anna liked it that Marka spent time with him. "George isn't a church-goer, but he's a good man," she'd say. When they arrived at George's favorite fishing spot, they climbed down the embankment and unpacked their fishing gear. George opened his black metal lunch box packed with sandwiches wrapped in wax paper. He opened his thermos and poured them each a cup of hot coffee. Marka snuggled inside her jacket and took a sip.

George sniffed the cool, crisp air, his nostrils flaring, and then he opened his mouth and exhaled. "Ah, life is good."

"Anna told me you were the luckiest fisherman she ever knew."

"Luck's involved, but so is skill and knowledge. You've got to know what tackle and lures to use, what bait is working, and mostly, a fisherman's got to know where to find fish. Here, hold this pole. Remember how I showed you how to tie the hook on the end of the line? The hook should always be sharp." George touched the hook with his thumb examining it. "If the point is even a little rusty, you might as well throw it away cause the fish will spit it out. Remember what I told you about the size of the hook?"

"Yes. The size you use depends on the size of fish you want to catch. You use small hooks for fish with small mouths, and for big fish, big hooks."

George said, "The last time Jonny and I went fishing at the dam, I caught a big walleye. The thing weighed fifteen pounds."

Marka put a large hook, a worm, and sinker on her line, and then walked to the edge of the bank and cast out into the moving water. "Now all I have to do is sit and wait."

The sound of muffled thunder caught their attention as a beet company truck rumbled across the bridge.

"That truck reminds me of an article I read in the paper about sugar beets," George said. "The farmers are planting a new type of beet seed. It's a hybrid that's supposed to cut the demand for manual labor."

"Why's that?"

"Because each new seed will produce a single plant instead of several plants together and that means it will eliminate the need for thinning." George set his cup down on the ground and took a pipe from his shirt pocket. "In the past, it has taken three to four weeks just to thin a field. Farmers here are putting in forty-five hundred acres with the new seed. They say it will even produce a higher yield." George stuffed a small pinch of tobacco into the pipe bowl.

All the talk about sugar beets made Marka wonder if Buddy had seen the article. She thought of him saying how he wanted to go back on the farm. A person ought to be able to do what they want with their lives. Anyways, what was she doing worrying about Buddy?

"Ridley needs a good crop this year. The town may not be able to hang on if the sugar beet industry goes. There's been a drought the last few years and then last year an early frost during harvest." George struck a wooden match against the side of the lunch box and tried to get his pipe going again. "If the depot closes, there goes the grain elevator and the stock yards. The sugar beet factory in Clayton is what keeps the railroad running through here.

Marka said, "I hope that doesn't happen."

"Railroad closings are many times the deciding factor as to whether or not a town will be able to stay alive. Could be serious."

George took small puffs off his pipe. "Oh, did you hear the news? Senator McCarthy died unexpectedly."

"Anna won't be sad," Marka said. She'll be relieved."

"Your people aren't exactly dangerous radicals."

"Does Anna have a reason to worry?" Marka asked.

"The KGB can make people disappear. McCarthy was right about the Communists infiltrating this country. The FBI needs to do its job."

"Anna is uneasy about the changes in Russia especially if it affects the German Russians. She is critical of the Russian government. She always warns me not to write anything down about my family. In the late 30's, her cousin sent money to his family in Russia, and when Stalin's men found out, they arrested them. They sent them to Siberia. And then in the early 40's, many of our relatives were sent there also. The other night she was going on and on about something Jonny told her. He said this McCarthy thing is turning into a witch-hunt. And something about Thoreau's writings being removed from the U.S. Information Services libraries throughout the world. He told her they have air raid drills in school. The kids get under their desks. She's afraid of the Russians, George."

George took sandwiches out of his lunch box and handed one to Marka. "Here, I made us Dagwoods. Well, McCarthy said Communists are going to undermine the American way of life, but I do agree with Anna. It's character assassination. Let's hope this is the end of it. Sometimes I think this whole "Red" scare has gone too far, like all the missiles sites going in around here. Guess we're supposed to feel protected. Underground silos with missiles pointed directly at Russia. I understand we can't just let Communism take over the world, but how smart is it to put bombs right on your land? Seems to me that makes us a prime target."

Marka unwrapped her sandwich and looked inside. George had used bologna, ham, and salami. "Tell me about your family."

"My family came from Denmark. My dad and his brother left there around 1882. They set sail for America. Both of them ended up getting jobs with Union Pacific Railroad. It was building its way west. Funny. Almost all our family ended up working for the railroad."

"George, why did you stay here after you retired?"

"Well, my dear lady, a person's got to live somewhere, and I couldn't think of a better place." George smiled and took a big bite of his sandwich.

The river ran swift. It churned along, swirled around tree trunks, and threatened to loosen the brush stuck tightly to the muddy riverbank. Many years ago, trees had been torn down by the fast waters of spring and lay straddled across one another, their roots sucking in the water from the river. The chokecherry bushes scattered along the riverbank were in full bloom, and the willow trees had sprouted new leaves.

Marka sat quietly and listened to croaking frogs and to the whistle of bobwhite quail. "George, what do you think of Stella Erlich?"

"I think she's snooty and unfriendly."

Marka said. "Bodie told me she killed a cat the other day. He said she threw a rock at it, and it fell dead."

George put his pole in a holder and stuck it into the soft, wet ground. "She killed a cat?"

"That's what Bodie told me. Then she dragged it by the tail out to the street to make it look like a car had run over it."

"That's the action of a small-minded person," George frowned.

Marka felt a hard tug on her line and asked George what she should do.

"Give a quick jerk," George said. "You got a fish. Don't let it get away. Now, tighten up on your line. Good, good, now reel it in. Looks like you got the first catch of the day."

"Just like you showed me," Marka said a little out of breath and triumphant.

"Look, a big old catfish. He didn't fight much. You did a good job bringing him in. Put him in the bucket and cast out again. See if he has any buddies."

After Marka cast out her line she resumed the discussion of Stella. "Stella doesn't like me."

"Sometimes I wonder if she didn't just catch the first train that came along when she married Buddy," George said. "She doesn't seem very happy living here."

"I feel kind of sorry for Bodie. I'd like to sell him my house just so he could get away from Carl. He wants to buy it even though he complains there's too many things that need fixing."

"What's he telling you?"

"That the roof leaks and the plumbing is bad. He says the house needs a coat of paint."

George said, "When Anna found out you were coming, she asked me to give the house a once over. Looks like the picture window has a hole from a bee-bee gun. The south side is faded and there's cracking. Maybe it could use some paint, but not the rest of the house. Sometimes does more harm to just keep putting on coat after coat of paint. My opinion, paint the south side and wash down the rest. Scrub it with soapy water, then put your hose on full force and wet it down. The main thing to remember is to make sure you work from the bottom, up. That prevents streaking. If you start at the top all the dirt runs down and makes it worse."

"I'm going to start on the house next week. Anna says it will be warm enough by then. I'll be so busy. Hope Anna won't bother me about Ladies' Aid. I know she's just trying to help me get reacquainted, but I won't go."

George opened his thermos and asked Marka if she want some coffee.

"No thanks. Anna wants me to go to the Home Demonstration Club. She thinks I need to learn to be a homemaker. I told her that I'm not even married. 'But, you can learn about things,' she said. I think it's so funny how the men hang out at the saloon and pool hall discussing world affairs and the women attend their clubs and talk about recipes, children, and gardening. I wonder if they ever talk about whether or not they are happy. Probably not."

"You're being a bit of a cynic, aren't you? Things that tough?"

"Well, I just don't like all the questions. Their biggest concern seems to be that I'm not married. I really don't think it was nice of them saying those things in front of Anna. Do they call her an old maid?"

George laughed. "I have to be honest, I've heard some chatter about you being in the saloon."

"Oh, I should have known that was a mistake. Why haven't I ever seen you there?"

"I swore off liquor a long time ago. I don't drink. It affects my moods. I'm a teetotaler."

"So, what other gossip have you heard about me?" Marka asked.

"Just that you're chaperoning the prom with Jonny."

"Is that where you heard I was in the saloon?"

"No, heard that in the pool hall."

"It's no one's business. Don't they have anything better to do?" Marka stomped her feet.

"Women gossip, men discuss." George laughed.

"Sometimes I wonder if it was a good idea to come back here. I always wanted to live in a big city, but things didn't work. George, do you think a person can ever go back home?"

"It's my feeling that we should always move forward with our lives, and maybe sometimes a person has to go back to go forward. Like backing a train down the track to hook up another car."

"Maybe I should just sell the house and move some place like Chicago."

"Sounds like you're trying to run away from something. Don't know what you want?"

Marka shrugged her shoulders. "I feel like I'm trying to be someone else, someone who really isn't me."

"Look at the river how it moves along and it is what it is, a river," George said. "It's not trying to be something else. I've learned this much, be what you are and try not to buck the stream. I used to, but now I go with the flow, it's much easier that way. Think things over before you do anything too drastic. Let me tell you something about people. Don't worry too much what they're thinking. Most people are too busy living their lives to really care. Oh, they won't miss the opportunity to discuss everyone's business just for fun. You gotta be thick skinned, Marka."

"I'd be running away again if I left, wouldn't I?"

"I've lived in a lot of different places being a depot agent, and I've found that people are the same wherever you go. You gotta learn how to live with them."

Early dawn turned to mid-morning. Marka lay in the grass looking up at the tall cottonwoods shimmering in the sunlight. A light breeze rustled their leaves. She closed her eyes. It sounded like falling rain.

George caught five channel cats and Marka caught the big catfish. He told her he had a rule about fishing. No matter who caught what, they always split the fish, each took half. He took a six-inch two-by-four out of his fishing bag and placed it on the ground.

"I'll clean the fish this time, but next time you have to help. Watch close." He made a slit at the back of the catfish and took his knife and ran it along the backbone, holding the fish carefully by its head. "See how I'm holding the head like this so I don't get stuck by its horns." He took pliers and grabbed a corner of the skin and peeled it back. When the skin was off, he cut off the head, turned it over, and pulled out the guts.

He noticed a bulge in the intestines. Maybe it swallowed a lure. "Look at this." He held up something shiny.

"What is it?" Marka knelt on the ground beside the block of wood that George used to clean the fish.

"It's a ring—a wedding band. And it was in the fish *you* caught."

"An omen?" Marka giggled. "Suppose it means I'll be getting married?

"Marka, the last thing you have to worry about is being an old maid."

CHAPTER 15

Marka dropped the scrub cloth into a bucket of soapy water and hosed down the windows. She held her thumb firm over the end of the hose directing a powerful stream of water against the cobwebs under the metal awning over the large picture window. The swallows had returned to their nests under the eaves. She was careful not to disturb them. Marka did as George told her, washing one side of the house at a time, working from the bottom up to prevent streaking. She trusted George about how to clean, and she trusted him about only the south side of the house needing paint.

While working on the north side of the house, she solved the mystery of why the cellar door slammed shut the day she had come over to search it. She surmised that the wooden door collapsed because it was soaked with moisture from winter snows. The extra weight pulled the hook loose from the side of the house. She found it lying on the ground next to the entrance of the cellar.

When she finished spraying the house, she washed the windows until they sparkled like diamonds in the sun. There was still so much to do before she could move in. She had to call the phone company and the power company to check the swayback lines that ran from the pole in the alley to the house. The clothesline wires needed tightening and the brick planter needed planting with petunias and pansies. She had decided against putting in a garden because Anna told her she could use help with hers. "Besides," Anna said, "I always have so much I end up giving most of it away."

The last couple weeks had been exhilarating, in spite of a few mishaps. One day her finger got in the way of a hammer and her fingernail turned black. This happened while she and Herb were putting new shingles on the roof. Anna said she would most likely lose it. Another day, she accidentally rubbed her hair against wet enamel while painting. Anna helped her get it out with turpentine.

113

Her hands were red and rough from all the cleaning. Day after day she rolled up her sleeves and got to work.

Every evening, Marka collapsed into bed. Anna was supportive of her efforts, but didn't understand why she wanted to do so much of the work herself.

"You should have Herb doing more. There's enough to do on the inside. You're working way too hard. Besides, you have the money to have the work done for you," Anna said.

"George and Bodie have helped a lot too, but they won't take any money. I pay Herb five dollars an hour and that's what I'd pay them, but they won't take it."

"When I ask the men folk for help with the heavy work, I offer to pay them or bake a pie. Usually, they take the pie," Anna chuckled.

"Okay, let's bake some pies," Marka laughed.

Tuesday night, Marka went to bed right after supper. She thought about all the work she had yet to do. A feeling of gratitude swept over her. She finally felt like she had a purpose, like she was working towards something good.

She thought she would ask Anna if she could borrow her car and drive to Clayton. Mother's Day was almost here and she needed to buy something nice for Anna. Maybe a new set of dishes so she would stop collecting the ones from the detergent boxes. And she needed to shop for a dress for the prom even though Anna offered to make her one.

"I won't promise any sewing to Stella for a while," Anna told her. But Marka thought back to what happened before Easter and told Anna she would just as soon buy a dress that way they didn't have to feel rushed. Really, it was that she didn't want to be disappointed again. And she didn't know if she could trust Anna after what she told her about Denver. Anna seemed to be taking it in stride, but Marka wasn't sure she was out of the woods. Anna could sometimes hold a grudge.

On Wednesday, Marka walked through the house and opened all the windows. The house filled with the songs of meadowlarks. Clean fresh spring air rushed into the rooms pushing out the stale smells, leaving the scent of lilacs and sweet Williams.

Bodie had made the house sound as if it were decayed. It wasn't that bad. Now it was shaping up and Marka thought she would be happy here. George put a new gasket in the leaky faucet in the bathroom. There was an ugly yellow stain from the dripping faucet and a nasty ring in the toilet bowl from the anti-freeze Bodie had put in the tank when he winterized the house. George brought over a pumice stone for her to use. He said she could put some putty in the hole of the large picture window where the BB pellets had gone through. The kitchen sink was clogged with grease and soap. George coached her on how to remove the trap and snake out the drainpipe. She was grateful he took the time to show her how to do the things for herself.

While she and Herb were on the roof replacing shingles, he swept the chimney. He filled a burlap bag with rags and two large rocks and tied it to a long rope, and then dragged it up and down. He warned her that the stovepipes would be packed with soot so she better clean them out right away.

After the outside work was finished, Marka would tackle the inside. She shared her plan with Anna. "I'll strip the wallpaper from the living room walls and tear off oilcloth in the kitchen. I'll have Herb fix the cracks in the plaster walls, then I'll paint all the rooms."

"Make sure you take down the stove pipes and clean them before you paint," Anna warned.

"Yes, Herb told me."

Marka was about to climb the ladder she had leaned against the wall next to the cook stove when Bodie drove up in his faded green pickup. She watched him from the kitchen window. He always walked slump-shouldered like he was carrying a heavy load. He walked with a shuffle, because of his bum hip. She noticed his blue jeans and plaid shirt were clean, and he was wearing polished cowboy boots instead of his usual engineer boots. Bodie seemed to be taking better care of himself. She found herself liking him in spite of one bothersome thing—the way he stared, not saying a word while she talked as if he were taking in everything and memorizing it.

"You look spiffy today." Marka hollered through the screen door. "Why are you all dressed up?"

Bodie's black hair was parted and combed and he smelled soapy.

He opened the door and stepped inside the kitchen. "I'm going to Clayton to get a fishing license. I thought, well, maybe you'd like to ride along and buy a new water heater. You said you needed one." He handed her the *Clayton Post*. "Wards has a big sale on. They got a twenty gallon one for $72.88, and a thirty-gallon for $89.88. Not that much more for the bigger one."

Marka took the paper out of Bodie's hand and read the ad for herself. "Glass lined tank - safety cut-off - AGA approved. Yes, I think I'll go with the thirty gallon. I'll need to stop at the bank first and get some cash."

"They'll put it on time payments. Five dollars down will hold it layaway, and then you can pay them five dollars a month. That's what it says here in the paper."

"No, I really need to bring it home today. I have to have hot water to clean. I took all the curtains down, they were full of dust and cob webs."

Bodie climbed the ladder and gave the stovepipe a shake. "I'll give you a hand with this Marka. Hand me that screwdriver, will ya? I'll loosen the top, you hold onto the bottom so it won't slip out."

"Get down, Bodie. You'll get your clothes dirty. I can do it myself. Besides, I want to show you something." Marka reached into her jean pocket and took out the ring she found in the big catfish. "George and I went fishing and look," she slipped it on her long, thin finger and spun it around.

Bodie got down off the ladder. He cocked his head looking at what Marka had on her finger. "It's Stella's wedding ring."

"What? Are you sure?"

"It's Stella's ring all right, she complained about it enough. Said it looked like it came out of a Cracker Jack box. Take off the ring and I'll show you something. See here." Bodie took the ring and rubbed his fingernail against the underside. "She took it to a jeweler and had him engrave these hearts. She said he did a sloppy job, ruined the ring and should replace it, but he wouldn't go for it."

Marka said, "Will you give it back to her? Say you found it somewhere." Marka felt a twinge. Do something nice for Stella?

"She wouldn't want it now, because Buddy bought her a brand new one, a big diamond. She wouldn't let up on him until he did." Bodie started to laugh. He laughed until tears ran down his cheeks.

Marka had never seen him like that before. It warmed her heart to see him happy even if it did have something to do with Stella.

"Know what this means, don't you?" Bodie couldn't stop laughing. "She threw it in the river."

"You think?"

"And a fish swallowed it. Ha! Ha! Ha!" Bodie roared. "If Buddy ever finds out, he's going to be pissed."

"I'm going to hide it away somewhere," Marka said, thinking that it might just come in handy some day to make Stella squirm should she ever threaten to tell what she knew about the man in Denver. "Then, let's keep this our secret."

"Boy, if that don't take the cake," Bodie climbed back on the ladder.

"Well, if you insist on helping me," Marka said, squeezing between the stove and the wall.

Bodie gave the pipe a slight tug and a twist. It was stuck tight.

"Where's Anna today?" He tugged more on the pipe.

"She's listening to *Helen Trent*. She won't miss her favorite radio programs. Her spirits are high these days. The whole McCarthy thing."

"Huh?" Bodie scratched his head.

"Oh, never mind. She's getting ready to put in her garden. Henry Campbell is going to plow and she's getting a load of manure. She's anxious to get her seedlings planted." Marka positioned herself under the stovepipe and tried to help Bodie break it free from the wall. "The other day she came home from Extension Club with the door prize. Guess what it was? A rake," Marka laughed. "Anna puts a garden in every year and she has enough canned stuff in her basement to live on forever."

"Marka what you gonna do that with all that stuff down in your cellar?" Bodie asked.

"Throw it out—I'm afraid to eat any of it, it's so old. How's it coming up there?"

Bodie took a screwdriver out of his back pocket and used the handle to tap around the stovepipe, the way you would around the lid of a jar to break the seal. He gave the pipe a hard tug and it broke loose from the wall.

"Oh, No!" Marka sputtered as black soot dumped down like an avalanche of snow. It landed right in her face.

117

"You all right?" Bodie called down.

She spit soot out of her mouth and shook it from her hair. She kept her eyes closed brushing it from her face. "Be careful you don't get soot all over your clean clothes," she coughed.

"Too late," Bodie said looking down at his soot-stained shirt and jeans.

Marka scooted out from behind the stove continuing to rid herself of the black grime.

"You look like a raccoon," Bodie laughed.

Only moments later Buddy drove into the yard. He walked to the house, knocked on the screen door, and peeked inside the kitchen. Wide-eyed, a smile broke across his face. "If it isn't Amos and Andy. What the heck happened? All I see is the whites of your eyes."

"We had a soot explosion," Marka giggled.

"Hate to spoil your fun, Bodie, but Dad needs you to unload a big delivery that just came in."

"I was gonna go to Clayton to get a fishing license and Marka needs to pick up a water heater."

"You better get down to the store," Buddy said.

"Last time he made me take all the cans down and dust the shelves. What about the water heater?" Bodie moaned, and walked out of the house brushing soot from his clothes.

"I'll drive you over to Clayton if you clean up first," Buddy chuckled. "I'm going to the Bootery." He put his hands in his pants pockets and rocked back on his heels.

Marka said, "Oh, no, I can manage a few more days. I mean, I don't think you should be taking me places."

"If I didn't need the boots, I'd let you borrow my pickup, drive over and get it yourself."

Marka reasoned with herself that she really did need the water heater. How would she clean with cold water and how would she do laundry? Yes, she'd let Buddy drive her to Clayton.

They loaded the new water heater in his pickup. At the Bootery, Buddy tried on boots and Marka bought Anna a pair of Daniel Green slippers. She'd get her new dishes another time. Then she walked to the dress shop and looked for something to wear to the prom, but nothing struck her fancy. She'd let Anna sew for her and maybe this time it would work out.

On the way back from Clayton, they stopped at A & W for burgers, fries and root beer floats. Buddy's gaze was intent while she ate, and when a couple of fries dropped from the paper dish onto her lap, he quickly retrieved them and popped them into his mouth. She pushed another fry off her dish, gave him a big smile, and then snatched it before he could.

The next morning Marka rose early. The eastern horizon was on fire, its orange and gold streaming across the sky. Anna was still in her bedroom making her bed. Marka thought back to the previous day and how she had gone to Clayton with Buddy. She had to admit she did have feelings for him, feelings that were different from how she felt about Jonny. But she wouldn't let it go any further. She'd go to the dance with Jonny and give him a chance.

Friday afternoon, Marka went to Ruby's apartment.

"I want to do something daring," Marka said. "I want my ears pierced like yours."

Ruby laughed. "People will think you're a Gypsy!"

"I don't care."

Ruby was wearing a black sweater and paisley ankle-length skirt. Her face was made up with the usual orange rouge and an opaque face powder that lightened her swarthy, mahogany skin. Her lips were smeared with bright red lipstick.

"The first thing I have to do is freeze your lobes."

Fedora flew down from the top of her cage and landed on Ruby's shoulder.

"Mind if Fedora watches?"

"She's not going to bite me again, is she?"

"No, I had a talk with her. I told her if she was not nice to you, you would never come see me again and that would make me sad."

Marka pulled her shoulders in a little and took a deep breath. "I'm a little scared. Oh, I guess I'm ready. Jab away." The thought of that needle going through her flesh made her cringe.

Ruby placed her right ear lobe between two ice cubes. "So you're going to live dangerously and go out with the school teacher.

There's an old Gypsy saying that goes like this: A life without danger is emptier than a life without love."

"I wouldn't exactly call Jonny dangerous," Marka giggled. "What I did in Denver was dangerous. Oh—oh, I can't feel my ear, Ruby."

"That's because it's frozen," Ruby laughed. She rubbed Marka's ear with alcohol, marked a dot with an ink pen where the pierce should go, and then placed a raw potato behind it. She took a long, sharp needle and quickly jabbed through the flesh, into the potato. "Did you feel that?"

"Yes, but only a pinch."

Fedora flew back to her cage. Ruby put a hoop earring through the freshly punctured hole. "I'm giving you these earrings. They were once special to me. I want you to have nice ones to wear to the dance. I won't tell you how I came to have them." Ruby handed Marka a mirror.

"Thank you, Ruby," Marka said, looking into the mirror at her ear. "Anna is going to be upset. She has such old fashioned ideas. She doesn't even like earrings. She says they're worldly."

"Older people are set in their ways," Ruby said.

"I don't like going against Anna, but I want to be my own person and not always do what she thinks is best."

"You need to stop trying to be something you're not. You worry too much about Anna. Don't apologize for who you are. Let's do the other ear. Isn't this better than tightening screws against your ears or clipping something on?" Ruby pressed ice cubes against Marka's other ear. "Now what is this about Jonny Sanders?"

Marka sat straight in the chair and held her breath as Ruby jabbed. "He's nice. But, I am more drawn to Buddy. It must be, because we knew each other from high school."

"You had a thing for him back then, huh?" Ruby rubbed a cotton ball soaked with alcohol across the fresh puncture.

"Maybe a little, but I can't let things go any farther."

"That's a good idea. I see another person inside you. You haven't discovered her yet. She is strong and wise. Her name is, Mia. Yes, that's what I am going to call you from now on, because you are getting to be like a daughter to me—telling me your secrets. Mia! It's a Gypsy name for Mizelli. I always thought if I ever had a daughter that is what I would have named her," Ruby's voice softened. "Mia, stay away from Buddy. Stella will do you great harm if she gets wind of anything."

"What do you mean?"

"When I am around her I notice that there's something that overpowers me." Ruby raised an eyebrow. "Sometimes I wonder what dark past she is hiding. Have you ever noticed the hollowness of her eyes? "

Marka said, "I'm going to tell you something, but you have to promise me you won't say a word about this to anyone."

"I promise."

"Well, the other day George and I went fishing and we caught this fish, and well, George likes to clean them right there on the riverbank, and when he opened the fish, there was a ring inside. A few days later I showed it to Bodie, and he said he was sure it was Stella's. The one she said she lost."

"See, I told you she is devilish. Wait a minute, I must get something for you."

Ruby went into her bedroom and came out with two copper pennies. "Here, these are lucky ones," she said pointing to Marka's loafers. "Put them in your shoes and make sure you wear the shoes whenever you're around Stella. Are you wearing the scapular I gave you? My mother-in-law told me her priest blessed it. Do whatever you must to ward off Stella's evil."

Marka left Ruby's apartment knowing she and Anna would have an argument about what she had just done. Pierced ears? What had possessed her? They ate supper and then Marka put on the dress Anna sewed for her.

"Ouch, that pin stuck me." she yelped. "You're upset over my pierced ears, aren't you?"

"Ach, you have such a thing for people who are different— people who do strange things. Hold still or I won't get the straps straight. Jonny will be here in an hour and I don't have his shirt ironed yet. Maybe you could do that while I tack these straps on."

"Thank you for the dress, Anna."

"Yah, you're welcome." Anna placed a straight pin between her front teeth and secured one strap. "You should really have a merry widow to wear with this dress," she forced the words out between the pin and her teeth.

"The strapless bra will do," Marka said.

Anna pinned the other strap. "Do they feel tight enough?"

"You stayed up half the night working on this dress. It's perfect."

"I'm glad I had this piece of pink taffeta," Anna said.

"I just love the tiny lavender flowers and you made it hit right at the knee."

"It could have been longer, shows too much of your leg."

"Let's leave the T straps off."

"Ach, no, not good for a chaperone."

"It's the fashion. I'm not a little girl. Ruby said a coiffure hairdo would be better then wearing my hair loose. What do you think?"

"Humph! Coiffure? You mean a French Roll? There now, take the dress off. Jonny's shirt is in the plastic bag in the bottom of the refrigerator. I sprinkled it this morning so it should be good and moist.

"Are you happy I'm going out with Jonny?"

"Yah, sure! Too bad he isn't German Russian. It's always better to go with one of your own. He does go to our church though and that's good. People are talking you know, ever since Easter when they saw the two of you sitting together."

"But, he's not one of my own," Marka teased. "One of my own would be, Bodie!"

"Ach, Gott, no!"

"You don't like Bodie and Buddy much do you, Anna? Is it because of Carl?"

"Leave it go. I don't want to talk about it." Anna stiffened and stared off into the corner of the room.

Anna finished sewing the straps on the dress while Marka ironed the white short-sleeved cotton shirt for Jonny. She had let Anna win. She would not wear a strapless dress to the school dance. Marka unrolled the shirt, dampened it more with a sprinkler, a coke bottle with a special stopper, and then she tested the iron with a wet finger. Hot! She felt a little nervous ironing a shirt for Jonny. How would she ever do as good as Anna, ironing it without a single wrinkle? It felt good doing something for a man. It made her heart stir a bit.

Anna chewed the inside of her cheek watching Jonny pin a gardenia to Marka's dress. Marka pinned a boutonniere to the lapel of his coat; a pink carnation with sprigs of fern and baby's-breath. She couldn't help notice how handsome he looked in his white jacket, black slacks and loafers.

Jonny nestled his nose against Marka's neck. "I like."

"Evening in Paris," Anna intruded. "Smells better than any you could buy from the Watkins man." Anna bubbled like champagne. She was pleased with herself. "You two make the perfect couple."

Marka's heart softened. She had made her aunt happy. Anna fussed with the straps on the dress, caressed Marka's hair and touched her bare ear lobes absent of the hoops she wore earlier that day.

They left for the dance at 7:00 p.m.

"I want to get there early so I can make sure the kids have finished decorating the gym," Jonny said.

As they went out the door, Marka whispered to Anna, "Are the seams in my stockings straight. Do I look okay?"

"You look beautiful," Anna smiled.

Queen Neptune and King Fish led the promenade through the arch decorated with crepe paper and balloons. Streamers of green and white hung across the gymnasium from wires that looked like strings on a violin. Marka thought of her senior prom and remembered it was not an evening of magic. Her date was Thomas Rayborn, only because no one better had asked her. She had been rude to him—doing everything she could to discourage his interest in her. She could not stand the thought of marrying him and ending up in Ridley for the rest of her life, a farmer's wife.

Jonny held her tight during the slow dances. Her heart stirred again like when she was ironing his shirt. Now they were so close, she could smell him and feel his soft cheek against hers. Her heart didn't race like when Buddy touched her, but she knew something about that was wrong. She respected and admired Jonny. But what did it matter? This would be the only time he would ask her out. It was more than likely a favor to Anna. Stella said he received perfumed letters from Texas. She would know working in the post office. Anna said it couldn't be so, but Anna saw things the way she wanted.

After the dance, they went outside to the playgrounds and talked. Jonny was concerned that the high school might close. "June third the town is having a special meeting and will vote on whether or not to close the school. If they close, I'll be out of a job and will have to move to another town."

"I'd vote for the school to stay," Marka said clapping her hands.

"Thanks for your support. Wish you were on the board. I heard there's never been a woman on the board before."

"No women in the saloon, no women on the school board. Keep them in the kitchen with a bunch of babies, right?" Marka fumed.

"I didn't mean to upset you. We haven't talked for a while. How are you getting along in Ridley?"

"There's a few people I wish didn't live here. Stella's one of them."

"I told you she was a handful."

"Guess I have no choice but to take her as she is."

Jonny said, "The other day, I read something interesting. It was a quote from Goethe. Goes like this: If we take people as they are, we make them worse. If we treat them as if they were what they ought to be, we help them to become what they are capable of becoming."

"You want me to apply that to Stella?"

Jonny laughed and kissed her lightly on the lips. Marka's heart leapt for a brief moment. Maybe Jonny was the one. No. She wouldn't consider it. She just wasn't sure about anything right now.

CHAPTER 16

Saturday morning, Stella telephoned Anna and insisted she needed her dress; so Anna spent the entire day at her sewing machine pumping the treadle fast and hard. Maybe she's finally realizing the price she has to pay to keep Stella as a customer. Marka felt smug watching Anna being careless with the delicate fabric.

She did all the chores while Anna sewed. She washed clothes even though it wasn't Monday. She hung the clothes out on the lines to dry just the way Anna taught her. Later in the day, she gathered them in her arms and brought them into the house. She tried to visit with Anna while they folded the sheets, her holding one end and Anna the other.

"There's a nice breeze today so the clothes dried fast. They smell so fresh and sweet," Marka said.

Anna's usual response would have been, "There's nothing like fresh sheets off the line." Instead she said, "Were there any clothes pins left in the bag? The kids steal them so they can pin playing cards to the spokes of their bikes. Bring the clothes pin bag inside when you are done," she snapped.

Anna went back to her sewing machine after they folded the clothes.

Marka asked her, "Are you upset about something?"

"Yah, it's wrong for Stella to hold this over your head. I told her I knew the whole story. I told her I wasn't going to do sewing for her anymore. She got mad and said some not so nice things about you."

"What did she say?"

"Just forget about it. I sure could stand some nice, fresh fish. Go call George. You two go fishing."

Anna grumbled for the rest of the morning; so Marka called George as soon as she finished waxing the kitchen floor. She liked George and felt safe when she was with him. She looked forward to hearing his opinions and appreciated the way he never came across like some sort of authority—although he did have clear and definite opinions about certain matters.

George showed up around 1:00 p.m. He picked fat angleworms out of Anna's rich garden soil and put them in a coffee can. A half hour later, they cast their lines out into the water and sat down on a plank by the water's edge.

"Don't I need a fishing license, George? Bodie told me he was disappointed he couldn't go to Clayton to get his, and I just wondered if I needed one."

"Women don't need one, but he better get his. Most people aren't aware of how much jurisdiction a game warden has. That's why I make sure I never go over the limit: ten trout a day—May through September. You can't have more than twenty fish in your possession."

"Think we'll catch another one with a ring in it?" Marka laughed. "Every time I see her flashing that big diamond I want to laugh."

"Who?"

"Oh, George, I forgot to tell you. I showed the ring to Bodie, and he told me it was Stella's wedding band. He said she told Buddy she lost it so he would buy her a new ring."

"Really convinces me she's devious," George said. "But, I'm more interested in you. Jonny will be jealous if he hears you went fishing with me again."

"I don't think so." Marka blushed.

"Heard you had a fine time the other night."

"Jonny doesn't dance much. Mostly slow ones. I had to beg him to jitterbug with me. Yes, we had fun."

"This is nosy, I know, but does Jonny have a chance with you?"

"Sure. I'd be crazy not to like him, but he's too smart and sophisticated for someone like me."

"That's a lot of baloney. If you think that, you don't know Jonny."

Marka wanted to tell George that she wasn't interested in Jonny that way, but she said, "He's someone to talk to once in awhile. He comes over to Anna's to pick up his shirts, and we talk about books and the high school track team." She couldn't tell George what was going on in her life concerning men. There are some things you can talk about with certain people and not with others.

"George, what do you think about Ruby Swain?"

"I don't have much to do with her. She's rather bizarre. Kind of strange that a woman would want to run a pool hall."

"Anna doesn't like Ruby, because she says she's superstitious. What do you think?"

"Being superstitious is just plain primitive."

The channel cats were supposed to be biting. They never had a nibble; so they gave up around four. The sky had clouded over and it looked like rain. "Heavy showers are predicted," George said.

Anna was disappointed that they returned empty-handed, but her mood had improved, and she was doing Saturday baking. She was bubbling like the yeast in her big crock bowl. She held up Stella's dress. "Finally, finished!"

"So, that's why you're so happy."

Marka dusted the furniture and ran the carpet sweeper. Anna asked if she would walk to town and get some flour.

"Sure. I may stop at the cafe and talk to Millie."

"Don't be too long, cause I need the flour," Anna said.

For some reason, maybe out of boredom, Marka ended up at the saloon. She kept walking after she got to the grocery store; she walked past the post office and Millie's Cafe feeling drawn to the saloon like a moth to the light. She ordered a Vodka Collins and almost bought a pack of cigarettes, but then remembered what she promised Anna. No more smoking.

There were only a few men in the saloon, one being Buddy, who joined her at the bar. He straddled the stool next to her and ordered Marka another Vodka Collins and a beer for himself.

"How you coming on the house? Cleaned any stove pipes lately?" he laughed. "Bodie told me you haven't moved in. Still at Anna's, huh?"

"Haven't spent my first night. Plan to move in after Memorial Day."

"I suppose Anna got her garden in. I just took the coffee cans away from my tomato plants. Hey, did you hear I got elected to the town board?"

"Congratulations," Marka put out her hand.

Buddy took her hand in his and wouldn't let go.

"Buddy, don't." She pulled it away.

Elton spread the *Clayton Post* across the bar. "Listen to this: Beet growers will be getting payment this week." He ran his finger down a column. "Says the Utah & Idaho Sugar Company will make its first payment of more than $100,000 to beet growers on May 24. Payment is for 1956 beets delivered to the company."

"Damn, I wish I was still on the farm." Buddy pounded his fist on the bar. "The saddest day of my life was when Dad sold the farm. Damn it all. I feel, well, kind of like things just ain't been right since."

Elton folded the newspaper and put it under the counter. "Shearing and lambing must be over. Look who just walked in— Ole and old Boss right at his heels."

"Looks like Ole got himself a new pair of cowboy boots," Buddy chuckled. "Walks like he's got a cob up his ass. Ole has a scar that runs across his entire forehead," Buddy whispered to Marka. "It happened one night when he was in here buying drinks for an Indian woman. Her husband, Running Rattle, came into the saloon and saw them making out down at the end of the bar. He pulled a knife and tried to scalp Ole. Look at it when he takes off that Stetson."

"I don't want to see it, besides, I have to go."

"No, wait. You gotta meet Ole." Buddy took hold of her arm and wouldn't let her leave.

Ole walked over to them and sat on a barstool. Boss curled up on the floor by his feet.

"Hey, look what the wind blew in," Buddy joked.

The first thing Marka noticed was the brown ring around the collar of Ole's undershirt and how his belly hung over the belt of his ripped and faded pants. Ole looked at them through squinted eyes, trying to focus through the thick layer of smoke in the room. He smiled wide. He had no teeth. He spoke with a heavy lisp.

"Poor old Boss." He reached down and patted the old sheep dog's head. "I promised him a beer, Elton."

"I have two rules here: You got to be of age to buy drinks and dogs aren't allowed to have booze. It goes to their heads." Elton wasn't joking.

Ole took off his hat and rubbed the top of Boss' head with the heel of his cowboy boot. Boss looked up and then laid his head back between his paws.

"So, let's hear some bragging about how Boss is the best damn Border collie around," Buddy said, trying to get Ole going.

"He's the best fetcher, and the only time he barks is when he gets a whiff of a coyote," Ole said. "Damn, I need a drink. Gimme me a bottle of Kentucky Straight," he rubbed his chin whiskers.

"Hey, when is the last time you had a bath?" Buddy asked. The paint's going to peel right off the walls in here."

"Had a bath the last time I came to town. Last winter to be exact."

"You smell real bad. Looks like you got some new boots," Buddy said. "His clothes may be ragged, but he always wears good boots. Right Ole?"

"Me and Old Boss, we had us one hell of a time this spring." Ole unscrewed the cap of the whiskey bottle and took a big hit. "Aw, that's what I needed." His beady eyes widened, and he rubbed his hand across his chin. He took another swig, closed his eyes, and shook his head. "Hrrr, damn good."

"Let me buy that bottle for you. Elton, put this on my tab. How are things on the range? How'd the lambing go this spring? Heard the coyotes were giving the ranchers a time of it."

"We been losing about six a night. The sons-a-bitching rattlers are more a problem than the coyote. Other day, Boss and I were rounding up sheep, and I heard buzzing and hissing all around me. They were coiled, their rattlers shaking."

"Aw, come on Ole," Elton poured himself a cup of coffee. "You're kidding, right? I enjoy your stories as much as anyone, but I'm never sure if you're telling the truth or just hallucinating."

"Damn truth. Boss charged one of the snakes, grabbed it in his mouth, sunk his teeth into the damn thing, shook his head a few times and threw it aside. It would have got me, and that's not my— magination!" Ole dug inside his shirt pocket and tossed a burlap tobacco pouch onto the bar. "See here," he boasted and emptied the bag. Dried rattlers rolled across the counter sounding like crinkled tissue paper. "There's about fifty of them. Count 'em if you don't believe me. Look at this, girlie. Want a couple for a souvenir? Here, I'll give you this rattler with eight buttons."

Marka pulled herself as far away from Ole as she could get.

"What's the matter, girlie? Look at these marks. There's where I got bit one time. I had to tie a handkerchief around my arm, cut myself, and suck the poison out."

"Damn it, Ole, that's a lie. You would have died if you got bit like that. Trying to impress the lady, aren't you?"

"You really killed all those snakes?" Marka squirmed, twisting her body around on the barstool.

"Hell, I ain't lying." Ole drew another mouthful of whiskey.

"So, Ole, you scared with all them snakes around you? Bet you were scared," Buddy teased.

"Scared? I ain't scared a nothing. Not even you, you little son-a-bitch."

"Now, Ole don't get riled up. You know what happens when you lose your temper." Buddy slapped Ole on the back.

Ole tried to rub his hand across the top of Buddy's head, but Buddy ducked. "Oh, shit. You're as quick as a blue belly lizard," Ole laughed. "We had a two-headed lamb born. Had a normal body, but the skull was divided and it had two faces."

"I've gotta go." Marka had had enough bar room chatter. She set her empty glass down. She felt perturbed and sick to her stomach.

After Marka left the saloon, she went to the store, picked up a sack of flour, and then headed back to Anna's. The sky was filling with dark clouds. George was right about the rain.

Thoughts played havoc with her mind as she thought about Buddy and the old sheepherder. Buddy acted as though Ole were some kind of hero. Surely this was an indication that they saw things differently. What did she and Buddy have in common anyway? Nothing!

She vowed she wouldn't go to the saloon again. She remembered what Elton told her. The first time she came in he said, "Women don't belong in the saloon, not in Ridley anyway." He was right. The Ridley saloon wasn't like the nightclubs in Denver. What was she thinking? Even Millie knew better. What possessed her? Was it Buddy, or the need to have alcohol? She pledged she would not end up like her father. It wouldn't happen to her, needing to drink. She would never go there again, she vowed. No. Never again.

CHAPTER 17

It took all the courage Marka could muster to spend the first night in her house. The June evening was silent, but she heard sounds. The walls and floorboards creaked as the house cooled from the heat of the day. Crickets kept up their steady chirping, and insects occasionally flew against the window screens.

Marka lay in bed fighting off fear. She hadn't told anyone about the odd things that happened every time she came to the house, and she hesitated to tell Ruby too much, because she knew Ruby would say it was just her father's restless spirit causing it all. "He isn't ready to leave this world. You have not made your peace," she said once, and another time, she said, "Your father has a trapped soul."

Had it all been her imagination, seeing ghostly shadows on the walls? Had she been influenced by Ruby's remarks? She was certain there were cold spots, especially in her parent's bedroom. At times, a window in a room would be open a crack when the house was warm, even though she was certain she had closed it. Sometimes, she felt cold air pass over her arm. And things around the house were moved. She'd find objects in different places than she had placed them. Marka knew if she mentioned any of it to Anna, she would just laugh. But tonight there was a spooky quiet to the house. She chided herself. Go to sleep! She squeezed her eyes shut and pulled the sheet up to her chin. Just as she was about to drift off, the hooting of an owl echoed through the trees. Her first night in the house was going to be a sleepless one. Her mind started in again. What was in the house? Should she stop wasting time speculating on what her mother told her? If she was meant to find it, whatever it was, she would.

Going through the house made all the bad memories come back. She would think about her parents and their lack of enthusiasm for each other. There was always silence and tension in her home. Her mother wouldn't leave her father, because divorce was frowned upon. Besides, she couldn't support herself, and she had no education. What drove her father to drink and what fueled his rage? He would push, shove, hit, and say hateful things. The thought of all this made the anger at her father boil like oil. Marka remembered how she felt afraid when alone in the house with him. When she lived in Denver, she lived with constant worry about her mother.

Anna told her to put the past behind, which meant bury it and forget. And Ruby told her to make peace with the past. But, what did that mean? How would she do that?

Marka fluffed her pillow and straightened the sheet. From now on she would get along with Anna. After all, Anna was only trying to help her be a part of the town and to get to know Jonny better. Anna kept telling her that Jonny stopped by and asked about her. "Jonny's a good man, and he likes you," she'd say. But Marka didn't care for him in a romantic way. He was more like a brother. His kiss didn't excite her. When she shared this with Anna, Anna came back with a warning: "This may be your last chance to get a man. He will stop coming around if you don't show him you're interested. What do you expect—your heart to flutter all the time?"

It was true. She was resisting him. She had ignored him—and she had been too busy hanging out with Ruby and working on the house. She'd try harder to fit in around Ridley. She would go to Ladies' Aid and Home Demonstration Club if that was what Anna wanted. She'd even try harder to be nice to Stella. She'd put their first meeting out of her mind and trust that Stella was not going to say a word to anyone. She'd even compliment her on her new diamond ring. This made Marka feel lighter. She had to admit that it was an odd coincidence about the ring, but things like that happened in life. Probably more times than anyone took note. No harm was done as long as Bodie kept it their secret. As far as she was concerned, it was between Buddy and Stella.

Sleep. Sleep. She must get some sleep. Tomorrow was her first day at the cafe. Marka yawned and rolled over on her side. It was quiet now; she'd go to sleep. She took a deep breath and let it out slowly.

Mice scratched in the wall next to her bed. "Oh, No!" She pounded hard to scare them away. Well, thank goodness it was over with Rex. It all started with him being there to console her after she returned from her parents' funeral in September. One event had led to the other. She had driven straight through from Denver to Ridley, intending to spend a week with her parents. She arrived late Friday afternoon. Mrs. Raver, the next-door neighbor, had seen her car and had come running over. There had been a terrible accident the day before. "We couldn't get hold of you. Your folks were in a head-on collision. Your mother is in critical condition."

"My father?"

"He was killed instantly."

She arrived at the hospital and was told that her mother was bleeding internally and that she had been sedated. Marka was taken to her bedside.

Marka tossed and turned. The mice had quieted. She couldn't stop thinking about things. On Memorial Day, she and Anna went to the parade in Clayton and then, to the cemetery. They placed pink peonies from Anna's yard on her parents' graves. At the parade, she had bought a red crepe paper poppy from an old veteran in a wheelchair. This, Marka stuck in the ground next to their marble headstone.

Anna said the cemetery visit would be a good idea to help finish their grieving, but it only stirred things up in Marka's mind. And why had Anna lingered at the gravesite of an infant? The words: **Baby Jacob—Born and Died 1901** were engraved on the light-colored, sandstone marker. Anna told her the headstone had a swan motif, because that represented either an unborn baby or child who died young.

"There's no last name. Whose baby?" Marka asked.

"It was the baby of a friend of mine."

Anna looked unhappy after that. The visit to the cemetery made them solemn. Anna didn't say a word the rest of the time they were there, and whenever Marka looked over at her, her jaw was tight, and her lips were quivering.

After the cemetery, they went to the picnic at the city park put on by the Ladies' Aid. The women had outdone themselves. The tables were covered with plates of fried chicken, bowls of potato salad, fancy Jell-O salads, cakes, cookies, and there was a big jug of lemonade.

Marka tried her best to be a part of the festivities. She and Bodie led the children's games of roll the egg with your nose, three-legged race, and the gunny sack race. She made sure she stayed a safe distance from Stella and Buddy, and whenever they walked by her, she gave them both a warm smile.

After the Memorial Day festivities, they drove home with their headlights on. Marka felt sad and couldn't get the thought of her parents out of her mind. It seemed to her that visiting the cemetery had only made her and Anna feel sad. The one happy event of the day was when Ruby's name was drawn as the winner of the quilt the Ladies' Aid had made. Tomorrow, after she got off work at the cafe, she would deliver it to Ruby. She would not tell Ruby that the ladies were upset, because she had won. Actually, they were disgusted and outraged that she won on only one ticket. Anna rebuked them and said Ruby won it fair and square. Marka had to hold her tongue when tempted to tell Anna that Ruby kissed the stub and said she had a vibration that it was a lucky ticket and she would win. She would not say anything to dissuade Anna's newfound tolerance for Ruby.

At two in the morning, Marka finally fell asleep. At dawn, a wind came up and blew branches against the side of the house. Marka woke feeling exhausted. How would she get through her first day at the cafe?

Marka discovered that working at the cafe was hard. The first day, she did dishes and rang up cash register slips. She made mistakes counting out change, but Millie made light of it. Millie made people feel comfortable in her cafe, smiling at everyone, heaping plates full, and topping off coffee cups.

The second day, Marka did dishes again and cleaned up while Ida and Millie cooked and waited tables. "After a few days, you'll feel more comfortable waiting on customers," Millie told her. She told Marka that Ida would be working full time in the cafe now that school was out for the summer. "It's either she works at the cafe or stays home with mother."

Millie told Marka she didn't have to wear a uniform; she could do as Ida and just wear a skirt and blouse, and a half apron. Like Ida, Marka refused to wear a heavy black hair net. Millie warned them that if the health inspector came in, she would get into trouble, but they wouldn't budge.

Millie wiggled in her pink nylon uniform when she waited on the men. "Ida, you take care of those women over there," she would say.

Breakfast was busiest from 8:00 a.m. until 11:00 a.m. The customers hung around until the mail was sorted. At noon, the siren at the Fire Station blew, and the lunch crowd arrived. The cafe bustled until closing time, around 4:00 p.m.

A week after Marka started work at the cafe, Jonny stopped for coffee. The breakfast crowd had thinned out so Millie told Marka she could take a break. She and Jonny sat in a booth at the back of the cafe.

"I'm going to Texas to spend the summer with my mother," he said. "Anna told me you moved into your house and were working here. I've got some books out in my car that I've been wanting to drop off for you, but I've been so busy getting grades recorded, and sports gear checked in. I'm sorry I haven't been over to see you."

"That's okay. I've been busy too. The house was sort of a disaster and took a lot of work. You'll have to come over for supper when you get back from Texas."

"How do you like working for Millie?" Jonny nervously rocked the coffee cup around in its saucer.

"Fine. Fifty cents an hour isn't much, but it will give me something to do for now. I'm going to apply to Deerfield Teacher's College. Hope to get in this fall. I really want to be a teacher."

"That's great, I'll help you any way I can."

"You were right about Ridley being quiet," Marka laughed. "I rather like it, though. Life in Denver was fast and hectic. I like the way people knock on your door and yell, "Yoo-hoo." Anna says that wouldn't happen in a big city."

"Sounds like something Anna would say. I'm really going to miss her. I'll miss both of you," Jonny stammered. "And, George, too. He told me you are settling in."

"I finally feel like I belong in this town," Marka said.

Jonny said, "I'm feeling unsettled. June twelfth is getting close, and the town votes on whether or not to close the high school. My future is in their hands."

"George told me he was sure they wouldn't close. He said they always get nervous when budget time rolls around."

"Say a little prayer for me. I had trouble fitting in when I first moved here, but, now, this is where I want to be."

"*You* had trouble fitting in?"

"Sure. It isn't any easier for a man than a woman. It's difficult when you come to a small community like this. People don't want things to change. When you're in the position I'm in, you find that most people don't want to hear your new ideas. Being a coach, you get a lot of advice. You know, an outsider is a handy scapegoat, and they take their frustrations out on you," Jonny laughed.

"At times I feel like I've never really been away. Nothing has changed much except for a few new people. I was a little disappointed when I first came back. I didn't expect a band or a banquet thrown in my honor, but the only person who really made me feel welcomed was Ruby. Anna tried to help me feel a part of things. In many ways, it was my own fault. I will always wonder if it had something to do with Stella." Marka flushed remembering that she never told Jonny about Denver, about Stella, and the plane ride. "I hate the way she treats Bodie. I tell Bodie to stand up straight and hold his head high. 'Look her straight in the eye when you talk to her. When you look down, she thinks you're weak,' I tell him."

"Bodie's kind of a lonesome dog."

"I feel sorry for him. He told me that when he was a kid, the other kids in school made fun of him."

"Kids can be cruel," Jonny said.

Marka walked Jonny to his car, and he gave her five books. Then something unexpected happened. He hugged her good-bye, held her firmly in his arms, pressed his lips to hers, and held the kiss for a long time. She wasn't sure why, but she felt her stomach flutter, and it took her breath away. Maybe he was more than just a friend. She felt secure and sure of herself in his arms.

She watched him drive away and asked herself if she cared that he was leaving for the summer. Yes, for some reason she did, and she felt a little disappointed that if there was to be anything between them, it would have to wait until fall.

CHAPTER 18

After the breakfast rush, the cafe smelled of hot buttered toast and coffee. Marka finished filling the napkin dispensers, salt and pepper shakers, and sugar jars. She wiped down the counter and tossed the dishrag into the dishpan. Soapsuds spilled out of the pan, landing on the floor. Millie frowned.

"I'll wipe it up," Marka said. "Boy, you're sure a Grumpy Grundy this morning. How was your date last night?"

"Just another Wildroot Cream Oil Charlie," Millie chewed her fingernails. "All he wanted to do was talk about himself. He loved to hear the sound of his own voice." Millie sniffed the air. "Smell that? Some old honyonker came in here with manure on his boots. Ida, go and tell those guys over there that one of them has—"

"Millie, don't ask Ida to do that. You really are in a nasty mood."

"Ida, come here!" Millie barked. Ida was bent over the selector buttons of the jukebox, a shiny mass of yellow, red and orange, with fancy chrome scrolling.

"Hold your horses," Ida said, putting a nickel in the coin slot. The Wurlitzer came to life and Billy Williams began dishing out *I'm Gonna Sit Right Down and Write Myself a Letter.*

"You spend all your tips in that darn jukebox," Millie pinched her lips together and wrinkled her large nose. "And you look like a skunk with that white strip across your bangs. You got to wear a hair net. The health inspector will come in and—"

"Millie, stop picking on Ida," Marka pleaded. "Ruby and I were watching American Bandstand, and the girls are stripping their hair with peroxide. Think back to when you were fifteen—and I hate hairnets too; I don't want to wear one. You're really in a state this morning."

Marka slipped hand-written menus between plastic covers. The lunch menu was simple: fried chicken, beef-steak, mutton and pork chops with all the fixings, hamburgers and fries, and hot dogs. On

Fridays, fish was added. There were only two dessert offered: chocolate cake or a slice of apple pie.

Bodie shuffled into the cafe and sat down at the counter.

"Someone gave you a terrible haircut," Millie whined. "Your head looks like a thatched roof. And where'd you get that shirt, the dime store?"

Bodie shrugged his shoulders.

"I'm just kidding. You look nice today." Millie pinched him on the cheek. She reached under the counter for a cup and saucer, and then filled the cup with coffee. Marka noticed that Bodie's presence seemed to lighten her spirits.

"So, Marka, are you sad Jonny has left for the summer?" Millie asked.

"We only went out one time."

"I've been trying for a whole year. Tried every trick in the books to get his attention, and you get a date with him right away. Is he a good kisser?"

"Millie. He just needed someone to help chaperone the prom. He is a good friend to Anna, that's all. Besides, he may have to move if the town votes out the high school."

"They won't close the high school," Millie said. "See those farmers up in the front booth. They've been talking to everyone who comes in here about voting to keep the high school open. Most of them have been here since eight this morning—drinking up my coffee!"

"Millie, go home. Ida and I will finish up. You hate everyone this morning,"

"It's the damn news. All I got to do is eavesdrop. This morning it's been—'Did you hear that the man in Custer was found guilty of killing his wife?' And this one—'A hired hand out on the range was struck and killed by lightening'. "

"Those are awful things," Marka said putting more dishes in the dishpan.

"How about—'there's a registered Hereford bull auction in Clayton. And twenty-seven carloads of wool were shipped to the east coast." Millie shook her head. "You wonder why I long for some romance and adventure in my life. All I do all day is listen to these honyockers."

"Enough!" Marka said.

"You are in some mood today," Bodie said, studying the menu on the wall.

"Hurry up and order. I haven't got all day," Millie's voice softened teasing Bodie.

"A burger and fries," Bodie grinned.

"A burger and fries; it's always a burger and fries," Millie smiled.

The cafe door opened and a handsome man walked in. He wore a black suit, a brightly colored necktie, and had a thin black mustache. He sat down in the first booth, closest to the jukebox.

"Marka put a hamburger on the grill for Bodie," Millie said. "Eugene just walked in. I'll take his order." Millie filled a glass with water, and unbuttoned the top buttons of her uniform to expose the soft curves of her breasts. She pinched her cheeks so they would look pink and removed the pencil from under her hairnet.

"She acts like she's preparing for battle," Marka said to Bodie. "She's going after the heart of some poor unsuspecting man. Good. Maybe it will change her mood."

"Nice looking suit. What will you have this morning, Eugene?" Marka heard Millie say. She watched Millie bat her eyelashes as she laid the menu down on the table.

Millie bounced back to the grill. "Marka, Eugene wants the pork chop meal, but first he wants dessert." She grabbed a slice of chocolate cake out of the case. "I gotta refill coffee for the guys up front. You should hear his voice," Millie swooned. "Soft and soothing. The kind of voice that gives you the feeling you can really trust the guy."

Marka shook her head and stabbed a fork into an already grilled pork chop. She heaped a big pile of mashed potatoes next to them. "She's back to normal," she said to Bodie who sat quietly taking the whole thing in.

Eugene walked over to the jukebox and dropped in some coins, and then, he came over to the counter, snapping his fingers and swinging his hips. "Say, you got change for a dollar?" He winked and raised an eyebrow at Marka. He slid the bill across the counter. Marka opened the cash register, counted out change, and then placed the coins in his hand.

"I've never seen you here before. You new in town?" Eugene asked.

"No," Marka answered, "but I just started working here."

Eugene put the change in his pocket and held out his hand. "Names Eugene Karlson. I'm the Watkins Man."

Marka extended her hand. He still had hold of her hand when Buddy and Stella walked into the cafe.

"You're burning Bodie's burger," Millie snapped at Marka. "Take your cow eyes off each other."

Eugene let go of Marka's hand and walked back to his booth.

"Look who just waltzed in—you take their order, Marka. Look at her majesty, the queen. Every time I see her she's got on something new."

"Millie, Ida can wait on them."

"Look, Buddy can't seem to take his eyes off you," Millie said.

"Just like Bodie can't take his eyes off you," Marka retorted.

"What you talking about? That dingle ball doesn't know a woman from a heifer."

"Don't be so sure. If you weren't always looking for prince charming, you'd notice that Bodie really likes you."

Millie took hold of Marka's arm and dragged her to the back of the cafe. "Let me tell you about the available men in this town. There's Bodie—he's no Burt Lancaster. Then there's those old bachelors—who live up above the saloon. They live on disability checks—drink it all up and then hang around the saloon waiting for one of the farmers to come in and offer them a few days work." Millie leaned close to Marka. "I heard that on occasion, Buddy drives them up to Deadwood to the whore houses."

"Millie, I don't want to hear this. What's the matter with you?"

"You should see your face," Millie giggled. "It looks hot enough to fry an egg. You ask Buddy about it some time."

"Are you upset with me over Jonny, because if you are—" Marka chewed her lip. "Guess that means you won't be coming to the party Anna is giving for me tonight."

"Marka. Eee gads. I'm a regular bitch, aren't I? I can be so damn ornery. It's just that, last night, well, shit and Shinola—I wouldn't miss your birthday. Anna knows I'm coming, right? She does, doesn't she?"

"Anna insisted I invite all my friends, including you, Millie. Marka laughed. "She even said I could ask Ruby. Anna and I have been getting along lately. I agreed to her inviting some of the women from the church. She also insisted I invite Stella. So, don't do anything stupid, you hear," Marka said, looking over at Buddy and Stella.

Marka left the cafe at 3:30 p.m. She went home and changed out of her work clothes. Then she walked to Anna's. Anna was in the garden picking green beans. Marka couldn't help thinking how Anna tended her garden like she took care of her soul, with care and dedication. Anna started to complain about the cottonwoods. "The ground is covered. It looks like a piece of flannel."

Marka picked a few long, lean green beans and put them with the others in the middle of Anna's apron.

"This morning there were white, puffy clouds sailing across the sky," Anna said. "Now look. There's a dark bank coming in from the west. Looks like there's a rainstorm moving in. That's good, because the garden needs a good soaking. I don't like to put the sprinkler on. A plant needs to grow its roots real deep in the ground. Won't do that if you keep putting water only on the surface. Just like a person. Need to put down deep roots," Anna said, placing more green beans in the middle of her apron, and then bunching it together into a bundle.

Marka asked Anna if she could cut some peonies for the table.

"Yah, sure."

"They smell like the sweetest perfume," Marka said. She left the stems long. She flicked off the ants with her finger.

They went inside the house, and Marka sprawled in a kitchen chair while Anna cleaned carrots, and peeled potatoes and onions to add to the pot roast cooking in the oven.

The house smells good, Marka thought. Like bay leaves and garlic. Anna had baked an angel food cake and made her famous 7-minute frosting. When Marka asked Anna if she could help with preparations, Anna said, "No, you sit and rest."

Anna went down to the basement to get dill pickles out of the crock. Marka's favorite. She said she'd also bring up a jar of sweet pickles, watermelon rind pickles, and pickled beets. Marka set the table. She smoothed the wrinkles out of the white tablecloth, and then put the beautiful pink peonies in a vase on the table.

The phone rang, one short and one long. Before she realized that it was not Anna's ring, Marka picked up the telephone. It was for someone on Anna's party line. She started to place it back on the receiver when she heard, "Hi, Nettie; it's Stella. You going to the birthday party for Marka?"

Nettie said, "Yes."

"Well, I'm not! It's time the people of this town wised up to Anna's niece."

Marka's heart pounded. She held her breath so they wouldn't know anyone was on the line.

"What are you talking about?" Nettie asked.

"It's a disgrace the way she hangs out at the saloon. I wonder what Anna would think of her precious Marka if she knew. It shouldn't be a surprise. I guess Marka's dad was a boozer too."

"Anna will be hurt if we don't go, Stella."

"Anna should know her niece is a home wrecker," Stella's voice was cold and seething. "She has a thing for my husband, you know. They actually meet at the saloon. Buddy doesn't think I know what's going on. I just can't take it any more Nettie," Stella fumed. "Buddy hasn't been the same since she came to town."

"I had no idea," Nettie said. "She seems like such a nice young woman. Are you sure about this? I heard that she and the English teacher are dating."

Marka searched her mind. Nettie? Oh, yes. She's the one who sided with Stella the night of Ladies' Aid. Well, it's all over. Her reputation would be stained. Stella just told Nettie and that was like telling the whole town.

"This isn't the first time she's gone after someone else's husband." Stella said.

Marka waited for them to hang up, then she put down the receiver. What was she going to do? If Stella and Nettie didn't come to the party, what were the chances that the others would come? Should she tell Anna what just happened? No. Anna had gone to so much work putting together a birthday supper. Well, she hadn't wanted those women coming anyway. That was Anna's idea. Yes, she was glad they weren't coming, and if Stella were going to tell everyone, well, all right! Bodie, George, Millie, and Ruby. They were her real friends.

Marka heard Anna coming up the basement stairs. She couldn't still her pounding heart. She felt as if there was a tornado going on inside her head. She ran to the living room and got her purse, looking for something to distract herself. "Look what I bought from the Watkins Man. Beauty cream." Marka held the small jar out for Anna to see.

"Ach, that stuff is no good. I use Pond's cold cream," Anna said putting the pickle jars on the cupboard.

Marka sat down at the table feeling a bit calmer. At least she had caught her breath without Anna noticing that something was wrong. She couldn't tell Anna what happened. It would spoil everything. "Um...the roast smells so good. And the cake is just beautiful."

Anna used a wet dishrag to loosen the jar lids. "Look at those clouds out there; they're getting black. Hope it waits to storm until after the party."

Ten minutes later, the black clouds clustered. An explosion of thunder shook the floor and rattled the windows. Lightning flashed across the sky, and it began to rain. Water beat against the house. Then the rain turned to hailstones the size of ping-pong balls. The hailstones, like an enemy, pounded the plants in the garden. It hailed for a few minutes then rained again. The thunder and lightning grew less, and as suddenly as it started, the storm passed and the sun came out. A rainbow arched across the sky.

"The garden. Ach, I hope the hail didn't do too much damage," Anna gasped, rushing out the door.

"Oh, Anna. Your garden."

A mist hung in the air and water dripped from the leaves of trees. The rain had cooled the air, and a sweet smell lingered. Marka and Anna stood at the edge of the garden. Cucumber vines, carrot and turnip tops, and tomato plants were battered from the hailstones.

"I thought for sure we'd been wiped out," Anna panted. "But, it doesn't look too bad. All is not lost. The roast! Hurry Marka, into the house. We can take care of this later." Anna quickened her steps; Marka followed. When they got to the house, they wiped the mud from their shoes and went in.

Only twelve people showed up for the party: Millie, Ruby, Bodie, George, Katie and Herb, Sophie, Reverend Thurber, his wife, Louise, and their three children. They played games with the boys: Hot and Cold, Button-Button-Who's-Got-The-Button, and they dropped clothespins into a milk bottle by kneeling on the chair above. The boys always won the bottle game. Millie said it was, because they were closer to the floor.

Reverend Thurber and George talked about fishing. Louise talked about vacation bible school and how it was to start in three days. "It will run the seventeenth through the twenty-first," she said.

Ruby and Anna talked about sewing. Ruby told Anna that she made most all her clothes. "No kidding," Anna said. It delighted Marka to think of them having something in common.

Marka tried hard to concentrate on the conversations and the games, but Stella's words echoed in her mind. When it was time to blow out the candles on her cake, twenty-six of them, she made a wish. She wished that Stella would decide she wanted to move back to St. Louis and that she and Buddy would pack up and leave Ridley.

Anna gave Marka a beautiful broach for a birthday present. "It belonged to *Mein Grossmutter*, My Grandmother," Anna said. "She carried it all the way from Russia in her sewing basket." Anna eyes twinkled. "Saw you eyeing it the day we looked through my treasure box and old photos."

Millie gave Marka a bottle of perfume; one that she bought from Eugene. Snake oil, Marka thought to herself, trying to add humor to her mood. Bodie gave her a pearl choker. "Buddy helped me pick it out at the jewelry store," Bodie said. George gave her a tackle box, and Reverend Thurber and Louise gave her a new Bible, King James Version. It was white leather with gold gilded pages. Katie embroidered a set of tea towels, and Herb gave her a new hammer. And Ruby gave her a pair of dangly rhinestone earrings.

Anna seemed pleased when Marka asked if she could stay overnight. She told Anna she felt unsettled from the storm, but really it was the telephone conversation between Stella and Nettie. Marka helped Anna straighten up the room and do the dishes after everyone left.

"Thank you for a lovely birthday party and thank you for letting me invite Millie and Ruby."

"Ruby's not as queer as I thought she'd be," Anna said. "I'm sorry I've complained about the time you spend with her. And, the earrings, they are nice. Boy, that Millie, she sure likes to give Bodie a bad time. Wonder if she can tell that he's sweet on her?"

"He is, isn't he?" Marka said. "I told Millie, but she thinks she's too good for him. She's waiting for her ideal man."

"It was a good birthday then, yah?" Anna sat down and rested her head against the back of her armchair. "I think it's kind of strange that none of the ladies from church came. Maybe the storm kept them away."

"That's not why they didn't come to the party. Anna, I have to tell you something. I promised myself that I would not lie to you anymore." Marka sat in the chair next to Anna. "While we were getting ready for the party, and you were down in the basement, the phone rang: one short, one long."

"That's Nettie's ring. Mine's one long, one short."

"I picked it up by mistake. It was Stella and Nettie talking and— Oh, Anna—Stella said some terrible things about me." Marka slumped in the chair. "Stella told Nettie that I was trying to steal Buddy from her and then—she said—it wasn't the first time I did something like that. I think she's going to tell everyone what I told her on the plane."

"*Eli du! Eli du!* Oh, dear! Oh, dear!" Anna gasped. What will people think? This will really stir up a hornet's nest."

"I'm not a home wrecker," Marka sobbed. "I'm not doing anything to lead Buddy on. He's the one who won't leave me alone."

"You and Stella have been at war with each other ever since you got here!" Anna's voice grew loud.

"I haven't done anything to her. She's the one—" Marka sat quietly. The guilt was eating away at her.

"Anna, I haven't told you everything. I've gone to the saloon and the pool hall, and, I did let Buddy drive me home from the dance in Deerfield. Another time, he drove me to Clayton to pick up a water heater. I'm sorry, Anna. I shouldn't have kept things from you. Are you upset with me?"

"I am Marka! The saloon! Why would you go into that place? If you only knew how your mother felt about that stink hole, you'd never darken its door."

"I didn't think it was such a terrible thing; not everyone goes to the saloon to get drunk."

"So you don't care for a man unless he's married, huh?" Anna asked harshly. "Is that why you never got interested in Jonny, because you had eyes for Buddy?"

"I didn't think he was interested in me." Marka felt stunned. Why had she trapped herself in a web of lies? She never should have lied to Anna about Denver—about smoking—about the saloon. Why hadn't she been honest with Anna? Was it because her deepest fear was not being loved? Anna, the one person whose love she needed the most. Would she turn her back on Marka?

"I don't want you to go in there—no more! They should just burn the place down." Anna's voice was stern. "Everyone says how the town needs the saloon for revenue, but let me tell you something. No one ever thinks about this; there are men who just shouldn't drink. They try to drown their sorrows, escape their problems. They have a few drinks, and all of a sudden they feel like a king. So many problems it caused your folks—if you only knew. Your mother was so ashamed and hated what people thought."

"I'm tired of worrying about what other people think. I'm sick of it!"

"People talk, Marka. I told you right off that you have to watch everything you say and do in this town. And what about Millie? I suppose she goes to the saloon too. I told you to stay away from her, that she was man crazy. Now, see what's happened."

Marka's nostrils flared. "Millie isn't like that. Besides she has changed a lot since I've met her. And she doesn't go to the saloon; I went there by myself."

"Well, if Millie's been trying to mend her ways, she's been using some mighty thin thread. Don't tell me she's changed. I saw her teasing poor Bodie. Anyways, we're off the subject. What about you going in the saloon?" Anna shook her finger at Marka.

Marka cried. "I thought you were different from my mother. She never listened to what was important to me. She never stuck up for me. Just like you over Stella." Tears streamed down Marka's cheeks. "Stella deceived me. She sat right there and let me spill my guts to her. Now she's going to tell everyone."

Anna sat quietly, wringing her hands. "I thought you told me you would never be so stupid as to get involved with another married man. You've played right into Stella's hands. You'll have to reap what you have sown. You probably lost your chance with

Jonny. Maybe that's why he went to Texas for the summer—he heard about Buddy and you going to the saloon."

"Anna, Stella has had it in for me from the first day I arrived. You don't believe me, do you? You believe her, but you don't believe me. Here!" Marka unpinned the broach Anna had given her for a present and put it in Anna's hand. "I can't take this. It just doesn't feel right now." Marka's heart felt like it had been crushed with a heavy stone.

Anna tightened her fingers around the broach; the veins stood out on her hand. "Wait here, I have something that belongs to you." She stormed into the bedroom, and then returned with something in her hand. "I found this in the dresser drawer after you moved back into your house. This is idolatry you know," Anna held up the scapular that Ruby had given Marka. "God protects you—not some piece of cloth."

Marka just couldn't let Anna have the last word. "Your precious Stella. I never wanted to say anything about this, but know what else she did? She ditched her wedding ring into the river and told Buddy she lost it. That's why she got a new one."

Anna was still sitting in the chair when Marka packed up her gifts and left. Marka thought how Anna's eyes looked like dark holes.

When she got home, Marka flung the door open, ran to her bedroom, and threw herself across the bed. She sobbed. She felt so alone. There never had been, nor ever would be, anyone in the world who truly understood or loved her. And, Anna, the closest person to her, had turned away. Wails of sadness filled every corner of the house. Pain ran deep in Marka's soul. She felt like her life was draining away.

"Have some breakfast," Millie put a plate of eggs, bacon, and toast in front of Marka.

"I can't eat. My stomach hurts."

"Too much cake last night, right?" Millie cracked her gum.

"Millie, remember when I told you that something happened to me in Denver involving a man. Well, you'll be hearing about it. Last night, before the party, I overheard Stella and Nettie talking about me."

Marka told Millie all about Denver, what Stella had said to Nettie, and about her terrible argument with Anna.

"Oh, honey. Are you okay? Go home. I'll handle the café by myself. Ida can stay on longer."

"I'm okay. I feel awful about Anna though. Oh, why did I pick up the telephone and listen?"

"Hey, be glad you did. At least now you know what is going on. Forewarned is forearmed. You and Jimmy Hoffa. I can't believe it," Millie laughed.

"What are you talking about?"

"I heard Hoffa is being indicted by the grand jury for wire-tapping. Seems he was tapping the phone of the union headquarters in Detroit."

"That's not funny, Millie. I don't make a habit of eavesdropping on conversations. If Stella ever found out, she'd probably have to report me to the government."

"Worse than that, she'd turn you into the phone company," Millie giggled. "I'm just trying to cheer you up."

"This is serious. She's really out to get me."

"Stella's jealous of you, that's all." Millie threw her gum in an ashtray.

"If I were a turtle, I'd draw in my limbs and stay that way forever," Marka said.

"Stella and her henchmen will be out to get you all right, but, you have Anna on your side. No one will believe Stella."

"No, I don't have Anna. Not anymore." Marka felt her throat tighten. Her eyes turned red and watery and a tear rolled down her cheeks.

Millie patted Marka's hand. "Hey, you have me. Stella better watch out or she'll find herself in hot oil." Millie pointed to the deep fat fryer over by the grill.

"Don't kid around. Even Ruby is leery of her. She warned me not to cross her. Oh, why don't I ever listen?"

"I know," Millie whispered in Marka's ear. "You could report her for reading everyone's mail. I'll send a post card through with some kind of funky story, wait for her to read it, and start some false gossip around town. We could catch her at it."

"Millie. No. Don't."

There was a disturbance in the street. They heard hooting and hollering and a car horn honking.

"Look. There's a fight in the street in front of the saloon." Millie grabbed Marka by the arm and pulled her to the front of the cafe. "It's Ole and Danny Deer Ears. They're going to bust each others' heads." Millie gasped.

Marka watched Ole throw Danny to the ground and then she walked away from the window. "I don't want to watch this. Fighting upsets me. I'll clear the tables and then, I'm going home. I'm exhausted. I didn't get much sleep last night."

"Now Danny threw Ole to the ground," Millie cheered. "Don't you want to see this? Oh, look, there's Buddy. Danny could have a knife."

Marka sat down in a booth. "What's Buddy doing in the middle of it? Knowing him, he couldn't resist the urge to show off. Hope he doesn't end up getting hurt."

"Ole and Danny are dancing around each other swinging their arms. Oh, they butted each other like two rams. Danny struck Ole square in the face with his fist," Millie said, excited. "Ole just followed with a quick right, and caught Danny on the jaw. Now, Danny's on the ground, and Ole's on top of him, punching."

"Millie, that's enough. You sound like an announcer at a boxing match."

"Ole's going to kill him," Millie said. "Oh, good, Buddy pulled him off. It looks like Danny is going to walk away. No, he isn't, he lunged at Ole. Now, they're both on the ground rolling around."

Marka went to the window. She felt disturbed watching the two of them roll around the oil-soaked gravel in front of the saloon. She was about to go back and clear tables when Ole stood upright, drew back, and landed a punch that knocked Danny out cold.

"Shouldn't we call Solly?" Marka asked.

"You go call him," Millie said keeping her eyes on the street. "Wait, he just drove up. The fight is over now."

They watched Buddy wrap Ole's bloody knuckles with a handkerchief. Elton wiped Danny's bleeding mouth.

"Looks like Ole may have knocked out Danny's front teeth," Millie said.

149

Buddy came into the cafe. "How did it start?" Millie asked pouring him a cup of coffee. She wiggled over to the warmer, set the pot down, then came back to hear the story.

"Ole came into the saloon and asked if anyone had seen his dog. Jake egged him on saying that Danny probably caught Old Boss and made stew out of him. Before any of us knew what was happening, Ole walked up to Danny, grabbed him by the neck, and threw him to the floor. Elton reached under the counter for the club he keeps there just in case things get out of hand. He told them to get outside. He knew there was going to be a fight," Buddy said, out of breath.

"I think it's awful," Marka said. "Men fighting like that."

"It was all Jake's fault," Buddy said.

"I feel sorry for Danny," Marka said, recalling the story Solly told her about how her dad used to bring the little Indian kids to their house for something to eat.

"Aw—she feels sorry for him," Millie teased. "Why don't you take him home with you. He's familiar with your house."

"Ole is an animal. So is Jake. They don't even act human. I hope Solly locks Ole up," Marka said.

"How do you know so much about Ole, anyway?" Millie asked. "He's never been in the cafe. He only comes to town a few times a year, and the last time was after lambing."

"Let it go, Millie." Buddy said. "Pour me some more coffee."

"You're still going to the dance with me Saturday night, aren't you Marka," Millie asked overfilling Buddy's cup. It ran into the saucer.

Marka frowned. She walked to the back of the cafe and waved Millie over to her. "Why did you say that in front of Buddy?" she said, scolding Millie.

"I did it on purpose so he'd know you were going to be there."

"Millie, you're just trying to make things worse for me. I told you what Stella said to Nettie. I don't want to be anywhere near Buddy. Just having him in the cafe makes me nervous."

That night Marka couldn't sleep. She tossed and turned, finally got up at 1:00 a.m., and drank a glass of milk. The thought of the violence she had witnessed the previous day made her body ache. She hated any kind of fighting or bickering. Marka thought about her argument with Anna. Not with fists like Ole and Danny, but with words, and words hurt as much as hitting, or stabbing with a knife. Anna hadn't even called the cafe once all day to tell her she was sorry.

Marka worried about Stella and what she would do. Things were getting out of hand, just like in Denver. And Anna held her responsible for all of it. Stella had made her a target. Marka laid her head on the kitchen table and wept. Her throat felt tight; she felt like she couldn't breathe. Hot tears stung her eyes. She wished she had a place; a foxhole, she could hide in. She couldn't stay in Ridley if Anna was angry with her; and if Stella talked, the whole town would turn against her. Anna worried what other people thought more than she cared about her own niece. There would be no peace for either of them if she stayed. Stella would make life miserable. No telling what she'd do next. The only thing to do was to leave town.

Marka went to the bedroom and got her suitcase out of the closet. She pulled clothes off hangers, opened drawers, and threw clothes across the room. One minute she was angry; the next she was sobbing. Her broken heart couldn't move as fast as her mind, trying to figure out what went wrong.

The next morning, Marka went to see Ruby. She ran up the flight of stairs.

"I'm leaving. When I first came here, I thought everything would be okay, but now, I don't think so. I should have known, you can never go back home."

"So, you're going to run again, just like when you left Denver," Ruby's voice was stern.

"I don't know why I came back anyway," Marka sobbed. "I hate this town. I always wanted to live in a big city and look at me. Stuck again in this hole. Maybe I should just sell the house and move to—"

"Where?" Ruby asked.

"To Chicago—back to Denver. Oh, I don't know."

"Did you ever think about this? Maybe you came back because you needed to make peace with your past. Aren't you doing the same thing to Anna that you did to your parents? Maybe you need to stay here and work this out."

"I don't have a choice. I'll never be accepted now. Stella will make sure of that. She's telling everyone that I'm trying to steal her husband, and she'll tell the rest—about Denver!" Marka took deep breaths between sobs. "Besides, Anna wants me to leave. She knows about me going into the saloon; she knows about Buddy. I've been so stupid."

"Okay, Mia, I tell you what we will do. You and me; we are both outcasts, right? We can move away together. Anna is a nester; I am a wanderer, a Gypsy. I'm not content to stay here; I want to find my brother."

"No, Ruby."

"Well, then. Anna doesn't hate you. She's family. All you got. She doesn't want you to suffer. The night of your birthday she told me about when her family left Russia. She wants you to have a good life. She's afraid of any kind of trouble. Afraid that the government will send all the Germans back to Russia."

"Anna has too much pride. She's always worried about what other people think. She never approves of anything I do. Oh, Ruby, she reminds me of my mother. Sometimes I feel like I am going through my childhood all over again. I can't do anything I want, because of Anna." Marka felt herself churning as the anger ran through her.

"How's Anna stopping you from doing what you want?"

"Anna doesn't love me," Marka sobbed.

"You say Anna has too much pride and doesn't love you. Maybe it isn't Anna that has too much pride. And as far as love goes, you don't just turn it off. Maybe she is angry and hurt, but that doesn't mean she doesn't love you. Okay, Mia, you go ahead and leave. Move to Chicago maybe, huh? George used to live there; maybe he can tell you where to find a place to live. What will you do with your house?"

"I'll sell it to Bodie."

"And, then, he can find what your mother so longed for you to have, right?"

"Ruby, I know what you're doing. You're trying to trick me. I thought you were my friend."

"Care to hear what I think? You are your own worst enemy. Listen to your heart, to your feelings. I don't really think you know who you are. You are a stranger to yourself. Listen to your yearnings and don't let others control your life. Be honest with yourself about who you are."

"But—I."

"Listen," Ruby took hold of Marka's hands. "You spend your life trapped in dark corners with silent forces pulling you. You need to make peace with your past, Mia. You need to feel the pain around your heart. Stay and battle this out. You're no longer a child. You have the power to choose what you want," Ruby pleaded.

"Ruby I have to go home. Millie asked me to go to the dance with her tonight, and I have to get ready. Maybe it will help me get my mind off things." Marka pulled her hands away from Ruby.

Ruby took Marka in her arms. "I know it's hard for you to hear these things, but it is only because I care about you."

"You don't know everything there is to know about me or my life, Ruby."

"I don't think you should go to this dance tonight." Ruby closed her eyes and took a deep breath. "I am getting feelings, like something terrible is going to happen. Promise me you won't go to the dance with Millie."

CHAPTER 19

Millie's old black Chevy chugged up the washboard gravel hill, made a left turn onto Highway 212, and then sped along the blacktop past haystacks, silos, and fields planted with alfalfa, corn, and sugar beets. Just before Clayton, they passed the sugar beet factory, a huge building with a tall smokestack.

It was 7:45 p.m., too early to arrive at the dance hall; so Millie suggested they stop at Dairy Queen for a milkshake. Marka asked if she brought any liquor.

"I have a bottle of rum under the seat."

"You have a milkshake," Marka said. "I'll have a spiked soda."

At 9:15 p.m., they pulled into the parking lot of the Veteran's Club. Marka spotted a shiny red pickup.

"Oh, no," she swallowed hard, "Buddy's here. I knew you shouldn't have said anything about us coming to the dance tonight."

"Why not?" Millie looked in the rear view mirror and smoothed on a heavy layer of bright red lipstick.

"If anyone sees us near each other, they'll believe Stella."

"It baffles me why he stays with her," Millie wiped a smear of lipstick from her tooth with her finger and then blotted her lips on a tissue. "Listen, honey, don't worry about it—just have fun. God knows you deserve some fun after last night. Tonight, I'm going to meet Mr. Wonderful," she swooned.

Marka unwrapped a piece of spearmint gum and chewed it to kill the smell of liquor on her breath. "If Buddy shows up, I'm staying clear of him."

Marka did try to discourage Buddy. She turned him down three times when he asked her to dance. She even avoided him by ducking into the ladies' room, but her efforts were in vain. While she was slow dancing with someone else, Buddy came up and tapped the guy on the shoulder.

"Cutting in," he took hold of Marka's arm and plucked her away from him. At first Marka resisted and then decided not to cause a commotion. What would one dance hurt?

They slow danced. Buddy pressed himself close, and touched his face to her cheek. She tried to push him away, but he held her tight. "I thought maybe you'd be with the school teacher." He smiled.

Marka felt warm and happy in Buddy's arms, but she thought of Anna's angry face. The liquor she drank before the dance made her lightheaded. She couldn't think straight. She pulled away and kept a distance between them until the song ended. The bandleader announced it was intermission. "I have to find Millie," she said and quickly walked away.

Millie was outside the hall waiting for Marka all excited about some guy she just met. She took Marka by the hand and led her over to her car, opened the front passenger door, and shoved Marka in beside a guy named Dennis, who was behind the wheel. Then she climbed in the back seat with a big burly guy she called Earl.

"This dance is a damn bust—band's lousy," Earl said tossing Millie's car keys over the front seat. "Let's drive over to Woodland. There's supposed to be a dance over there. Dennis, you drive."

"Millie, we can't stay out too late," Marka turned around and looked in the back seat. Millie was curled up in Earl's arms, kissing him and cooing.

Earl broke away from the kiss. "Don't be a square."

Has Millie lost her mind? Every time she's interested in a man she gets crazy. It's hopeless to try talking to her now.

"Dennis, are you okay to drive?" Marka asked.

Dennis held his finger in front of his face, slowly brought it to his nose, pulled it back, and then put his finger in his mouth. "I'm okay," he laughed. "I've only had a couple beers."

They were five miles from Woodland when Earl told Dennis, "Take this next turn. It's a short cut."

"A short cut—to where?" Marka asked, concerned.

"Dennis just drive," Earl ordered.

They drove down a narrow dirt road that led to a group of pines. This is no short cut, Marka fumed inside. It's just a way to get the car off the main road so they can park and make out.

"Park this thing," Earl commanded.

"I thought we were going to the dance in Woodland. Why the change?" Marka asked.

"The square is a chicken too," Earl roared with laughter.

"I'm no chicken," Marka huffed. "I just thought we were going dancing."

Dennis pulled over to the side of the road, and turned off the ignition. He turned on the radio. *Warm up to Me Baby* by Jimmy Bowen and the Rhythm Orchids was playing. Marka laid her head against the back of the seat, tightened her arms across her chest, and closed her eyes like she was going to sleep. Dennis seemed like a nice guy, but she would not make out with someone she hardly knew. Marka was glad when Dennis turned the radio louder to drown out the moaning sounds coming from the back seat. Millie and Earl were slobbering all over each other.

Dennis reached into his jacket and brought out a half pint of Four Roses whiskey. He unscrewed the lid and offered Marka a swallow. At first, she hesitated and then she took several sips. They burned her throat and made her stomach feel on fire. Tomorrow she was going to tell Millie that this was a bunch of shit! Marka felt angry and disgusted for having been put in this position. I'm going to come right out and tell her that when she is with a man, she acts like no one and nothing else matters. Marka took a couple more swallows of the whiskey when Dennis offered it to her.

Dennis tapped Marka on the shoulder. "Let's go for a walk."

Marka sighed a breath of relief and nodded yes.

They got out of the car and walked up the dirt road. The moon cast enough light so they could see where they were going. Dennis told Marka that he and Earl were in the Air Force, stationed at Ellsworth near Rapid City. They worked at the missile sites that were being built in the area. "I'm from Nevada," Dennis said. "Earl's from Texas. Earl and I aren't that good of friends."

They walked and talked for a half hour. The cool air helped clear Marka's head. Oh, why had she drunk the liquor? One sip led to another until she couldn't keep count.

When they got back to the car, Dennis tapped on the hood. They waited a while then he opened the door on the driver's side and climbed in behind the wheel. Marka got in the passenger side and sat crammed up against the door instead of sitting in the middle.

Millie and Earl were asleep. Marka laid her head back on the seat and closed her eyes.

Earl awakened her. He leaned over the front seat. "Hey, party poopers. Wake up—let's party! The night's still young."

Marka winced at the smell of his repugnant breath.

Earl opened the car door, stepped out, and pulled Millie, half asleep, out of the car. He opened the front door, grabbed Dennis's arm and pulled him out too. The keys were in the ignition. Before Marka knew what was happening, Earl jumped into the car, started it and drove away, leaving Millie and Dennis standing there alone in the night.

"What in the hell are you doing?" Marka gasped her head pounding.

"Thought me and you should get acquainted," he slurred. He sounded cold and uncaring.

"You turn this car around right now!"

Earl kept driving. He drove for a few miles, and then pulled the car over to the side of the road. The moonlight shined in through the car window. Earl's eyes were like a hawk, ready to devour its prey.

It was a desolate, solitary area. No other cars had passed them. Earl must know these back roads well, Marka thought. Her heart pounded in her ears. What did Earl have in mind? The fear of him overpowered her, made her panic.

"Don't act so innocent, little missy. You wouldn't be with Millie if you weren't a fun-time girl too. Now, let's have a kiss." Earl's expression grew crafty and cruel. He slid across the seat and pushed his face against Marka's cheek. He pressed his hot, wet lips against hers, and stuck his tongue in her mouth. Marka pulled away. She pinched her lips tight and stiffened her jaw. The taste of his saliva in her mouth made her retch. This infuriated Earl. He glared, and then forced another kiss on her, this time biting her bottom lip.

"Ouch! You're disgusting!" Marka cried and slapped his face. She touched her lip with her finger; it felt wet. She rubbed her tongue around her mouth; she tasted blood.

Marka found the door handle and pulled hard. She jumped out of the car. Earl was right behind her. He yanked her arm and threw her against the front of the car. She felt a stabbing pain as the hood ornament gouged her in the small of the back.

Marka fought back punching Earl in the Adam's apple. He coughed and staggered away. Her heart beat rapidly; her palms were sweaty, and her hands shook. She knew the frightening truth. Earl planned to have his way with her. She'd rather die first.

Earl got his bearings, stood up and lunged at Marka. He flung her to the ground, landed on top of her and glued himself there. "You think you're too god damn good for me, don't you, you little bitch," he said clenching his teeth.

Marka stiffened her body. Earl hit her cheek, and when she turned her head to the side, he pulled her hair so he could look into her eyes. His eyes were glaring; his breath was heavy with the smell of liquor. She wanted to holler for help, but who would hear her? It would probably just make Earl angrier. Will tonight be my time to die?

She felt the pain in her back, the sting on her cheek. She lay still for a moment, knowing the hopelessness of a struggle. God, if you're real, I need you more now than I ever have in my life, Marka prayed. Please, God, help me. Marka drew in a deep breath. He's not going to get away with this. Maybe he's drunk enough so that I can throw him off track.

"Okay, okay, wait a minute," Marka's voice softened, but her heart raced. "You don't have to force me. Give me a chance. Can't we get to know each other first?" Only an egghead would fall for a trick like that, she thought.

Earl bit. His body eased, and he lessened his hold. He let go of her shoulders, rolled away, and lay on the ground beside her. Marka lay looking at the black sky pitted with stars. God, help me, God, help me, she prayed over and over. She prayed God would send a car, or, better yet, a sheriff.

When Marka felt it was safe, she got to her feet and straightened the wrinkles from her skirt. How was she going to get away from Earl? It was impossible to outrun him. He was a big bull. There's only one way, she thought. Get him away from the car, distract him and then make a run for it, hoping he left the keys in the ignition.

"Let's walk farther into the woods. It's not private enough for me," Marka motioned to Earl.

They walked a short ways, and then Marka sat down on a bed of pine needles. They stuck to her bare legs. "Dennis said you were part of the missile crew. You're from Texas, and he's from Nevada. I know someone that went back to Texas to visit—"

Marka swallowed hard thinking about Jonny; she wished she were with him or with Buddy, right now, and anywhere, but here, in this dark place, with Earl. She must make small talk. Keep her voice calm. "How do you like the area?"

Earl didn't answer.

"Do you have a girlfriend back home?" Marka asked.

"They're nothing but a bunch of bitches." Earl looked down at the ground.

Marka had a sick feeling in the pit of her stomach. There was no one to help her in this place. Earl was calm now, and if she could keep things that way, she would have time to devise a plan. "Do you think I'm a bitch? Millie isn't a bitch, is she? Wish we had a blanket, it's not very comfortable here is it?" Marka forced herself to relax.

"Quiet. What was that?" Marka said softly and got to her feet.

"What?" Earl pulled his shoulders back and sat upright. He looked over his shoulder. Marka gave him a swift kick in the groin. He curled up and made a guttural noise.

She ran for the car. God, please let the keys be there. She ran as fast as she could, gasping for air, her heart pumping fast. The moon cast soft shadows, and then something inside her took hold. Her legs felt strong. She held her arms out in front of her as she ran, and looked up at the sky. Faster and faster she ran. Something told her that she would be all right.

Marka reached Millie's car. She tore open the door and the dome lights came on. The keys were in the ignition. Oh, God, thank you, God. Marka turned the key, and the engine started. She slid across the seat and pushed the locks down on all the doors. She turned on the headlights, then put the car in gear and pushed hard on the gas pedal. The car fishtailed on the gravel.

She drove a mile or so, took a right, and then drove another mile. She hoped she was back on the main road.

"Oh, please, let Millie be standing by the road," she prayed. She turned the headlights on high beam and watched both sides of the road as she drove slowly. Finally, there they were, walking down the road, thumbing for a ride. Marka honked the horn and pulled over to the side.

"Get in!" she shrieked. "Get in! We have to get the hell away from here!"

Dennis and Millie jumped in the front seat. "Where's Earl?" Millie screamed as they took off.

Marka took one hand off the wheel and held it high in the air, the middle finger pointing upward. "See this," she screamed, "this is what I think of your Earl!"

No one said a word all the way back to Clayton. Marka pulled into the parking lot of the Veteran's Club where Earl's car was parked. "I left your friend back in the woods. Go after him if you want, but if I were you, I'd leave him there to die," Marka said to Dennis.

Millie drove back to Ridley. "What happened back there?"

With the tension of the escape still eating at her, Marka could not control her feelings. "We shouldn't have gone with them," she screamed at Millie. "It was a stupid thing to do. I shouldn't have let you talk me into it. I don't want anyone to find out about this, you hear?" she sobbed.

"Earl had too much to drink, and I know he is kind of bossy," Millie said. Did he try something with you?"

"Yes. He tried something!" Marka felt wild with rage.

"Oh, honey. I'm sorry. Millie slammed her hand against the steering wheel. "The bastard lured me to get to you. I was just the bait! It was you he wanted. I swear every time I start to have feelings for a guy he does something stupid."

"Oh, Millie, can't you think of something else for a change?"

"What do you mean?"

"Never mind." Marka felt a lump in her throat. This was the blackest night of her life.

"We'll go to the café, and you can call Sheriff Kelly."

"No. It will come out that you made it with him. Then I'm supposed to convince the Sheriff that I hadn't agreed to it? It will be my word against his. Just get us back to Ridley. I want to forget this night ever happened. It's not all your fault. I had too much to drink. Drinking always gets me into trouble."

Sunday morning, rain poured. The thirsty earth soaked in the much-needed moisture. Sasha paced back and forth across the room several times, then jumped onto the bed and curled up next to

Marka. Anna's cat had taken up residence at Marka's shortly after she moved into her house, merely because Marka let her stay inside any time she wanted and fed her canned tuna.

Marka gently stroked Sasha's silver-gray fur; the back of her head and down her back, but Sasha became indignant and unappreciative, and pouted like a small child who couldn't go out to play. She delivered a pitiful mew, got off the bed, and jumped to the windowsill, looking mournfully at the rain.

Marka started to cry again. All night she shivered and cried. The thought of Earl sickened her: how he kissed her, how he pressed his body close to hers. She thought of his smelly breath. It made her shudder. She had never felt that kind fear before last night. It was a fear that ran through her entire body.

She would *never* go to another dance with Millie. Last night, Earl might have—Oh, God. Marka pulled the sheet over her head and pulled her knees to her stomach. She needed to take another bath to soak out all of Earl's ugly, dirty touches.

At 8:30 a.m., Anna telephoned. "Marka, will you come to church with me?"

"I don't feel well, Anna. I must be coming down with something."

"I'm sorry, *madchen*, for the way I acted on your birthday. Can I come over after church? I feel so bad about everything."

"Not today, Anna. I'll call you when I feel better and then, you can come over." What would Marka tell Anna about the bruise on her cheek? Everything was such a mess. What was she going to do? Millie won't be able to keep her mouth shut about last night, Marka fretted. The only sane thing Marka could think to do was to call Ruby. She couldn't hide out all day in her bathrobe.

"Ruby, could you come over? I need to talk to you. I'll explain everything when you get here."

Marka got dressed and closed all of the drapes in the living room.

Ruby knocked on her door, opened it, and hollered. When Marka came to the door, Ruby put her arms around Marka. "Mia. What happened to your face? How did you get the bruise on your cheek?"

Marka told Ruby everything. "First, Buddy was at the dance, and he wouldn't leave me alone until I danced with him. Millie convinced me to leave the dance with her and these guys. One of

161

them tried to have his way with me." Marka's eyes filled with tears. "You warned me not to go to the dance, but I wouldn't listen."

"Why didn't you say, NO to Millie?" Ruby asked.

"Anna told me right from the start to stay away from her. Oh, what am I saying? I had too much to drink. It was my fault. Ruby, please tell me what to do," Marka sobbed. "Is Earl going to kill me for leaving him out on the road like that?"

"Let's sit down," Ruby took hold of Marka's hand and led her to the couch.

"It really started on my birthday. First, Anna's phone rang. Her ring is one long, one short. My phone rings one short, one long. I got confused. I guess I was excited about the party. Then, hearing Stella say all those awful things about me and then I had a terrible argument with Anna. Oh, Ruby."

"Yes, Yes, Mia."

"I should have known something awful was going to happen yesterday, because I did everything backwards. It's like getting out of bed on the wrong side, you know," Marka rambled on, hardly stopping for breath. "I usually make my bed, then do the dishes. Only I did it the other way around. I always put on my make-up, then do my hair, but when I was getting ready for the dance, I did my hair and then put on my make up."

"Backwards or bad luck or maybe it all happened for a reason," Ruby said. You're not at peace, Marka. I told you that. You have to stop fooling yourself about who you are."

"I don't know who I am," Marka sobbed.

"You tell me how you are always lying to Anna. I think you lie to yourself too. And you don't share yourself with anyone."

"Yes, I do. I've told you lots of things about me."

"But, you never tell me how you feel. How do you *feel* inside, Marka?"

"I feel empty. Like an old junky trunk."

"You were drinking?"

"Well, maybe a little. Oh, damn, a lot!" Marka stood up. "I'm scared. I'm scared!" She felt like the wind had been knocked out of her.

"Mia, I will help you. You are not alone." Ruby said. "You need to see the truth. Evil is always full of lies. Tell the truth."

Marka paced around the living room. "I tell myself I'm not going to smoke or drink, but that's all I can think about. I feel guilty, because I lied to Anna. Right now, I want to have a drink. When I was living in Denver, I drank every night except the days I bargained with myself. Sometimes, I would go a week without drinking, and I felt I was all right. I would watch my drinking, because I never wanted to be like my dad. I'd have drinks every day after work. When I came to Ridley, I promised myself—no more, but I went to the saloon the first chance I got. I don't know why I did that. I don't understand any of the things I do." Marka wrapped her arms tightly around her stomach.

"Mia, you have to stop fooling yourself. The more you keep hidden, the more you don't know who you are. How am I going to get to know the real Mia if you don't share with me who you really are?"

"I'm afraid you won't like me if you know what I'm really like—what I really think. The things I do—all the bad things I have done."

"What about the good things you do? You are a good person. Be who you are and be proud of it. Come, sit on the sofa with me."

Marka said, "When I was a kid, well, I was always angry, because I wanted my parents to get along. Why couldn't they just like each other? They were too busy arguing to notice me. I wanted them to care about me, to be there for me. My mother kept herself busy around the house. When Dad came home, they got into arguments. I always worried about them. I tried to be good so they wouldn't fight. I use to blame myself if they were unhappy. I thought it was my fault."

"Fighting is about who will control the other. That's how people are. You didn't have a carefree childhood like I did, Mia. A child shouldn't have to worry about taking care of her parents. It is supposed to be the other way around," Ruby consoled Marka.

"I always felt there was something wrong with me for the way I felt. Maybe I was a disappointment to them," Marka sobbed.

"You need not be ashamed of your feelings." Ruby touched Marka's shoulder. "Mia, the first day I met you, I told you that you were haunted with bad memories."

"Ruby, please tell me what to do. Here, read my palm." Marka put her hand in Ruby's hand. "You know what the future holds for me. Please, Ruby, I need you to tell my fortune. You told me not to go to the dance with Millie, and I didn't listen to you. See what happened, something bad. What will happen to me next? Please, Ruby, tell me," Marka pleaded.

"Mia, I cannot foretell what will happen. Yes, I did tell you not to go to the dance with Millie, because I had bad feelings. That's all it was, bad feelings."

"Ruby, you told me you have powers like your mother."

"Mia, listen to me. I will tell you something I never told anyone before," Ruby whispered. "Yes, my mother saw things no one else saw; she had the gift, but I don't. Sometimes, I tell people what I think they want to hear. I listen close to what people say; I watch them with an eagle's eye. I am good at reading people, but it's only feelings that come from some place deep inside me. Maybe it comes from what I want, Mia; I can never be truly certain."

"Ruby, are you telling me that everything you said to me wasn't true? Marka took her hands away and covered her ears.

"I will admit that, at first, I was playing with you like a cat plays with a mouse. I did tell you things I thought you wanted to hear, because I needed a friend. The more we became friends, well, from then on, all the things I told you were from the wisdom of my heart. Mia, I never once allowed you to cross my palm with silver. You are my friend, but I would never tell you something just because it's what you want to hear. The day you arrived in Ridley—it was good luck for me. I had been thinking about leaving. Then you arrived."

"Ruby, you're talking in circles." Marka felt confused. She wanted to understand. George called her bizarre. Anna said she was queer. But, Ruby had an understanding of things.

Ruby took off the white lace shawl she was wearing and wrapped it around Marka's shoulders. "I want you to have this."

"You don't have to give me anything, Ruby."

"When someone's life is falling apart, you try to do something to make her feel better."

"I do feel like I did in Denver. Oh, no. I can't go through that again."

Ruby sat close to Marka on the couch, and touched her bruised cheek. "It's outrageous. Earl must not get away with this. The government employs him, right? They will lock him in the stockade."

164

"What can I do about it? I'm afraid to tell Anna. She'll say that I should have listened to her. She tried to warn me about Millie, but I wouldn't listen. Why don't I ever listen? Anyway, no one will believe me. They'll probably say I led him on, and I was with Millie. She has a bad reputation. People will say that I'm like her. It's my own fault. Now I really will have to leave Ridley. It's the only thing I can do." Marka pressed her hand against her forehead. "And if Stella finds out about this, she will spread any rumor about me she wants, and people will believe her. See, that's why I can't say a word about what happened last night."

"Everything that happened to you was for a reason. Maybe there is something you need to learn. You have been on a deadly course. That is what I really wanted to tell you the first day we met. My feelings told me so, but, people want to hear what is good, so I didn't tell you."

"You say that you don't have powers. You knew right away I had a problem with my parents. I never told you this before, but the day before I left home, Dad and I had a terrible fight. He couldn't understand why I wanted to live so far away from them. Denver, to him, was on the other side of the world. Why couldn't I work in Clayton? He kept asking. How could I just leave my mother like that? I got angry and told him that I was leaving, because I couldn't stand his drinking and their constant fighting. I wanted to get as far away from them as I could. Oh, Ruby. It was never the same between us. After the argument, they were so distant."

"So, you see then, Mia, you came back to make peace. Their spirits are tormenting you, because you have not asked for their forgiveness. The evil spell on you must be broken."

"Ruby, you said I needed to be more honest about things. I can't keep this secret any longer. This is something that not even Anna knows about."

"What, Mia?"

"One night, my folks were having a terrible argument. I was in my bedroom playing with my dolls. I heard a crash and my mother screamed. I snuck out of my room and went to the dining room, and my father was breaking furniture and smashing pictures. Then, he grabbed my mother by the throat. Ruby, I think he would have strangled her if I hadn't been there. I screamed and screamed. He turned his head and looked at me, his eyes were full of rage. He stopped and let her go."

"How old were you?" Ruby asked.

"I was ten. Anna knew I was upset about something, but I was afraid I would get into trouble if I told. And, I was ashamed. I didn't want anyone to know how crazy things were in our house."

"My little, Mia." Tears welled in Ruby's eyes. Her mascara mixed with the tears and looked like dirty water running down her cheeks. "You have had this hidden deep inside you all these years. You will feel better now that you have told someone. You no longer have to hide what happened. You have let light shine on the secret you had shut away."

"What do you mean, Ruby?"

"When we hide things we feel shame, a shame that's not really ours. When we tell, we are free. The house was scary, and you saw ghosts, because of what happened when you were a little girl. You are a sensitive creature, Mia. That is why all of this has haunted you."

"I want it to go away, Ruby."

"Yes, now, the curse has been broken. Their ghosts will no longer torment you. They are at peace. They will no longer slink around in the shadows. Now, you can be free to be what you want and to do what you want to do. This is where real freedom lies."

Marka laid her head on Ruby's shoulder. "I promise you something, Ruby. No more drinking."

"And, no more lies," Ruby said.

"No more lies. I promise."

Monday, at 6:00 a.m., Millie telephoned Marka and asked if she would be coming to work.

"I can't come to work with my cheek bruised like this, Millie! I need a few days off. No, I can't just cover over it with make-up." Marka felt angry. Hurt rose from deep within. She wanted to tell Millie that she was never coming back to the café, that she hated her, that she was nothing but trouble. She wanted to tell her that Anna was right about her, that she was the town whore. She wanted to tell her that she was going to quit her job at the cafe and look for an office job in Clayton. She wanted to, but she couldn't. I can't blame Millie for everything: the drinking and the lies. It was as much my fault. No, it was more my fault. It's time for me to grow up. "I'll be back to work as soon as I pull myself together," Marka said softly.

That afternoon Marka spread a blanket on the grass. She put on her dark glasses to keep out the bright sun. She closed her eyes and listened to the rustle of the trees. She heard clatter and thumping coming from George's house. Then, she heard a whirring sound from his electric saw. George. What would he think about all of this? He just can't find out.

Marka reflected upon the things Ruby said the day before. Yes, she did keep things to herself, and no, she hadn't been in touch with her feelings. Not for a very long time. She was glad she told Ruby about that terrible night. I want to tell Anna about it, but I'm afraid she won't want to listen.

Marka fell asleep, and when she woke, she realized she had let the sun burn her. She was about to go in the house when Anna walked up. When Marka saw her, she burst into tears. "This is just one more thing gone wrong," Marka sobbed. "Anna, I've got a bad sunburn."

"Let me put a towel soaked in tea on your burnt legs," Anna said. "If you don't, the skin will peel just like bark off a tree. *Madchen*, what happened to your cheek?"

"It's a long story. I'm sorry for everything that's happened. I have told you so many lies. I lied about not smoking, and I didn't tell you I went to the saloon. I have a problem with drinking, too, Anna. I am trying to figure things out."

"Marka, my, Marka," Anna's lips trembled.

"I wouldn't listen to you about Millie. The other night I went with her to the dance in Clayton and, well, we ended up going with these guys. Anna, something terrible happened. One of the guys attacked me. He tried to force me to—to, then he hit me on the face," Marka cried. "I'll leave Ridley if you want. I'll sell the house to Bodie if he still wants it. I'll leave. I've been thinking about Chicago. Maybe things will be different for me there."

"*Ach, Gott im Himmel.* Anna touched the bruise on Marka's cheek. "Your lip! Are you okay?"

"Yes, but maybe I should call Sheriff Nader."

"No, then everyone will find out. We don't want people to talk. We can't bring attention to us. You are right about me; I worry too much what people think. I don't want you to leave. I've done nothing but think about you for the last two days. I know you have much anger towards your folks. Life wasn't always the easiest for them. I think holding on to all this anger is what is holding you back from being happy. Please go and talk with Reverend Thurber. Maybe he can help you."

"He wouldn't want to hear me say that I hate my parents for not loving me, for not wanting me, for wanting a son. I hate my name. From now on I want to be called Mia. It's a name Ruby gave to me, and I like it better," Marka said, spitting the words out from gritted teeth.

"Ach, your dad did favor boys. But don't pay any attention to what he did. No, you were named after my *Grossmutter,* Marka Annaliz, my mother's mother. They called her just Marka. She died when your mother and I was young."

"I was named after your grandmother?"

"Ach, you mean your mother never told you that? I should have told you then." Anna hugged Marka and patted her softly on the arm. "Your mother kept so much to herself. She didn't like to talk about things that were hurtful. But, she should have at least told you about your namesake. Names are important. I was named after the Anna in the Bible. The one who announced in the temple that Jesus was the fulfillment of all God's promises, and who thanked God that she had been allowed to live to see it."

"Mom never talked about any of her family."

"Well, anyways, I was sixteen when our mother died, your mother was only four. Our mother was run over by a thresher. The horses got spooked and took off. They pulled the machine over her body. Our father married again, this time to an older woman with two grown sons. Well, anyways, it was because of our stepmother that we even learned to read. And she taught us to sew and cook. She kept us out of the beet fields some of the time. We would have had to help with the thinning in the spring and the harvest in the fall. I loved my Baba's wife. But, your mother, well, she never got over her grief for our mother."

"I never knew any of this, Anna. Why didn't mom ever tell me anything?"

"Your mother had so many problems with your dad. She tried to keep it quiet, about his drinking. She was a proud woman. But, in a small town like this everyone, knows your business. I think she knew the whole town was talking. She was ashamed."

"They fought all the time, Anna. He'd shove and hit her. I always went to your house when things got really bad. I just couldn't stand it. Mom would tell me not to say or do anything to set dad off, and then she'd say something wrong. I'd come to your house. Didn't you ever wonder about all those times I came over to your house?"

"I know your dad drank, but he never hit her. Your mother would have told me if anything like that was going on. All your mother told me was he drank too much. I knew how she hated the saloon and his drinking, but she never told me about him hitting her."

"Well, he did! I'm not making it up! The only reason I'm telling you this is, because I can't live with these memories anymore. No one ever talked about any of it. One time I thought he was going to kill her. He had his hands around her throat! I remember how I was so afraid."

"*Lieber Heiland*, Dear Lord," Anna shrieked. "What are you talking about?"

"You would have helped me if you had known, right, Anna? I needed to talk to someone about it, but there was no one to listen."

"Marka, don't talk like this."

"I always felt like they didn't love me. I tried to be good all the time, not make trouble or ask for things. What was so terrible about me that they couldn't love me? I could never please them. Was I a bad girl?" Marka felt fragile, like a piece of moth-infested cloth. The lump in her throat made it hard for her to breathe. "I felt like there was something wrong with me."

"Marka." Anna held her close. "I am so sorry that your mother and father were so tangled in their problems that they never stopped to think about how it was hurting you. It was the drinking. It had nothing to do with you. You were a good little girl."

Marka and Anna stood with their arms around each, and sobbed. They clung to each other for a long while.

"When your father drank, he felt like the wisest person in the world. Your mother would try and stand up to him, but his anger made him stronger. She would back down. Ach, it's just like two

169

countries at war with each other trying to prove who is the most powerful."

"I remember him, red-faced and glassy-eyed from all the liquor. I never really understood what they were arguing about," Marka said.

"Your dad thought he knew it all. He wouldn't listen to anyone. Your mother resented that. She wanted a say in things too. They were both stubborn. They put down roots of bitterness. They devoted so much of their energy to their war they had no time for you—they did love you. Yes, I saw what was happening but there was nothing I could do except to be there for you as much as I could. That is why I always had you stay with me so much of the time. You'd always come by me every chance you got. My Gott. Many times I wished you were my child." Tears flowed down Anna's cheeks.

"I wished you were my mother. I felt close to you. Mom just wasn't there for me. I can't remember her playing with me or doing things with me. She'd tell me to go to your house, because she was busy. That hurt me when she said that. But your house is really where I wanted to be. Do you think she'll forgive me for that?"

"Yah. Yah." Anna said. "Things hurt so much when you're a child."

There was a long silence.

"They did love you, in their own way," Anna said.

"I'm a failure at everything I try to do. I failed in Denver. I thought I could have a new start here. I was beginning to feel like I belonged in Ridley."

"You belong right here with me. First, stop feeling sorry for yourself. And forgive your parents. We've all been hurt in life. It's up to us to bury the blame and anger. Remember the commandment, to honor your father and mother. No matter what, they were your parents. And you must change your ways. No more going to the saloon."

"No more drinking," Marka said. "I don't hate my name anymore, Anna. Is it all right if Ruby calls me, Mia?"

"Yah. I will make us some tea. That is another thing you may like to know about my *Grossmutter*. Back in Russia, she was a *brauche*, a healer. Sometimes they had no doctor, and she would use herbs, and say prayers over people. She was a deeply religious person."

"I don't understand why you find Ruby so strange."

"Yah. You're right about that. I apologize. I won't judge her anymore."

"Tell me more about your grandmother."

"Let me think, now. Oh, yah. Her household duties kept her very busy, but at night, after Grandfather read from the Bible, she would make up stories in her head and tell them to your mother and me." Anna reached into her apron pocket and brought out the broach she had given Marka on her birthday. "Here, this belongs to you. And now you know that it belonged to the *Grossmutter* you were named after. And, Marka, I want you to know this—*Ich lieben du*, I love you." The lines on Anna's face relaxed.

Marka asked Anna if she could sleep at her house for a few nights. She was afraid Earl would come to Ridley looking for her. Every time she thought about Earl, she shivered.

"He better not bother you," Anna said. "Put it out of your head, and stay away from that Millie. She's trouble. Tell her you quit the café."

Anna made chicken-noodle soup and butterballs for supper, and even though it was a warm evening, it still tasted good. It was one of Marka's favorites and the first nourishing thing she had really had in several days. They talked more about Marka's parents. Finally, she said, "I'm really tired. I'm going to bed."

She slept heavily for several hours and then was awakened by a dream. The dream felt so real. She got out of bed and went outdoors into the warm summer night. She walked through the cool grass, and looked up at the black dome of the sky filled with a million stars. It dazzled her eyes. The stars seemed so close she could touch them. The Milky Way. She remembered how she and her mother loved to look at it together. Her mother would spread a quilt across the grass. Marka would put her head in her mother's lap. She would point to the sky and say, "Look, there's the big dipper." It's good to remember the good parts of childhood. She was tired of feeling angry. She thought of the time she and her mother watched the aurora borealis, a beautiful display of lights in the northern sky. Green-gold lights flashed bright as daylight and stretched from one end of the sky to the other, reaching high toward the zenith. "It's the Northern Lights," her mother said. "It's the most beautiful thing I've ever seen."

"What makes it Mama?"

"It's God's fingerprints all over the sky," her mother whispered softly.

Marka stood looking up at all the stars and realized she would never again have to grope in the darkness. God did exist. God had always been there, but she had been too angry to notice. She thought about the wind, and how she could not see it, but she knew it was there. Marka felt a compassionate touch. Something wrapped warmth around her, and for the first time in her life she truly felt safe. She felt a peace, she had never known. She finally believed there was something powerful even though she couldn't totally grasp it.

CHAPTER 20

Marka woke early the next morning. The sun was just coming up over the horizon. Anna was still asleep. The birds had begun their morning song, and far off in the distance, Marka heard the roar of a tractor working a field. She ran water into the coffee pot.

She fried an egg, and a slice of bologna, and then sat at the table waiting for the coffee to perk. Marka reached back to her childhood for the meal blessing. "Come, Lord Jesus, be our guest, and let these gifts to us be blessed," she said. It felt good, and breakfast seemed to taste better. The world felt quiet and motionless. She felt certain things would work out.

The coffee perked; brown liquid bouncing up and down in the glass top. Marka poured herself a cup, then snuggled into Anna's favorite armchair. It had her smell, and this comforted Marka. She pulled her robe up around her neck. The time had come for her to accept responsibility. Like a weaned child, she knew it was time to grow up, to depend on herself, and not to blame her parents for how her life had turned out.

Ruby said, "Tell the truth." The truth is that she had made mistakes. It would be easy to blame her parents for everything that went wrong in her life, but she couldn't. Not after what Anna told her about the way they had been toward each other.

"Things go way back," Anna had said. Anna told her that her father had kept all his feelings bottled up inside of himself. He was nothing but an emotional junk collector covering his feelings with booze. He was full of rage, and when things didn't go the way he wanted, he exploded. And then there were the times when he threatened he would kill himself. He would sit with his head hanging. Marka thought how she felt relieved having told Anna about that terrible night. The night her father almost killed her mother.

"Your mother confessed to me many times that she would like to trade places with me," Anna had said.

"She told me she envied my freedom. She had no say about things. I think your mother just finally gave up."

Marka thought how her parent's inability to show love had bred insecurity in her. She had grown up afraid and unsure of herself. Her upbringing lacked words of encouragement and praise. Perhaps, some of it had something to do with their culture, Marka thought. There wasn't time for pampering, because there was always work to do. And if she disobeyed, she got hit. That made her afraid of her father, who reminded them that the man was the head of the house. He would pound his fist on the table. "I am the father!" And then there were all the secrets. All those things you couldn't tell. Sometimes it meant you had to tell lies.

Anna tried to help in her own way. She wanted her to marry a nice Lutheran, German Russian and if not that, there was Jonny. Instead of being appreciative, she had been rebellious and prideful. She had been defiant towards her parents, towards Anna, and towards God.

She had let herself be blown about without any direction of her own. She was like the cotton from the cottonwood trees that floated through the air, landing wherever the wind carried it. She had let other people pull her in the direction they wanted her to go: Rex, Millie, and Buddy, but, no more. I will no longer let life just happen. No more putting my needs aside or letting others discount my feelings, and, I'll not blame the folks any more. I am an adult now, and it is time to take responsibility for my life and my decisions.

After breakfast, Marka went over to Ruby's and told her that she and Anna had made up. "Ruby, you were right about the things you said. I had a dream. You're good with dreams, Ruby. Listen to my dream and tell me what you think."

Marka told Ruby about the dream. "I was outside, working in my garden. When I came back in the house, there was a little girl banging on the keys of my typewriter. I felt irritated and yelled at the child. 'You can't just go in someone's house and mess with her things. Don't you have any place to go? Why aren't you in school?' The girl said that school was out for the day. 'Then, why don't you go home?' The girl said, 'I don't want to. I'll just have to go to the cellar.' I felt pity for the child. I picked her up and held her close.

174

'Don't you have anyone to take care of you?' The child said, 'No.' Then, I told the child, 'You will never have to go to the cellar again. I will take care of you forever'."

"You always hated the cellar in your house, didn't you?" Ruby said. "You told me it was cold and dark and full of creatures. I think the dream means the child wants to be free. The little girl in the cellar is you, and she wants to be loved and to be herself."

"I'm staying in Ridley, Ruby. No more running. I ran away from Ridley, but I took all the memories with me. Look what happened when I came back. I made the same mistakes again; only the difference is this time, I'm going to learn from them. I'm finally getting to know more of the real me. I am a strong person, Ruby. Sure, I've made mistakes, but I won't blame anyone else."

Marka told Ruby how she felt the presence of God. How she felt it in the depth of her being. "It was a powerful abundance of love. No words can describe it, Ruby. The night Earl attacked me, well, I called out for help, and God helped me. I heard a sound that night, a rustle in the bushes. It gave me the idea to sidetrack Earl's attention long enough to put him out of action."

Ruby smiled and hugged Marka.

"I'll fix my life just like I fixed the house. I feel ashamed for the way I dishonored my parents, and for the way I encouraged Rex and Buddy."

"You can now be free from the past," Ruby said. "You will find what it is your heart desires. The ghosts of your past life will no longer haunt you."

One week after these happenings, Millie came over to Anna's to visit Marka.

"That night was a close call," Millie said. "He could have really hurt you. You know what I mean? I should have known better. Earl Guttler! I'm sorry, Marka. I won't ever do that to you again. I promise."

"I can't go to any more dances with you. Buddy shows up. It's wrong. He's a married man." Marka felt a gnawing in the pit of her stomach. She would never let what happened in Denver happen again.

"Are you coming back to work in the cafe?"

"Yes, but if Buddy comes around, I don't want to wait on him."

"What are you going to do when Jonny comes back from Texas?" Millie asked.

"I don't think he's interested in me. Anna wants to get us together. She's doing match making. Jonny and I mostly talked about the books he reads."

"As soon as Jonny gets back, you ought to put your heart and soul into making him yours," Millie chuckled.

"If I do, it will be the first time in my life I've gone after a guy. Usually I just let things happen," Marka said.

"Come over to the house tonight at 7:30 p.m. and watch *Jimmy Durante* with Ida and Mother and me."

"Not tonight, Millie. I need to do some serious thinking."

"What good will thinking do? You need fun in your life. If you'd rather do something else, Ida's been bugging me to go to the drive-in. She's crazy about Debbie Reynolds. The movie, *Tammy and the Bachelor* is playing." Millie persisted. "Leslie Nielson—he's such a hunk—please say you'll go. We can go a little early and get a spot right up in the front row."

Marka said, "No. I have to—think."

That evening Marka told Anna she was tired; she went to bed before dark. She propped pillows against the headboard and pulled a sheet across her legs. The first thought that came to mind was that she hadn't wanted to see certain things about herself. Like how she wanted things her own way. She was just as responsible as Rex was for what happened in Denver. It was time she paid the consequences of her actions. Marka thought about the money she took from Geraldine and how she didn't deserve it. After all, Rex was a married man. He didn't belong to her. But her pride had been hurt, and the money made it seem less painful. Tomorrow morning, first thing, she would call Rex and tell him that she wanted to send the money back. She thought about how self-righteous she had been about her parents. And, yes, even about Stella. How arrogant she had been, thinking she was perfect and everyone else was to blame.

"Where shall I mail the check, Rex? To your house or to the office?"

"What money? I don't know what you are talking about," Rex said over the phone.

"I have to give the money back," Marka insisted.

"Will you be quiet a minute and listen to me," Rex said. Why did you leave like that? Listen, Geraldine and I are getting a divorce. If that's why you left, because you didn't think I could divorce her, well you were wrong."

"Knowing you—you've found another woman by now," Marka said.

"No," Rex laughed. "Geraldine found another man."

"I still have to send the money back," Marka said.

"Marka, I don't know anything about the money."

Marka took a deep breath and gripped her fingers tight around the receiver. "Geraldine said it wasn't the first time you had become involved with your secretary. She told me to take the money and leave Denver. I know how stupid I was, but it's in the past now. Listen, I need to return the money."

"I don't want you sending me the money. Consider it money you earned."

"You bastard. What a horrible thing to say. I feel like hanging up on you for that." Marka felt a lump in her throat. She was on the verge of tears.

"What I mean is that you gave up everything—your job, and your friends. I was the one that messed up, but why didn't you at least say good-bye. After I heard you were gone, I wrote you a letter, but you never answered."

"I didn't get a letter from you. Rex, I need to make a clean start. I need to give the money back."

"Geraldine gave you the money. Give it back to her or to charity if that'll make you feel better. Well, if that's all you called about, I guess we're done. Good bye, Marka, and I wish you the best."

Marka slammed down the receiver. Her heart was beating fast. She felt a little dizzy. She sat silently for a while trying to absorb all Rex said. She had to be strong and stick to what she knew was right. Rex said he wrote her a letter. It was probably the one Stella sent to the dead letter office. Why had she phoned him? Did she want to talk to him one last time? It really didn't matter. She was determined to set her life on a new course.

CHAPTER 21

A warm, dry wind blew across the garden. "I hope this wind lets up, or it will dry out everything," Anna said, setting down the watering can. Anna wore a man's long-sleeved shirt and a straw hat with a large brim to protect her from the sun.

"I planted too much again this year. So much to take care of."

Marka said, "You need some new gardening gloves, Anna. Look at the calluses on your hands."

"Ach, they all have holes in them. Yes, I need new ones." Anna picked up the watering can again and sprinkled the plants. "Everything is so dry."

"Anna, you're working too hard. It's hot out here in the sun. Let's go inside and I'll help you in the garden this evening when the sun goes down. There's something I want to talk to you about. I telephoned Rex, the man in Denver. Well, I told him I wanted to give the money back that his wife, Geraldine, gave me. He said he wouldn't take a cent of it—told me to give it to charity. Anna, I never told you how much money it is. It's enough to do something nice for the town and still have money for something else. I was thinking I would like to donate a new organ to the church, and, I want to buy you an electric sewing machine."

"No, Marka, I don't need one."

"Yes, you do! And, what would you think if I started a bakery in the back of Millie's cafe?"

"You aren't going to go into business with that Millie, after what happened?" Anna huffed.

"Anna, I can't blame her for what happened. It's time I take responsibility for what happens to me."

"Well, you know, Carl gets most bakery things into the store. You think you can compete with American Beauty Bread?"

"Millie told me, that at one time, her mother did baking for the cafe. It would be a little competition for Carl—that should give you a chuckle. You don't seem to like him much."

"He's just a stubborn, bull-headed old German," Anna laughed.

"Maybe you could give us some of your recipes and some baking advice. There's a big oven and baking pans in the back of the building, so all we would really need are staples. We can go to Clayton and buy things in bulk."

"Do you really think it is such a good idea? What about all that education you have and the experience working in an office? I think you can do better than this. Why don't you want to go to work in Clayton? I thought I heard you tell Jonny once that you wanted to go to Deerfield Teacher's College. You thought you'd like to be a teacher."

"I can't go until I get an application in and get accepted. I need something in the meantime. I want to try something different," Marka said.

"*Madchen,* do whatever you want. And, yes, I will give you my recipes. If this makes you happy, then it makes me happy too."

"I called Reverend Thurber and asked if he would see me this afternoon," Marka said.

"Marka, that's good." Anna's eyes lit with pride.

When Marka arrived at the parsonage, she was greeted at door by Louise, who led her to a room in the back of the house, a room that had been made into an office. Jordan Thurber was sitting at his desk, writing, when she entered. Marka thought about what Anna told her; one of the reasons Jordan got the pastorate at the church, was because he spoke fluent German.

Marka sat down in the chair across from him. She told him about the night she had gazed at the Milky Way and how she and her mother had loved the northern lights. "I remembered something special about my mother, and I felt like I experienced the presence of God. I feel so much better now."

Then, Marka told Reverend Thurber about Rex and Buddy, and she told him what happened with Earl.   They talked about her parents, especially her father.

"You seem to have problems with men," Jordan said.

Marka told him about the anger she always felt towards her parents. How she felt she had broken the commandment to love and honor them. "Anna has helped me to understand things and I can truly say that I've forgiven them."

"That's good. God forgives all our transgressions too. Sometimes our troubles come from distracting thoughts, thoughts that won't let us live in the present. Sometimes we have to face the ugly side of our personalities. No one is perfect," Reverend Thurber said.

"We all have a good side and a bad side, right?" Marka said. "Ruby told me that it's important to know who I am."

"Ruby is right. Those who know themselves, find that people can work together for good."

"I can see that now. I can see that I don't need to be perfect," Marka said,

"We have to be careful not to dwell too much on how we felt as children, because children have such strong feelings. As children, the memories are that much worse. Our thoughts can change our lives if we think about good things, like how God loves us."

"I understand," Marka said.

"Our enemy is fear. Faith and prayer are what keeps us going. Prayer is how we connect with God, how we take care of our spirit."

"That night, with Earl, I really believe God heard my prayers. He showed me I am a strong person."

"It's hard for us to understand, but God does have a purpose for our lives. We just can't see it until it unfolds. We don't need to understand everything if we learn to trust. Letting go of the past so we can handle this day, that's what I think is important," Jordan said.

Marka walked out of the parsonage feeling on top of the world.

Two weeks had passed since the argument with Anna and the incident with Earl. Every day, Marka felt her heart mending. The dark times, the nights her mother and father fought, and the times she felt alone, all were fading from her memory.

She and Anna spent nights looking through old photos. One day, they spent the entire time talking about the happy times. Marka felt she was beginning to get a glimpse of her true being. The bits of memories from her childhood were fitting together, making a nicer picture, like when a cloudy sky clears and you can see the beautiful day beyond.

Marka felt it was time to go back to work at the cafe. The bruise on her cheek had healed enough so that she could cover what remained with a layer of make-up. Millie called every day, complaining about how she and Ida had to work their tails off just to keep up.

Marka walked down the sidewalk towards town and noticed all the ordinary things she had never noticed before, like the chatter of birds, the sound of the leaves clapping in the breeze, the smells of sweet flowers, and the sound of barking dogs. She walked by vegetable gardens and took special note of how large the fruit had grown, and how vines sprawled across the ground. She noticed the large white cloud formations, and felt the warm sun on her skin.

She thought about Jonny. She couldn't wait to write and tell him that on June 19, the voters had rejected the proposal to close the high school. The count was 30 in favor of closing, and 112 opposed. George told her there were 7 spoiled ballots, and 1 unmarked one.

"Now, who do you suppose pulled a stunt like that? Submitted a ballot with nothing on it," George laughed.

Marka felt grateful for George. He was always doing things for her. The night before he brought over two wooden planter boxes he had built and a mess of trout he caught while fishing in Deerfield Canyon. "This one weighed eight and a half pounds, and is twenty seven inches long," he said holding it up for Marka to see.

Marka felt grateful for Anna too. She thought how excited Anna was that morning about the ornamental gourds she had planted. Last fall, she saw an article in *Good Housekeeping* that said you could use them as birdhouses, fruit baskets, nut dishes and even sewing baskets. What would she ever do without Anna?

Breakfast rush was over by 10:00 a.m. There were a few farmers sitting around the cafe talking about whether or not they would see a good profit this year on sugar beets. The new monogerm hybrid seed had eliminated the hand labor, and they were expecting to see an increase of at least three tons of beets an acre. The sheep ranchers were upset about their sheep bloating. The vet told them that the bloating was from them eating too much alfalfa.

Marka and Millie sat in one of the booths drinking coffee.

"What do you think about my idea of starting up a bakery in the back of the cafe?" Marka asked. "You told me once that your mother had one going at one time."

"Years ago, before Mother's stroke. Yes, I remember it was popular with the people," Millie said.

"Maybe we could get it going again. Anna is always baking. She could give us some hints, and some of her recipes for *roggenbrot, kaffee-kuchen.* She used to cook lunch at the dormitory, you know."

"We'd have to get up so damn early though to get the baking done," Millie whined.

"Anna taught me to get up with the birds. I'd come down early, and get the baking done before the breakfast crowd arrived. I'd work the morning shift. You and Ida can handle the rest."

"The baking pans and flour bins are still in the back room. Maybe it would work," Millie said.

"Can you image how business in the cafe will pick up when the wonderful smell of baked goods hits the street?"

Millie frowned. "It will cost some money to get started. Where we going to get the money?"

"I have a little nest egg. I'll make the initial investment. We'll work it out."

Marka felt excited about starting the bakery. That would put the money Geraldine gave her to good use. She'd still give some of it away to charity. One thing she wanted to do was to pay Sophie's bill at Carl's store. She stopped in on her way home from work and gave Carl the money. Carl gave her Sophie's book of charge slips and stamped them—Paid. He seemed uninterested in the whole affair, and more interested in telling her about the article he read in the *Clayton Post* about an eighteen-year-old man who was killed when his gun went off accidentally. He mumbled something about Buddy and his hunting rifles.

Marka went to the parsonage and handed Jordan a check for a new organ for the church.

For the next few weeks, Marka and Millie worked at the cafe during the day and spent the evenings cleaning up the back room. They asked George to check out the gas ovens. He replaced some of the valves and told them that everything else worked fine.

The first morning, they made cinnamon rolls to tempt the palates of customers. The aroma drifted into the front of the cafe. They were sold out by 9:00 a.m.

Marka was filling the coffee machine with water when Millie walked over to her and whispered in her ear. "Don't look now but trouble with a capital T just walked in the door, those guys from the dance. Dennis and Earl." Millie raised her eyebrows, and twisted her upper lip over her bottom one.

"Oh, Millie." Marka cringed. "What if he does something in here?"

"He doesn't have the balls," Millie said putting her hand on Marka's arm, trying to make light of the situation. "They are sitting down in the booth by the front window," Millie said, looking over her right shoulder. "I'll wait on them. You stay here behind the counter."

Millie threw her shoulders back and took a deep breath, then walked over to them. Marka finished making coffee and started clearing dishes off the counter, moving along so she could get closer and hear the conversation Millie was having with them.

"What can I get you?" Millie stood, scribbling on her order pad.

Marka heard Earl mumble something and then Millie said, "Sorry we are fresh out of blood this morning." Millie just can't resist being sarcastic, Marka thought.

Marka heard Earl say, "Tell your friend over there she better not go out walking alone at night. Never know what may pop out of the bushes."

When Millie returned to the counter, she told Marka to put two hamburgers on the grill. "Make his rare. He emphasized the word, rare, and smiled an ugly smile. Then, you know what he said? He said, 'How about you and me going for a nice ride tonight, baby?' Marka you better watch your backside. This guy could be dangerous. You better tell Buddy about what happened."

"Are you crazy? That's the last thing I'd do!"

"What about Bodie? No, on second thought, he couldn't fight his way out of a paper bag. Marka, you've got to tell someone."

"Who is going to want to take on a guy that size?" Marka asked. "Just serve him his food."

"Should I bat my eyes at him or show him my bust line?"

"No, don't do anything dumb. I think the best thing to do is to ignore him." Marka felt irritated with Millie.

After work, walking home from the cafe, Marka thought about Earl and how it looked as if he were going to start harassing her.

Who could she talk to? Who could she trust? Millie wasn't going to be any help in dealing with Earl. Maybe Ruby, Marka thought. Yes, she would go over to Ruby's apartment after supper and talk to her.

They stood by the large window facing Main Street. Sunlight poured in and outlined Ruby's body as she swirled paint around on the palette with her brush. "I just can't seem to get the eyes right," she said. "Henry had beautiful eyes, and I want to do him justice. I almost had them right, but not quite." She dabbed a flesh tone over the canvas where the eyes were to be.

"What am I going to do to get rid of Earl? I didn't turn him in; so now he thinks he can do anything he wants."

"Mia, you got to watch out," Ruby said. "You're right, Millie doesn't use her head. She thinks with a different part of her body."

"Give me a while to think on it, Marka." Ruby chewed on the end of her paintbrush. "Did he threaten both you and Millie, or just you?"

"Just me."

"Well, there you have it. The guy can't stand being turned down."

"Ruby, what about your brothers? Gypsies take the law into their own hands, right?"

"Who told you such a thing? Besides, I don't have any idea where my brothers are. I never told you I had brothers."

"I'm sorry. Once, when Herb and I were talking—I guess he told me. I'm not thinking straight today. I just don't know what to do."

"Aw, the next time I see Herb—aw! It's okay. You are my friend. A better friend even than Herb," Ruby laughed. "Now, I will tell you things that even Herb doesn't know." Ruby laid the palette and paint brush down on the table beside the easel. "Let's have tea. I will tell you."

Ruby put the kettle on the stove and Marka sat at the table. Fedora flew down from her cage and landed on Marka's shoulder.

"Be nice, Fedora." Ruby said. "The truth is, I don't know where my brothers or mother are. I wish I could see them again, but the day I married a *gaje,* a white man, was the day I became an outcast from my people."

"Ruby, I'm sorry."

Ruby became melancholy. "Our caravan was moving across the Dakotas. We stopped in at the ranch and asked if they had work. They did. Branding cattle. My father and brothers worked for them for a week; then, a drunken cowhand turned up dead, and they said my father did it. They took him off to jail and his bail was high. He said we were not to use the money we earned. My mother did what she had to. She could tell that Henry was taken with me; so she got the money from him. It is our custom that the groom pays for his bride, so my mother approached Henry, and we got married. My mother and father and brothers took the money and skipped out. I stayed on the ranch. I haven't heard from them since. Marriage is forbidden to a *gaje*, but my mother was desperate."

"That's terrible. Ruby, did you even love him?" Marka got up from the table, came around the back of Ruby's chair, bent down and put her arms around Ruby's neck. "I am so sorry."

"We were in love. That's the funny part. We were trying to figure out how I was going to stay with him and not go back to Toledo, where we were from. I was born there, but I never had a birth certificate. You need to show your certificate to get married." Ruby laughed and laughed. "I didn't have one so we forged his sister's. Such a life I've had, but I did have a good childhood."

"When were you born?" Marka softly stroked Ruby's hair with her hand.

"Some time in November, I think."

"Do you miss your people and the Gypsy life?" Marka asked.

"Henry was good to me. It's our custom that when you marry you take an oath: Free one another when love has left the heart. Not once did I want to leave Henry." Tears came to Ruby's black eyes. "We were happy together, but I will never be permitted to rejoin my people. Life is life. That's what my mother always said when she had to accept something even though she didn't want to."

Marka wished she could make it all better for Ruby.

"Try not to worry about Earl, Mia. I'll try to think of something."

"I feel like a little bird around a cunning cat," Marka said.

"But, cats can't fly—birds can. A bird is okay as long as they remember to stay away from the cat," Ruby said.

In the middle of the night, Marka was awakened by noises, outside. She lay still and listened intently, trying to figure out if she was just dreaming or had really heard something. She thrashed around in her bed for a while, then went back to sleep. In the morning, she found a dead raccoon on her front step. She called Bodie and asked him to come over to the house.

"Hasn't been shot," he said. "Looks like someone hit it with a car."

"Bodie, there's this creep, Earl, that came into the cafe, yesterday. He's one of the Air Force guys that work at the missile sites. He told Millie he was going to hurt me." Marka found herself wanting to tell Bodie a little lie. How could she tell him the truth? She promised herself she would tell the truth from now on. But, there are times when you just can't.

"I wouldn't dance with him one night, and now he's holding that against me," she said crossing her fingers behind her back, deciding this was a time when the truth would lead to too many questions, and Bodie wouldn't know how to handle it."

"Tonight, I'll sleep in my pickup, and if Earl comes around, I'll shoot him." Bodie stood tall with his shoulders back.

"No. Don't do that. He probably won't bother me again. The stunt with the raccoon probably satisfied his anger."

The next day, Wednesday, Marka woke to find Bodie slumped down in the seat of his pickup. He had kept watch over her just like he said. He was there on Thursday morning and on Friday.

Then, Friday afternoon, right before they were ready to close the cafe, with only two tables left to clear off, Earl and Dennis came in and sat down in a booth. Marka stood behind the counter while Millie waited on them.

"Why do you keep coming in here?" Millie stood, biting her nails.

"There a law against it?" Earl snapped.

"Guess not—but, we are about to close," Millie snorted.

"Well, I'll have a big old piece of you then," Earl said, raising his eyebrows and squinting at Millie. Dennis squirmed and put down the menu.

"How about a piece of rat pie, topped with whipped cream flavored with strychnine?" Millie snapped.

Earl decided to order a hot roast beef sandwich. Dennis said, "Burger and fries."

Marka ladled gravy over slices of roast beef and mashed potatoes, and told Millie that she would take the order over to the booth. "I've got to show Earl I'm not afraid of him."

Millie tried to argue her out of it, but Marka would have it no other way. She marched over to their table, set the plates down, and turned to walk back to the counter. That's when she saw the turquoise car, shiny, with big chrome fins. "Oh, God! It's Rex!" Marka could hardly wait for Millie to finish rounds with the coffee.

When Millie walked behind the counter to brew another pot, Marka pulled her into the bakery room. "See that guy that just walked in and sat down at the counter," she whispered in Millie's ear.

Millie peeked around the doorway. "The gangster-looking guy?"

Marka couldn't help but laugh. Yes, Rex did resemble a gangster with his dark hair slicked back, tiger-eye ring, and open-necked sports shirt. "Millie, that's Rex, the guy from Denver. Remember? I told you about him."

"Yes. But, he's a hood?"

"He's not. Oh, never mind. I have an idea. Let's just go back out and act like nothing is unusual. I'll go sit next to Rex, and maybe he can help get rid of Earl."

Marka sat down on the stool beside Rex. "Before you say one word, do me a big favor. See those two guys over there—I'll explain later. That big one with the red and gray plaid shirt—he's been hassling me." Marka cleared her throat and said loudly, "Yes, it is good to see you too."

Rex put his hand on Marka's arm. "Doll, whatever you want." Rex walked over to the jukebox, put in a nickel, and punched *With All My Heart* by Jodi Sands. Then he walked over to Earl and Dennis' booth. Marka watched as he leaned close to Earl and whispered something in his ear. Earl's eyes bulged, and then he pulled bills from his wallet, and laid them by his half eaten lunch.

Dennis, Earl, and Rex walked out of the café. Millie ran to the door and stuck her head outside.

Marka kept busy washing and stacking plates and cups.

Millie rushed back over to her. She was grinning and excited. "Whew! That gangster-looking guy, I mean, Rex, well, he slammed Earl up against the side of the cafe. He pressed one hand against

187

Earl's windpipe and grabbed him by the balls with the other." Millie began to roar. "He looked Earl right in the eye and said, 'Stay away from Marka if you want to keep these.' Dennis and Earl took off like bats out of hell leaving a cloud of dust behind them."

Marka left the cafe with Rex. They drove over the railroad tracks to the stockyards at the edge of town.

"Sorry I had to bring you here, but this is a small town, and I've caused enough of a stir since I arrived, and if your car is seen parked by my house, the whole town will be buzzing. I can't afford that right now. I feel like I am walking on thin ice as it is."

Rex reached across the seat and touched Marka's cheek. "I still love you, you know. I told you in the letter I wrote that I would divorce Geraldine. Why didn't you write me back?"

"I didn't get the letter. It's a long story. Doesn't matter now anyway, I have no intentions of taking up where we left off."

"How many times do I have to say this? Geraldine is divorcing me. We can be together now. Come back to Denver."

"I have a life here. I moved into my house, and I have started a bakery." She wouldn't let herself be blown away in the wind again. Endings aren't easy, but they are necessary, she thought to herself. She had learned a lesson. She must take care of herself. She must move forward and not be stuck in the past.

"There's someone else, isn't there?"

"No, not now, maybe not ever. My aunt Anna never married, and she's made out all right for herself. I'll probably follow in her footsteps."

"What about that guy in the cafe. Does he think he has a chance with you?"

Marka laughed. "Never! He's just someone I met at a dance. He liked me more than I liked him, that's all."

"Liking you is easy to do." Rex slid closer to Marka and kissed her cheek.

"Don't." She glared at him. She turned her head towards the car window. "Don't!"

Rex slid back behind the wheel. "Remember when you called me about the money? Cause Geraldine's really putting it to me, kicking me out without a penny."

"Oh, I get it. You can have what's left of the money. I spent $1,000 of it. I don't make much at the cafe, but I'll manage. You can have the damn money. I told you that before. I don't want anything from you."

"Marka, damn it. I don't want the money. I just said that so you would feel sorry and come back to Denver with me."

"Rex, I'm a different person now. I can see you're up to the same old thing. Why did you come here anyway?"

"Because I need you. I've missed you. Marka, come back."

Although Saturday was not baking day, it was the busiest time at the cafe. Anna shook Marka's shoulder to wake her up. "Marka get up. It's that Millie on the phone. She wants to talk to you."

Marka groaned and turned over in the bed. "What does she want?"

"I don't know. Come on, get up."

Marka dragged herself out of bed and went to the phone.

"Marka. Guess what? I can't believe it—you won't believe it! My prince did show up after all. I'm leaving town—with your *old* Rex." Millie was excited; she could hardly get the words out fast enough. "He said you didn't want him anymore, and well, I figured that meant it was okay. We stayed together last night at a hotel in Rapid. Marka, I'm in love. I'm really in love this time. Will you go over and help Ida? The two of you will have to run the cafe from now on."

Marka hung up the phone and slumped in the chair. She covered her eyes with her hands until all she saw was darkness. Just when she thought things had settled down. What now?

"What in the world is going on? Anna asked.

Marka told Anna how Rex showed up unexpectedly at the cafe and how he scared away Earl. Then she told her what Millie said on the telephone.

"Ach, see I told you. That Millie is crazy when it comes to the men. That Rex just better quit fooling around and go back to his wife."

Marka got dressed and went over to tell Ida the news. Ida was making breakfast for her mother. Ida took Marka into her bedroom so her mother wouldn't hear them.

"I can't believe she did this," Marka said.

Ida took bobby pins out of her thick uncontrollable hair. "If you knew Millie like I do, you wouldn't have trouble believing it. Millie will shack up with anyone that will have her. I never want to be like her."

"Ida, what are we going to do about the cafe?"

"Guess we have to open. People will be wanting coffee and breakfast." Ida put on a skirt and sweater and brushed out her curls. "We ought to just put a big sign in the window—Out of Business. That would serve her right. This isn't the first time she's done this." Ida yawned.

They opened the cafe. Anna came down and helped out with the cooking. "I'm no spring chicken, just a determined old hen. Sure, I can help," she said. She and Ida got along so well that Anna offered to teach her how to sew. Ida said she was interested in being a fashion designer.

Monday morning, Millie was back at the café apologizing to Marka.

"Millie! How could you?"

Millie shrugged. "I'm just too desperate, I guess."

CHAPTER 22

After the last ring of the church bell, Reverend Thurber walked in and sat down in front of the choir. Katie played the opening to *Onward Christian Soldiers*, and then the congregation joined in. Marka sang especially loud this morning thinking how the new organ had been purchased with money she gave Reverend Thurber, under the condition that she, the donor, would remain anonymous.

Carl, Bodie, Buddy, and Stella walked in together, and sat down in the pew across from her and Anna. Buddy took up the rear, which put him directly across the aisle. Marka watched Stella fold and refold her white linen gloves.

Marka sat attentively listening to the Reverend's sermon.

"We have to learn to live with imperfection in ourselves and others," he said. "We need other people, and they need us. We all have faults. Like the Bible says, 'If we say we have no faults, we deceive ourselves, and the truth is not in us.' Life can sometimes seem like a river of sorrow, but no suffering is unbearable if we can lean on others." The Reverend glanced at Marka. "And, of course, it goes without saying that we always have God's shoulder. Troubled waters will be in your life, but look for the blessings," he said with a stern voice. Marka thought of Anna, George, Ruby, Bodie, and even Millie, and how they all had been a blessing to her.

Half way through the sermon, Marka noticed Buddy's eyes were closed. His head fell forward, bobbed towards his chest, and then he jerked upright. Marka hoped Buddy hadn't come to church just to remind her of the dance in Clayton. He certainly wasn't interested in the sermon. Marka thought to herself how she wanted to be finished with the whole sordid thing—Buddy and Stella. Rex was out of her life, thank God. Surely he had too much pride to contact her after running off with Millie. And, she'd gotten over her fear of Earl. She felt certain he would never bother her again.

Things had finally settled down. She had gotten through the worst of it. She thought how she used to feel like a baby bird out on a limb that was about to break. She didn't feel like that anymore. She had wings strong enough to fly.

Monday, after working at the cafe, Marka helped Anna with chores. She felt the warm sun on her arms as she sprayed water around the plants in Anna's manicured garden. She cooled the tall spires of hollyhock with water from the hose. "Hey, don't get so angry," she said talking to a bee buzzing around her arm.

Anna heard the grumbling and warned her not to get carried away with the water. "We're going to be irrigating next week," she said. "Then the garden and lawn can get a good soaking."

Reverend Thurber's oldest son, John, rode up on his bicycle.

"Say, do you happen to eat Wheaties? The reason," he said, "is that I have two box tops, and if I get one more, I can order this submarine." He showed them a picture from a cereal box. "You load the boat with baking soda and the soda makes it move and bubble around in the water, one more box top and a quarter with it, then I can send in for it," he said.

"How about you getting rid of those weeds over there along the garden." Anna handed him the hoe. "Marka, go in the kitchen and look in the cupboard. I do have a box of that cereal. There's a quarter in my change purse. He can have that too—for hoeing those weeds."

Later that evening, after Anna and Marka ate supper, they went into the front room.

"I paid close attention to what Reverend Thurber said in his sermon on Sunday," Marka said. "He talked about living with imperfection in ourselves and others. I always thought we were supposed to be perfect."

Anna went over to the oak buffet and got her Bible. She sat in her armchair and opened it to a place she had marked. "This is what Reverend Thurber read Sunday in *kerich*, church. 'If we say that we have no faults, we deceive ourselves, and the truth is not in us'." She closed the book. "It's when we think that we are perfect that we get ourselves into trouble. Pride goeth before a fall."

"I think the church is full of hypocrites. There are the men who hang out in the saloon, and the women who gossip. They looked so pious. Buddy slept through most of the church service."

Anna chuckled, "Look at it this way. How bad would they be if they didn't go to church at all? Maybe they'd be worse," she laughed. "Maybe, if even for one hour a week they think about godly things, it's better than nothing at all. If we were perfect, I guess we wouldn't have a need for church. That's the way I see it," she folded her fingers tightly around the Bible.

"You're close to perfect, Anna. I was full of anger, shame, and guilt when I arrived in Ridley. Now, I can see how wise you are, and; if I had only listened to you in the first place. You were right about Millie. I asked her how she could lower herself to sleep with every guy she meets, and she said, 'Look at me. I'm not pretty. I have to do something to interest a guy'."

"Ach, that floozy. That's an excuse. Well, you don't have to work at that cafe. Put in your application at the Court House or how about the sugar factory?"

"I still think the bakery is a good idea. I want to go to Deerfield Teacher's College if they accept my application." Marka thought how when she went to work for Millie, it had not met with Anna's approval, and now she showed resistance to the bakery. Marka thought about how she had forged ahead out of rebellion. She felt different about things now. She would like Anna's support but didn't need her approval.

"Yes, but, you haven't given up on marriage and children have you?"

"I may never marry. I may stay a single woman like you. Is that so bad?"

Anna raised an eyebrow and pursed her lips. "Come with me. I want to show you something."

Anna went into the kitchen for the flashlight she kept on the counter by her refrigerator. She walked down the hallway and took the broomstick with a bent nail in the end from behind a door. She used it to hook the metal ring that was secured to a trapdoor on the ceiling. The pull-down ladder, which led to the attic, came down and rested on the floor. Anna climbed the small stairway. "Come."

Marka stayed close behind, just in case Anna lost her balance. They stepped into the attic. The room was hot and stuffy. There were no windows, only small louvered openings for ventilation. Just enough light filtered through so Anna could see to make her way over to a large black trunk. She shined the bright flashlight on the lid, lifted it, and started to rummage around until she found a bundle wrapped in yellowed tissue paper. She handed the flashlight to Marka. "Shine it here." She let the tissue fall to the floor and closed the lid. Next, Anna spread a dress across the lid of the trunk.

"Mom's wedding dress!" Marka ran her hand across the shear netting that overlay the once white, now yellowed, satin. "I recognize it from the folks' wedding picture." Marka gently picked up the dress and held it close to her. "I wonder how Mom felt the day she wore this. She must have loved Dad, or she wouldn't have married him."

"They were so in love," Anna said. "Yes, in the beginning, they were, but they let things get in the way. Life can be hard at times. We may never know what someone else is going through. Take me. I use to be a very angry person. I would rant and rave about good for nothing men, and your mom would always say to me, 'Anna, leave it go.' She was right. Sometimes things happen to you and you just have to leave them go."

Anna took another bundle from the trunk and removed the tissue paper. "This is the christening gown you wore when you was baptized." Anna held up the small dress made of white linen, trimmed with elaborate lace. "I was going to use it for my baby. At one time I had a baby you know. I even thought I might get married."

"A baby. Anna, I didn't know."

"Yah, that's why I'm telling you now. Well, anyways, this goes way back. When I was a young woman, I was in love with a German Russian boy. He loved me too, but his parents wanted him to marry someone else. They did things like that you know, decided who their children were going to marry. It not only had to be someone who was German, but also went to the same church. My stepmother warned me not to get serious about him, but we loved each other, and that was that. Then, I was in the family way, but I never told him, because he married someone else."

"Oh, Anna, how awful for you. Who was he?"

"I don't want to say."

"That's okay. I understand, Anna."

"Well, I ended up living with my papa and stepmother. She said she would say the child was hers. A late-life baby. Well, she was a heavy woman so no one would suspect.

"Where is your child, Anna?"

"He's buried at the cemetery in Clayton. Remember the little grave we stopped at on Decoration Day?" Anna's eyes welled with tears. "That's his resting place. Well, anyways, my stepmother was a good woman. I already told you that, didn't I? Yes, I did." Anna wrapped the small dress back in the tissue and put it in the trunk. "She kept me in the house with her and taught me how to cook and sew. That was my job; I cooked for the hired help. I had the baby, a boy. It was a stillbirth. I named him Jacob. We had a quiet funeral for him."

Marka put her arms around Anna and held her close. "I'm so sorry. I had no idea all of this happened to you."

Anna's eyes were red and teary. "So, you see I'm far from perfect. All I know is, I will not feel pity for myself. I have always tried to be grateful for everything no matter what. There now—the secret is out. My stepmother always said that secrets make us sick." Anna took a hanky out of her apron pocket and wiped her eyes. "Shortly after, there was a job turned up at the school. They needed someone to cook school lunches and to fix breakfast and supper for the teachers and students living in the dormitory. Because Hannah, that was my stepmother's name, had taught me to be such a good cook, I did okay. I moved into a little room in the dormitory and lived there. Ten dollars a month for rent. Can you believe it? Well, anyways, when people found out I could sew, they hired me to make dresses, coats, and curtains for their houses. I saved up my money and bought myself this little house. Hard work. That's all I know."

Marka sat quietly, taking it all in, thinking how hard this must have been for Anna.

"Your mother was six years old when all of this happened. It was hard on her when the baby died and when I left the farm and moved into town. That was hard on her too."

"The baby buried at the cemetery; the little headstone with just the name Jacob, and the year 1901. Oh, Anna," Marka sobbed. "I am so sorry."

"I always wondered how much it all affected your mom. When you were born, well, I always thought that she let me have so much of you to make up for my loss. It's funny. In all those years, we never talked about my baby. It was like he never existed. Your dad didn't like it because Rachael and I were close. She would hold back her affections from him. I use to tell her that. Many times I saw her push him away. Then he'd end up going to the saloon. Peace in your home depended on his moods. He could be loud and abusive. But she never complained."

Marka said. "I'd see her crying some times. Then she'd tell me to go to your house. And, you always had time for me. You would stop whatever you were doing. You'd get up from your sewing machine and get me milk and cookies. You always had cookies."

"You were like my own child," Anna said, wiping away more tears.

Late Saturday afternoon, after Marka had cleaned her house and Anna's, she sat quietly in Anna's kitchen reading *The Scarlet Letter*. She found herself immersed in the story ever since Anna told her about her baby. Hawthorne's Hester had to wear a bright red A over her breast, because she had been convicted of adultery. She raised her illegitimate daughter, Pearl, in a town that looked upon the child as some kind of evil spirit who had been conceived out of an unholy passion.

I will never tell Anna's secret. Marka thought how she would have to rethink everything she ever felt about Anna. Why did life have to be so complicated? It wasn't only the things you knew that caused confusion, but the things you found out later on, things of great consequence. It was hard to understand it all.

Occasionally, Marka looked up from her book and watched Sasha lunge and paw at the shadows on the freshly waxed linoleum. The sunlight danced around the curtains and shone on the particles of dust floating in the air. I will never again do anything to cause Anna grief, Marka vowed.

The telephone rang. It was George. "He wants to talk to you," Anna said handing the phone to Marka.

"Fishing. I'd like that. Yes, it has been slower at the cafe this month. The farmers are cutting their hay. Yes, the ovens are working fine. Um, hum, the bakery idea was a good one. Okay, I'll be ready in fifteen minutes." Marka hung up the phone.

"Anna, George said ever since we started the bakery I haven't had time to go fishing with him. Said maybe I'd like to come along today and see if we can catch some bullheads before the sun goes down."

Anna handed Marka a bucket as she headed for the front door. "Pick some chokecherries while you're at the river. I'll make some syrup and jelly. Here, put on a long sleeved shirt and keep it tight around your waist so the chiggers don't get you."

"Yes, Anna, Yes, Anna." Marka smiled and thought how she had no resistance to Anna's constant care. It felt good to have no more resistance.

Marka and George sat on the riverbank. There was a light breeze blowing across the water. Marka baited her hook, threw the line in the water, and stuck the handle of her pole into the soft mud. Then she found a shady spot where the trees cast shadows on the grass. She lay down, took off her shoes, and wiggled her toes.

"The sun won't be setting for a couple hours," George said pulling his hat down to his brow. He sat quietly with his pole in the water, ever so often reeling in his line to check the bait. "Fish must be sleeping again today."

"Worms from Anna's garden are good, aren't they?" Marka asked.

"Yup. Must be the coffee grounds and egg shells." George bit the stem of his pipe. "Anna has got one of the best gardens in town."

"She's about the best at everything. If I could be half the person she is. She's been through a lot, and still she has so much faith. I haven't treated her right."

George said, "You worried about something?" He reached into his pants pocket for a jackknife and then walked over to the edge of the bank to cut his fishing line loose from the tangled weeds. He returned to the spot under the tree where Marka sat. "About Anna. We all get out of sorts from time to time. The way I see it, Anna is maybe too worried about you. She's trying too hard to make things good for you, and maybe you resent it."

"I feel like I'm going crazy trying to figure things out," Marka said running her fingers through her hair and rubbing her temples. "George, you don't go to church?"

"I never been big on church."

"Do you believe?"

"Sure. There's no proving it, but I'm convinced. Guess I see a lot of love around. Sometimes you got to look for it, but it's there. Look at Anna. She forgets about herself and is always there for others. I call that love, but I can't help you out as far as offering proof about whether or not there's a God. It's not my job to set others right. That's the Reverend's job. But I will say this—the truth will defend itself. My business is to be a good person and treat others well. Every human being has the right to choose a higher power and the theology they follow, be it Christianity, Indian, or Eastern."

Marka thought about the night she saw the Milky Way. She was sure that was the night things started to turn around. She felt as if she were going in a new direction. "I like Jordan, the minister at our church. I wonder why he decided to be a preacher."

"Guess a man's got to follow his calling. Couldn't be a minister if he didn't have people to preach to."

"You never heard him preach then?"

"No." George cast his repaired line into the water.

"Do you talk to God?"

George answered. "Sure. People who never talk to God are probably afraid of what He might say. You aren't paying attention," George pointed to Marka's pole. "I thought I saw a tug on your line."

Marka gave her line a little tug to see if there was something on it. There wasn't. George seemed to want to fish, but she wanted to talk. "You asked before if there was something wrong. There is. I really need to talk to someone about things."

"Okay, go ahead. I'm listening." George took an empty pipe out of his shirt pocket and gritted it between his teeth.

"You don't drink, do you, George? You said you don't go to the saloon."

"Is this talk going to be about me?"

"No. I don't know how to say this. Well, I guess I'll just have to say it. I have a drinking problem. See, when I was in Denver, I got into the habit of going into the lounges and—" Marka struggled to find the words. She better just tell him the truth. That's what Ruby said she needed to do. Not be afraid to tell the truth. "When I lived in Denver, I got drunk a lot. I got involved with my boss, a married man. I had to leave. I came back here to make a new life for myself."

"Let's pull in our lines," George said, stuffing the pipe back in his pocket.

They pulled in their lines, and Marka continued her story. "Everything has gone wrong since I got here. The night of my birthday, Anna and I had a terrible argument. She found out I had gone to the saloon a couple of times, and she hit the ceiling. We talked about my parents and how my dad's drinking destroyed our family."

"Marka, the reason I don't drink or go to the saloon, is because I'm a recovered alcoholic. I haven't had a drink in ten years. I understand people who have a problem with booze.

"Oh, I can't imagine you with a drink in your hand. How did you stop? Was it hard?"

"I spent time in the funny farm. First, I had to admit that I had a problem and then accept the fact that I needed help. See, that's why I said before that I do believe. I just don't think going to church will make that much difference for me. I think being honest with myself is important."

"Yes," Marka said softly.

"Takes a strong person to admit when they're wrong. Takes a person of integrity to want to make up for things. My suggestion to you is you better quit drinking before you find you can't quit."

Marka and George sat by the river, and she told him everything. "It's true. Once I start drinking, I don't want to stop. It makes me feel good, and then I can't get it out of my mind." She told him about Rex and the night Earl attacked her. She even told George about Buddy and Stella.

"I don't understand if I really have feelings for Buddy or if I just did it to get even with her," she said.

"Well, you better figure it out, cause if you don't, you'll never be able to stop drinking. Two wrongs never make a right. If Stella is hurting you, she will eventually pay for it. It's not your battle."

"But she's waged war against me. Ever since I came to Ridley."

"Have you ever tried talking to her?"

"That's what Anna thinks I should do. George, do you think I could be an alcoholic?"

"From what you've told me, sounds like you could be well on your way."

"I feel so ashamed. How could that happen to me especially when I hated my dad's drinking so much?"

"Your dad's alcoholism probably meant you would be a prime candidate," George said.

A slight breeze caused ripples on the water. "Don't move. Just listen," George said. "I go fishing, because I like the quiet. I stick a tree branch into the ground close to the water's edge, rest my pole between the V in the branch, and lay the other end of the pole on the ground at my feet. I sit and watch the moving water or keep my eyes to the ground and watch the bugs crawling in the grass. I take in the wonder of nature. That's my church. Try it sometime."

"Okay, I will." Marka sat quietly, not moving a muscle, but it was a struggle for her. First, she thought a spider fell in her hair from the trees above; then she was sure there were ants biting her heel. She was determined not to let George think she couldn't be still. She took a deep breath, let it out slowly, closed her eyes, and thought about nothing. She heard the slight roar of the water and smelled the sweet air. After a few minutes, she became fidgety again and said, "I'm going to walk along the river and look for chokecherry bushes. Anna wants them for syrup and jelly.

"I'll help you. Fish ain't biting anyway."

"Thanks, George. I love Anna but I hate the chiggers," Marka said, putting on her shoes and picking up the bucket.

They found bushes loaded with berries half mile down the river. They picked until the bucket was three quarters full and then walked back to their fishing poles.

"Look," George pointed to the water. "There's a carp. Look at his fins on the top of the water."

They headed towards the bridge. Across the river on the other side of the bridge a flock of small birds swooped down and landed, then took off again. "When birds do that, there is a storm coming," George said.

The setting sun cast beautiful yellows and reds in the sky. Marka and George looked over the side of the bridge and watched eddies swirling in the water.

"George, you're like a father to me. Thanks for listening."

Marka thought how George was one of the most wonderful men she had ever known. Today, he had taught her how to listen to the birds, the trees, and the water.

At three in the morning, Marka and Anna woke to a loud roar. Thunder crashed and rumbled. It shook the house and rattled the windows. A flash of lightning ripped across the sky. Rain pounded against the roof of the house.

They looked out a window and watched the whipping wind rip leaves and branches from the trees. "It looks like the storm is coming from the northwest," Anna said.

"Do you think we should go to the cellar?"

"I think we better stay here for now," Anna said taking Marka by the hand and leading her over to the corner of the dining room. "We better stay away from the windows."

Marka shivered. "I hope it's not a tornado."

They stood in the corner of the room away from the windows and waited for the wind to die down. It seemed it would never stop blowing. They listened to the swishing of the trees. The wind banged on the windows and doors, and then it quieted as quickly as it had started. Anna went to the kitchen and stuck her head out the door. "The wind is gone, but the air is chilly," she said. "Bet we're going to get hail."

It did hail, huge stones, the size of a baseball. "My garden," Anna moaned. "There will be nothing left. Look at the size of those hailstones."

The hail pounded against the roof and went through the metal awning above the front room window. Anna looked worried. "Just so the wind don't come back and we get a bunch of broken windows. The garden is probably gone."

The storm finally ended. Marka was glad she had decided to sleep at Anna's; that she was with her during the storm. Marka flipped the light switch. There was no power to the house. She checked the telephone. The line was dead. She wondered how much damage had been done to her house.

In the morning, power was still off; so they couldn't listen to the radio. They went over to Marka's house. A big tree branch had broken off and was resting on the roof.

Later that afternoon, they had power and listened to the news report. The radio announcer said that the storm had battered the Ridley area. It struck in full fury. The hail stones measured three inches across. The storm left houses with shattered windows, cars with huge dents and broken windshields, but the most serious loss was to the crops. Some of the farmers lost their whole crop of corn. Sugar beet fields were leveled. Not everyone got hailed out; others had bumper crops of grain, corn and beets unharmed.

Anna was saddened over her garden. The hail broke branches off the bean plants and pounded the leaves of red beets, turnips and carrots. Some of the tomato plants had branches severed where the hailstones cut through. But, luckily, only about half the garden had been damaged.

"Only a temporary setback," Anna said. "Nothing like the farmers have to face."

Although the garden would come back, Anna's roof sustained damage. She and Marka would have to hire Herb. First, the branch from Marka's house had to be removed.

The hail had also damaged the roof of the grandstand, pavilion and exhibit halls at the fairgrounds. They would have to work long hours to get them fixed before the fair was scheduled the middle of next month.

CHAPTER 23

The water truck made numerous trips back and forth from one end of Main Street to the other. It went up the hill to the highway and back down again, spraying water until the dirt and gravel were packed tight to keep the dust down. The next couple of weeks there would be heavy traffic, because of the fair. The Butte County Fair brought life to the town. The fair's claim to fame was in 1927 when it made national news. President Coolidge came as guest of honor for three days. The Homestake band of Lead played the three days and each night for the bowery dance. New tractors and automobiles were displayed and demonstrated. Airplanes flew overhead for entertainment.

The tall grasses in the ditches beside the road to the fairgrounds were mowed, as so were the vacant lots around town. By the end of the week, the whole town smelled fresh and looked tidy.

Preparing the roads and cutting the grass were only a few of the things that needed to be done in preparation for the fair. The fairgrounds had to be cleared of debris, over-grown weeds, and remnants of last year's fair. The hail damage to the roof of the grandstand, pavilion and exhibition halls had been repaired. Herb and his crew worked seven days a week to get the work completed. The pavilion even got a fresh coat of paint.

Bodie was hired by the fair board to help get things ready in the livestock area. He spread straw around the animal pens and all over the inside of the livestock barn that would house the 4-H entries: sheep, goats, swine, and cows. He repaired the cages in the poultry house for the prize chickens, and rabbits. He helped set up booths for food, games, and trinkets.

Millie's Café was especially busy. Day after day, there was a rush of customers; people wanting breakfast before they went to the fairground to set up their displays. Finally, at 10:00 a.m., the cafe had cleared out.

"Mail came in a little while ago," George said, stirring cream into his coffee. "Stella really surprised me this morning. She gave me her copy of the *Clayton Post*. Now, that was sure nice of her." He winked at Marka.

Millie and Marka cleared the counter and all the tables of dirty dishes and wiped everything down. Millie turned the grill down and scraped bits of crusted food off to one side. Marka neatly stacked dirty cups and saucers, glasses, and plates into the large bin under the wash sink.

"Does it say anything in there about the county fair? About the shows, the exhibitions, or the dances?" Marka asked. "The dances in the pavilion were fun."

"Well, let's see." George readjusted his reading glasses and spread the newspaper across the clean counter. "It talks about the Harley Motorcycle Races in Sturgis this month. Oh, this isn't so good. A ranch hand found dead—a suicide—shot himself in the head." George lifted his cup. "Can I have a refill on the coffee, Millie?"

Millie cracked her chewing gum. "Shooting yourself in the head. That beats all. Does it say anything about the dances?"

"Here it is," George said. "Says that fair preparations are now in full swing in Ridley. The Television Vanities of 1957 stage show will be Thursday, Friday, and Saturday nights. It's a musical comedy show with magic tricks and a controlled balancing act." George blew on the coffee and took a couple large sips. "Hey, $500 in prize money for horse racing Friday and Saturday afternoons. That's where I'll be. At the track."

"And—and—the dances?" Millie lit a cigarette, took a puff and laid it in the ashtray. She filled George's cup and offered Marka a cigarette. Marka shook her head, no.

"Oh, that's right. You don't smoke, and you're a church goer now," Millie said sarcastically.

George read out loud: "Evening show at the grandstand starts at 8:00 p.m., first with the 4-H style review and then a stage show. Here we go. The pavilion dances are planned for Friday and Saturday nights and start at 9:30 p.m."

"We gotta go." Millie put her arm around Marka's waist and bumped into her hip.

"I don't want to go," Marka said, remembering the last time she went to a dance with Millie. She shrugged her shoulders and raised her eyebrows at Millie.

"You just said what fun they use to be."

Marka thought how it would be fun to go to the dances, but not with Millie. Something bad was bound to happen. Ruby and Anna would hit the ceiling if she said she was going to a dance with Millie after what happened with Earl. She wished Jonny had come back from Texas, so she could go with him. That is, if he would ask her.

"Why don't you take Ida to the dance?" Marka asked. "She would love to go and show off all the new dances she's learned on American Bandstand."

Millie frowned. "Ever since that show started on TV, she rushes out of the café to get home. It's just a bunch of kids jumping around. All I hear any more is Buddy Holly, Chuck Berry, Paul Anka, and Neil Sedaka. People say it's the devil's music."

"You aren't serious." Marka laughed.

"Says here," George continued to read out of the paper, "the fair draws high interest for its inclusion of the annual West River 4-H Sheep Show, in which all West-River 4-H members are invited to compete for educational trips to the National Western Livestock Show and 4-H Club Round-Up in Denver."

"Well, ain't that interesting." Millie took a drag on her cigarette.

Marka said, "The smell of chokecherry jelly is filling Anna's kitchen, and she is making her famous bread and butter pickles. She's received a blue ribbon every year so far. She's counting on a ribbon again this year."

"What else is she going to enter?" Millie asked. "The tri-state milling company is having a bread baking contest. She should enter her Russian rye. That's the first thing we run out of from the bakery."

"We should enter her Russian rye," Marka and Millie said in unison.

George piped in, "Maybe you gals ought to bake a cake. It says here: Lady Baltimore Cake Contest sponsored by the Utah & Idaho Sugar Company."

"Anna is going to enter something for the crochet contest," Marka said. "Yesterday, she soaked a doily in sugar water. Said that's how she gets them so stiff. All that sugar—U & I Sugar should offer a prize for that," she giggled.

George laughed. "Sorry, it's got to be a cake."

The week was scorching. The temperatures held steady in the high eighties. The nights stayed warm, too warm to sleep, and the mosquitoes ate at you when you went outdoors. There had been a rainstorm in the Mud Butte area, and some small hail covered the ground around Mule Creek. Fortunately, this time Ridley had been untouched, but there was always a fear this time of year that at any moment a storm could come through and leave devastation.

In spite of the heat and storms, August was a glorious time of the year. It was harvest time. During evening, a big moon loomed in the sky, and crickets in the tall brown grass sang steadily. It was the busiest month of the year in Ridley; the hay was bailed, the corn was cut. Women tried to outdo each other canning vegetables, pickles, jellies, and preserves. Basements and cellar shelves were lined with rows of mason jars. Entering a jar in the fair was a sure way to judge the quality of the produce and the skill of the canner. The ladies of the county competed to see who could put up the most jars and whose were the best.

Ruby suggested to Marka that they go to the fair together, and that they invite Anna along. Marka said that Anna wanted to go, but heard on the radio that the temperature was going to reach 93 degrees.

"If it gets too hot, she may want to come home a little early," Marka said.

"We could take her home if she wants, or maybe she could catch a ride home with someone else," Ruby said.

"She really does want to go," Marka responded. "She wants to check on her pickles and crocheted doily centerpiece. See if they got any ribbons. Let's go right after lunch. Then, we can get there in time for the parade. It starts 1:00 p.m."

Anna did go to the fair with them. After the parade, they walked through the pavilion and looked at the exhibits. There were entries for handicrafts, hobbies, baked goods, sewing, photography, and painting. Ruby and Marka filled out a ticket for a free television set that the fair committee was giving away that night. They tried to persuade Anna to fill one out, but she declined, saying the last thing in the world she wanted was a TV.

"Wouldn't it be fun to have a TV, Anna?" Marka said.

"Ach, they are too expensive. Anyways, we got a good radio."

"Oh, Anna."

"If I win, I'll give it to you," Ruby said.

"Ach, no."

"Oh, you two," Marka smiled glad Ruby and Anna were getting along.

Marka and Ruby wanted to walk around the fairgrounds and check out the booths. It was getting too hot; so Anna stayed inside the pavilion.

"Ruby, why didn't you enter anything in the fair?" Marka asked. "Your paintings are beautiful."

"Wanted to enter my portrait of Henry, but I still can't get the eyes the way I want them. I thought about entering the lovely quilt—the one I won in the Ladies' Aid raffle. But of course, I didn't make it," she teased.

They walked past the shooting gallery, the penny toss, and carnival rides. The merry-go-round calliope played *East Side, West Side, All A round the Town*. There were tents full of kewpie dolls, prizes, and pennants that said "South Dakota". At the end of the fairway, the Ridley Ladies' Auxiliary had their booth. A poster board advertised lemonade, hamburgers, and fries.

Stella was running the booth and was prancing around like an ostrich. Ruby insisted they go over and buy something. Marka resisted, saying she felt as if she would be going into a war zone. Ruby persuaded her. They walked up to the booth.

"If it isn't Madame Butterfly," Stella said, smirking at Ruby, puffing out her chest as she filled the large jar with lemonade. She was wearing a crisp starched, ruffled apron.

A shiver ran from the top of Marka's head right down to her toes. She felt tempted to slap Stella's face and tell her she was despicable for spreading rumors around Ridley, but she smiled sweetly.

"What you ladies peddling this year?" Ruby asked.

Stella glared at her with unconcealed loathing. "May I help you?"

"Two lemonades," Ruby said, putting her hands on her hips.

Stella poured a glass of lemonade and handed it to Ruby. Then, she filled another glass and when she handed it to Marka it slipped out of her hand, landed on the ground and splashed on Marka's shoes.

Marka stood, confident, and looked at her with an unmoving stare. Katie, who was working the booth with Stella, grabbed a dishtowel and handed it to Marka. "Oh, dear, how clumsy of me," Stella said. "I'll pour you another one."

"Never mind," Marka said, bending over to wipe the cold sticky drink from her shoes.

"Marka, tell Anna I have some material and a pattern I would like her to sew for me," Stella said, making light of what had happened. Marka had an irresistible urge to stick her tongue out and walk away.

The telephone rang just as Marka stepped into her house.

"Marka, this is Millie. The dance tonight, what did you decide?"

"I don't think so. I went to the fair today with Ruby and Anna. Anna is a little down—she didn't win the crochet contest, but her pickles won another blue ribbon."

"Who won the crochet contest?" Millie asked.

"Some lady from Clayton. It was a tablecloth."

"The dance, the dance." Millie persisted. "Go with me, please."

"I don't know," Marka hesitated.

"At least go to the grandstand show. We can decide about the dance afterwards. Listen. I'm reading from the paper now: The stage show—The O'Dells and Jackie, a control balancing team recently returning from a 40-month world tour. Imagine that!" Millie laughed and kept on reading. "The Cycling Saxons in trick riding and juggling and V-Roy and Company featuring acts of illusion. What do you say? Come with me, please."

Marka agreed to the grandstand show. She'd go only if Ida could come along. Millie and Ida picked her up at 7:30 p.m. After the show at the grandstand, the winner of the television was announced. It was Carl Erlich. Millie waved her arms in the air and shouted catcalls. "It would have to be him who won," she hollered.

Millie begged and pleaded for Marka to stay for the dance and finally Marka gave in. "I'll stay, but so help me—if you take off on me or try to talk me into going out to the car with anyone."

Millie put her hand on Marka's shoulder. "I promise; I won't. Not after what happened. Is that why you were holding back about coming to the dance?"

"Yes. It did cross my mind!"

At 9:30 p.m. the band began playing, but it was after 10:00 p.m. by the time the guys got up their courage to ask the ladies to dance. A trip or two behind the pavilion for a drink usually loosened them up. Marka always felt uncomfortable standing around, smiling charmingly as the guys walked by eyeing her. She felt like a piece of meat in a slaughterhouse. Millie doesn't just stand around. She asks the guys to dance, Marka thought. But then, Millie is fast.

Marka and Ida leaned against the wall of the pavilion and swayed to the music. By 11:00 p.m., Ida had only danced once and Marka eight times. Marka couldn't understand why Ida hadn't been asked to dance. She was a little plump, but she was pretty with large brown eyes, thick lashes, and small pointed nose. She looked nothing like Millie. Marka was about to go out for a breath of air when someone tapped her on the top of her head.

"Wanna dance?"

"Buddy, what are you doing here? Where's your wife?"

"Home. She talked Dad out of the television he won. She's hot on having one in the bedroom. Seems to fit. Good company for her and her terrible headaches. I said to her, 'Go home and take your television to bed,' and so she did."

Marka sniffed Buddy's breath. "You've been drinking."

Buddy pinched his thumb and forefinger together and held his hand in front of Marka's face. "Just a little—tiny—bit," he slurred.

"Let's go outside. You could use some air," Marka said.

The night air was warm and the stars, a million brilliant lights, were dazzling in the sky. The carnies had shut down their game booths; the concessionaires were taking down their tents and packing up.

Buddy pointed to the busy workers. "This afternoon they turned me away after I won five teddy bears at the shooting booth. I made some little girls mighty happy. They finally caught on that I was no amateur. I'm the best damn shot in the county. Antelope season— hell people take me along just to get their kill. Can't wait for the season to open," Buddy bragged.

Marka and Buddy walked around the fairgrounds, past the empty livestock pens and implement dealers. Buddy had to examine the tractors and combines. "We had a McCormick combine just like this one for cutting wheat, and we had a fairly new John Deere. I wish Dad hadn't sold the farm. See that shiny green tractor over there? It's an Oliver. When I was a kid, I used to play on the one we had."

"You and Bodie probably have some good memories of the farm. He doesn't talk about it like you do though," Marka said.

"Bodie wasn't interested in the farm. Not like me. I'd like to save up and buy another one. I'd raise sugar beets. They say that the sugar beet factory is going to close, because the beets aren't doing well, but that's a lot of hogwash. You know what? Our old tractor is still out there on the place. Out behind the big barn. I really think it is great the way you listen to me talk," Buddy slurred. "Did I tell you I really miss the farm?"

They headed back towards the pavilion. The Ferris Wheel stood against the night sky. Buddy grabbed Marka by the arm and pulled her behind one of the steel pillars beside the huge ride. The moonlight cast a shadow across his face. Buddy had broad shoulders and stood only a few inches taller than Marka. His eyes were glassy. His skin looked leathery and tan under the lights.

"Marka." He had a mischievous smile on his face and he swayed from side to side. "I got one hell of a crush on you, and I get damn jealous of Bodie, cause he gets so much of your attention. And that goddamn teacher—what's his name? I suppose he'll be back, hanging out at Anna's again just so he can see you."

"Buddy, you are drunk. Cut it out."

Buddy straightened his slumped body and put his hands in his pants pockets. "I'm not drunk. I'm stone sober. I want you to hear what I have to say. It's more than a crush," Buddy said. "It's love and Stella knows it. God, I hate her. That first day I saw you in church; I lost my heart to you." He teetered back and forth. "Guess I am a little tipsy."

"You're drunk, and I don't want you to say anything else."

Buddy drew Marka to him and kissed her. He held her close and patted her behind.

"No." Marka pushed him away.

"Don't get all huffy. I know you're hot for me too." Buddy kicked at the dirt with his boot. "The way you act when you're around me. Come on. Admit it. You have feelings for me too."

"I like you. You made me feel at home in Ridley, which is more than a lot of people did. I'm sorry you took it wrong. You're a married man, and, well, there's a lot about me you don't know."

"But, I do know, Buddy said. "I know about that guy in Denver."

Marka's heart skipped a beat. Here it comes. How many sordid details had Stella shared?

"Marka changed the subject. "Why did you marry Stella if you didn't love her?"

"Because I was lonely," Buddy kicked the dirt again. "It was shortly after Mom died—Bodie was in Korea. Dad was distant; I felt like I would die of loneliness. I met Stella, and she was crazy for me."

"She wanted you. Were you crazy about her?"

"No. She was a warm body. I don't feel bad about saying that, cause she just wanted to get away from her mother. Damn it all. If I had gone to Korea with Bodie, I wouldn't be in this mess, but Dad kept me home to work the farm. He told the Draft Board he had to have me. When Bodie joined up, Dad was glad. Bodie was always an embarrassment to him."

Marka laid her hand on Buddy's shoulder. "You're talking crazy. If you had gone to Korea, you might have been killed. Look at Bodie; he could have been killed just as easily as wounded."

"Life just ain't fair, you know. I want to be on the farm, and I can't. There's no way Stella would ever let me have my freedom."

Buddy started to cry. He put his arms around Marka and held her close. Her head was reeling. She was drawn to him for some reason. She felt the heat of his body burning out of control, like a blazing fire. The word echoed in her ears—Stop! You're going to get burned. Marka pushed Buddy away and ran towards the pavilion.

"There you are," Millie hollered across the fairgrounds. "Whew, I'm all danced out. Ready to go home?"

Marka walked faster towards Millie and Ida. She wondered why she always let things go so far with Buddy. "Yes, let's go home now." She tried to sound cheerful.

"I didn't even have anything to drink tonight, and I didn't go out in the car with anyone. I promised myself I wouldn't let you down," Millie whispered in Marka's ear.

"Thanks, Millie." Marka thought how Millie and Ida had come just in nick of time.

"But what about you, Marka? Who was with you outside the pavilion? Couldn't have been Buddy, could it?"

CHAPTER 24

"Stella has something on him," Marka said quietly to herself as she rolled over on her stomach and ran her hands across the warm grass. She pulled a long blade from the ground and chewed on the tender white root. "Why else would he stay with her? He doesn't love her. He told me so. Oh, no," she moaned, "it's happening all over again. Only this time it's Stella and Buddy instead of Geraldine and Rex."

Marka pounded the ground with her fists. The things Buddy said the night of the fair were the same sort of things Rex said about Geraldine. Rex stayed with Geraldine, because of her money. She had finally figured that out. But Buddy. Why would he be willing to lead such a miserable existence being married to someone like Stella? He didn't love her. Oh, why was she even thinking about all of this?

And what if someone saw them together outside the pavilion? They were sure to tell Stella. Maybe they already had. Marka thought about the day before in People's Grocery.

She and Mildred Johnson crossed paths in front of the meat counter. Mildred stopped right in her tracks and stared at her, then looked over her shoulder as Marka walked away. Marka saw her out of the corner of her eye; it was either the sight of her or the smell of bad meat that made Mildred frown.

She also heard Nettie and Charlene whispering to each other at the magazine rack. When Marka walked over to the rack, Charlene waved her arm in front of Nettie's face and said "Oh, look at my new Elgin wristwatch."

A group of birds chattered and dove down from a tree branch and then swooped up to the other side of the tree. This momentarily interrupted Marka's thoughts, and then she went back to her fuming. She sat up, crossed her legs, and wiggled her toes in the grass. She watched the birds, dive and dart about, fighting to set the pecking order. The larger, stronger ones were in charge; the smaller, weaker ones got out of their way. She thought how small and weak she felt, compared to someone like Geraldine and Stella.

So, what does she have on him? Maybe it has something to do with Carl? Maybe Carl would never stand for a divorce in the family. Pious Carl went to church every Sunday and held tight to his beliefs and interpretations of life. That's what Anna said about him. How he follows all the rules. That was probably it then; divorce was out of the question. Not that any of it mattered anyway. She was through with Buddy.

Marka lay down on the grass again and rolled over on her stomach. Her long hair swung forward around her face. If she had any feelings for Buddy, they ended Wednesday afternoon when he came into the cafe. She thought she had made it clear the night of the fair that she wanted him to leave her alone. But there he stood, all sure of himself. He walked over to the jukebox and made selections. He tapped his fingers on the top of the machine and carefully chose songs. Then, he walked over to the counter where she was filling salt shakers and said, "Hey, those earrings are keen." He took hold of her hand and asked her if she liked Jerry Lee Lewis's song, *Whole Lotta Shakin' Going On.*

She shooed him away like a fly and told him she was busy.

"It's been on the charts for weeks," he added, touching her arm. She pushed his hand away. "What's the matter?" he asked. "When you going to another dance with Millie?"

"Never!" She went back to the bakery room and told Millie to go out and get rid of him. "Tell him I'm busy; that we have work to get done. Tell him—"

"For cripes sake, what do you expect? You're always leading him on."

"I am not." Marka defended herself.

"You'd have to be stupid not to notice that he can't take his eyes off you."

"You're exaggerating."

"Why don't you go for him? You know you got feelings for him."

"He's a married man."

"So what? Stella doesn't deserve him. If you put half a mind to it, you could have him—take him away from her." Millie curled her

214

lips. "Little, double-chin Stella, and her husband is making a play for you. I saw you two cuddled together the night of the fair."

"Millie, stop it. It wasn't like that at all. I don't mean to lead him on. Honest, I don't."

But how could she think no one would notice or that Stella wouldn't find out? She knew everything that went on in town.

"Stella snoops at people's mail," Millie whispered in Marka's ear. Bodie told me she reads the post cards. She knows about all catalog orders, and bills people get. I'd sure like to fix her. Hey, I have an idea. Let's send a post card from a secret admirer to you, from Clayton. Make it real mushy."

"No, Millie." Marka leaned on the doorframe, peeked out into the cafe, and watched Buddy for a while. He strutted around like a rooster. He'd walk up to someone, shake their hand and slap them on the back.

"Everyone's little Buddy's friend," she said softly to herself and smiled.

Marka stopped her daydreaming, got up off the ground, and walked towards the house. How had this happen again? She couldn't blame anyone but herself. "It's not men I can't trust; I can't trust myself!" she declared. The night of the fair she felt sorry for Buddy; she let herself be taken in. She made the same mistake with Rex. She had to busy herself with other things. Anna told her Jonny was back from Texas. "He got back a week after the fair," Anna said. "You know, school will start August 29."

The aroma of cloves, allspice, and cinnamon filled Anna's kitchen. She finished spooning red beets into sterilized jars. Marka sat at the table drinking a glass of lemonade and watched Anna wipe the rims with a dishrag, and then twist the jar lids tight.

"Now, I want to make an apple pie for us, and one for George. He came over and fixed the hose on my washer." Anna made several trips to the cupboard and brought back flour, lard, rolling pin, pie tins and a bowl of apples.

"I've been thinking." Marka said, "Since we didn't win the television at the fair, what would you think if I bought one? You could come over to my house and watch with me."

"Ach, wouldn't you know that someone like Carl would win," Anna said wiping her hands on her apron.

"And, you know who ended up with it?" Marka said.

"Who?"

Marka knew she had to tell Anna the truth. There would be no more lies between them. "I saw Buddy at the dance the night of the fair, and he told me Carl gave it to Stella."

"Oh."

Anna handed Marka a knife and told her to peel apples. Marka sat at the table, peeled, and watched Anna make crumbs out of flour and lard. Anna added some cold water to the mixture, and then formed a round ball. She sprinkled flour on the counter of the Hoosier and rolled out the piecrusts and placed them in pans.

"Jonny hasn't even bothered to call," Marka said.

"Maybe he's busy getting the boys ready for football." Anna sat down at the table. "Here, let me show you how to peel apples." She ran a knife around the apple and ended with an unbroken ring of peel. She cut the apple in half, removed the seeds, and placed the halves into the bowl of lightly salted water.

"He probably doesn't want to see me anyway," Marka said. "Maybe he and his old girlfriend..."

"Ach. You don't know that. Invite him to supper Saturday night."

Marka thought about it while Anna rolled out crust for the top of the pies. "Yes, I think I will. It's time for me to get my life going again. Will you help me make a special dinner?"

"Yah, sure," Anna smiled.

By Saturday, Marka felt exhausted. It had been a long week. Monday was washday; Tuesday she went to the cafe early to get the baking done before it got hot. Wednesday, she worked past 4:00 p.m. to clean the café after closing time, because Ida went to Rapid with a friend to get new clothes for school. Thursday, she drove Anna and Sophie to Clayton. They shopped at Smiley's Market and Piggly Wiggly. Marka went to Woolworth, while they went to J.C. Penney for pillowcases to embroider.

Friday had been especially busy at the cafe. The irrigation was completed for most farmers; so they came to town. They sat around and talked about their hopes that the beets would be good this year. They hoped to have a large yield, and hoped that the beets would have a high sugar content. Fritz Weimer bragged about his corn being twelve feet high and that was with only irrigating it once. Some of the men complained that they were sick of the government paying them to let their fields lie fallow.

Everyone was in a tizzy over the newspaper article about the strangled nurse. She had been found dead in her apartment. "Crimes happen in big cities like Los Angeles. Nothing like that ever happens around here. Probably some jealous man, or maybe even the wife of some guy messing around," Harry Paddock said.

Marka felt a chill run down her spine. Something like that could happen here as well as anywhere. She gathered her tips off the counter, put them into her apron pocket, and then cleared away the dirty plates and cups.

Jonny showed up for supper at 5:30 p.m. on Saturday. Marka answered the door. He stepped into the kitchen. He hugged her tight and kissed her on the cheek.

She felt glad she had taken extra time getting ready, wrapping her hair into a French roll and using an eyelash curler. She even dabbed Evening in Paris behind her ears thinking how he had liked it the night of the prom. Anna helped her get supper started; a pork roast with potatoes and carrots. And Anna brought over a rhubarb pie.

"Let's sit down at the table while supper finishes cooking," Marka said. "Tell me all about your trip." She opened the oven door to check the roast.

"It was nice to see old friends. I painted mother's house and got her car running right. Changed the spark plugs, put on new tires, things like that. Her biggest concern was—me—was I ever going to settle down and get married?' Jonny chuckled. "She asked me, 'Isn't there anyone in the whole state of South Dakota that is wife material?' Then she invited one of my old girlfriends over to her house.''

The muscles in Marka's neck tightened. So, he did have an old love interest just like Stella said. Why was it every man she met had to come with a set of circumstances? She had to take it slow with Jonny or risk getting hurt again.

"I'm so grateful the high school didn't close," Jonny said. "I hated the thought of leaving Ridley. Well, you know how I felt about that. I wrote about it in a letter. "

"I never got a letter from you."

"I sent you a letter shortly after I got to Texas."

"Really? The mail is slow, I guess. I sent my application to Deerfield teacher's college for spring semester. I should have heard something by now. I wonder if I should call and ask them if they received it?"

"I remember distinctly mailing it," Jonny said. "That's right, I mailed it along with my mother's letters. You really should have gotten it by now," Jonny said with a puzzled look on his face. "So you really want to become a teacher? That's wonderful. Why don't you come and sit in on one of my English literature classes?"

"Would it be okay? I'd like that."

"Absolutely."

They went to the dining room where Marka had the table set with china dishes and her mother's good silverware. Jonny settled into his chair while she went to the kitchen and arranged the roast and vegetables on a large platter and then placed it on the table.

"The books I left. Did you read any of them?" Jonny asked.

"Yes, a couple and I finished *The Scarlet Letter*. I found it to be very chilling. People can be so cruel."

"Shows what happens when a community meddles in other people's lives," Jonny said. "Hester was definitely the heroine of the story. I felt that Hawthorne didn't mean for it to be a romance novel, but more to point out the condition of a people's hearts." Jonny sliced a chunk of roast, put it in his mouth, and chewed. "This roast is wonderful, Marka."

"Anna helped me."

Marka sat straight in her chair and smoothed her napkin across her lap. "It is really good to have you back."

"How was your summer?"

"Very quiet," Marka said.

"Good. Good."

What she just told Jonny wasn't true. Ruby had told her one of her problems was that she wouldn't let anyone know who she really was. How she wasn't honest.

"Not all men from Texas are nice like you, Jonny. I met a guy this summer. His name is Earl. He's a friend of Millie's. Oh, it isn't important."

The truth? Not this time. If she were to have a chance with Jonny, well, telling him about Earl could ruin things. He might think it was her fault. It would complicate matters. Maybe she'd tell him someday if they got to know each other better. Maybe there are times when things are better left unsaid.

"I think it is dandy that you want to go to college, Marka. They offer scholarships. Perhaps I could help you find out about them."

"I plan to work in the bakery and cafe until next spring. Anna still thinks that I should take a job at the courthouse. I don't want to. I have some money saved, and as long as I don't have to buy a car and can use Anna's, I'll be okay."

"Saw in the paper where they want $2,500 for a new Rambler— radio, heater, V8, and white walls." Jonny wiped his mouth with the linen napkin. "A '57 Plymouth Savory Hardtop with whitewalls, automatic transmission and for the same money. I'd like to buy a new car."

Jonny left shortly after they finished supper. She had hoped for more from him, more from the evening. Something has changed since his trip to Texas, she thought. Maybe he wasn't interested in her romantically but only as a friend. If only she had gotten the letter, she would be able to figure it out. Jonny said he sent her a letter. He wouldn't lie. That wasn't like him.

The next morning, she went to the post office and asked about the letter. If Stella were nosey like Millie said, she knew every piece of mail that came in and went out. Marka thought how she would be cordial and try very hard to be nice to Stella. She would ask Stella to help her track down the letter. And this would be her chance to make amends, as George put it.

Stella got angry and shouted at Marka. "Are you accusing me? How dare you! You can't face the fact that Johnny could never be interested in someone like you." Her words cut deep into Marka's heart.

Marka stood up for herself. "The letter you sent to the dead letter office, well—I know who sent it. You did me a favor." She was referring to Rex. "For your information, he's out of my life!"

That night, Marka couldn't sleep. Her thoughts were of the newspaper article about the strangled nurse. She couldn't get it out of her mind. Harry Paddock said there was a photo in the paper of the woman sprawled across the bed, her nightgown pulled up around her neck and a silk stocking around her throat. Nothing like that could happen in Ridley, could it?

She had to think about her future. What she really wanted to do with her life. Anna wanted her to go to Clayton and get a good job, but she wanted to keep the bakery going and then start college. She had enough money to see her through at least one year. There would not be time in her life for romance. Her destiny, well, she would probably end up like Anna, a spinster. From now on, she would think only of becoming a teacher.

CHAPTER 25

It was under a dazzling, starlit sky that Marka first laid eyes on George's son, Jack. She and George were sitting on George's porch talking about school starting in a few days and how the town would bustle again. There would be lots of traffic on the streets. People would go to football games, dances, and school programs. Marka told George that Jonny asked her to sit in on his English literature class.

"I told him I applied for admission to the 1958 spring semester at the teacher's college in Deerfield," Marka said.

The rungs on the rocker squeaked as George gently tipped back and forth. He'd stop occasionally to fuss with his pipe, to stuff the bowl full of sweet smelling tobacco and to relight it.

"Listen," George stopped rocking. "Hear that car engine? Never heard it around town before. You heard it before?"

"I don't know," Marka said. "I never pay much attention to the sound of a car."

"Well, I do, and there's someone new in town." George put his hand behind his ear. "The car's got kind of a purr to it."

They sat and listened to the steady singing of crickets. Nothing moved but bugs darting through the air. The summer warmth clung to their skin as they sat content, unconcerned over the sound of the unfamiliar car on the other side of town. Then the sound of that car engine stopped. It started again, and soon headlights approached. Gravel crunched beneath the wheels when it stopped in front of George's house. The streetlight lit up the car.

"It's a '57, Plymouth Fury. Look at all that chrome and those fins. Looks like it's ready for flight. I can't tell who the heck it is." George shrugged his shoulders and got out of his chair. Marka rose too and leaned over the rail, trying to improve her view. The car door opened, and a tall, thin figure emerged. A man walked slowly towards the house, his eyes looking straight ahead. George turned on the porch light, and, immediately night moths danced around the bulb.

"Dad?"

George gasped, "Is that you, Jack?" He put his hand over his heart.

A young man climbed the porch steps and thrust his long arms towards his father. Marka stood silently by while they hugged.

"Jack," George chuckled, "by gosh, I can't believe it's you. What a surprise! Oh, this is my friend, Marka." George reached out and touched her arm.

Marka fixed her eyes on Jack. He had blonde, wavy hair, smiling eyes, and a wide smile. He made her stomach flutter.

"Son," George's eyes sparkled. What a surprise. By gosh, I can't believe it. Why didn't you tell me you were coming?"

"It was a spur of the moment thing," Jack said. "I haven't taken vacation for a long time; so I just got in the car and started driving." His voice was soft, like the call of a dove. He turned his head from side to side as he talked, looking at George and then at Marka.

"Well, I'm sure glad you did. I just can't believe it," George said shaking his head in disbelief. "Jack works at Cape Canaveral in Florida," he said. "How you guys coming on getting a satellite to outer space? Too bad the Russians beat us in the space race."

Jack answered. "We're working on it."

Marka said, "I should get going, George. Nice meeting you Jack." She stepped sideways down the porch steps, eyes still on Jack's wide smile. "You probably won't want to go fishing in the morning now, will you, George? That's okay. I'll just tell Millie that I'll be in early after all."

"The long drive probably wore Jack out," George said. "I could go with you and let him sleep in."

"I've never been fishing in my life. Mind if I go along?" Jack asked.

"We go mighty early—just as the sun starts to rise. Best time, this time of the year," George added.

"Okay by me," Jack said.

"I'll bring a thermos of coffee and something to eat," Marka said.

"And I'll bring the bait. Are you sure about this son? We can give you a day to rest up." George lightly punched Jack's shoulder.

"I didn't drive that far today. Sure, I'll be ready to go."

Marka lay awake waiting impatiently for the sun to peek over the trees, announcing the break of day. It had been one of those miserable, summer nights, too hot to sleep. Just as she would start to drift off a mosquito, would buzz in her ear. She'd pull the sheet over her head; then she couldn't breathe.

Dawn finally came and with it the song of meadowlarks. They know the exact instant to start their morning music. Marka rolled out of bed and went to the kitchen and put on a pot of coffee. She sliced the *kuchen* Anna made for her in perfect oblong pieces, selecting the ones from the middle of the pan, because they were moister. She wrapped the pieces of *kuchen* separately in waxed paper.

She brushed her hair, pulled it over to one side into a ponytail, and then secured it with a rubber band and small red nylon scarf. Her big blue eyes asked, "And what are you up to?" as she stared into the oak framed mirror. She removed the scarf and band and repositioned her hair into a tomboy tail in the back of her head. She tossed the scarf on the dresser.

They walked along the bank through thick foliage to where the river cut wide. The sun ascended, its rays streaked with gold. The river moved silently. The morning air was fresh and warm. Off to their left, a mallard landed on the open water.

"The fish are going to bite today," George said putting two plump angleworms on his hook.

"No wonder," Marka laughed and shook her head in amusement. "The way you're loading on the bait."

"What do you mean? Got to give them something worth going after." George winked at Jack. "Here, Jack, use this pole. I'm gonna put some cheese on mine and make the fish curious." George slipped cheese on his hook and then put a small split-shot sinker about twelve inches above it. He placed the other pole in Jack's hand. "Cast out your line. Keep your finger on this lever and then release it as you bring your arm forward."

Jack let go of the lever too soon; so the weight and baited hook fell on the ground.

"You just need some practice, that's all," George assured him. "I'll make a fisherman out of you. Here, throw it out again."

"Your Dad taught me everything I know about fishing," Marka said.

Jack gave it another try. This time it was a perfect hit. The line went way out and fell in the middle of the moving water.

Marka held her pole tightly as she reeled in her third catfish. "You should have seen me when I was learning to fish. It cost your father a lot of flies and sinkers." Marka thought of the first time she went fishing with George, and how they opened the fish and found Stella's wedding ring. She laughed out loud.

"You think it's funny, do you?" George asked.

"I was thinking of our first time fishing and how we found the ring."

"What did you ever do with it?" George asked.

"It's in my jewelry box."

Fish flopped around in the metal bucket. The catch of the morning: four catfish and two bullheads. The crappies they caught were small; so George threw them back. Marka slipped off the long sleeved shirt she wore to protect her from mosquitoes and used it to dab the sweat from the back of her neck.

"It's getting too hot for the fish to bite," George said. "We won't catch any more unless we find a shady spot where the water is cooler. Let's move out of the sun—down where those cottonwoods are shading the water."

George led the way through the tall grass and brush. Marka walked behind him, and Jack followed. She felt self-conscious wondering whether Jack was looking at her shapely behind in her tight denim jeans.

A garter snake slithered across the grass in front of them. Marka stopped short, and Jack bumped into her. She felt a flush of excitement.

"If I had a swimming suit, I'd go for a swim," Jack flirted.

"Swimming season's over," Marka said. "It's dog days."

The next morning, Marka went to the café early to do the baking, then came home and put on a white cotton blouse and a pair of plaid Bermudas. It was another scorching day. She telephoned Anna and told her she would mow her grass later in the day when the sun went down.

After she ate supper, Marka walked over to Anna's, cut her grass, and raked the cuttings. George and Jack waved to her from George's porch. George hollered for her and Anna to come over for lemonade. She searched outdoors for Anna.

"Anna," she called. Sasha came running to her and rubbed her long, soft hair against her bare legs. Marka heard Anna call to her from the garden. She joined her there.

"The garden has started to die back. Help me pick the last of the cucumbers. We'll have *gummere salat,* cucumber salad for supper."

"Anna, did you know George has a son? His name is Jack. We went fishing yesterday morning."

"Who? Jack? Jack who?" She moistened her lips with her tongue.

"George's son, Jack Hanson. Did he ever mention to you that he had a son?"

"No, he never did. Come, help me with the hydrangea," Anna said and headed for the west corner of her house.

"There's something about him that I really like, and, he's so handsome; he looks like Alan Ladd. Oh, George invited us for some lemonade."

"I thought we was going to help Ida cut out the material for that wool suit she's making for the "Make It With Wool Contest". Here, hold this branch while I cut the string," Anna ordered. "I better hunt for some more rusty nails or these blooms will turn pink next year, and I love the blue." Anna gently moved the blooms toward her and tied them around the downspout that ran down the corner of the house. Marka stood patiently as Anna fumbled with the string. When she finished, she reached into her apron pocket and took out a handkerchief. She removed her straw hat and wiped the beads of sweat from her forehead. "These things are just like people," she said. "Sometimes they need holding up. Just like Ida needs help with making that suit for the wool contest."

"I know, Anna."

"I think it is good George's son has come to visit, but he's here just for a visit, right? Then, he will go. Ida is more important, yah? And, what about Jonny? You give up on him?"

Marka hung her head and stared at her sandals that had sunk into the warm dirt of the garden. Jonny! Anna just wouldn't give up on getting them together. But, really, Anna is right. Jack will be leaving. What was she thinking anyway? Besides, she had her life planned out now. The bakery was going well, and she would start school in Deerfield as soon as she got her acceptance. She had promised to help Ida with the suit. The "Make It With Wool Contest" would be the middle of September.

For the next week, Marka tried not to spend too much time with Jack, but, despite her efforts, they spent almost every evening together. He came to Ridley to visit his father, but in the evenings, George was either going to bed early, or he wasn't feeling well, because he ate too much supper. Once, George developed a terrible headache. Jack wandered over to Marka's house, and they sat outside in the warm night air, drinking iced tea, and batting at the mosquitoes.

Marka confided in Jack, because she knew he would soon be leaving to go back to Florida. This was not the old Marka, keeping everything to herself. She told Jack about Rex and Buddy; how she felt like a failure when it came to judging men. She told him about Stella and how she spent months fearing the repercussions from what she told her during their plane ride. "She let the cat out of the bag a couple of months ago, and nothing much came of it," Marka said. "Guess the people in town had too much work to do this summer to spend time gossiping, and, I spent all that time worrying."

Marka told Jack about Jonny, how Anna had her heart set on them getting together. Of course, this idea was a compromise for Anna, because marrying outside the clan was frowned upon. "Anna told me that my aunt, Tillie's mother, married an outsider, an English, and she had nothing but trouble. Anna is always trying to convince me that Jonny is a good catch. And if I were a teacher too, well… that would be a good profession for me. That way wherever he got transferred, I would always be able to get a job. I do have a certificate from Secretarial School, but I don't want to do that kind of work anymore. I want to teach."

"Sounds so practical," Jack said. "It's commendable that you want to get more education. I always had a tough time in school. I felt like such a dumb kid, because I couldn't read. I saw the letters in reverse—b and d would always be in the wrong place. They didn't know what was wrong with me—couldn't I even read or spell? In college, I found out that I had a learning problem. Hell, Rockefeller and Einstein had the same thing," Jack laughed.

"I always got straight A's in school," Marka said. "But it didn't do any good when it came to my dad. He thought education was a waste of time for a girl. I always felt like he wished I were a son; someone to take fishing and hunting. I always tried to do things with him, but he didn't even notice. He'd tell me, 'Get to the house! Girls are supposed to stay inside and cook and clean.' In other words, women are valuable only when they take care of a man."

"My father had a son, but he never took me fishing. Never had time, always too busy. It kind of gripes me to see him having the time now—the way he has all the time for you."

"It doesn't seem like we are talking about the same man when you talk about your dad. He's not like that anymore."

"He used to drink a lot." Jack said. "Did he tell you about his drinking days? Last time I saw Dad we walked the halls of the veterans' hospital detox ward. He was getting dried out. I had just finished college and took a job offer as an engineer with NASA in Florida."

"That's something you and your father have in common," Marka said. "He is always talking about the space program."

"I know. That's one of the things we have been talking about. My dad likes politics too, but that's all we talk about. I can't seem to talk about anything personal with him. Guess I have too many bad memories."

Marka had always kept a degree of distance between herself and men. She never really gave her heart totally to anyone. She felt differently talking to Jack. She wanted to know everything about him, and it was good letting someone know all about her. No more lies or secrets.

"Why don't you ask him about things?" Marka asked.

"Why can't he just tell me? He tells you everything."

"Can't you just start over with him? I know it's probably hard to forget the bad things; I've been going through some of this myself, but, well, guess I've had a lot of help from others: my friend Ruby, your dad, and my aunt. When I asked Anna why my folks never told me things, she said sometimes young people don't like to hear what the old ones have to say. When the time is right, then things will surface. Maybe you and your dad just aren't ready to talk about things." Marka's throat tightened, and her tongue felt thick in her mouth. She wiped away the tear that ran down her cheek. How she wished Jack knew his father the way she did.

Jack had a faraway look. "I can see you have a good relationship with him."

"Maybe it's because I don't have any expectations. I accept him just as he is. He did tell me about the drinking. He told me he had many regrets in his life. Now, I know what he was talking about," her voice softened.

"I didn't mean to upset you. I'm sorry."

"Your father and I talked about many things, but obviously you were the part of his life he didn't want to talk about. Maybe it seems I see only what is good in your father, but I've had my own problems with alcohol. It's something that can sneak up on you and, before you know it, it has control of your life. I understand where he is coming from, I guess."

"So, you think I only look for the bad in my father? My father was one of the most selfish people in the world. Things always had to go his way. You didn't know him the way I did," Jack was indignant.

"What about your mother, Jack? You haven't said much about her."

"My mother had her fill of my father. She divorced him when I was ten. I lived with her until I went away to college. What about your folks?"

"My mother didn't have time for me. I remember her shaking her finger at me and saying, 'Shame, shame.' I felt as if I were just a bother to her, and, my parents fought all the time. My dad drank a lot too. I worried about them all the time. I spent half my life at Anna's house, but I've finally dealt with my anger towards my folks. Anna helped me see things about them. Now, I know they did the best they could, and things didn't always go right for them either. I needed to forgive and honor them as my parents. That's what Anna said. My friend, Ruby, said that all those old memories were nothing but ghosts that haunted me. I feel free now."

"Do you think our parents would have corrected their mistakes if they had realized what they were doing?" Jack asked.

"Yes. I think they would have."

"I hated my father's drinking, but I hated them getting a divorce more," Jack said. "What about your parents? Did they stay together?"

"My folks may have been unhappy with each other, but according to Anna, as German Russians, you stay together no matter what! You stick with your own kind, and you don't divorce."

"Gee, I've never talked about any of this before. Thanks." Jack touched Marka lightly on the hand and gazed into her teary eyes. "Look at all the stars. There must be a billion," Jack said, making things seem happier.

"Look, a falling star," Marka gasped. She playfully slapped his arm. "Make a wish." Marka closed her eyes and made her wish. She wished Jack didn't have to leave Ridley next week. She thought how the falling star appeared from nowhere, just like Jack had that night she sat on the porch with George, then how quickly the star vanished, just like Jack would, for he'd be going back to Florida to his job, to his life.

After Jack went back to George's, Marka stayed awake and thought about things. She and Jack had talked for hours about their childhoods. It bothered her that Jack didn't know his father the way she did. His childhood memories were of a father who was drunk and absent; a father who worked all the time and didn't take him fishing. The George she knew was different. He was caring and patient and certainly did not put work ahead of spending time with people. And, he wasn't judgmental. He accepted people the way they were. He had a handle on life and knew how to cope, and, he hadn't had anything to drink in ten years. That said a lot.

She felt as though she knew more about George than his own son did. Jack seemed surprised when she told him how his father had always wanted to be a professional baseball player.

"Your father told me he was a good hitter, but his father wouldn't let him sign up with a team when they offered a spot. He insisted that he stay and work in the family butcher shop."

Jack didn't know that his grandfather was a cruel, abusive man. George also told her that he married a cold, abusive woman, but she didn't tell that part to Jack. So, why don't we ask our parents about their shattered dreams? Marka wondered. Why don't parents tell their children more about their lives?

CHAPTER 26

August thirtieth would be the last night of the dog races at the Black Hills Kennel Club. George came into the cafe and asked Marka if she would like to go with him and Jack while the races were still running. "He's getting tired of going fishing and listening to the radio with me."

They drove to Rapid City to the Greyhound track. Marka stepped up to the pari-mutuel window and put two dollars down. She bet the third race, number eight. It was a long shot, but she ended up winning $25. She told Jack she would use the money to take him to a fancy dinner club the last night of his visit.

The next morning in the cafe, Millie told her that she was becoming the topic of conversation. "Buddy gets up and leaves whenever someone starts to talk about you and this Jack fellow," Millie said. "What's going on with you and this guy anyway?"

After Marka got off work at the cafe, she went to see Ruby. She ran up the wooden steps to Ruby's apartment. Ruby opened the door and pulled Marka inside. "Fedora is not herself today. I'm afraid she will fly right out the door."

Ruby had Fedora wrapped in a towel and held tightly against her chest. "She's sick, I think. She's making sneezing noises. Every time I place her on the hot water bottle, she goes wild. I don't know what else to do for her." Ruby held the bird tighter. "Where have you been lately, Mia? You haven't been over for a couple of weeks."

"Ruby, the most wonderful thing has happened. George Hanson's son, Jack, has been here for a visit, and I'm crazy about him. I just can't get my head out of the clouds."

"Do you hear music that no one else hears," Ruby laughed.

"Yes!"

"You are smitten. You've got stars in your eyes."

"It's the way his hair falls over his forehead and the way he pushes it back with his fingers, the way he closes his eyes when he laughs. I love his nose, his chin..."

"He sounds wonderful," Ruby held Fedora tight against her chest and stroked the bird's head with her finger. "Poor Fedora, it will be all right."

"Millie said there's gossip going around about Jack and me."

"So what? I thought you didn't care what other people think."

"I've made so many dumb mistakes when it comes to men. Guess I'm just scared."

"Don't be so worried about making a mistake. Go for your hopes and dreams. Be alive."

"I do feel differently when I'm with Jack. I'm not afraid to tell him things. Remember when you told me that I won't share who I really am. Well, I do that with him. And, in telling him, I understand myself more. Ruby, I am beginning to feel like I really know who I am, and I can trust who I am."

"You are different. Your voice is softer. You don't seem angry anymore and you have stopped feeling sorry for yourself. Fedora even likes you better," Ruby laughed.

"Good. I like myself too. Ruby, I have to face that Jack will soon be leaving to go back to Florida. Anna will be glad. The other day she told me, 'Jack will be going soon; besides, he's not one of us, not a German Russian.' The only way I can get her to stop is by saying that neither is Jonny, and if I had to marry a German Russian, then Bodie would be the most likely candidate. She didn't laugh when I said that. I don't like being disrespectful to her."

"Is standing up for yourself being disrespectful? I don't think it is. Aren't you just defending yourself?"

"You're right, Ruby. Thanks for being such a good friend."

"So, what is going on with you and Stella? Have you finally got Buddy out of your blood?"

"Yes." Marka told Ruby about Rex and how he scared Earl off. "He told me he sent a letter, but I never received it. I never received the letter Jonny sent either. When I asked Stella, she raged at me. I decided to drop the whole thing."

"So, Stella sending that letter to the dead letter office was doing you a favor," Ruby roared.

Thursday night, Marka and Jack went to the drive-in theater. When Jack picked her up, Anna reminded them to leave early, because it was family night. "That means you pay by the car and not the person," she said.

At dusk, the movie started. Marka slid over to the middle of the seat on the pretext that Jack wouldn't have to turn the speaker so loud. The movie, The Vintage, subtitled, "When the Time is Ripe for Love," starred Pier Angela and Michele Morgan. Ida had told her that morning at the cafe, "The movie is about an innocent girl and a fugitive caught in the madness of the vintage season."

Marka couldn't concentrate on the movie. The smell of Jack's aftershave teased her nose. She was glad when he moved closer and put his arm across the back of the seat. Then, he touched his cheek against hers. It was so soft, like a feather brushing across her skin.

His lips found hers, and she felt her stomach fill with butterflies. He hugged her tight, and Marka held him, not wanting to let go. Was this feeling love? Would the feeling stick, no matter what happened? Their kisses continued into the night, and when the movie was over, they drove back to Ridley. Jack turned the radio to KOMA - Oklahoma City. He sang along with the song playing, "I've got a gal and Marka is her name."

Jack's two-week visit with his father had finally come to an end. For Marka, the dreaded day arrived; Jack was leaving in the morning. She phoned George's and reminded Jack that she had promised to take him to the supper club in Clayton. She would use the money she won at the dog races.

They decided to have an early supper and spend their last night together watching the sun go down at the river. It had been one of the places where they spent much time together: fishing with George and just the two of them, sitting on the bank, talking.

Marka put on her white linen sheath and pointed pumps. She brushed her hair and let it fall loose around her shoulders. She penciled in her eyebrows to make them look thicker and put on eyeliner. She wore the hoop earrings and white shawl, both gifts from Ruby.

Jack reached across the table and touched Marka's hand. He looked handsome in his gray tweed jacket. "You look beautiful, he said. "Remember the day you told me about Ruby piercing your ears?"

"Yes, in fact, these are the earrings she gave me. I don't know what this means, but she said that I shouldn't ask her where she got them," Marka giggled. "Do you think that means she stole them?"

Jack took a small velvet box from his inside coat pocket and handed it to Marka. "Open it."

Marka opened the box and inside was a pair of Black Hills Gold earrings for pierced ears. "Jack, they are the most beautiful things I have ever seen. I am going to go to the ladies' room and put them on."

"I thought about ordering a bottle of champagne in a bucket of ice," Jack said. "I decided against it."

"I appreciate that. Thank you, Jack."

After dinner, they drove back to Ridley. Marka sat in the middle and snuggled close to Jack. When they reached the river, they parked on the other side of the bridge and walked down the well-worn path that led to the water. The sky looked like it was on fire, the pink, flaming orange, and gold stripes of the sunset reflected on the water. The water rippled and moved slowly along the riverbank, and it seemed as though it whispered.

Jack put his arm around her shoulders. They stood silently until the sun went down, and then, Jack spread a blanket under the cottonwood trees, and they sat there and waited for the sky to fill with stars. Something that looked like a neon light darted out of the thick grass blades. "What was that?" Jack stood up.

"It's a fire fly. Haven't you ever seen one?"

"No."

"When I was a kid, we use to catch them and put them in a jar."

"In downtown Chicago, where I grew up, we didn't have such things." Jack sat back down on the blanket and hugged Marka close to his side.

"I guess I was lucky to have grown up here. We use to catch grasshoppers and hold them between our fingers to watch them spit."

"You're kidding. They actually spit!" Jack laughed. "Sounds like you were a tomboy. Wait until I tell Dad that story."

Marka became quiet. "He's going to miss you, Jack. He's really been happy since you've been here."

"I know. I'm glad I came. Really glad I came." He cupped Marka's face in his hands and gazed into her eyes. "I'm glad I came back to see my dad. We had a good visit and I got to meet you. I've had this gnawing in the pit of my stomach for the last few days. I don't want to leave, Marka. I love you. I love you so much, I ache inside." Jack gently took Marka's hand and put it against his chest. "Feel my heart. It's pounding."

Marka nuzzled her head into his chest and wrapped her arms around his neck. "I never showed you one of my favorite spots," she said. "We could walk from here. The sky is glorious with stars tonight."

"Good. I was hoping you wouldn't want to go home yet," Jack said.

"I don't want the evening to end either." She caught hold of his arm and gave him a quick kiss.

"Do you love me?" Jack asked, his eyes deep and serious.

"I think I do," she answered.

They walked the short distance to Marka's spot under the willows. Jack spread the blanket. The black dome of the sky was filled with stars close enough to touch. Marka sat down and pulled her legs underneath her. Jack untied his tie and loosened the button of his shirt, and let the tie dangle loose around his neck. He put his arm around her. Marka loved to feel Jack holding her. He leaned close and kissed her eyelids, then her lips. The kiss felt dangerous and forbidden, but she let herself relax, and her body melted into his. They kissed, and his hands were hungry to touch every part of her body. Marka wanted Jack to keep his lips pressed to hers forever. Jack rolled close to her and laid one leg between hers. Her heart pounded; her mind told her to stop.

Jack unbuttoned the back of her dress and slid it down to her waist. He kissed her bare shoulders, her neck, and her breasts. There was the faint hoot of an owl, a rustle in the tall grass. Their passion grew. They could not stop until their desire for one another was fulfilled. They lay nestled together, silent.

Suddenly, dawn was all around them. The tree branches above their heads danced in the light breeze that blew softly across their bodies. Their glorious night together had come to an end. It was a new day. They would say their parting words and Jack would be leaving. Marka pushed the thought from her mind.

"I feel differently than I have ever felt in my entire life," Jack said, running his finger across her lips. "All my life I've looked for something real. I feel like I finally found it."

"I'm a little confused...yet...I feel at peace with the world," Marka said.

Marka watched the branches overhead. She thought of Jack being George's son. George told her that when he was a young man, he thought he had all the answers to life. Then, as he got older, the truth was he knew very little and could only guess when it came to figuring out people and happenings. Would she ever see Jack again, she wondered?

"This may sound corny, but I feel like I finally found someone who touched my soul," Jack whispered. Marka wondered if she would ever feel this way again. In the silence of the early morning, all she cared about was the feel of Jack's body pressed close to hers.

In a soft voice, he asked, "Are you my girl?"

She said, "Yes."

In the days that followed, Marka felt without direction. She felt a lack of motivation and desire. A part of her felt missing. How could she go on without him? Every time she closed her eyes, she saw his face. It made her heart feel light, but, he wasn't real anymore; she couldn't touch him. He could only be in her memories. Tears streamed down her face and her heart felt heavy. The whole thing seemed so unfair—to be touched by someone in a special way and then to have them gone from your life.

CHAPTER 27

The September sun was strong. It scorched the tall prairie grass and pastures that spread across the flatlands, turning it a golden brown. Threshing crews showed up, and the combines cut wheat. Farmers cut their hay and laid it down in windrows across the fields. They bound their corn into bunches and bragged that they produced more bushels per acre than ever before, filling cribs with the tawny golden ears. The harvest was nearing completion, and the calves were put into the feedlots.

On September twenty-six, the sugar beet receiving stations opened. Farmers started bringing in loads of sugar beets. Trucks loaded with beets rolled into town and roared down the hill, headed for the beet dump. They drove onto the platform beside the one-room scale house and dumped their load. The silver white roots tumbled onto the huge berm alongside the railroad tracks. The train made its daily pick up of beets. The sound of the whistle and the clicking wheels were heard as it rolled through town.

It was autumn, but it felt more like spring. Indian summer, one last warm spell after the first September frost would hold back winter. It would last through most of October, maybe even as late as November, turning the cottonwoods to hues of brilliant gold. For now, the gardens were resting from their summer's work. Some geese were already heading south for the winter. The young ones seemed unhurried, never having been south before. They filled their bellies with the corn left in the fields. Once fed, they rose off the land, honking, and gracefully flapping their wings. Hunters were waiting for October when pheasant, duck, and goose hunting would begin. For now, they were hunting antelope; the season had opened mid-month.

Early Monday morning, Marka went to the cafe to do the baking. By 8:00 p.m., Main Street was lively with cars and trucks, parents driving their children to school. The school bus brought the country kids to town. Marka watched as children walked by the cafe carrying their school books. She thought about Jonny and how she had not seen him in weeks. Anna said he picked up his shirts Sunday morning and said to tell her that he had been busy with his football team, and he wanted to ask her whether she would help him chaperone the homecoming dance.

"And he wanted to know if you would have time to help some of the kids work on the floats for the parade," Anna said.

Marka felt disappointed that Jonny was always so busy he couldn't tell her himself.

Millie told Marka to close the cafe early. "Ida needs to go to Clayton to buy shoes. She is in the glee club and needs black shoes to wear with her black gown."

Marka closed the cafe but didn't feel like going home; so she walked to the river. She went down the hill, walked the well-worn path of stomped weeds. She walked until she reached the spot where she and Jack spent their last night together. She sat on the grass and pulled her knees under her chin. The suns' rays peeked through the trees and shone on a spider weaving its web in the tall grass.

Her heart ached for Jack. Would she ever see him again? If not, those two weeks of happiness would have to do. She never felt this way before. She gave up Rex without a struggle, what she felt for Buddy was confusing and wrong, and Jonny seemed more like a friend. Finally, she found someone, not bound to someone else but free to love her.

Life plays mean tricks. Tears streamed out of the corners of her closed eyes. They felt hot against her cheeks. Each time she walked past George's house, she thought of Jack. She wondered how George was feeling. She couldn't get it out of her head how the George she knew was so different from George—the father—Jack talked about. Jack said he was rigid and selfish. That's not how she saw him. He was always open to new ideas and very caring. He always had time for her; he was always glad to see her any time she dropped in on him. Bodie, Buddy, and Herb, all told her they thought her father was the greatest guy in the world. Maybe it boils down to this: children and parents never really get to know each other the way they should. Maybe that's how it is between Jack and George.

Marka thought how selfish she had been about not helping Ida with the wool suit for the contest. Anna and Ida made a red, two-piece with an extra long jacket, and Ida had won second place. First place was a trip to the national finals in Phoenix, courtesy of F.W. Woolworth. The first place winner in Phoenix would go on a two-week trip to Europe.

"Ida had her heart set on winning and, I let her down," Marka chided herself, and Anna had no sympathy towards her blues over Jack. "I warned you this would happen," she said. The only comforting thought Marka had was that she had sweet memories of a brief romance with someone she loved and who said he loved her.

Tuesday morning, sparrows and blackbirds chattered outside her bedroom window. It sounds like a war going on. They're probably fighting over food and territory, Marka said to herself. Oh, who knew what birds argued about anyway?

She got out of bed and watched the birds from her window. A blackbird swooped down and flapped his wings at two sparrows that were pecking at something in the grass. The sparrows flew away. Then, the blackbird flew away. The sparrows returned, and again, the blackbird was back. Who decides who's in charge? Why do the sparrows fly away when the blackbird comes? Marka groaned. She felt irritable and sick. Her stomach had been upset for days. If Millie offered her Sala Padica one more time, she would scream.

"Oh, no, I'm going to be sick," Marka cried and ran to the bathroom.

"He's always here the same time of day. You could set your clock by him," Millie whispered in Marka's ear as she was clearing the counter of dirty dishes.

"How are you today, Clarence?" Marka asked.

"People think I have one foot in the grave, but they don't know what the hell they're talking about." The grooves around his mouth deepened. "Ever since I had that stroke, they think I'm worse off than I really am." Clarence pulled on his goatee. "I got a bad ticker, a little erratic, but I'm going to be around for a long time. Maybe that's what worries them," he laughed.

Clarence took off his brown felt hat, laid it on the stool next to him, and put his old hickory walking stick down on the floor beside his stool. He always wore a long-sleeved shirt buttoned to the collar, and he carried a couple of Old Stogie cigars in the shirt pocket. "Life is what you make of it, and what you make it is up to you," he said.

Marka chuckled. "You having the usual?"

Clarence tipped his head to one side and smiled.

Marka filled a cup with coffee and slipped two jelly donuts onto his plate. "Don't tell Millie I gave you an extra." Marka laughed, knowing it was a game she and Millie played with Clarence. Millie gave Clarence an extra helping of whatever he ordered. She told Marka to keep filling his coffee cup until he had his fill. Marka thought about how Millie always gave the Ellis kids an extra large scoop of ice cream. Millie is a good person. She just has a problem with men. Maybe we are birds of a feather.

Anna's garden was on its way to seed and the last of the crops needed picking. She had a bumper crop this year, way too much to can. Marka asked if she could take Clarence some vegetables. Clarence lived in a tarpaper shack on the edge of town. She wanted to clean his house and do his laundry. "Doesn't anyone care how he's living?" she asked Anna. But Anna said, "Just leave it alone. You worry too much about other people, like you are always worrying about Bodie. Sometimes you have to just let things be. Take Clarence some food, but stay out of his house. He might try something with you."

"Hey, girlie," Clarence motioned to Marka. "Ever wonder why that mail lady always keeps that dog of hers in the post office with her?" Clarence cocked his head back and put his thumb under his suspender strap.

"Why?" Marka leaned close, and then backed away a little, the smell of cigar smoke in his greasy hair made her feel nauseous.

"She's afraid he'll disappear again. I kept that damn mutt locked up in my garage once for three days. Kept coming around pissing on my spirea bushes. Fixed its little ass."

Marka thought back to the night Anna took her to her first Ladies' Aid meeting. Stella was upset that her dog was missing. Marka laughed and laughed. She laughed so hard she had to go back into the bakery room.

At 10:00 a.m. the cafe was noisy. Farmers were talking about the fall round up, saying it was time to cut out the fattened animals and ship them to slaughter. They were anxious to see whether the new beet seed would produce the high sugar yield that it was supposed to.

"Antelope season opens today," George said, folding the newspaper in half. "Hunters will be invading the whole area."

Henry Morganson sat down at the counter next to George. "Course most hunters will get their kill the first few days if it's like past years," he said.

"Listen to this," George said reading from the *Clayton Post*. "The air force announced that it will set up its first intercontinental guided missile squadron late this year. The squadron will be equipped with Snark missiles. And, get this; a Russian airliner landed at McGuire Air Force Base after a 5,570-mile flight from Moscow. It was the first Russian plane to land on American soil since World War II, and it was carrying twenty-four cases of vodka and employees of the Russian delegation to the United Nations."

Henry laughed and asked, "Are we going to shoot them down or get drunk with them?"

"Oh, Marka, honey, you look white as a ghost," Millie poured George and Henry more coffee. "She's sick again," Millie said to George.

"A little early for the flu," George said, concerned.

"You better go to the doctor," Millie said. "I'm worried about you."

"I made an appointment with Doc Sellers."

"For when?" Millie asked.

"Monday morning. I was going to see if you could get someone to help you out in the cafe."

"Don't wait. You're sick as a dog," Millie insisted. "You take my car, and go to Clayton."

"But, I haven't got an appointment. I can't just walk in."

"Then, call right now. Tell them you can't wait until Monday. You look awful. Don't fool around with this, Marka. My Aunt Thelma, was all right one day and dead the next. She had spinal meningitis."

"Millie," Marka shuddered. "Don't scare me like that."

"Then, call the doctor's office."

Marka filled out the health history form the nurse gave her. The nurse scanned the paper with a suspicious eye, occasionally looking up at Marka. She handed Marka a glass jar and said, "Take this to the ladies' room and urinate in it. Bring it back to me when you're through."

After Marka did as she was told, the nurse led her to an examination room, took her blood pressure, and told her to take off all her clothes. "Put this on," the nurse said and tossed Marka a faded, turquoise cotton gown. "When was your last menstrual cycle?"

"I can't remember. My periods aren't regular. Sometimes I go a couple of months without having one."

"Are your breasts tender?"

Marka pushed the tips of her fingers against her breast. "They do feel a little tight."

"Doc Sellers will be in when he's finished with his other patient," the nurse said.

Doc examined Marka. He looked into her eyes, her throat, and felt her neck. He told her to lie on the examination table, and then pushed on her breasts and stomach. He adjusted his glasses, and then wrote something in Marka's chart.

Marka had only been to Doc Sellers, their family doctor a couple of times. First, there was the time she had an accident with her bicycle and sprained her elbow. He made a sling for her to wear. The time she had poison ivy on her face, he gave her some terrible green liquid to rub on the blisters. She always liked him. He had a way of making her feel at ease.

"I would like to have a couple of blood tests done," he said. "There was a case of polio reported—a ten year old boy who had not received inoculations."

"Do you think I have polio?"

"No," Doc Sellers laughed. I guess I just had it on my mind."

"Then why the blood tests?"

"It's just a precautionary thing. Don't worry," he said patting her on the arm. "I'm going to check a few things I think it could be."

The following Wednesday afternoon, Millie told Marka to go home early. They had been busy at the cafe with more than the usual farmers having breakfast, visiting, and waiting for the mail. "I'm still feeling a little nauseous," Marka told Millie.

Anna brought a loaf of fresh baked rye bread over to Marka. "It's not cooled all the way, but you like the heel. Here, I'll cut it for you."

Marka hugged Anna. "You always remember I love the heels. You are the sweetest person in the world, but I just don't feel like eating, Anna."

"I brought you the paper," Anna handed Marka the *Clayton Post*. "Look, the wool grower's parade is this Saturday, in Garrison. Wouldn't it be fun to go? Ida will be riding on one of the floats."

Marka read from the paper. "Saturday, October fifth merchants are invited to enter floats in the parade. Floats will show the various phases of the "Make It With Wool Contest". The theme is—what wool means to the tri-state area."

The telephone rang. Marka answered and listened carefully as the nurse said, "Doc Sellers would like to see you in his office as soon as possible."

"Well, yes. Is there something wrong?"

"No, nothing serious. It hasn't been long enough to see if the rabbit died, but Doc Sellers is pretty sure you are going to have a baby."

"What?"

"You're going to have a baby."

Marka hung up the phone. She felt dizzy and hot. A baby! She was going to have a baby?

She lay down on the couch, and stared at the ceiling trying to think of something to take her mind off the thought of a baby. When she was a kid, she used to pretend she was walking on the ceiling. She would have to step over the stovepipe. A baby? No! Back to thinking about the ceiling. She'd walk towards the dining room where the molding would be ankle height and then she would have to lift her foot high in order to step over the arched wall between the two rooms. She was going to have a baby? She felt frightened, then happy. She started to cry. Me and Jack. Marka wiped away the tears that had collected along her chin. She lay still and focused on the big black spider that was slowly edging along the windowsill trying not to be noticed.

Anna came into the living room, noticed the spider also, picked up the newspaper, and swatted it. It rolled into a ball and fell on the floor. "You can tell fall is here, because the spiders want to come inside," Anna said. "So, Marka, who was on the phone?"

"I have this way of messing up my life," Marka said. "Just when I think I have things figured out." She sat up on the couch and pulled her sweater down over her hips. "It was Doc Seller's nurse."

"What is it? Something serious?"

"Yes, it's serious. I'm okay. I'm not sick," Marka stammered. Marka pulled her knees to her chin and hugged them tight against her. "Guess there's only one way to say this. Anna, I'm going to have a baby."

"Oh, my Gott. You're in the family way."

"How could I let this happen? Just so you know right off, Jack is the father."

"Ach, Gott, Marka. Don't worry now. It will be all right. Just don't tell anyone. If you let it out that you are going to have a baby, it will be like opening up a pillowcase full of duck feathers. The gossip will fly all over this town."

Marka's face grew pale. "I could go to a home. I could say I'm moving back to Denver. I'll leave before I start to show. No one will ever have to know. I'm going to have to leave Ridley for sure this time, Anna. It's the only way."

"No, *madchen*. Well, now, let me think. Yah, it will be all right. This is the kind of news that gets out though." Anna unhooked the wires of her glasses from around her ears and wiped the tears with the corner of her apron.

"Why are you crying, Anna?"

"I'm crying because it brings back much of my own pain. Well, you know the story." Anna closed her eyes and took a deep breath. "You can't leave, you and I are family. We stick together."

Marka went for a long walk. She smelled chimney smoke and burning leaves. October started out cool and crisp. The blaring sun of summer was gone, and now the sky was overcast, covered with smoky gray clouds. Grass poked through the layers of wet brown and yellow leaves. There had been a frost during the night, which meant the end of summer.

Marka pressed her hands against her belly and thought about how happy she felt. Anna convinced her to stay in Ridley and have the baby.

"Where else would you go?"

"But people will talk. "I've let you down, haven't I?"

"No. We will get through this together. I don't care anymore what people think. Are you going to tell Jack? What about George?"

Marka thought of the passion she and Jack had felt for each other the night before he left. "It wasn't a cheap fling, Anna. I care for him in a way I have never cared for any man. Yes, I'm going to tell George."

That afternoon, Marka went to see George. She walked slowly across George's front yard. What would he think of her? Would he think she was a tramp? Oh, God, please let him understand. In a few months, her belly would swell; she would outgrow her jeans. There would be no hiding it from anyone.

Marka knocked on the screen door. "George, George."

George hollered for her to come in. He was listening to the radio and rolling cigarettes.

"Come sit down," George waved his arms towards her. "Where have you been? Sit down here." He patted the chair next to the radio. "Mind if I listen to the rest of Paul Harvey? He's talking about the Soviet firing of Sputnik. He said Dulles issued a new warning to Russia. The U.S. will retaliate against the Russian homeland if Russia wages war in the Mideast. We got to constantly be on guard, Dulles said." George sprinkled Bull Durham tobacco on the tissue paper and rolled it tight. He licked one side and pinched it together.

Marka sat in the chair next to George's rocker and tried to listen to the rest of Paul Harvey, but her thoughts were of the baby and what George would say when she told him.

"They made a 500-pound birthday cake for President Eisenhower. A five tier creation frosted with his favorite, yellow roses." George lit the cigarette he had rolled. "And—good day to you, Paul," George laughed and turned off the radio. "So, what do you think of that? Russians keep pushing for more."

"Anna always tells me to be quiet about our Russian heritage."

"Maybe she's right. Not to scare you, but we are always at war with them. So, what you been up to lately?" George asked. "How's the bakery going?"

"It's doing very well. Millie's been doing most of it, because I've been busy helping Anna with the last of the canning. Marka reminded herself she had to tell George, but the words wouldn't come. "Bodie and I went to the sawmill in Deerfield to get wood for the cook stoves, a load for Anna, and one for me. We had to sort and stack it."

"I'd have helped if you had asked."

"Bodie helped. You do so much for Anna and me, George."

"Looks like we're going to have one heck of a football team this year," George picked up the newspaper. "Read where Ridley beat Garrison 73 to 42. Jonny's got a good bunch of boys to work with this year. That Raymond Brieson is a fast runner. Say, how about going to a football game with me sometime?"

"Sounds fun."

She had to tell him now! Marka felt butterflies in her stomach. She rubbed her temples. She had a headache, because she had stayed awake half the night, worrying about what George would think. While eating breakfast, she heard the wild geese flying over and they inspired her. She listened to them beat their wings and cry out their honking sounds. She thought about how George told her once that as soon as there was a shortage of food in the fields, the birds would make their annual fall trip to their wintering ground. The flocks would form into V formations and begin their southward flight. Those geese had given her an idea. This was how she would explain it all to George.

"So, you and Anna been acting like a couple of squirrels, storing up for winter," George laughed.

"George, there's something I have to talk to you about." Marka crossed and uncrossed her ankles. That morning she rehearsed the speech over and over, but now the words had completely gone out of her head. Her mind felt empty.

"George, have you ever thought what it would be like to be a grandfather?" Marka felt a knot in her throat. "Having a little fishing buddy?"

"I've come to know you pretty well over the months, and I've developed a healthy respect for you. I can tell by the tone of your voice that something serious is going on," George said.

"George, remember when we were fishing down at the river, and we heard the wild geese? They were flying over, and you told me they were on their way to Canada. You said they would nest, breed, then raise their family there."

"Yes, that's how it works." He said, and a smile began to take over his face. He sat patiently and waited for her to finish her speech.

"I really liked the part about how they stay together, how they don't mate with another bird, just the one they've chosen. And even when one of them dies, the other never mates again." Marka felt like she was delivering a speech in biology. The gnawing pain in the pit of her stomach grew stronger.

"You and Jack are getting married?" George gasped. "So, that's why all this talk about geese."

Marka was quiet. She got out of her chair and stood close to George. "I don't know about the married part. We are going to have a baby." Her cheeks grew hot. She touched her belly. "There's a baby growing in here, Grandpa."

"George got out of the chair and hugged Marka. "My son will do the right thing. You've told him, right?"

"I'm going to write him a letter tonight. I haven't heard from him since he left, have you?" Marka asked.

"No, but I didn't expect to," George said. "Things didn't improve that much between us during the time he was here."

"It's my fault," Marka said. "I spent too much time with him; time he should have spent with you."

"No, that's not it." George sat back down in his chair. "You can't change the past just by changing yourself. The old memories are still there for other people."

"I wish Jack knew you like I do, and, I want to know more about Jack. What was he like as a kid?

"I'm sorry, Marka, I can't tell you much. I was too busy working and drinking to notice." George hung his head. "I have a lot of guilt over it."

CHAPTER 28

Occasionally, Marka would look up at the blue sky and watch the leaves dancing on the branches of the cottonwood trees. The gold speckled leaves shimmered in the breeze, the sunlight magnifying their beauty. She held the envelope containing the letter she wrote to Jack tight in her hands. She would go to the café, tuck herself in the corner of a booth, and read it one more time before she mailed it.

The cafe smelled of coffee and bacon frying. Marka made herself a strawberry milkshake and told Ida to add it to her tab. Then, she tucked herself into the corner of the booth and spread the letter out on the table. The night before she turned off all the lights and lit a candle. In the shadows of candlelight, she wrote the letter to Jack.

Marka wrote that, at first, she had doubts about having a child when she had just begun to discover herself. She said that when she thought about the baby inside her, it made her feel like she was experiencing new growth in her life. Her past anger that caused her to feel that everything was wrong with the world, and the fear, which told her that nothing she ever did was right, had slowly faded away. She wrote Jack that she would be giving birth to a baby, and the baby would be giving rebirth to her. She ended the letter with, "Do you feel the same way?"

She stabbed a straw through the strawberry shake and swirled it around. She read the last paragraph of the letter. "The days seem endless since you've gone. Mostly, I just sit and stare. Everything seems wrong. I go places we've been. Your face haunts all my dreams." Sounds corny! I can't rewrite this again, Marka whispered to herself.

Ida came over to the booth and sat down. "Did you get bad news in a letter, Marka? You look so serious."

Marka decided that no one would know about the baby except for Anna, George, and Ruby. She wanted to tell Ruby, and Anna said she wouldn't mind if she did, if she was sure she could trust her. She couldn't tell Ida and certainly wouldn't tell Millie. Ever since Millie ran off with Rex, Marka felt a loss of confidence in her. There was one thing she learned about Millie: you couldn't trust her. A great deal of Millie's life hung on finding a man to marry, and Marka had learned not to be surprised by anything Millie decided to do. "I'm just looking over this letter I wrote before I mail it," Marka said.

"I'll leave you alone then," Ida said getting up out of the booth.

"Thanks, Ida."

Marka mused about Jack: his smooth face and the clean smell of his aftershave. She felt excited when she remembered the tender kisses and comforting hugs. She thought about their last evening together, dinner at the supper club, the earrings, and the river. There had been chemistry between them, not a frivolous passion. She felt sure the love between them was real, and, the answer to this letter would let her know if Jack felt the same way, if he had the kind of love for her that would stick.

The cash register rang and the drawer sprung open. Ida took a quarter and plugged the jukebox. "Marka, there's the big sugar beet dance over in Garrison tonight. Wanna go?"

"No thanks." Marka slurped the last of her milkshake.

"You don't like going places with Millie anymore, do you?"

"I'm just not into dances these days." Marka thought about the baby and how she was going to be a mother. Now, going to dances was out of the question. Besides, she had more important things to think about, like Jack, marriage and a home for the baby. She had a purpose to her life.

"That's right," Ida said. "You've been sick. Are you feeling any better?"

"Yes, much better. Thanks, Ida. Well, I've got to get this letter to the post office. It's already 10:30 a.m; so this probably won't go out in today's mail." Marka ran her tongue along the glue on the envelope and pressed the flap with her thumb. The milkshake made her queasy stomach feel better.

When Marka got to the post office, Stella was sweeping the floor, and Bodie was unloading mail sacks from the delivery truck. Marka turned the combination on her mailbox. There was a bill from the Black Hills Power and Light Company and a green slip for a package. Marka closed the box and walked over to the teller's window. She slipped the letter she had written to Jack into the mail slot.

Bodie was stacking canvas mailbags in the corner of the room. Marka heard Stella reprimand him. "What an asinine thing to do, you stupid cluckhead. Why did you say that to Henry? It makes people think that I open their mail and read it."

Marka heard Bodie say to Stella, "I see you reading post cards."

"If you start shooting your mouth off, I could lose my job. Worse yet, I could get sent to prison. I've never opened anyone's mail and read it." Marka saw Stella shove Bodie, and he hit his shoulder on the wall.

"Stella, how awful! Stop that! You stop pushing Bodie around."

"Oh, it's just you. Don't stick your nose where it isn't wanted," Stella's voice was cold.

"I have a package to pick up," Marka laid the green slip of paper on the cold metal counter under the teller's gate.

Stella walked to the back of the room where the larger parcels were kept.

"Psst, Bodie, come over here," Marka whispered.

Bodie came to the window.

Marka's complexion was white and her nostrils flared. "Why do you let Stella treat you that way?"

Stella walked back to the window. "Bodie, get back to work. Here's your package. From Spiegel's, huh?" She lifted the gate and slid the package underneath. There was no remorse in her eagle-gray eyes.

"I need to talk to Bodie about something." Marka stood straight, hugging the package.

"He's supposed to be sorting the mail for me. Talk to him when he's not on work time." Stella sneered and slammed the gate down hard.

"Stella, it will only take a few minutes. I need to talk to him now!"

Stella relented. She called for Bodie to come up front, and then she walked to the back of the room.

"Bodie, you still want to buy my house?" Marka whispered through the gate.

"Yes."

"After supper come over to Anna's so we can talk."

Bodie's smile widened and his eyes flashed. "Okay. Okay. After supper," he said in an excited, hushed voice.

Marka went over to Anna's at 4:00 p.m. She was making *wurst,* German garlic sausage. She untangled long, opaque casings that had thawed out in a dishpan of salt water. She blew one open, stretched it onto the metal nozzle, then turned the handle to fill the casings with a mixture of beef, pork, salt and pepper, and lots of garlic. "Get the string and scissors over there on the table," Anna said turning the handle of the sausage stuffer.

"I did it," Marka said. "I mailed the letter to Jack telling him about our baby, and, I talked to George last night. He seemed happy about it—I really think he is, Anna."

Anna washed her hands and dried them on her apron, then took a hanky from the pocket, lifted her glasses, and wiped her eyes.

"You're crying. I thought you'd be glad to hear this."

Anna sat down at the table. "Yah, I am." She blew her nose and shuffled her feet under the chair.

"I stayed up half the night writing a letter to Jack. George says he is sure Jack will do the right thing. Don't cry, Anna. Everything will work out."

"I'm crying because I am happy, that's all," Anna folded the handkerchief into a perfect little square and put it back in her apron pocket. All I ever wanted was to see you happily married with children. She picked up the brown paper package from the table. "What is this?"

"A dress I ordered from Spiegel's catalog. I was going to wear it to the homecoming dance that Jonny asked me to chaperone with him. I ordered it before I knew about the baby. I will send it back."

"Yah, Jonny is pretty much out of the picture now, huh?" Anna said.

"We were just friends anyway, Anna. Oh, Anna, guess what else I did? I told Bodie that I would sell him my house. I thought about what you said about me living by myself in the house during the winter, and you're right. It wouldn't be a good idea. Besides, Jack will probably want to live in Florida after we are married. It would be best to sell the house right now if I could. I won't abandon it again."

"Are you sure that's what you want to do? What about what your mother said, something in the house. You haven't found it yet, have you? Ach, what am I saying? You do what you have to. How are you feeling today?" Anna asked as she gently laid her hand on Marka's tummy."

"Anna, there wasn't anything in the house. I don't know what Mom was talking about. I would have found it by now. Besides, I can't think of anyone I would want to have the house more than Bodie. He has to get away from his dad and Stella. I hate the way she treats him." Marka held up her hand. "Don't tell me to stay out of it, Anna."

"Yah, now I know Stella has a cold heart. There's no tenderness in her."

"Anna, I'm glad we don't argue about Stella anymore."

"How about a piece of cake?" Anna walked over to the cupboard to get plates.

"Anna, you're always feeding me."

"Yah, and, now you're eating for two," Anna joked. "So, anyways, George was happy about the baby. Good."

"Yes. Jack and George don't have the best relationship. George told me he made a lot of mistakes in his life. He used to have a bad drinking problem, but he doesn't drink any more. George is a different person now."

Anna set a slice of cake in front of Marka. "Just because he doesn't drink any more doesn't mean he didn't hurt his family. Sometimes, it takes a long time to heal that kind of wound. You know that from your feelings about your dad."

"This is different. George and my father are two different people." Marka put a large piece of cake in her mouth. "I don't care about any of that anyway, Anna. I only care about the baby."

"Marka, you have to be quiet about being in the family way. Don't tell anyone just yet. You know what the people in this town are like.

Marka laughed. "Ruby said that when the women find out, they'll cluck and cackle like a bunch of hens."

CHAPTER 29

The evening was quiet. Anna and Marka ate supper, washed the dishes, then went into the front room and listened to *Fibber McGee and Molly*, one of Anna's favorite programs. After it was over, Anna turned off the radio.

"I don't mean to stick my nose in your business, but don't give the house away to Bodie. He may act stupid, but he's not. Still waters run deep, you know. He's not poor. He gets a government check every month plus what he makes doing odd jobs around town. He lives with his dad, so he doesn't have to put out any money for that. Don't let him swindle you," Anna said.

"I've never been comfortable back in the house," Marka said. "I had to rid myself of things that haunted me in childhood, and now I want to rid myself of the house. Anna, I want to sell, and I want Bodie to buy it. He does have to pay Carl rent. He told me so." Marka leaned her chin on her hand and looked at Anna with determined eyes. "There's something I want you to think about before Bodie gets here. He was in a war; he was shot. The Korean War was about Russia too. It was the North Koreans, and they are communists. Anna, Bodie has something in common with you—he hates the Reds too. Let's give him a break, okay?"

There was a knock on the door, then it opened a crack, and Bodie hollered, "It's Bodie. Come to talk about the house."

Anna got up from her chair and went to the door. "Bodie, not so loud. We don't want the whole town to hear. Come on in."

"Turn on the porch light," Bodie said. "Look what I brought you."

Anna turned on the light and looked outside. There stood Bodie with two pheasants, one in each hand.

"Ach, Gott. What's this?"

"Buddy and I went and got us some pheasants."

"Ach, hunting season hasn't begun," Anna said.

"We shot them right in the neck. Got them with one shot, so they wouldn't be all full of buckshot."

"Yah. Well, lay them somewhere back of the porch and come on in."

After Bodie finished hiding the pheasants, Anna took him by the elbow and pulled him inside the kitchen. "I'll dress them out tomorrow. Maybe make a pheasant potpie and have you over for supper. Looks like we might have something to celebrate. Marka tells me you want to buy her house. Come on in the living room and sit down," Anna motioned to Bodie to sit in the chair close to her. "Marka, you stay comfortable on the sofa."

"Why you want to sell? Bodie asked. "You moving back to Denver?"

"Ach, no. She's moving back in with me," Anna answered.

"Oh." Bodie said.

Anna couldn't help but get down to business. She promised not to stick her nose in, but Marka could see she was going to.

"So, Bodie, why do you want to buy the house?" Anna asked right away.

"My house," Marka quickly added.

Anna waved her hand at Marka, motioning her to be quiet, then pulled herself forward a little in her chair and planted her feet firm on the floor. "Marka says she wants to sell—her," Anna nodded at Marka, "house to you. So, how much you think you ought to pay for this house?" Anna watched Marka out of the corner of her eye.

"I don't have much money, but I want the house real bad," Bodie said, shuffling his feet. "Marka told me a long time ago that if she ever did sell it, it would be to me."

"Yah. Sure. Okay. But, she can't just give it away, you know."

"There's lots of work needs to be done on that house," Bodie groaned.

Marka felt she had to move things along. She'd throw out a number. It was a little like, how George taught her to bait up a hook, and then cast it in the water. She'd see if Bodie was ready to bite. "How about $4,000?" Marka asked.

"Whew. That's a whole lot." Bodie scratched the back of his head.

"I don't think it's enough," Anna piped in.

"Are you including the furniture in that price?" Bodie asked.

"What!" Anna exploded.

"Gee, I hadn't thought of that Bodie. Yes, you will need furniture," Marka said.

"He can always buy himself furniture," Anna said.

Anna is making things too tough on Bodie, Marka thought. Even if they agreed on a price, Bodie may not go through with the deal. He had spent his entire life under his father's roof except for the time he spent in Korea. Carl would probably do everything he could to prevent Bodie from leaving the apartment. After all, who would do the dirty work around the store and post office? Stella will have a fit when she hears about this. He's got to get out on his own. It really is best for Bodie, Marka thought.

"I have $5,000 in my bank account. It's all the money I have. It'll take at least $300 to put on a new roof. That's what it needs, you know." Bodie hung his head. "After the hailstorm, Herb and I really only patched it. I'd have to hire someone, because of my bum hip."

"All right, all right, Bodie." Anna put her hands over her ears and shook her head.

"I really want Bodie to have the house." Marka put her hands on her hips and gave Anna a stern look.

"What would you say to $4,000 including the furniture," Anna blurted. "But, we want the lace curtains in the bedrooms, and some of the special things like the china cabinet my sister kept her cup and saucer collection in—special things like that. But you could have the beds, tables and chairs."

Bodie sat quietly cracking his knuckles, first on one hand and then the other. "I'll give you $3,800 for the house. I don't need all the furniture. You can have an auction. That would give you more money." Bodie sat straight in his chair. His eyes sparkled with satisfaction. "Well, what you say?"

"It's a deal," Marka held out her hand. "Let's shake."

Bodie got up from the chair and strutted over to Marka like a lame bandy rooster. "It's a deal."

"Maybe things are moving kind of fast," Anna said. "Why not sleep on it?"

"No," Marka insisted. "I want to settle this now. Bodie, get your money together. Oh, I'd like to be a fly on the wall when

Stella hears you're moving out of Carl's and into your own house," Marka gloated.

October was a month of excitement for Bodie and Marka. Bodie took on a new look; he walked with his shoulders back, which made him look taller. He told Carl, Stella, and Buddy that he was moving into his own home.

The cafe buzzed with the news about Bodie. Millie placed a big cinnamon roll in front of him and filled his coffee cup. "What did they say when you told them the news?" she prodded.

"Dad said, 'Well you're almost thirty. Maybe you do need a place of your own.' Almost knocked my socks off. Buddy was happy for me, but—Stella. When I told Stella her eyes got as big as saucers." Bodie tossed his head back and stuck out his chin. "I'm as happy as a pig in mud," he laughed.

"Heck. You might even want to get married some day," Millie smiled and batted her eyelashes. "You don't want to be an old bachelor, do you?"

Marka joined their conversation. "Bodie's going to be his own boss from now on. No one is going to order him around and treat him like an errand boy."

Marka felt happy. Jack should have gotten her letter by now, she thought as she packed her parents' clothing into boxes that were going to the church basement to be stored for the Ladies' Aid's next rummage sale. This task she never got around to. Ruby would say that she wasn't ready to do it until she made peace with herself. It felt right tearing the house apart. It's been a long time coming.

There was a sense of urgency that prompted Marka to get to work clearing out her house for the auction. On one side of the room she stacked things that were to be sold. She put special things like her mother's cedar chest filled with crocheted and embroidered things on the other side of the room.

"Yoo—hoo," Anna called from the kitchen.

Marka heard her slowly moving through the rooms, first the kitchen, then the dining room, living room, and then back to the bedroom where Marka was working.

"Anna, I am so glad you are here. Look at the dresses I found in the old trunk in the garage. They were wrapped in this bed sheet. Look at all of the beadwork. They're beautiful."

"They belonged to our *Grossmutter*.

"Markaliz?"

"Yah," Anna said, running her hands across the small black beads.

"We must keep them," Marka smiled.

"Ach, no. They will bring money at the auction. Let's get some money out of all this old stuff."

"Are you sure, Anna? Let's keep them if they are special to you."

"They are just a couple of old dresses."

"All right. I'm grateful for any advice you can give me on what to sell, what to keep. Bodie had a good idea about having an auction, don't you think?"

"People will come from all over the county. Let's just hope the weather stays nice," Anna folded up the dresses and laid them on the pile of things that were to go for auction. "It's a good time for a sale, because beet season will be winding down and the sale won't interfere with deer season. It runs the whole month of November."

"Mom really loved hats, didn't she?" Marka retrieved three large boxes from a high shelf in the closet. "How do I look in this one?" Marka pulled the netting down around her face.

"Ach, you look old in that one."

Marka sorted through the rest of the hats in the box until she found a black pillbox. "Should I try this one on?"

"Yah, go look in the mirror."

"I like it." Marka's eyes sparkled. "I feel kind of funny about wearing Mom's things though."

"Your mother is looking down on you, and she's smiling at you wearing these hats," Anna said.

"All these dresses and coats will go to the rummage sale. Anna, take anything you want. I'm glad you told Bodie to keep mothballs in the closets. They would be full of holes after all these years. I'm going to keep some of Dad's shirts to wear over my dungarees. They will come in handy as I start to show. My jeans are getting tight and, I'm losing my waist."

Anna took a brown wool coat with the fake fur collar from the pile. "It won't fit me. Your mother was much larger than I am, but she always loved this coat so much," Anna said.

"Maybe you could do some alterations and make it fit. I want you to have Mom's cup and saucer collection and her set of china. Put them in your cupboard. They will look pretty through the glass doors, and, get rid of those detergent box dishes. You'll have nice ones now."

"Won't you need these things to set up housekeeping?" Anna asked.

"No, I will buy new things."

By the end of the day, Marka and Anna had sorted through all the closets and drawers. Anna encouraged Marka to keep certain things; other things she said to get rid of. Anna told her to keep her mother's jewelry and crocheted bordered handkerchiefs, tea towels, and pillowcases. "Keep your folks' wedding picture," she said, pointing to the large framed photo hanging over the chest of drawers.

"I'm going to take it to your house and hang it in my bedroom. I will get a special frame for the picture of Grandmother Markaliz," Marka said.

"Don't drop that mirror or you'll have seven years' bad luck," Anna warned.

"Anna, did you hear what you said? How is that any different than what Ruby says? Superstition—hunches. It's all the same thing."

"How about this old radio?" Anna asked. "Want to take it over to the house too?"

"It doesn't work," Marka said.

"Maybe you could get it fixed. Maybe it only needs some new tubes."

"I'd like to have a radio to listen to. You go to bed early, and I could listen to it in my room." Marka tipped her head to one side and studied the radio. "I don't know where it came from. It's not the one I remember the folks having. That one had a beautiful mahogany veneer. This radio looks like a piece of junk. I remember the night that Jack and I tried to get it to work," Marka giggled. "We ended up making up our own songs and singing to each other."

"Bet your dad bought it at an auction and then realized it didn't work," Anna said. "Your dad always tried to get something for nothing. Served him right."

"I think I'll have Bodie haul it to the dump, along with all the other junk," Marka said. "What collectors they were." Marka held up a Prince Albert tobacco can. "This thing is full of keys from coffee cans. In the garage, I found coffee cans full of used nails that Dad had pulled out of boards and straightened with a hammer."

"Your folks were frugal. I think that's how they say it, frugal."

"Yes, I think I'll have Bodie take all this stuff to the dump," Marka said.

Anna shook her head. "Aw, why not see if you can get a few bucks out of that radio? Maybe someone else will think it works."

"You aren't serious, are you? Oh, well, I will."

"So, after going through everything in the house, you never found anything that could be what your mother was talking about?" Anna asked.

"I've reached the conclusion that there is nothing. I've been through everything. There's nothing here. No hidden treasure."

Auctions were usually held at the Legion Hall, but Ruby offered the use of her pool hall. "We can move the card tables and chairs to one side and use the pool tables. I'll cover them with sheets so you can use them to display the smaller items like dishes and knickknacks," Ruby said. "There will be enough space for the auctioneer's podium and for the people to stand during the auction."

"Thank you, Ruby."

"I think it is good you are getting rid of the house, but, leave Ridley. Never! Jack will have to leave Florida. I cannot let you go, Mia."

"What happened to all your talk about freedom? Don't I have anything to say about it? Don't I even have a choice?" Marka giggled.

"You know, I'm just teasing, Mia. I want you to be free to choose whatever you want."

"This is the first time in my life I really do feel like I'm making my own choices," Marka said. "I feel free and strong."

"You are. Free from the past. You have made peace with your parents, and now, they are protecting you from the other side. You also have their strengths."

Marka put her arms around Ruby. "It's because of you. You've been a true friend. You never judged me, and yet, you didn't pamper me either. You told me the truth about myself. I'm grateful to you, Ruby."

"Is Anna worried about what the women will say and do if they find out? Just remember, Anna loves you. You must try to understand her."

"I don't think she cares anymore what people think. She's changed."

"Are you regretting your night of passion?" Ruby asked. "Was it a full moon that night? Sometimes the moon can cause us to do strange things."

"I can't blame the moon. I am through blaming fate or people for the things that happen to me. I made my own choice. I have no regrets."

Ruby took Marka by the hand and led her over to the front window where she kept her easel. She removed a cloth covering. "Because I have been inspired by your courage, I have started a new portrait of Henry. I am going to leave the eyes until last, but I have a feeling that this time, I will get them right."

Marka smiled. "You will, Ruby. You will."

After supper, Bodie stopped by Anna's and told them that he and Buddy had gone to Clayton and talked with Ed Davis, a lawyer, who would draw up the papers on the sale of the house. Bodie placed an ad in the *Clayton Post*. Auction: Household of Philip and Rachel Becker. Saturday, November 9, 10 a.m. to 2 p.m.— Billiards' Hall, Ridley.

Marka told Bodie to take whatever he wanted from the tool shed. "It's my way of showing gratitude for all your help."

Bodie smiled and said, "I'll split the carpenter tools with George. He could use some claw hammers, and screw drivers. I'll keep the hand saws, clamps, files, and spirit level."

"The only thing I want is the wooden fold-out ruler," Marka said, "a keepsake from my dad."

By Friday afternoon, almost everything had been moved out of the house into Ruby's pool hall and to Anna's basement. Bodie kept the stove, refrigerator, table and chairs, couch, recliner, and one bed. He kept some of the linens, bedding, and some of the dishes and cooking utensils. Marka asked him if he would like to have the scenery picture that hung above the sofa. "I want you to have it, Bodie, because you said it gave you a certain feeling whenever you looked at it, and, what about the old buffet? Would you like to have that too?"

Bodie shook his head. "No, I don't have any fancy things to put in there. Don't have any use for it."

"You may decide to get married some day, and your wife may want it," Marka teased.

"I don't think so. Auction it off. One more trip should about do it. I'll go get George and have him help me load the buffet onto the pickup."

"I haven't done anything with the cellar. There's just a bunch of canned goods down there. You can have them. My mom always labeled the jars with the year she canned it, but make sure you don't eat anything too old. If there's anything crusted on the side of the jar that means the seal broke, and it is leaking. Oh, Anna wants all the empty jars."

Bodie and George loaded the buffet and took it to the pool hall. Marka swept the cobwebs off the wall where the buffet had stood. On the wall there was a skinny cupboard that had been hidden by the buffet. That small cupboard had always intrigued her. Her mother told her that there was a pull down ironing board built into the wall.

Marka opened the small door to the closet. Inside was a wooden ironing board just like her mother had said. She pulled the top of the board. Something fell onto the floor. A bundle wrapped in brown paper with twine wound round it.

Marka took the package over to the window to get a better look. She slipped off the twine and opened the bundle. Inside there were papers. In an envelope, there was the deed to a parcel of land. Marka read: *Town of Ridley Lot 1 Block 4 1st recorded document: Pioneer Townsite sold to Julius Becker who assigned his interest to Jacob Becker, July 10, 1924. Warranty Deed Book 4 page 10.*

Marka stood frozen like she was encased in a block of ice. Was this the treasure that her mother told her about the day at the hospital? She would never have looked behind the door if Bodie had decided to keep the buffet. Her heart raced. What should she do? Oh, God. This has to be it," she squealed and danced around the room.

Marka took the package of papers over to Anna's house. "I have something to show you, Anna. You better sit down."

Marka opened the manila envelope, took out the papers, and handed them to Anna. "This must be what Mom wanted me to find. Bodie moved the old buffet away from the wall and you know the little door, where the ironing board is, well, these were stuck behind it. Can you believe it?"

Anna held the paper close to her eyes and squinted trying to read. "Ach, I can't read this. You do it, Marka."

Marka sat in the chair next to Anna. "It seems that in 1924, there was a community lot sale. It says here in this newspaper article that people flocked from all directions to try and buy the lots." Marka sat quietly and read, and then she spoke. "The four downtown corner lots sold for one thousand dollars. This paper says that Jacob Becker owns the one in Block Four. Who was Jacob Becker, Anna?"

"Ach, that was your dad's father."

"It looks like it was signed over to my dad. Look here." Marka pointed her finger at a signature. "This downtown lot belongs to me now, as well as my folks' house."

CHAPTER 30

By 9:00 a.m., cars lined Main Street. They nosed in vertically against the sidewalk, the best way to park on the small street when a crowd was expected. On auction day, it was likely that twenty-five cars or more would show up.

The men paced the wide sidewalk in front of Ruby's Pool Hall. They stopped now and then trying to peek behind the sheets that covered the large plate glass window. They discussed the latest news about the missile sent into outer space.

"The Russians have launched another satellite. This time they put a dog in it." George announced to the crowd.

Harry Paddock yelled for everyone to hear: "Hey, did you see President Eisenhower speaking on nationwide television? Well, he held up the nose cone of a rocket for all to see, and said: 'This has been hundreds of miles into outer space and back. Here it is, completely intact'."

The men discussed the fact that the Russians beat the United States to outer space with their Sputnik. Who is more powerful the United States or Russia?

"How the hell are we going to keep ahead of the Reds?" Joe Stobner asked. He just happened to have the *Clayton Post* tucked under his arm. He proceeded to read from it. "Listen to this: The most difficult problems in perfecting an intercontinental ballistic missile are the obstacle of firing it into space and bringing it back without having it burn up from friction." Joe put the paper back under his arm. "Hell, if I understand Eisenhower right, our scientists and engineers have solved the problem."

George was standing beside Joe and Harry. He told them and everyone else standing in front of the Pool Hall that his son, Jack, was an engineer and worked for NASA.

The women sat in their cars doing crochet and embroidery work. Some read *Ladies' Home Journal*, *McCalls*, or *True Story*. Now and then, they would look up and yell at their kids, who skittered about, chasing one another up and down the sidewalk.

Stella was tending the store for Carl. She removed the CLOSED sign and opened the door to the anxious shoppers, mostly children interested in Hershey bars, jawbreakers, and the little wax bottles filled with sugar water.

Marka walked into the store behind the children. She needed paper napkins for the *grebble,* donuts. Anna had been up since the crack of dawn, frying and sugaring. She said it was a way for Marka "to make a little extra money." She said people would pay 25 cents for two.

"Don't you kids be running around in here," Stella yelled. "Just get what you want and get out." Marka watched her as she tied the white apron tightly around her waist and walked over to the mirror that ran along the wall above the small freezer containing ice cream bars and popsicles. She watched Stella lean across the freezer to get a closer look at herself in the mirror while she re-did her hair combs.

Several children lined up next to the cash register laying pennies, nickels, and dimes on the counter.

Stella took the nickel from Cherry and then leaned down and gently tapped her freckle-covered nose. "I just love that red hair of yours. This candy should last you all day if you suck on them slowly—one at a time." Stella held the roll of Neccos in front of Cherry's eyes.

"Can we get it moving?" Jimmy Caldwell yelled from the end of the line.

Stella dropped a nickel into the cash register. She pursed her lips and squinted as she hurried the other children through.

When Jimmy got up to the register, Marka heard her say, "Don't give me any of your crap, or I'll tell your mother what you were doing out behind the store the other day. And, if you're the one that soaped the windows Halloween night, well, I have ways of finding out things."

Jimmy paid for his candy and ran out of the store.

Marka thought Stella could be so cruel, but she promised herself she would be cordial. She didn't want to make any more trouble. Besides, she wasn't feeling well this morning and the day would drain all of her energy.

"Are you coming over to the auction?" Marka asked.

"No. I'm not interested in second hand stuff," Stella sneered.

Marka felt her face and neck redden. She wanted to say, "Well, you're married to a second-hand man." She thought it through. No, she couldn't. If Anna were here she'd say, "When it comes to Stella, just leave it go. Don't get into it with her."

Marka thought she would be leaving Ridley with Jack. Why continue the war with Stella? She put the money for the napkins down on the counter, turned to leave, and couldn't resist saying, "Isn't it wonderful that Bodie bought my house? Just think how happy he is going to be." The words came out before she could stop them.

The doors to the pool hall opened at 9:30 a.m. so people could examine the goods. They pushed their way into the large room. Anna's grebble and coffee were good sellers. People walked around eating and jotting down numbers on paper donated by the auctioneer.

"This gasoline lantern is very old," Anna convinced one man. "It came from the old country. It's probably worth a lot of money to an antique dealer."

After the man walked away, Marka whispered in Anna's ear. "It came all the way from Russia?"

"No, I didn't say which old country, did I?" Anna giggled and winked at Marka.

Slim Anderson, the auctioneer, asked Marka whether she wanted to go past 2:00 p.m. if things hadn't cleared out. She said to go as long as it took to sell everything. Otherwise, George and Bodie would have to haul it back to the house.

At 10:00 a.m., Slim whacked the podium with his gavel and held up the first item for bid. Hands went up, numbers were called out. Slim yelled, "Going once, going twice, sold."

The auction moved along without a hitch and when the thirteenth item came up, it was a pair of porcelain lamps with white satin shades still covered with plastic. Marka never removed the yellowed plastic covers, because it seemed like a violation of her mother's wishes. She stood and studied the lamps and thought about what Anna said the day before, suggesting she keep some of the things to put in her new home. The more she thought about those lamps, the more she wanted them back. Besides, they were rather beautiful, and the picture of the 17th Century couple dancing reminded her of her and Jack.

The couple wore white wigs, the kind worn by English parliament. The lady looked elegant in her apron-fronted dress. She wore pointed shoes with ribbon ties. The gentleman wore a red, double-breasted coat over a ruffled shirt. He had on Hessian boots and held gloves in one hand. The lamps were too romantic to let go, she thought. Besides, they were something her mother had cherished. She could keep them in her bedroom at Anna's, and then she and Jack could put them in their home.

Marka walked to the back of the hall where Ruby was standing. "Ruby, see the lamps that Slim is about to auction off. I can't let them go. Bid on them for me."

"How high you want to go?"

"Start out with five dollars. Go as high as fifteen if you have to. I'll pay you back."

Ruby walked to the front of the room and began bidding on the lamps. Marka thought again how the couple painted on the lamps made her think of Jack. She wondered if he received the letter. It had been ten days since she dropped it into the mail slot at the post office. Marka slid her hand across her belly and noticed it was beginning to feel tight. She had been so busy the last week clearing out the house; she hadn't even noticed the changes taking place in her body.

"Sold," Slim said as he hit the gavel on the podium, "to the lady with the big smile in the brightly flowered dress." Ruby bought the lamps for nine dollars and fifty cents.

"Oh, Ruby, thank you," Marka hugged her tight. "It seems silly, I suppose, but I felt a certain attachment to these."

Ruby leaned close to Marka's ear. "It was fun. Did my Gypsy show through?" Ruby's dark eyes danced.

By 2:30 p.m., most everything had been auctioned off except for a few curtains and the old radio. Marka told George, "I hate to have Bodie make a special trip to the dump for these things. Have him bring it over to Anna's. Anna said the old radio might only need a couple of tubes."

The days that followed the auction were blustery. People were busy raking leaves into heaps for burning. The smell of smoke filled the air. It got colder each day, and the wind howled through the cracks in doors and around the windows of Anna's house. The trees stood naked against the blue of the sky. The last geese flew over, heading south.

Rain delayed the first week of beet harvest, but the farmers were satisfied because, for the most part, the harvest progressed steadily. In another week, it would be completed. They were ecstatic with the yield the new beet seed produced.

Everyone seemed to sense the changing of the season. Some people welcomed the change; others complained about the prospect of another bitterly cold winter. There was talk around town about Bodie Erlich, the proud homeowner. How he walked with his shoulders back, head held high. Some people thought Bodie had made a good decision to buy a house of his own. "Maybe he'll even get married someday," Anna said.

Others said he should have stayed with his father. Why waste all that money keeping up two places? Bodie was pleased with himself, and went about his business. Carl and Stella couldn't ride herd on him.

"Dad is moody and ornery to customers when they come into the store. He grumbled at me when I said I wanted to put my groceries on credit. He even went so far as to post a sign by the cash register that read: 'Bills Must Be Paid End of Each Month'. Stella is hibernating at the post office. After she sorts the incoming mail, she just sits at the desk in the back reading magazines."

"I'm happy for you, Bodie," Marka said.

"I like to be at the store more now that I don't live there. I go to work in the afternoons. I unload the delivery trucks and stock shelves. I even unloaded the mail truck for Stella, but, now, I make her pay me. Buddy comes over to the house and spends time with me. I think he likes to get away from Stella," Bodie laughed.

This one event, Bodie buying a house, kept conversation going at the saloon and cafe for quite a while. There was another event to occur.

Only a few people knew that Marka was going to have a baby. She was putting on weight and growing in places that would soon make her condition obvious. She fretted to Anna about needing loose fitting clothing and that she still hadn't heard from Jack. George asked her every day, and every day she saw the disappointment in his face when she said, "No."

266

"I tried to telephone him a couple of times, but there was no answer," George said. "The only thing that makes me smile is my excitement over becoming a grandfather. I love you like a daughter, Marka."

Marka would leave the cafe and walk to the post office after 10:00 a.m. rush. Every day, still no letter from Jack. Ruby keeps telling me not to give up, but what if Jack never cared about me the way I care for him? The night at the river, he told me he loved me. Has he changed his mind? How could his love for me burn out like a match?

Anna took care of Marka, making sure she ate right and got plenty of rest and she never pestered Marka about not hearing from Jack.

One afternoon after Anna and Marka listened to Anna's favorite radio drama, *The Secret Life of Helen Trent,* Anna said, "I was thinking I should buy one of those TV sets. Ida told me there is a soap opera on television called *Love of Life.* Anyways, I've been dreading the thought of long winter nights."

"That would be fine, Anna."

Each day, Marka felt her heart sink deeper, because she wasn't hearing from Jack. She put her pride aside and phoned a couple times, but there was no answer. She thought Jack was probably busy with another missile going into space.

"We could stay up late and watch TV until it goes off the air," Anna said. "Ida likes Wild Bill Hickok. She said I would like to watch Lawrence Welk. He's German Russian, you know."

"It costs a lot for a television. Let me buy it with the money I got from the auction."

"I have the money. I can get a nice TV for around four hundred dollars. Besides, you'll have to quit your job at the cafe soon. You need something more than a radio. Jonny hasn't brought you over any more books, has he? Well, the Bookmobile comes once a month."

"Jonny only said two words to me the day of the auction. Anna, has he even asked about me? He's probably angry, because I told him, no, to chaperoning the homecoming dance. Maybe he has taken up again with his old girlfriend in Texas."

"Yah, he asks about you, but I don't tell him much. I told him that you might be moving in the spring—maybe back to Denver, I told him."

"People are going to wonder why I'm quitting the cafe. When they don't see me around town, they'll ask. Will I have to spend all my time in the house? I am not ashamed of what happened. I fell in love."

"Marka," Anna gasped, "don't talk like that. For shame."

"Shame on what? You of all people, Anna, should understand. What about when you got pregnant with your baby?"

"Ach, don't use that word; it sounds so awful. So, now I'm thinking I shouldn't have told you about my baby."

"I'm sorry; that was a horrible thing to say. I'm so wrapped up in myself right now. Forgive me, Anna."

November sixteenth was a cold Saturday. Bodie brought two jackrabbits by, skinned and cleaned. He told Anna and Marka he checked his traps that morning and had caught four. "I'm going to take the pelts to Heider Brothers. They had an ad in the paper for deer hides, mink hides, and rabbit pelts," Bodie said.

After Anna got her bread dough mixed, she had Bodie drive her to the Coast-to-Coast Store in Clayton, and she bought a television; an Admiral for $399. Herb offered to install the antenna. "Bodie can't crawl around up there, because of his bad hip, and George has no business being up there. I'll be careful not to walk around too much, or Anna will need a new roof come spring," Herb said.

"What is that you said about a new roof? Gott, I hope not. I spent all my money on this TV."

"Your roof is in good shape. I was just giving you a hard way to go," Herb laughed.

Jonny walked by the house, noticed all the commotion, and stopped in.

"How about you stay for dinner, and then, we'll watch some TV," Anna said. "Think I'll call Bodie and George, and we can have a TV celebration."

"I'd never turn down your cooking." Jonny stood with his hands on his hips looking up at the roof. "Wonder what's taking Herb so long?"

"Maybe someone should go and look around the other side of the house. Hope he didn't fall off," Anna said.

Herb walked to the crest of the roof and yelled down for someone to go into the house and check the reception on the television.

Jonny went in, came back out and said the screen was still snowy. "Turn it southeast towards Rapid City," he yelled up at Herb.

Supper was usually around 6:00 p.m., but tonight they ate at 7:00 p.m. Marka and Anna served fried chicken, mashed potatoes, and hot biscuits. Marka sat next to Jonny. Anna made sure the men dished up first, and then she and Marka sat down to eat.

"The new '58 Ford is out," Jonny said trying to make casual conversation.

"Sometimes, I wish I would have kept my car," Marka joined in. "Gads, I practically gave it away when I left Denver."

"Anna told me you are thinking of moving back." Jonny kept his eyes on his plate.

"It's not for sure," Anna blurted.

George changed the subject. "The stores in Clayton are wanting everyone to register for free prizes. Be in town on Friday for the opening of Christmas season. That's what everyone is saying."

"Hey, Bodie, Santa Claus will be dropping by the Bootery at 7 o'clock Friday night," Herb teased. "You're going aren't you?"

Bodie finished his last bite of chicken. "Me and Buddy are going deer hunting next week."

After supper, they all sat in Anna's front room and watched television. When it was time to go, Anna had plates piled high with leftover food from supper for them to take home. They left happy with their bellies full.

A week later, the ground was covered with a layer of frost. It clung to the grass, to the dead vines in the garden, and to the rooftops, and it stayed most of the morning until the sun melted it away. Anna said she was glad she covered some of her plants with straw.

"I saw on TV news that we're going to be getting a snowstorm, at least five inches," Anna said, stuffing a couple of pieces of wood into the cook stove. "Sasha is driving me nuts bringing those dead mice to the kitchen door."

The next morning, Marka stood at the kitchen window and watched heavy snowflakes float through the air. They looked like goose down shaken from a pillow. During her appointment with Doc Sellers, he told her that the baby was doing fine. Despite her heartbreak over Jack, she felt safe and content with Anna. Maybe it's time to wipe Jack from her memory. Marka felt a lump in her throat. She hugged her stomach feeling protective of the growing child inside her. She looked over at Anna, who was busy washing dishes and thought how understanding Anna had been about Jack, never once scolding her for what happened.

"*Madchen*, how is your crocheting coming along?"

"One more sleeve, and I'll be finished. The stitches are so small. Thank you for buying the television set, Anna. It gives me something to look forward to in the evenings."

"Tonight is Ladies' Aid meeting. It's at Stella Erlick's house," Anna said.

"What will you say when they ask why I'm not working at the cafe?"

"Not that you're moving to Denver. I learned my lesson on that one. I feel bad that I lied to Jonny. I think he knew I was lying."

"I can't hide my condition forever."

"I'll sew you some sack dresses. Ach, now days they call them A-lines," Anna laughed. "I know people can be cruel, Marka. I know what you're going through. I had to keep hidden too. Don't get yourself upset. When the time is right we'll let people know."

"You are right," Marka said.

Anna walked to the window. She wiped her hands on her apron and gazed at the snow falling to the ground. "Why don't you call George and see if he wants to play cards tonight? I don't want you sitting around feeling sorry for yourself. That won't help a thing."

"Don't worry about me, Anna."

"I thought he could keep you company, that's all."

"Okay, I'll call him. He'd probably like to beat me at Rummy again," Marka laughed.

CHAPTER 31

Katie picked Anna up at 7:00 p.m. It was a glorious winter night. The moon cast its light across the newly fallen snow. The air was crisp, and there was a heavy smell of smoke from the chimneys.

Anna put on her coat and gloves, tied a wool scarf around her neck, and grabbed her pocketbook. Katie had the car headlights on high so Anna could see where she was walking. The lights made the snow glisten.

Marka gave Anna a hug good-bye. "Take it slow across the yard so you don't slip and fall."

George came over shortly after Anna left for Ladies' Aid. Marka laid a deck of cards on the kitchen table. "Anna doesn't like card games, but I do. Ready to have me beat the pants off you?" she laughed.

"First, let me tell you some gossip. Ole got arrested and charged with public intoxication."

"In Ridley? I can't believe Solly actually did it. He doesn't work that hard upholding the law in this town."

"Not Ridley, in Clayton. He got fined fifteen dollars and sentenced to thirty days in jail."

"It's about time he got put away for a while," Marka laughed. "I still remember that day he was fighting with Danny Deer Ears. He was like a wild animal. He should stay out on the prairie with his sheep."

"Today, I heard on the radio that Eisenhower is convinced the American people won't sacrifice security for a balanced budget. Ever since the Russians launched their second satellite, people are up in arms. Most people agree that Congress has to cut spending on domestic programs to finance defense needs," George went on, "but Eisenhower feels it is a distasteful thing to do."

Marka said, "Ruby told me that Sputnik is going to mess up the celestial-astrological atmosphere."

George shook his head. "I know she is your friend, but..."

"Oh, George. That's just because you don't know her. Ruby has been wonderful to me. You might as well know. I told her about the baby. I know I can trust her."

"Speaking of my son. I got a letter from him. He said to tell you "Hello". He never said a word about the baby. It makes me angry. I'm going to tell him."

"No. Don't spoil what you have going between you and Jack. You're just trying to find your way back to each other. This is my problem, George. I've tried to call several times, but he's never home. I probably won't hear from him.

Anna said, "Sometimes a man just has a good time and then throws himself back into his work. Anna says I must think of the baby now. I'll have to get over him."

"You aren't going to fight any harder than that?"

"George, I've never been comfortable with rejection. I don't go where I'm not wanted, and I won't push myself on anyone. And, I certainly won't play games to get what I want. It's plain to me, Jack doesn't love me, and he isn't interested in the baby."

"If there's anything I can do for you, you know you can count on me." George picked up the cards, shuffled them, and then dealt them each five cards for a game of Rummy.

"Financially, I will be all right. I had planned on going to college, but now I will be looking for a job after the baby is born. Anna said she would take care of him, or her. I didn't think she'd want me to stay in Ridley, because the shame of it, you know."

"Marka, don't give up on Jack," George said, dealing the cards. "I haven't."

Marka studied her cards and then remembered she had a favor to ask George. "Oh, George, there's something you can do for me." Marka got up from her chair. At night, I'd like to listen to KOMA. I decided to put that old radio in my bedroom. I plugged it in, even banged on it and shook it a little, but it won't work. Would you take a look at it? Anna said it might just need a couple new tubes."

George got up from the table. "Let's have a look."

They went into Marka's bedroom. George pulled the radio out from the wall and checked the plug. "Seems to be okay, no frayed wires," he said. Then he clicked the on and off knob. "Get me a screw driver, and I'll take the back off the thing. Anna may be right about the tubes. An old Zenith, huh?" George loosened the last screw, and then pried the thin flat board from the back of the radio.

"Hell and tarnation, no wonder the darn thing didn't work! Look at this!"

Marka's eyes opened wide. Inside the radio, where some of the tubes had been removed, were stacks of bills wrapped in small bundles with string.

"By God, look at all this money," George gasped.

Marka sat on the edge of the bed and put her head in her hands. She started to cry. "This must be what Mom was talking about that day in the hospital. She tried desperately to tell me there was something in the house. George, I can't believe it."

"You just hit a gold mine, woman!" George sat down on the bed beside Marka and put his arm around her shoulders. He wiped the tears from her cheeks with his thumb.

"I never told you this before, but right before my mother died, she told me there was something hidden in the house. I searched everywhere and nothing turned up; so I gave up the search. Then, I did find something the day we moved everything out of the house for the auction. An envelope stuffed in a cupboard. It is the deed to a piece of property here in town. I figured that was what my mother was talking about. George, how much money do you think is in there?"

George pulled out the bundles of bills squeezed in between what radio tubes remained. "Twenty dollar bills, fifties, even some hundreds."

"Oh, George." Marka clapped her hands.

They laid the money out on the bed and Marka counted the stacks while George recorded the amounts on a piece of paper. They were counting the last stack of bills when Anna arrived home. They heard the kitchen door open.

"We better break it to Anna gently," George said.

"There's nothing gentle about Anna when it concerns money." Marka chuckled.

Marka closed her bedroom door, and she and George went to the kitchen.

Anna seemed flustered. "Ach, that Stella. She was in a nasty mood." Anna sat down on a chair and took off her over boots. "First thing she did was to bring it to everyone's attention that you went to the saloon. And, 'Why don't we ever see Marka anymore? Why didn't she come tonight?' she said."

"Anna, sit down. I have to tell you something," Marka's heart was racing.

"Well, anyways, then during the business meeting, she argued about everything and insisted we have a Christmas tea to make money. She was so proud of her little finger sandwiches and cookies. I wanted to tell her that we couldn't enjoy the food, because of the smell of furniture polish. That pine scent filled every room of the house." Anna took a deep breath and started to tell them more. Marka couldn't stand keeping it to herself any longer.

"Anna, we found the treasure! The one Mom said was hidden in the house. George and I found it in the radio.

"What? A*ch du lieber*. What is it?"

"Money. Lots of money," Marka couldn't stop laughing. "To think that old radio almost went to the dump."

"*Gott in Himmel*." Anna put her hand over her heart and took a deep breath.

They went to the bedroom, and when Marka opened the door, Anna saw all the stacks of bills lined up neatly in piles on the bed. She clapped her hands and laughed. "The Lord has blessed you. How much money is there?"

"Looks like close to $10,000," George answered. "We haven't counted the last stack."

Anna put her hand behind her ear. "Tell me again. Did you say $10,000?"

"Yes, $10,000," George whispered loudly in her ear.

"My Gott. Yah, now I remember. The radio your folks had went on the blink and instead of getting a new one your dad bought that old radio at an auction. 'It looks like a piece of junk. It doesn't even work,' your mother said. 'He keeps saying that one of these days he will fix it'. Your mother wanted a new one so bad. To think it was sitting there all these years full of money."

"Could it have been your father's money? Since the Great Depression some people don't believe in banks, you know," George said.

"My dad would never have kept money like that around the house. He did believe in banks. He said our government had learned its lesson and what happened during the Great Depression wouldn't happen again. "

"Well, they obviously knew about the money, because your mother wanted you to know," George added. "Tell me more about the deed to a piece of property in Ridley."

"Remember the day you and Bodie moved the buffet out of the my house?"

George said, "Yes."

"Well, there is a skinny cupboard and behind the door is a pull-down ironing board. I opened the door, and a manila envelope fell on the floor. It had papers inside. I looked through the papers and there was a deed to a parcel of land in Ridley. It's Lot 1 Block 4. That's on the corner across from the flour mill."

"Well, if that don't beat all. Anna is right. You are one lucky woman. You can go to college and won't have to work." George put his strong arms around Marka and hugged her tight. "And I am one lucky man to have you, the mother of my grandchild."

CHAPTER 32

Bodie fell prey to Buddy's enthusiasm for hunting. Early Friday morning, before sunrise, they packed Bodie's pickup with rifles and tarps, and headed for the buttes. Buddy bragged to everyone that he would have a buck the first day out. With the knowledge that Bodie was away, Marka slipped her parka on and walked over to the house.

It was hard to imagine the house was no longer hers. It was now the property of Bodie J. Erlich. A new Deed of Trust had been issued, but that fact had not made it feel final. It was not until she stood face to face with the house that she realized it no longer belonged to her.

Contradictory emotions whirled through Marka's mind. She had worked hard to rid the house of its leaky roof and plumbing problems. She scrubbed and cleaned every room and moved the furniture around to her liking. She reacquainted herself with every cupboard, closet, and drawer. She made peace with the past, and the wounds from the heart of the small child she once was were beginning to heal. She made the house her own, and now she had to let it go, but she would keep the good memories the house held alive in her. Like the way the floor squeaked in front of the kitchen sink while her mother did the dishes, and the way the light streamed in through the large picture window when there was a full moon. She would always remember the smell of her mother's cooking, and the sight of her father sitting at the kitchen table, reading glasses sliding down his nose, reading the *Clayton Post*.

There was satisfaction knowing she had withstood all the bad memories. It's like Ruby said, she faced the demons of her past, and the ghosts were gone. She and Anna had talked things over so many times; the pain and anger were finally gone. She understood her parents more now, and she forgave them. And she forgave herself. There was relief in knowing that she left the house this time under different circumstances. She was not running away from anything. As the sun set, the house was a silhouette against the western sky, and it looked content. Yes, she made the right decision to sell to Bodie. The house needs Bodie as much as he needs it.

"Yes," she said softly. "It's time for me to move on."

"I still can't believe there was all that money in that old radio," Anna said. "Who'd have guessed? I feel hurt that your mother didn't tell me about it, though."

"Maybe she was going to and that's why she was so insistent that day in the hospital. I think she wanted *us* to know," Marka said. "Maybe Dad swore her to secrecy."

"All's I know is she did tell me your dad bought it at an auction, and it didn't work. Leave it to your dad to get lucky like that."

"And, I never told you this...Mom said something else to me that day. She said, 'Marka, I love you'."

"She did love you."

"I don't remember Dad ever saying it—not once in my whole life," Marka said with downcast eyes.

"People didn't say the words, I love you, unless maybe it was when they got married. It was a word used for romance. We just expected that our loved ones knew and didn't have to be told."

Marka said, "I do forgive him."

"That old radio having all that money hidden in it. It looks like a piece of junk," Anna laughed. "Yah, your mother wanted you to find it, and you did. That's the main thing."

Marka said, "I better get it to the bank. What about the deed to the town lot? There are probably taxes due. Who do I talk to? And why *didn't* the rancher take the money to the bank instead of leaving it in the radio?"

"Boy, oh boy, you've got the questions."

"Did the folks ever mention the deed to you, Anna?"

"No, but our people are secretive, you know."

"Oh, it doesn't matter. The point is I found many treasures since I came back to Ridley." Marka took Anna's hand. "I'm not talking about the money and the deed. I'm talking about you. In spite of all the horrible things I've done..."

"Ach, Marka." Anna pressed her hand against Marka's cheek.

"Ruby is a treasure too. I know she's kind of strange, but sometimes we have to overlook certain things about people."

"That's right," Anna smiled. "Don't judge a book by its cover; so maybe we don't judge others, because they look strange or have different ways from ours."

"George says not to throw a perfectly good apple out, just because it has a blemish. He's a treasure too," Marka said. "I'd like to think I've changed some since I came back to Ridley. I think I stand up for myself, and I'm beginning to understand myself better. If things had just gone right with Jack. No! I can't say that! I won't blame others for my mistakes."

Anna said, "Well, things certainly did not turn out like you thought."

The hunters returned late Friday afternoon. Bodie telephoned Marka and Anna, and told them to come over to the house and see the buck they shot. Anna was busy making *bierocks*, cabbage buns. "I will live without seeing a dead animal," she said.

"Look at the beauty we got here," Bodie said, stuffing his hands into the bib of his blue overalls. It was tan-brown with a white belly. "This one has a nice rack of horns," he bragged as he and Buddy pulled the big buck off the hood of his pickup.

"We drove to the top of the ridge and then walked down the hill to hunt," Buddy said.

"How far did you have to go?" Marka asked.

"About twenty miles north as the crow flies," Bodie said, standing tall and proud. "We hiked a couple of miles through thick brush and pine trees."

"We are going to dress it out. You may not want to watch," Buddy said. "Bodie, go get an old washtub, then we'll hang it in the garage."

"I'm going to keep the horns so I can hang them in my new house," Bodie said proudly.

Marka felt a twinge in her stomach. "Oh, swell. This is when I have to go. Congratulations," she said, and started to walk away.

Marka turned to look at the house one more time. Bodie would hang the rack of horns on a wall, and that would be the beginning of a whole new history for the house.

Buddy caught up to her and took her by the arm. "You have no idea what you're putting me through."

278

"Don't say that. I've got to go." She pulled the parka tight around her tummy and shook her head at him. If only he knew she was almost three months along and that Jack, George's son, was the father of her baby. He wouldn't be so interested in her then.

CHAPTER 33

Marka laid the baby sweater on her lap and watched the snowflakes drift down from the sky. She had crocheted two pair of booties and now the sweater, all out of multicolored Orlon yarn: pink, blue, yellow, and white. It was soft yarn made especially for babies. "All that really matters is the child growing inside me," she whispered softly to herself. She looked out the window and watched George shovel his drive way. Several months had gone by since she wrote to Jack telling him about the baby.

Anna kept referring to her as "being in the family way." There will be no father for my baby, but there will be a family, she thought, moving the yarn over her hook and fingers. There will be Anna, George, Ruby, Bodie, Millie, and Ida.

Marka thought of the previous day when she finally convinced Anna to let her go outside the house. "Anna, I'm not showing that much yet. I don't want to stay inside all the time. Please, can't I just go see George?"

"Yah, sure. You go see George, the baby's *Grossfadder*, Grandfather."

Marka walked across the street to George's house. She knocked on the door, opened it, and hollered in. He was at the kitchen table, drinking coffee and reading the newspaper.

"Come, sit down," he said.

"You reading more about the Russians?"

"No, I'm reading the funny papers—Dagwood and Blondie. So, Anna is letting you out of the house, is she?"

"I'm not going to sit around feeling sorry for myself," Marka wrapped her arms around her stomach. "I have so much to be grateful for, George—all that money in the radio. It will be more than enough for the baby and me for a very long time. Anna says, 'Tell Millie you won't work for her anymore'."

George got up from the table, paced back and forth across the room, with his arms held behind his back, hands clasped. "Do you still want Jack?"

Marka rubbed her hand across her belly. "It's hard to tell anymore. I'm determined to forget him. I keep thinking maybe it was just a chemical thing. Ruby said maybe it was the moon that made me loony and it was passion. True Romance magazine would say it was a lusty kind of love. Anna said I wasn't using my head, just my feelings. I loved Jack—that's all I know. We met under the right circumstances. We have much in common. George, I've never felt that way about any man before Jack."

"It bothers me that he never called you or answered your letter," George said.

"It was silly for me to think that he could love me. He probably thinks I'm just a hick gal from South Dakota."

"He could at least write to you if only a few lines. At least let you know where you stand and ask about the baby."

"George, it's over, and just because Jack is your son, well, it doesn't affect how I feel about you."

George opened a pouch of sweet smelling tobacco and stuffed small pinches into the bowl of his pipe. "I had a reason for asking about your feelings for Jack. Jonny and I have been talking a lot lately, and he is having suspicions about you. Thinks you have some sort of incurable illness. I hope I'm not out of line by telling you this, but he has feelings for you, Marka."

"I think the feelings are just friendship and we both love Anna. The night we all had supper at Anna's, the night she got the television, Jonny never said much to me. I think he got together with his girlfriend in Texas. Besides, he won't be interested in me when he finds out I am going to have a child. I've ruined my reputation by going to the saloon and hanging out with Millie—and now this. No, George. Jonny won't want anything to do with me when he finds out."

"Okay. I won't bring it up again. Say, I want to run an idea by you," George said, striking a wooden match on the underside of the coffee table, then lighting the tobacco in his pipe. "What the kids in this town need is an ice skating rink. If we had a piece of ground that is sort of undeveloped and flat, the town could flood it. Now, I was thinking; I know this young woman who happens to own a big corner lot."

"Oh, George, that's a wonderful idea. I don't know what to do with the lot now anyway."

"I already talked to Jonny about it, and he thinks it's a good idea too. He said he'd see to it that the ice is always cleared of snow, or the kids could take care of it themselves."

"You told him that I owned the lot? Did you tell him about the money in the radio?"

"I told him you owned the lot. I didn't tell him about the money. I wouldn't do that unless you said it was all right. There's a town meeting at the Legion Hall this Friday night. Let's see how people like the idea. The town would have to pay for the water; so people will have to agree on it."

"Anna won't like the idea of me going to the meeting. Besides, there are no women on the town board."

"You wouldn't have to go. I'll go and make the proposal to the town. Buddy is on the board. He told me how appreciative he is to you for selling the house to Bodie. He likes you a lot," George said, laying his pipe down in the ashtray.

"Well, it's my property now, and I guess I can do what I want with it. Yes, George. I like the idea. I don't know why my dad never claimed it. It's all such a mystery, just like the radio. I never knew my folks had so many secrets."

CHAPTER 34

The next morning, at half past eight, Anna sifted flour and kneaded bread dough. The white powder covered her apron. She pushed and pulled the dough with her small, strong hands.

It was another cold morning. The mercury had stayed below zero for the entire week. Heat from the cook stove filled the kitchen and spread to the other rooms of the house. Anna kindled the ashes in the cook stove, positioned two big pieces of wood in the firebox, and then put on a pot of coffee. The oil-burning stove in the living room could never put out enough heat to keep the house warm during a severe Dakota winter. She always kept water in the reservoir on the right side of the stove, and she used the compartment on top to keep things warm. Anna preferred doing her baking in this old range.

"I like the way the bread comes out of the oven," Marka said, "all hot and crusty, better than the bread that comes out of the gas ovens at Millie's café."

Marka pointed to her heavy woolen socks and then to Anna's. They both laughed at the same time.

"We're ready for winter, right?" Anna smiled.

Marka yawned and pulled her robe tight. She watched Anna place the dough in an oiled crock bowl, then cover it with a clean dishtowel.

"Does this remind you of working in the bakery?" Anna asked.

"Yes, it does."

Marka opened the kitchen door and stretched her neck out into the biting winter air. The sky spit snowflakes at her face. The predicted snowstorm had arrived.

"Sometimes, I miss Millie and the café," Marka said. "I want to tell her about the baby."

"What if she blabs to everyone? You know she doesn't always use her head."

"I'll tell her to keep it to herself. I just can't keep this from her any longer."

"Marka!" Anna pointed out the kitchen window towards Sophie's house. "Something is wrong! There's no smoke coming out Sophie's chimney. We must get dressed and go over." Anna pressed her hands to her chest. There was fear in her eyes.

Marka thought how Anna knew Sophie's habits.

"Yes, something seems wrong."

They got dressed. They quickly put on their heavy coats and zipped up their rubber boots. Marka held Anna's hand as they walked across the yard, blanketed with newly fallen snow. They had to make their own tracks to Sophie's house.

Anna pounded hard on the wooden storm door, and when there was no answer, she said, "We're going inside."

She turned the doorknob and stepped inside the kitchen. Marka followed her through the rooms to the bedroom. The drapes were pulled closed, and only a crack of light filtered through. Anna turned on a lamp. "Brrr. The house is freezing. What's going on here?"

They walked over to the bed piled high with quilts. "Sophie, are you okay?" Anna's voice quivered. She lifted the quilts off Sophie. Anna stiffened, her feet frozen to the floorboards. "She's gone," Anna said softly. Her eyes filled with tears, her lips trembled. "*Deire freinde,* Dear friend." Anna closed Sophie's eyes, then lifted one of Sophie's arms and laid it gently on top of the quilts.

They walked back to Anna's in complete silence except for Anna's sobbing. A snow-laden branch creaked above their heads as they walked under the cottonwood.

When they got home, Marka called the coroner's office and later that morning, they came and took Sophie's body away.

For the rest of the day, Anna sat in her bedroom with the door closed. Marka took her tea and tried to get her to eat some supper, but she only sat with her head laid back against the headrest of the chair. She stared into space. Her eyes were glazed over, her silver-gray hair disheveled, hanging loose around her face.

Marka sat at the kitchen table and tried to enjoy her soup, but the thought of Sophie, now gone, made her cry. Sophie was Anna's best friend and confidante, and she had always treated Marka nicely. Every time the three of them had tea together, Sophie and Anna had told her many things about their Russian heritage, how their families left Germany in 1763 when Catherine the Great invited Germans to colonize Russia. A manifesto was issued which promised—land and exemption from military duty for 100 years. Sophie and Anna talked about their recent feelings of anxiety over the threat of war with Russia and that they could be deported or locked up like many Japanese and Germans were during World War II. Anna said that, starting in 1936, in America, it was not wise to admit to being German. Now, in 1957, it was not a good thing to be from Russia. Marka thought of Sophie's tearful, anxious face when they talked about the family they still had in Russia. "I wonder how many are still in the Gulag?" she asked Anna.

"We have starving relations there you know. Those that couldn't or wouldn't leave when they had the chance," Anna said. "They don't have the freedoms we have."

Anna and Sophie's conversations about their people had given Marka a sense of belonging. Her parents, Rachel and Philip, were German Russian. Anna, along with all her grandparents, had been born in Russia and emigrated from Russia to America in the early 1900's. Anna had said once that made them Russian.

Marka knew it was best not to talk about any of this, or she would have to endure prejudices that a part of society held against them. Anna had convinced her of that.

Sophie's funeral was at 10:00 a.m. on Monday, three days later. Anna managed to pull herself together. She braided her hair and wound it into a knot at the back of her head. She put on her black dress and hat with the heavy veil.

After the funeral, Marka went to visit Ruby. She stayed a couple of hours, and when she came home, she found Anna in the kitchen in her housedress and a green gingham apron. She had made a kettle of *kraut suppe*, cabbage-vegetable soup, and it was simmering on the stove.

"Anna, are you okay?"

"What good is it for me to sit with my head in my hands?" She put her hand in her apron pocket and handed Marka a small crocheted doily. "Sophie made this for you. I forgot to give it…" Anna's hands were shaking. "See how small the loops are. She could do such fine work."

Marka smiled and hugged Anna tight. "Yes, she always had to give me something when I left her house. I'm sorry your friend is gone." Marka felt like she too had lost a friend and ally. Sophie always stood up for her where Stella was concerned.

Anna said, "I feel sad because I won't see her anymore. I will miss our visits and how we would always bake twice as much just so we had something to share with each other."

Anna sat down in a kitchen chair. "This morning, I went out to the woodpile to get some wood, and I looked over at Sophie's house. I saw her. There she stood."

"Anna, Sophie is dead. What are you talking about?"

"Ach, I saw her spirit. I know everything is okay with her now. Some people think it's silly, but, I feel at peace about her."

Marka put her arms around Anna and held her close. "I don't think it's silly."

"Thank you for paying Sophie's bill at Carl's store. He told me," Anna said.

For the next few days, Marka helped Anna with the housework. They did the washing, which was now more of a chore for Marka. She ran the clothes through the wringer getting as much water out as she could, and Anna hung them on the rope strung across the basement.

"It's too cold to hang out the clothes," Anna said. "They will get stiff as boards and our fingers will freeze."

Marka made breakfast while Anna went outside, sorted through the woodpile, and loaded the basket with various sizes: kindling to get the fire started, medium pieces to sustain the fire, and large pieces that would burn a longer time.

Several days a week, Marka walked to Ruby's pool hall. Ruby reprimanded her for walking on the icy sidewalks. "In your condition, you have to be careful you don't fall. I'm surprised Anna lets you out of the house."

"Anna doesn't object. She's mourning Sophie."

One afternoon, when Marka got back from Ruby's, Anna was in the kitchen, crying. Marka started talking about Sophie and what a wonderful person she was. Anna said, "Ach, I know. I'm not crying over her. It's Carl."

"Did the two of you get into another argument?"

"No. I've been sitting here thinking about Sophie and how the last time I saw her she was still teasing me over Carl asking me to marry him. You know, we was good friends, but I never told her the story about me."

"You mean about the baby?"

"Yah, I think it's time I told you the rest of my story. Carl and I, well, we knew each other as children. Our families came over from Russia together. We always wanted to get married someday, but in those days, you did what your folks said. Old man Erlick and old man Burgardt, that was Lydia's father, well, they decided their kids should get married."

"Anna, does Carl have something to do with your baby?"

"Yah." Tears filled Anna's eyes. She bit her lip. "I guess I never wanted to admit that I did love Carl. In those days, you didn't go against the old people. When we are young, we make choices that are not good for us, and then, we have to live with them for the rest of our lives."

"Is Carl the father of your baby?"

"Yah. I couldn't tell Carl. I've never told him to this day. I never married because I thought, well, if I can't have Carl, I don't want anyone."

"Anna, why didn't you marry him when he asked you, after Lydia died? You should have. You could have had some happy years together."

"Yah. I guess so." Anna hung her head.

CHAPTER 35

In the morning, Anna seemed happy and less sad about Carl and Sophie. Marka heard her in the kitchen, humming. She felt guilty enjoying the comforts of a nice warm bed while Anna was in the cold kitchen waiting for it to heat up. "Get lots of rest. You got to take care of yourself and the baby," Anna would say.

When Marka got up she went to the kitchen, and Anna was shuffling her feet, doing a little dance. She was bundled in her housecoat, wool socks up around her legs, and her hands stretched over the cook stove. Marka stood beside her and warmed herself too.

"Anna, how do you think your life would have turned out if you and Carl had married?"

"The things I said yesterday; well, I'm still suffering the loss of Sophie. It brings everything back to me—the baby, and Carl. The things I said about Carl before, all that came from my anger.

"Anna, did your folks like Carl? Would they have wanted you to marry him? Did you and Carl have a romance?"

"Well, now, all this goes way back," Anna said. "Did I tell you that our *mutter* died when I was sixteen? Your mother was just four."

"Yes. You told me."

"*Babe*, Papa, was a nice man, but he needed help on the farm; so I had to work very hard. I wasn't able to go to school, because we worked in the sugar beet fields. My knees got all blistered and dirt stained from crawling on the ground. If the family needed money, everyone had to work even at the age of five. Your mother had to come to the fields with us, because there was no one to care for her. It was hard without our mother; so, Babe got married again, and she was a wonderful woman."

"Yes, you told me this, Anna."

"No, I didn't tell you this part. Well, anyways, just listen. She insisted that I move to town so I could make some money and meet someone. I became the cook at the dormitory in town, and I became the cook and cleaning girl for the parsonage. The preacher's wife taught me how to sew and before long, I was doing mending and then, I learned how to read patterns. That's when I did sewing for hire. The preacher had so many books; he helped me with my reading. Carl would come into town and we'd go together after church."

"Is that when the romance started?"

"Yah, but the old man figured I wasn't good enough for his son."

"How did you survive it all, Anna?"

"Believe it or not, I was very rebellious at one time. What saved me was that I always believed someone was with me, like God giving me an angel."

Anna and Marka went to the table and sat down. Anna stiffened herself, cocked her head, and looked deep into Marka's eyes. "Don't talk about this with anyone. Don't talk about us being from Russia and the hard life we had. These are scary times what with the Cold War with Russia and all. We are better off to keep things to ourselves."

"I won't; I promise."

"Anyway, let's change the subject. Thanksgiving is next week. What about us inviting George to dinner?"

"And, Ruby?"

"Yah, sure, and, Jonny."

"It's Ruby's birthday. May I bake her a cake?"

"Oh, what day's her birthday?"

"I don't know what day—neither does she," Marka giggled. "She knows only that she was born in the month of November."

"Ach, that's crazy not to know the date of your birth."

"Anna, that's the way her people did things. Now, don't judge. We have been talking all morning about the ways of our people. How they told their kids who they could marry. Not all our ways were good ones."

"Yah, you're right. Well, that's the way it was. You did what you were told. You didn't go against the old ones. Well, anyways, let's forget about it now and make a list of the things we need from the store. I'll call out to Paddock's farm and tell them I want a nice big turkey hen. They can bring it into town so we won't have to be out on those icy, country roads."

"How about Bodie? Would it be all right to invite him without inviting Carl, or would you like to invite Carl too?"

"Ach, I shouldn't have told you all that. Now, you won't leave me alone. Carl always has dinner with Buddy and Stella. Yah, invite Bodie."

"Can't you just picture it, them all gloomy and sad, and us laughing and happy?" Marka laughed.

"Call Bodie and tell him we need him to come over and shovel the sidewalk; then we'll ask him," Anna said. "You go call the others. I'll make a list of things we need, and then, I'll have Bodie get them."

"I want to invite them in person," Marka said, rushing down the hallway to get dressed. "I need some fresh air."

"All right, then, go ahead. When you go out, take these crusts of bread and throw them in the garden for the birds."

George yelled from the living room, "Just a minute, I'm coming." He opened the door, and then kicked aside the throw rug that was rolled up on the floor in front of the door to keep the draft out. "Hey, what are you doing out in all this snow? Come on in and sit here where it's nice and warm." The wood crackled in his pot-bellied stove. Marka stomped the snow off her boots and shook out her parka.

George turned off the radio and sat rocking back and forth in his chair. The rungs creaked against the hard wood floor. "So, what brings you over? Jonny and I are going ice fishing this afternoon. We heard they're nibbling around looking for something to eat."

"What you doing for Thanksgiving, George?"

"Oh, I don't know, asking for a reason, maybe, like I'm invited for dinner?"

"Yes!" Marka smiled.

"In that case," George said, "yes, now I do have plans. A man would be a fool to turn down Anna's cooking."

"Jonny's invited too."

"Go call him. Use my phone."

"He's probably in school, George. I'll call this evening."

"Call the school. Call him before someone else invites him. Trust me on this one," George insisted. "Oh, by the way, the town is going to let us flood the lot to make a skating rink for the kids. I explained how you found the deed and wanted to let the town use it. How could they say no?" George winked. "Jonny was very happy about it."

When Marka got back to Anna's, she called the school office and asked the secretary to leave a message for Jonny. Later, when he had a free period, he phoned her.

"Anna and I want to invite you to Thanksgiving dinner. Oh, good. Say, could you drop by Anna's later today? I want to talk to you about something. I'm going to walk to town. I want to invite Ruby. Will you walk with me? See you then."

Snowflakes gently touched Marka's rosy cheeks. She tipped her head back and looked at the gray sky. Snow fell like a silk veil, quietly and softly. Marka gathered snow in the palm of her woolen gloves.

"Do you remember how we made snowflakes out of white construction paper in Miss Dilly's class and she said that no two snowflakes were alike?" Marka walked cautiously through the half foot of snow that fell the night before.

"Of course. We'd make little cuts, any design we wanted. I remember something about them always having six points. Isn't it funny the things you remember?" Jonny stopped, stood still, and let the snow gather in his hand. "Yes, look at this, six points."

Marka gazed down at Jonny's hand. She squinted her eyes so she could see. "There's nothing there. Stop teasing me."

"Listen," Jonny said, "snowflakes are an eternal thing. They are the same as they were a million years ago. Water is water, right? How old is water? It's been here forever. When water freezes, it becomes crystals, and crystals have six sides; so, snowflakes must have six sides."

Marka quickened her step. "This is why you are a good teacher—and you're—a good friend."

Jonny put his arm out and took hold of Marka hand. "Hold onto me. It's slippery."

Jonny was a good friend, and he was smart. Too smart not to have figured out that there was something different about Marka. She had to tell him about the baby.

"The reason I wanted to talk to you…I don't know where to begin," Marka said. "You haven't seen much of me…"

"George told me. I knew something was wrong, so I dragged it out of him. He told me you were going to have a baby, and he is the grandfather."

"Oh! I'm glad he told you," Marka felt relieved. "You're too good a friend not to know."

When they arrived at Main Street, the sidewalks had been shoveled. Jonny lagged behind and made a snowball, and as Marka started making her way up the wooden stairs to Ruby's apartment, he threw it at her. Ruby heard giggles and came out of her apartment to see Marka and Jonny standing at the bottom of the stairs.

"Will you join us for Thanksgiving dinner? Jonny, George, and Bodie are coming," Marka hollered up the stairway to Ruby. She wiped melted snow from her coat.

Ruby's eyes sparkled. "Come on up," she said hugging her warm sweater tight up around her throat.

They climbed the stairs and joined Ruby on the landing.

"We can't come in," Marka said. "I just wanted to invite you in person."

"When is Thanksgiving, anyway?"

"One week from tomorrow. Oh, Ruby, say you'll come. It will be such fun."

"Will I have enough time to get a catalog order? I want to wear something nice. Maybe even a suit. How about wool with—"

"Ruby, you don't have to impress anyone."

"Oh, Mia," she chimed. "Thank you. Tell Anna thanks."

Marka and Jonny trudged back to Anna's, and the heavy snow pack that had accumulated creaked as they walked.

"Anna really does want Ruby to come to dinner. I told her that Ruby feels like an outcast, but, she stays here because she can't go back to her people."

"Why not?" Jonny asked.

"Because she married a *gaje*, a white man. She will never be allowed to return to her people or her way of life. I told Anna that I

292

thought Ruby was one of the strongest people I'd ever met. Anna said that sometimes people seemed strong on the outside, but that there is a weakness on the inside."

"People can be fragile," Jonny said. "Glass is strong in a blown flask, but if it's hit in just the right spot, the flask will burst apart. It can be that way with people too."

On Thanksgiving Day, it had stopped snowing. The sky was a silvery blue; stillness lingered throughout the town. Everything was motionless, except for the smoke billowing from the chimneys, and birds pecking at the suet Anna put into a piece of netting and hung on the clothes lines.

"They need a feast today too," she said. "Just so the starlings don't make pigs of themselves and eat it all before the other birds get a chance at it."

Marka felt happy, content, and excited. "It's Thanksgiving Day my little baby," she said, waltzing around the kitchen. The aroma of roast turkey wafted through the house and made her hungry. The sweet potatoes were ready except for the marshmallows. Anna made her own, because they were out of them at People's Grocery. She dissolved gelatin in water, cooked in sugar and corn syrup, and then beat the ingredients until it formed peaks. She would spread the marshmallow over the sweet potatoes and brown them right before they were served.

Marka baked a birthday cake for Ruby, a Lady Baltimore Cake with Never Fail Seven Minute Frosting.

"How old is she if she doesn't even know when she was born?" Anna asked.

"She knows how old she is, just not the day of her birth. Anna, it doesn't really matter, does it?"

Bodie showed up first. When he arrived, he was standing with his stocking cap pulled down over his forehead and eyebrows. He stomped his overshoes to remove the caked on snow, and then unbuckled each one, and set them inside the door on the rubber mat. Ruby arrived next, and then George and Jonny arrived at the same time.

After they ate, the men retired to the front room while the women cleaned up the kitchen. Marka washed, Ruby dried, and Anna put away the leftovers. While Ruby was drying the silverware, she dropped a fork and said, "Oh, that means we will be getting company."

"What?" Marka laughed.

"I know that one," Anna said. "Drop a spoon means you will have good luck. Drop a knife and you will have bad luck."

"I dropped a fork; so, that means we will be getting company."

George walked into the kitchen about that time.

"See, here comes company," Ruby roared with laughter.

George said, "That's about as silly as saying as this one. If a horse grows long hair early in the fall, it's a sign that there will be a hard winter."

"Well, I suppose if the geese leave early in the fall it means the same thing," Anna joked.

"Guess we all have our superstitions," Marka winked at Ruby.

After the kitchen was clean, they had mincemeat and pumpkin pie with whipped cream, and of course, cake. They sang happy birthday to Ruby. She was taken by surprise and started to cry. Marka thought how lovely she looked in her black flowing skirt and red satin blouse. Ruby would have looked ridiculous in a wool suit.

The men wanted to play cards, but Anna said playing cards was looked on as being sinful. She relented and said, "As long as you don't play poker and bet money, it will be all right."

They played a couple of hands of Pitch, and then George went to his house and got his cribbage board. He and Jonny tried to teach Bodie the game.

Anna turned on the television, and Betty Furness was advertising the Amana refrigerator. This reminded Anna of something Stella had said at the last Ladies' Aid meeting about how she was going to be getting one. Marka thought how *she* could buy ten new refrigerators with the money she found in the radio.

Jonny came into the front room and sat down in a chair beside Marka and asked her whether she would like to go to the Sugar Dance with him in Garrison. "It's November 30, at the community hall."

Marka thought about being three months along, and although she had only a small bump of a tummy, she knew Anna would not think it was a good idea. She was about to say, "No" when Anna said, "She'd love to go with you. You know Ida was crowned Sugar Queen, and it would make her so happy if you went. Yah, that Ida has such a beautiful singing voice. When I die, remember that I want her to sing at my funeral."

"Anna, don't tease about that," Marka said.

Jonny changed the subject. "The school Christmas program is Dec. 14. The girl's glee club will sing, and the band will play. Ida is going to sing a solo. Maybe you and Anna would like to come to that. There's a thick layer of ice on the rink. The kids took shovels and brooms to it. We could build a fire in a barrel."

Marka said, "Yes" to the dance and to the Christmas program, but when Jonny asked her to go ice skating on the new rink, Anna gave her a look and said, "No," I don't think so, Jonny, not in her condition."

Christmas came and went without much excitement. Bodie brought them a small pine he cut in the hills. They set it in front of the living room window and decorated it. On Christmas Eve, they went to the church program. The children put on a pageant with shepherds, wise men, angels, and of course, a baby in the manger. They used one of Ida's dolls from when she was a child.

After the service, everyone received a brown paper bag with an apple, ribbon candy and an assortment of nuts.

Anna and Marka went home and exchanged presents. Marka surprised Anna with a brand new, Singer, sewing machine; a portable. Anna was happy. "I still want to keep my old treadle though," she said.

Anna had made a baby quilt for Marka. She had stayed up late at night. It was a well-kept surprise.

CHAPTER 36

Marka pulled the curtain back from her bedroom window. Ridley was quiet. Nothing moved except for the birds that hung around the treetops feeling the cold, occasional bite from the freezing north wind. The day before, smoky gray clouds had come from the west, and the night was cold and dark, but, this morning it was clear, and the bright sun made the snow sparkle.

She went to the kitchen, opened the door, and yelled for Sasha. The cat bounced across the snow and darted inside. This was the part of winter Marka loved; the idle ground covered with freshly fallen snow, nothing outdoors needed to be tended; the plants were dormant. She felt warm and snug indoors. She was about to close the door when she saw Bodie plodding along, walking toward Anna's house. He was wearing his red and black plaid hunting cap with the flaps pulled down over his ears. He cupped his hands together and blew on them.

"Haven't you any gloves?" Marka asked sounding motherly.

"I was in such a hurry to get out of there, I forgot them," Bodie said.

Marka told Bodie to come inside and shut the door behind him.

"Out of where? Take off your coat and boots. How about a cup of hot cocoa?"

Bodie sat down at the table. He took his cap off and laid it on the floor.

"Buddy and Stella just had a terrible fight." He unbuckled his over boots and tugged at the tops of his thick woolen socks. "I was at the back of the store, stocking shelves. They didn't know I was there. Boy, they sure went at each other. First, Stella asked Buddy why he hated her so much, and he said well, she wasn't what he thought she was when he married her. He said she was greedy and only thought about herself. She whined like a baby that he didn't know what it was like to be poor, to have to kiss up to people. He said she didn't have to kiss up to anyone in this town, and she said, yes, she did."

Bodie stopped and took a deep breath. "He said he warned her that living in a small town would be different than living in St. Louis. Then, Stella said that she was tired of Carl always making jokes about why they didn't have kids. What would he say if he knew they hadn't even been sleeping together? Then, she really laid into him. Gee, Marka—I'm scared to tell you the rest."

Bodie got up from the table and paced around the kitchen.

"What? Tell me." Marka got up from the table and walked over to where Bodie stood. She took him by the elbow and led him back to the table.

Bodie got tears in his eyes. He took his handkerchief from his back pocket and blew his nose. "Stella said, 'I know you cheat on me, but how could you have slept with Marka? Now, you have a bastard child on the way'." Bodie balled his fists and slammed them together. "She said that people saw you two leaving the pavilion the night of the fair dance."

Marka crossed her arms over her tummy as if to protect the child. She felt a ringing in her ears; the room seemed to be spinning.

"I shouldn't have told you, should I?" Bodie shook his head and pounded his fist on the table. See, all I did was upset you for nothing."

Marka reached across the table for Bodie's hand. "It's all right. I'm glad you told me. Part of what Stella said is true. I am going to have a baby. So, I guess this means the news is out. I hoped it could have waited until spring. I wanted to get through the winter without anyone knowing. I'm hardly showing," she said.

"Then it's true? You're going to have Buddy's baby?" Bodie looked confused.

"No, not Buddy's. I know Stella hates me, but she must not think that this baby is Buddy's. I've got to talk to her."

Anna was in the basement washing clothes, and when she heard the commotion, she came upstairs. Marka told her what Bodie had said.

"I'll go talk to her," Anna said. "Bodie, I don't want you talking to anyone about this, you hear. Marka is going to have a baby, and the father is George's son, Jack. Marka wrote him a letter about it, but he hasn't shown any interest, which means that she will be raising her child alone. That's bad enough. I don't want this whole town spending all winter gossiping over it."

Marka's shoulders felt tense. She sat with a wary gaze. She tried to turn down the noise in her mind. "I did have an affair with Rex, and then, there's Jack. I guess you can lie to others, but not yourself. The whole town probably knows by now. Oh, what difference does it make?"

"It makes a lot of difference! You have to be more of a fighter." Anna picked up the telephone. Her eyebrows drew together, and her nostrils flared. "I am going to call Stella and have her come over here and we are going to talk this out."

"What makes you think she will come over?" Marka asked.

"I'll tell her it's important Ladies' Aid business. She'll come or I'll go over and drag her here by the hair!"

Stella pointed her finger at Marka. "You're having my husband's baby. You couldn't land a man in Denver. You thought you could in Ridley. Well, not my man!"

"That's not true." Marka stomped her foot on the floor. "Where did you hear this? I want to know."

"From the nurse at Doc Seller's office. All I have to do is look at you, and I can tell it's true," Stella said.

"Bite your tongue, Stella," Anna's voice rose steadily in anger. "Marka is in a delicate condition right now, and the last thing she needs is a tongue lashing from you."

"So, it is true," Stella squinted her eyes, and she tightened her lips. Stella threw her head back, stuck out her chin, and put her hands on her hips. "Well Buddy isn't going to give you a cent. I'll see to that. Why don't you do the smart thing and get out of town?" Stella fixed an evil stare on Marka, and said, "You sniveling little whore."

"You have a hard heart, Stella," Anna said giving her a look of disgust. "The words you speak reveal more about you than what you are saying. I never knew you were so cruel."

"Stella, ever since I came to Ridley, you've had it in for me. From that first day after church, you've insulted me in front of others and you've threatened me. I won't tolerate any more from you. You are an evil person. No wonder Buddy is looking for someone else," Marka sobbed, ran to the bedroom, and slammed the door. "And I have no intentions of leaving town," she screamed through the closed door.

"The baby is Jack's; George's son," Bodie blurted. "If you think back, you'll remember that his son was here visiting this summer."

Marka came out of the bedroom. Anna put her hand up motioning Marka not to say anymore.

"So, where is he then—the father of your baby?" Stella sneered. She put her hand to her chest and coughed. "I'm warning you, Marka, it will be open season on you if you encourage Buddy. You are a husband stealer. This whole thing is upsetting me. I'm leaving."

"Upsetting YOU! If you have any decency, you won't spread this all over town," Anna said, following Stella as she stepped carefully down the slick porch steps, pulling her scarf tightly around her throat.

"Just remember, Stella, that when a bee stings, he leaves his stinger, but he eventually dies," Anna yelled at her as she stomped off down the street squawking like a bossy blue jay chasing all the smaller birds away from the feeder.

"People who go around saying hurtful things only end up suffering for it, because it boomerangs," Anna said to Marka.

"What did you mean, Anna, about the bee sting?"

"They end up feeling guilty for their unkind words and it starts to eat at them. They usually bring about their own destruction."

Marka began to cry. "I don't know what I ever did to her. All I wanted was to be a part of this town and she has done everything she could to hurt me. This is my town—not hers. This is where I was born and raised. How is it that I don't belong, and she does? I hate her. She's going to ruin everything for me. I hope something horrible happens to her."

Anna said, "I don't believe in revenge, but sooner or later the chickens come home to roost."

CHAPTER 37

No one expected the blizzard that hit the second week of February. No one was prepared. The day before, the Chinook winds had come in from the southwest and melted the snow, flooding the yard.

At 3:00 p.m., it started to snow, and by 5:00 p.m., the storm struck. A bitter wind stirred up and blew from all directions. It battered against the sides of houses and plastered snow against windows and walls of buildings. The powdery snow was so fine that the wind pushed it through the cracks in window frames and under doors. It drifted up against the houses, barns, and other out buildings, and in some places, it piled as high as five feet. The wind howled through the windows, and outdoors, the trees moaned.

The blizzard lasted two days. The temperature the night before had fallen below zero. Before the blizzard, it was so cold that a crust had formed over the powdered snow. During the blizzard, nothing had moved outdoors for two days except for a cottontail that ran across the yard. The radio said the highways were clear between Clayton and Ridley, Deerfield, and Garrison. The problem remaining was the livestock stranded on the range. They would have to go without food. Farm machinery would be buried in snow for weeks unless they had another warm wind blow in.

Anna stayed up late and fed the fire in the cook stove to keep the house warm. When she grew too tired she went to bed and set an alarm clock so she could get up early and get it going again before the ashes cooled too much.

Marka lay in bed, listening to Anna stoke the fire. She touched her tender, swollen breasts. She was five months along now, and sleepless nights were becoming a common thing. If she had her way, she would stay in bed most of the day, but she heard Anna call from the kitchen. "Marka, it's nine o'clock. Get up. The sun is shining. It's going to be a nice day after all."

Marka crawled out of bed, put on her robe, and opened the blinds. The sun streamed into the room.

Anna was in a clean housedress and apron. She had fried bacon and made *blinas,* pancakes for breakfast. "I hope we have enough fuel oil left to get through this cold spell. The gauge on the tank shows it's near empty." Anna poured bacon grease into a coffee can. "We don't want to risk running low. I'm going to call and have oil delivered. We must keep the house warm for you, Marka."

Marka held her hands over the cook stove, warmed them, and read aloud from the Farmer's Almanac that hung on the wall next to the stove. "February 12. 'Take care of the pennies and the pounds will take care of themselves.' I'm sure thankful that I don't have to worry about money, Anna. What a blessing."

After breakfast, Anna looked through the seed catalog and talked to Marka about what they should plant in the garden come spring. She would have to get her seedlings started for tomatoes, cucumbers, and cabbage.

Marka stood over the sink stirring her hot cocoa, looking out the window at the icicles hanging from the eaves of the house. Drip— drip—drip. A thick sheet of snow slid off the roof and hit the ground with a thud. The bright rays of sunlight hurt her eyes. "I want to call George. I wonder if he put the battery back in his car. I'm starting to go stir crazy. We've been cooped up in the house for days now."

"*Madchen,* where you want to go?"

"I thought I'd go to Clayton to Ben Franklin's and buy some more yarn. I almost have that sweater set finished, and I want to start another one."

"You are showing now, you know."

"I'll wear my coat. It will cover me."

"The radio said the roads are clear, but make sure you get home before it starts to get dark when the temperature drops and the roads get slick," Anna warned.

"I think the gossip about me having a baby is around. During the storm, no one from church even bothered to check on us. They are shunning us. I'm sad and discouraged, Anna."

"Yah. I'm disappointed, but not surprised. It's a good thing we have George to check on us."

After lunch, Anna called George and asked if he by chance was going to Clayton. He said he was now after she told him what Marka had in mind about needing to go.

"There's no sense in her being out on the roads," George said. "I need to go to Piggly Wiggly for a few groceries and to the dime store to get myself a new pair of reading glasses."

Anna reminded George about their combined stash of Red Stamps from Smiley's Grocery Store. "I'll take Marka to their store basement, and she can cash them in for baby things," George said.

George turned the heater in the car on high.

"Marka, what do you think about the satellite that's orbiting out there in space? About time the Americans finally caught up with the Russians."

"It's amazing, isn't it? Anna and I have been watching it on television. We invited Ruby to come over, but she said, no. She's not happy about all of this. "It will mess up the celestial, astrological atmosphere, she said."

"The woman is strange," George shook his head. "I know; I know; she's your friend."

"Ruby's thoughts are different from other people. Anna has a Farmer's Almanac and it has information about Aquarius, the Zodiac sign. Maybe Ruby does have some strange ideas, but I think she's right about Stella. She says Stella has a dark heart."

"Haven't seen much of her lately. Maybe she's cold-blooded like a fish. They slow down in the winter," George said.

"Anna says that Stella is still playing childish games. Will Stella tell everyone who comes into the post office about me? That's what worries me."

Anna had supper ready when Marka got home. They ate, and then Anna got Marka started on another baby sweater before she read her Bible. With outstretched arms, the book balanced on her knee. She peered over the top of her glasses. Marka looked up from her crocheting once in a while and watched how Anna touched her wet tongue with a finger, and then she'd turn a page.

"What does it say?" Marka asked.

"The upright are directed by their honesty; the wicked fall beneath their loads of sins. *Proverbs Eleven*. I was thinking about Stella and what could have made her so hateful. Tonight is Ladies' Aid, and not one person called to see if I was coming."

Marka lowered her eyes. "I've spoiled things for you. I'm a scorned woman, because I am going to have a child and have no husband. It's like the book Jonny gave me, *The Scarlet Letter*.

Anna closed her Bible and put it on the side table. "And what I did with Carl was wrong? I thought we was going to be getting married. Well, anyways…"

"I'm giving everyone something to talk about," Marka said.

"When they get their talking done, they'll forget about it. It's too bad you and Jonny never got together; that's all I can say. He's a good man. You two could still get together. He knows about the baby now."

"Anna! I know I am well past marrying age, but I will not let you push me into Jonny's arms. Besides, what are you thinking? Marrying outside the German clan is frowned upon." Marka put her crocheting aside. "He's not the right man for me. I won't marry the wrong man."

CHAPTER 38

March fourth was bleak. The sun was covered with a thick layer of clouds. The temperature fell and the wind blew all day. Only days before, warm winds had melted the snow. Then, the temperatures dropped, and the melted snow formed ice, deadly black ice, on the blacktop and bridges. It was on a patch of black ice, on the bridge between Garrison and Ridley, that ended Stella Erlich's life. The sheriff told everyone the skid marks indicated her car spun out of control. It fishtailed across the road and ran down into the barrow pit, the deep ditch beside the road.

Ruby telephoned Marka. "Did you hear what happened to Stella? There's talk going around the pool hall that there was an empty bottle of vodka in the car. The *Clayton Post* took photos at the scene of the accident. Somehow, Herb got a hold of them. Gads, you can't even recognize her face; there's so much blood."

After reporting all the gory details, Ruby added, "The funeral is on Friday."

"How awful." Marka felt a deep sense of sadness and confusion all at the same time. "Are you going to the funeral, Ruby?"

"I must. Just in case Stella had any feelings of hatred against me. I must make peace with her spirit. I don't wish for her to come back and seek revenge."

There was a knock on the door. Bodie came over to Anna's to tell them what happened. He was sobbing, but he managed to get the story out. Bodie told them that Stella's mother had been visiting since the middle of February. "Buddy said Stella and her mother argued all the time. It drove him crazy. I guess Stella's mother is a tyrant; he don't like her. He was glad when she left. He didn't even want to drive her to the airport in Rapid. Made Stella do it. Now, Buddy feels guilty." Bodie blew his nose on his handkerchief. "The Sheriff said Stella was drunk when she had the accident. Buddy's got himself locked up in the house and won't come out."

"What a horrible thing," Marka said. "Tell Buddy, I'm sorry." Her throat tightened, her eyelids lowered and reddened, and tears appeared in her eyes.

Anna was quiet the whole time Bodie talked. She stood with her eyebrows knitted together and her mouth pursed tightly. "Sounds like Stella was cut from the same cloth as her mother. She told me once that her mother was a drunk and a terrible person."

The church was cold the day of Stella's funeral. The furnace had broken, and there was not enough time before the funeral to have it fixed. During the service, everyone sat shivering in their heavy overcoats, hats, and gloves. Marka and Anna sat in back, because Anna felt uncomfortable. None of the women in Ladies' Aid had even bothered to call her to ask whether she would bring a hot dish to the church basement where they always had a meal for family and friends after a funeral.

"Look at them sitting up there wiping their noses and weepy eyes," she whispered to Marka. "It looks like they took her side."

Ruby walked in and went to the front of the church. She sat in the second pew directly behind the family: Buddy, Carl, Bodie, and Stella's mother. Her stride was slightly arrogant, torso straight, head held high. Her expression was that of confidence. She was wearing a red wool coat, long white gloves, and a black matador hat. The hat leaned off to the side of her head. Marka knew exactly what she was doing. She was dressing for the occasion.

Marka thought back to how naïve she had been when she opened her soul to a complete stranger on an airplane, not knowing that the stranger would turn out to be her worst enemy. She guessed everyone had a dark side. She certainly had one. She had frequented the Ridley saloon and drank at the bar, which she knew was not acceptable behavior for a small town. She lied to Anna about smoking and drinking, and, she had made a death wish against Stella.

While Reverend Thurber spoke kindly of Stella, Marka bowed her head and prayed to God. Please forgive me for all my sins. And, Lord, I am grateful for the good people in my life; for Ruby, who let me share my secrets. She never judged me, only said, "You have made mistakes, but YOU are not a mistake."

George told me his story and talked about a higher power. That helped me to turn my life around. I found the strength to accept the truth about myself.

Marka looked up and saw Ruby with her nose just slightly in the air and thought of one more blessing she could be grateful for—the ghosts of her past were gone.

Reverend Thurber concluded the funeral service with the Lord's Prayer, and then, they sang the "Old Rugged Cross", and everyone exited the church after passing by the casket and expressing their condolences to the family.

That evening, Marka and Anna sat quietly in the front room. They agreed to leave television off for the evening. It was quiet except for the ticking of the regulator clock and Sasha's purring.

Anna moved the crochet yarn across her fingers and looped it through the small end of the hook. She pulled a goodly amount of yarn from the ball and settled it on her lap between her legs. Marka turned the page of the book she was reading. She couldn't concentrate; she kept thinking about how Stella hated her from the very beginning.

"It all started that first Sunday after church, you know." Marka said to Anna, putting her book down. "Stella shunned me instead of saying, hello. The last time I saw her was the day she came over and accused me of trying to steal Buddy from her. Why did Stella feel so threatened by me?"

"Because Stella wanted to be the Queen of Ridley, and she wanted to be in control of other people's lives," Anna said. "Just like the Cold War between Russia and the United States." Anna put down her crocheting.

"I wonder whether things would have been different if I had not told her everything that day on the plane?"

"We must forgive and forget, Marka."

"I'll try, Anna."

Marka's attempt to forgive Stella was short lived. Two weeks after the funeral, Buddy showed up at the door. She and Anna were sewing blocks for a bed quilt, when Buddy came to the house and said he needed to talk to Marka.

They went into the front room and sat on the sofa. Buddy told her that he was going through Stella's belongings and he found two letters without a postmark. "One is to the Teacher's College in Deerfield, and the other is to Jack Hanson, in Florida. And there are two letters with cancelled stamps, one from Texas, and one from Denver. The Denver letter was postmarked March 10, 1957."

Marka took the letters from Buddy and slowly looked at them one at a time. Her hands started to shake. She screamed, and she tossed all but one to the floor.

"The letter I wrote to Jack," she gasped, and held it close to her chest. Her anger towards Stella flared. "How could she have done this?" Marka picked up the other letters and held them tightly in her hands, and then she turned the envelopes over and let out a moan. "She didn't even open them! These letters. My, God, they held— my life. How could she be so cruel?"

"I don't understand why she did this," Buddy said. "When her mother was here, I did overhear them talking and Stella said something like, 'I can't do anything right. I pushed Buddy right into her arms.' "

"I don't know what to say," Marka wept and hugged her stomach tight.

"She kept my letters, but she didn't even open them!"

Buddy said. "She must have figured as long as she didn't open them, she wasn't breaking the law. Stella had a weird way of thinking."

"Buddy—I—feel like I'm going to faint." Marka put her hand over her face. She heard a hissing in her ears and everything started to look black.

"You're white as snow. Lay down on the couch," Buddy's voice sounded far away like an echo, and the last words she heard him saying were, "Anna, you got to get in here quick!"

When Marka opened her eyes, Buddy was sitting on the floor beside the sofa, holding her hand, and he was crying.

Marka sat up.

Anna told her to lie back down. She covered Marka with a blanket.

Buddy didn't move from the floor. "I heard Stella tell her mother that she ran away with me out of spite. So, she used me. And I was god damn stupid. I didn't want to see how awful Stella was. Bodie told me about how she threw her wedding ring in the river just so she could have a new one."

"Do you have any idea what she's done to *my* life?" Marka sobbed.

"She was cold. If she didn't get her way, she'd strike like a snake. The only reason she married me was to get the hell away from her mother. They had a fight right before they left the house for the airport."

"I don't want to hear what she did to you!" Marka could not stop crying.

"I was tempted to burn all these letters and not even tell you."

"Buddy! No!" Marka covered her ears with her hands. "I'm glad you didn't do that. Maybe now I can make some sense out of things. I don't know whether I can, but I have to try."

Wednesday evening, Ladies' Aid was at Katie Weisson's house. Marka barged in on the meeting. She felt a knot in her stomach as she stood in front of them. She had never done anything like this before, but what did she have to lose?

She delivered her rehearsed speech. "Everything that has happened to me since I arrived in Ridley will not be swept under the rug."

She told them about her battles with Stella and how Stella held back her letters. "It seems to me that Stella was her own dead letter office. I take responsibility for all my actions, but let's just say my life would have turned out differently if she had not done this to me. I am very disappointed in all of you for the way you have treated Anna. You're hypocrites! You go to church, and you talk about how you pray and help each other. I don't see it that way. You gossip and judge. Well, everyone makes mistakes, but you can't seem to forgive a wrongdoing. When I came back to Ridley, I felt like an outcast. Now, my Aunt Anna feels like one. If you want to take out your wrath on someone, take it out on me, not Anna."

CHAPTER 39

Marka felt vindicated. She and George phoned Jack and Marka didn't hold back a thing.

Jack said, "You've been so wrong about me. You're much more to me than just a fling."

"Did you ever think of me after you left?" she asked.

"Yes, oh yes, my darling. I wasn't sure how you felt about me."

Her tantrum at the Ladies' Aid meeting had been effective. The women opened their arms to Anna, and apologized for their pettiness. Soon, Anna was busy with sewing jobs, and the church ladies dropped by to visit. It didn't take long for the news to get around that Marka and George's son, Jack, were to be married.

Anna became consumed with love for the baby growing inside Marka. Every day, she patted Marka's belly and talked to the baby. She kept saying, "That Jack is a good man even though he's not one of us."

Marka couldn't remember a time when Anna was as happy as she was these days. She wanted to sew a wedding suit for Marka; she wanted to have a shower for her and invite every lady in Ridley. In addition to taking care of Marka's needs, she was busy nurturing her seedlings. It was almost time to move them to the garden. "Look, already the geese are coming from the south," Anna said. "Spring is a time of rebirth—a time for growth and new beginnings."

Saturday, April fifth, the day before Easter, George drove Marka to the airport in Rapid City to pick up Jack. They left early in the morning. The first rays of sun rose over the horizon. The winter's moisture had turned the countryside to green. Pasque flowers pushed themselves up through the pasture grasses.

"My lady, look for that cloud with the silver lining. It's out there somewhere," George said.

"I don't suppose Jack will want to move to Ridley," Marka said. "He has a good job at Cape Canaveral."

"You're right. Best not hope for that."

"Besides, just because he's coming doesn't mean things will work out. We have much to talk about," Marka said. "But at least he knows about the baby."

"I hope Jack and I have a better go at it this time around," George said. "When he was here last summer, he resisted everything I said. He always took his mother's side in the divorce. This time, I want to tell him my side of the story."

Jack's plane got in at 11:00 a.m. When Marka saw him walking towards the arrival gate, she tried to choke back the tears so Jack wouldn't see her crying. The baby in her belly kicked.

Jack ran to her and scooped her into his arms. She looked into his green-gray eyes and saw that he was crying too.

George told them to go get a bite to eat at the coffee shop while he retrieved Jack's luggage. "I can surely handle one suitcase by myself," he said.

They stood outside the airport restaurant and held each other for a long time before going in.

"Marka, will you marry me?" Jack asked.

"Yes! I wasn't sure you'd ask," Marka could hardly get her words out. She wrapped her arms around his neck.

"I felt jilted when I didn't hear from you," Jack explained, then continued, "my stupid pride kept me from you. I have been a fool. I should not have let my insecurity keep me from calling you."

"You know, Ruby kept telling me not to give up, to keep sending good thoughts out to you, but I didn't believe her," Marka responded.

"When Dad called and told me how Stella held your letter, well, I thought I'd go crazy. I hope you know if I had gotten it, I would have come back and married you right away."

"When I didn't hear from you, I thought you didn't love me and that the baby didn't make any difference. How could I have been so wrong?"

"Let's stop blaming ourselves," Jack cleared his throat. "I had a long visit with my mother and told her about you and the baby. She admitted she had done a horrible thing by telling me only the bad things about my dad."

"It was good of her to admit that to you," Marka said. "Jack, have you forgiven your father?"

"Yes, I want to get to know him better."

"I've come to realize that my parents had their struggles," Marka said. "In the past, I held so much against them, but I've made peace with all that—but, not with Stella! My heart is still full of anger. I don't know whether I will ever be able to forgive her for what she did."

"To think she tampered with our lives," Jack's voice was low. "She took away so much joy, and, you had to go through all of this alone."

They stood silent for a long time, their arms entwined. Marka leaned her forehead against Jack's chest. She felt peaceful and happy. "So, you want to make an honest woman out of me?"

Jack took an engagement ring out of his jacket pocket. He kissed it and held it to his heart before he slipped it on her finger. "I can't wait a minute longer."

"I accept," Marka beamed like a ray of sunshine.

The next day was Easter Sunday. Anna gave Marka and Jack her blessings. She wanted to take Jack to church so she could show him off to everyone. Monday morning, George drove his son back to the airport. Jack's plan was to return to Florida and look for a house, then return to Ridley for his bride.

Ruby took hold of Marka's arm and pulled her into the apartment. "I have something to show you," she led Marka over to the window where the easel stood. "Look, I finished the portrait of Henry. I finally got the eyes right."

Marka got teary. "It's beautiful, Ruby. I knew you would do it someday."

"It's you, Mia. There's something about you that brought it out of me. I want to show you something else," Ruby said. "A package came in the mail for me. Wait here."

Ruby went into the bedroom. When she came out, she was carrying a black case. "This is my father's violin. When he played, I would be filled with joy."

"This means your family knows where you are. Do you think they will come for you?"

"I don't think so, Mia. But, that's okay. I know they have not forgotten me; so, enough about me. How are you feeling, Mia? Are you going to marry Jack and leave us?"

"Oh, Ruby, he loves me. My heart is so full. Every day I get a letter from him."

"For once, you are following your heart. Stella did an evil thing to you. We should never mess with the fate of another person."

"I hate her for what she did," Marka said.

"In a way, it is kind of mystical," Ruby looked serious. "The wrong thing happens for the right reason."

"What do you mean, Ruby?"

"The letter from Rex. It was good you didn't get it," Ruby laughed.

After Memorial Day, Anna had Harry Paddock plow her garden plot. She hired Bodie to rake it out smooth. Anna had been working way too hard, but Marka was in no condition to help. "You look like a springer, a cow heavy with calf," Anna teased.

On June Fourth, a Tuesday, Marka gave birth to a baby boy. He weighed eight pounds and three ounces. He had delicate pink skin and sky-blue eyes. Jack wanted to name him Dwight after Eisenhower, but Marka said, "No, that's going too far."

"Dad would like it if we named him George," Jack said.

"What about Fritz? Anna said.

"I want to name him, Jacob," Marka said, looking at Anna and thinking about the secret they shared.

Jack and Marka were married quietly in the home of Louise and Reverend Thurber. Marka considered having Anna alter her mother, Rachel's wedding gown, but then decided a suit more fitting for the occasion.

George, Ruby, Bodie, Millie, and Ida were all there. Anna took Marka and Jack's picture with her box camera, and she took a group photo. Ruby smiled wide beneath a hat with a big floppy brim.

Jack returned to work in Florida. Marka started packing boxes and storing them in Anna's basement. Anna kept telling her to go to the store and buy bread, because she didn't have time for baking. At the slightest sound, Anna would rush to the baby and pick him up.

As each day passed, Marka thought how good life was, and she was finding that the love for the baby was dissolving the bitterness she felt against Stella.

CHAPTER 40

That morning had been a glorious one. White, billowy clouds moved across the blue sky. Marka and Anna had finished hoeing the weeds in the garden while Jacob lay in his buggy and breathed the warm morning air. They thinned the carrots, beets, and turnips and marveled at how fast the tomato plants had grown, and how the cucumbers were already starting to spread across the ground. Anna was pleased her *schwarzbeeren,* black berry, and gooseberry plants were doing so well. Marka and Anna stood close to each other, resting on their hoes. Anna talked about how she loved laboring in the garden.

During the afternoon, Anna suddenly became ill. She said she didn't feel well and went to her bedroom to lie down. Marka checked on her an hour later. Anna lay still in her bed. Marka leaned close and Anna pointed to her mouth. Her mouth moved, but there were no words. Her face was twisted to one side.

Marka called Doc Sellers.

"Cover her with a warm blanket. I'll be there right away."

Marka covered Anna and sat on the edge of the bed. She put Anna's hand in hers and rubbed her fingers over Anna's hardened blisters.

Marka went to her bedroom to check on Jacob, and then to the kitchen window to see whether Doc Sellers had arrived. She paced back and forth between the kitchen and Anna's bedroom, trying to hold back her panic. She felt numb and disorganized. "It will be all right, Anna. Doc Sellers is on his way."

Her mind wanted to chatter about inconsequential things, but she had to be there for Anna. Anna looked into Marka's eyes but couldn't speak. "Anna," Marka said fervently, "you're going to be all right."

Marka wished Doc Sellers would get there. Anna just has to be okay! This was not how she expected the day to turn out. It had been a wonderful morning of working, talking and laughing, and then they ate lunch and listened to Paul Harvey.

Anna wasn't very hungry. "I feel a little woozy," she said. She didn't pick Jacob up when he whimpered. How could Marka have missed the warning signs? "Oh, why didn't I realize something was wrong," Marka reprimanded herself.

.

"She's had a stroke," Doc said. "I gave her a shot. I want her to go to the hospital, but she shook her head, no. You know how stubborn she can be."

"I'll stay right beside her," Marka said.

"Call me if anything changes. I'll be here early this evening."

At 7:00 p.m., Doc Sellers came back to the house to check on Anna. Marka had been in the room fifteen minutes earlier. Anna had her eyes closed; she was breathing, but things didn't feel right. She was too still.

Marka waited awhile and then went to the doorway of Anna's room and looked inside. Doc was slumped over in a chair, holding his head in his hands.

"Is Anna all right?"

Doc shook his head, no.

Marka walked over to the bed. Anna lay still, her chest wasn't moving; her head lay straight on the pillow; her face, colorless like wax. "Anna, Anna," Marka whispered softly. There was stillness in Anna's face that told her, Anna was gone.

"Anna's heart stopped shortly after I got here. I just wanted to sit with her for a while," Doc said. "I want you to know this; death held no fear for her. Not once did I see terror in her eyes. I knew her well enough to say this with confidence," Doc said.

Fear and sadness gripped Marka's heart. "She just can't be gone," Marka's cried. She slumped to the floor and knelt beside the bed. She felt dizzy and nauseous; she felt as though she would choke on the lump in her throat. She felt like the breath had been knocked out of her, and she felt like there was a heavy weight on the top of her head pushing her into the ground.

Doc said, "I sat here and closed my eyes for a while, and when I opened them, Anna's eyes opened wide like she saw her Maker, and then they closed, and then her spirit left her body."

"Anna spent her life near God," Marka choked on her tears.

"I'll call the coroner now," Doc said. There were tears in his eyes.

Marka's fingers shook as she dialed George's number. "George, Anna just died. Can you come over?"

George responded, "I'm on my way."

Marka said, "Thanks." Marka sat in the rocker with Jacob waiting for George. He came right over.

News traveled quickly in Ridley, and soon, Reverend Thurber was at the door. "Anna made all the arrangements for her funeral ahead of time," he said. "After Sophie passed away, she told me what she wanted for the church service. She had it all set up with the funeral home in Clayton. She even has a cemetery plot paid for. Oh, and she gave me her last will and testament."

Marka sat stone-faced. She didn't know what to say.

"Anna told me all about her child," Reverend Thurber said. She wants her headstone to read: Mother of Jacob.

Jack caught the plane to Rapid City the next day.

Marka ordered a spray of flowers for the casket. Ruby said that she wanted to gather flowers from Anna's garden and make some arrangements for the altar of the church.

Marka told her, "That would be nice."

The morning of the funeral, Marka brushed her hair back into a bun, and then looked through one of her mother's hat boxes. She cried when she remembered how Anna persuaded her to keep them. She picked a black one with a peek-a-boo veil. She pulled the veil down over her swollen, red eyes. Her body felt cold; heaviness descended over her.

Every pew in the church was filled and people had to stand in the back of the building. Tillie, Anna's niece came to the funeral. Even farmers took time from their work in the fields to come.

Ida Mae sang *Amazing Grace,* because it was a favorite of Anna's. Marka told her about the time Anna said, "I want Ida to sing at my funeral." Ida stood with her hands behind her back and cleared her throat a bit as Katie played the interlude. Then she drew a deep breath and closed her eyes. The words floated across the room: "Amazing grace, how sweet the sound, that saved a wretch like me! I once was lost, but now am found; was blind, but now I see." Ida's beautiful soprano voice resonated through the church.

Reverend Thurber stood behind the podium. "One day, Anna and I were talking and she referred to herself as an old fool," he said. "I told her that if she were any kind of a fool, she was God's fool, for she always kept true to what she believed about Him."

Marka thought of Anna and how her eyes would twinkle when she was happy. How her house had a Sunday dinner smell, how Anna always called her *madchen*. Marka hunched her shoulders and dropped her head. Anna always seemed so sure of what her life was about. She knew who she was; she knew what she cared about. She loved the people of Ridley even when she didn't agree with them. Anna's words wove themselves through Marka's mind to the fragile places in her heart. Anna had once said, "The Lord didn't put us here to just eat and drink. We are here to make the world a better place. We are here to do good deeds, and the Lord takes us out when He wants to. Guess that's why we better live each day to its fullest."

Reverend Thurber said, "Anna is gone from our midst, but she will always live in our hearts. She was generous and did good deeds for the people of Ridley. Anna, part of the fabric of this town, was born in Russia in 1882. When she was eleven years old, her family came to America. Her family worked sugar beets in the area. Her mother died, leaving Anna, her father, and her sister, Rachel. Anna cooked at the school, and the dormitory, and she was a seamstress. Anna and I talked about many things, and one thing I feel certain of—Anna is with the Lord. How often she told me how much she loved you, Marka."

Reverend Thurber ended the service with these words: "Jesus said, 'Do not be afraid. I've been to heaven, now I'm back. And I'm here to tell you that there is a place that has been prepared for you after you die.'"

Marka wiped the tears from her eyes. She recalled the day when she was a small child and brought a dead bird to Anna. Anna went to her bedroom and came out with one of her special embroidered handkerchiefs. She wrapped the stiff bird in it, and took Marka by the hand and led her outside. They dug a hole under the branches of a peony bush. Anna laid the bird in the hole and covered it up with dirt. Then, she said the Lord's Prayer.

"Anna, why do things die?"

"Everything must die. Plants, animals, birds, and people, but God has a very special place for all of them. He has a special place for birds."

Marka held Jacob close and felt a burning pain that he would never know his Great Aunt Anna.

The ushers removed the spray of flowers from the casket and lifted the lid for the viewing of Anna's body.

"Let me hold the baby while you go up," Jack said.

"No," Marka shook her head. "I want to take him. Come with me."

She was the first to pass by the casket. Tears streamed down her cheeks and her body trembled with sadness. It's not Anna in this satin-lined coffin. It didn't look like her. It is only the shell that had housed her soul. Her spirit had gone home. Marka felt her legs giving out and swayed to one side.

Jack steadied her. "Stay as long as you want. I'll be right beside you."

Bodie and Buddy walked up and passed by the casket. Carl lingered and began to sob. Buddy took him by the arm and led him out of the church. Marka's felt her heart rip open.

Marka took hold of Jack's arm. "I'm ready to go now," she said.

Marka couldn't grasp the idea that Anna was gone. After the service, people expressed their condolences, and said that it was good that Anna didn't suffer, that she went in her sleep. All Marka could think about was that Anna was gone, and she would never see her again.

Anna was buried in the Clayton cemetery. There was no plot available beside baby Jacob; she had to be buried in the newer section, but it was not far away. Anna's casket was lowered into the ground. Reverend Thurber picked up a handful of dirt and handed it to Marka. She tossed it on the casket. The sky darkened and clouds covered the sun.

"All this is done to cause us to think of our own resurrection," Reverend Thurber said. "Like putting a bulb into the ground, we look forward to spring when it will grow into a beautiful flower."

After everyone had left the cemetery, Marka carried her baby over to the light-colored, sandstone marker with a swan etched into it. Someday, she would tell Jack about Anna and *her* baby. She needed to. There was no shame.

Marka had made arrangements for a dark marble headstone to be placed on Anna's grave in the fall when the ground had settled.

A plant leaves a seed to bring forth a new life for another generation. But there were no children or grandchildren to keep Anna's memory alive. Marka promised herself she would tell her son all about Anna.

CHAPTER 41

The day after the funeral, Jack flew back to Florida. Marka got out of bed and tiptoed over to the crib. She lifted the blanket to check on the baby. Jacob was so still. She touched his cheek, and he moved. Jacob must be exhausted, Marka thought. Poor darling; everyone wanted to hold him and tickle his cheeks. She thought perhaps it was their need to touch this new life; a way to distract them from the loss of Anna.

A deep sadness gripped Marka. Anna was gone, and her life without Anna would never be the same. No matter what happened from here on, Anna would not be a part of things. How she longed to talk to Anna, to touch her. No more Anna in the kitchen before daylight building a fire. No Anna to make sure the food was on the table before Paul Harvey came on. Who would make sure that Marka always did her washing on Mondays? No more Anna to talk with, to laugh with, to sit and be silent with.

No Anna to see Jacob grow and walk and talk. What about all the things they wanted to do with the baby? Marka thought of the way Anna and Jacob looked at each other. They seemed to have an understanding, a language that only the two of them spoke. She thought of the day she took a picture of them and how the flashbulb had made Jacob flinch. Oh, why did Anna have to die just when she had a child to love? For all those years Anna grieved for her own child and she couldn't tell anyone. She kept everything inside. Marka swallowed the lump in her throat. Life can be unfair.

Marka scolded herself for letting Anna work so long in the garden that day. "It's too hot to work out here," she had said. But, Anna had said, "I'm a tough old bird. Don't worry about me."

Marka still agonized over that day. Anna had taken more rest breaks than usual. She should have suspected something was wrong.

Marka went to the kitchen and rearranged the pies and cakes on the table. After the funeral reception, the leftover food was brought to the house. The refrigerator was full of Pyrex dishes and bowls covered with cellophane. Marka noticed a brown paper bag sitting on the cupboard and opened it. Inside was a girdle and nylons.

She remembered Millie asking her, "Got something to put my girdle in? It's killing me." Marka thought how Millie always made her laugh.

After the funeral service, the men sat outside under the shade trees and drank coke spiked with whiskey. The women sat in the house, drank ice tea, and praised Marka for her strength. She was holding up so well.

Ruby called her aside and told her that was rubbish. "Go ahead and cry if you want to, Mia."

In the weeks that followed, Marka was grateful for her friends. Millie called every day to check on her. Marka told her that Sasha had disappeared and Millie said, "I'll keep an eye open for her, and if you need someone to watch the baby, let me know."

George told her, "I am the proudest grandfather in the county. You have made me very happy, because I have something I've always wanted, a family." George said that he thought Anna was one of the most remarkable women he had ever known.

"She lived life on her own terms," Marka told him.

Whenever Marka told Bodie she felt angry because Anna was gone, he told her she should work in the garden. "Anna wouldn't want her garden to die," he'd say. Twice a week, he showed up at Marka's door, usually around 8:00 a.m. when it was still cool enough for them to work in the garden. Marka thought how Bodie had turned out to be a responsible man. He had his own house, and he was out from under his father's thumb.

Millie told her that she had given up on going to dances, that she and Bodie had been going to the movies together. "Bodie is helping me make a new sign for the cafe. I'm finally getting around to changing the name from Millie's Cafe to Four Seasons Café."

I guess Millie realizes she will be lonesome when Ida goes off to designer school in the fall.

And Ruby was there to hold her close when she felt numb and ripped apart. Marka talked to her about all of the conflicts she and Anna had when she first got to Ridley. She told her that Anna had shared many things about their German Russian heritage and what they had to do to survive.

"I did have legitimate complaints about my childhood, but Anna helped me to see that my parents did their best. The conditions of their marriage made their lives difficult."

Ruby assured her that she would get past the grieving for Anna. "We never forget them, but we have to learn to go on without them," she said. "Remember when I showed you the portrait of Henry and said that I finally got the eyes right? I think I felt guilty for loving him. Like, I turned my back on my people. A Gypsy is supposed to remain faithful to her clan. I am free from the guilt. Henry was good to me. We had a good life. Neither of us always had to have our own way. Remember that, Mia."

"Ruby, what do you believe about death? Where do you think Anna is right now?"

"I think death is like this." Ruby said. "There is a candle burning—that is life. When the candle goes out, smoke filters through the air and goes somewhere. Then, the candle is cold."

"I had a dream about Anna," Marka said. "I dreamed that Anna was standing in my bedroom in the dim light looking as she always did in her flowered house dress and apron. I said, 'Is that you, Anna?' Anna touched my hand and took a hanky out of her apron pocket and placed it on my pillow. In the morning, I awakened and as I climbed out of bed, a white cotton cloth with pansies embroidered in one corner dropped to the floor. Am I going crazy? Was it a dream or wishful thinking?"

"It's a Gypsy custom to put food on the grave of a dead person for a while to appease them. Their ghosts can come back."

"Ruby, do you believe in God?"

"I believe the Divine gives me the freedom to choose. I am not bound by any rules, and yes I do."

Every night, Marka talked to her baby as she rocked him to sleep. She hugged his small, soft body and kissed his satin cheeks. She told him that he brought joy to her life, and how she had hopes and dreams for their future.

"Your daddy has found us a house, and we will soon be moving to Florida, my little darling." Tears streamed down her cheeks as she thought of Anna holding Jacob close and remarking that he smelled as sweet as lilac perfume.

"I love you Anna, and I always will," Marka said as she laid Jacob down in his crib.

CHAPTER 42

Marka stood on the bridge looking down on the river. Birds swept to the water's edge and momentary gusts of wind stirred the leaves of the cottonwoods. She thought she heard the trees and the clouds singing. Marka held her arms extended toward the sky and opened her palms. She felt alive, and truly free.

A river is always going somewhere, she thought. It comes from a place and has a destination. It winds and curves, laughs and weeps. It has a life of its own. Marka leaned against the cool metal frame of the bridge as memories of the past year moved within her like the free-flowing water.

So much had happened. When she arrived in Ridley, she didn't understand why she felt and acted the way she had. She wondered why she didn't know herself very well. She had been blind to her heart and mind and the truth about herself. She had made poor choices. She had grown up a desolate child caught in a world of fear and shame, because her parents were at war with each other.

And, why had she always felt the need to come back to Ridley? Was it because she did need to revisit old memories? She did need to feel the anger and sadness?

When she left Denver, she was determined to return to Ridley and make a life for herself. Was it like the geese going south in the winter and returning home in the spring? George had told her, "Geese have instincts; we humans sometimes cannot explain the actions we take. We feel motivated to do things, and we don't always understand the reasons why."

Marka had taken a hard look at herself. She had looked inward; she had examined her feelings, but mostly, she looked outward; she looked at how others reacted to her and her behaviors.

Anna had helped her to see many things about herself. Anna told her that lack of forgiveness would destroy a person's spirit. She thought about what she had learned from Anna about her ancestry. Anna found pride in being German Russian, and Marka thought she was beginning to. She didn't know what the future held for her and her people where the Cold War was concerned, but she felt strong and secure. No matter what happened, she knew she would be all right.

Marka had received a sympathy card from Jonny. He was spending the summer in Texas with his mother.

Then there was Ruby, who always told her, "You need to make peace with your past. Then, you will find freedom from the ghosts that have haunted you."

When Marka told Ruby that she had finally felt that peace, Ruby had to get the last words in when they parted. She told Marka, "What you choose to do with your life is who you are, and when you know who you are, you are free. And remember this, Mia. To live is to give your heart away. To love is to give yourself away."

Marka had hidden from the truth. She only saw what she wanted to see. She couldn't live a full life being a stranger to herself. Anna had said, "Just as this house sat in ruins, you've let anger and resentment towards your parents cripple your soul."

When Marka told Buddy good-bye, he told her he made an offer on the Nettleson place. He planned to raise sugar beets. Buddy told her that he tried to talk his father into moving out there with him, but Carl wanted to stay in town and run the store.

She had said her good-byes to Millie, Ida, Bodie, and Reverend Thurber. She told the Reverend, "Yes, I do need God in my life."

And then there was George. It was one of the hardest things she had ever had to do, to tell him good-bye. George, the man she loved most in the world next to Jack. He hugged her and held her and had tears in his eyes. Just when he and Jack had found each other, they had to part. George promised to visit them in Florida.

In her will, Anna left her house to Marka. Marka's cousin, Tillie, would be moving to Ridley, because ranch life had taken its toll on her. Marka wanted her to live in the house as long as she wanted.

Marka handed her the keys to the house, and Tillie said, "Anna wouldn't want you to grieve for her. She'd want you to be happy."

The sunset was turning to gold and red, and was reflecting off the flowing water. A car drove across the bridge and parked by the side of the road. Jack walked towards her carrying baby Jacob. He kissed her, and the three of them stood on the bridge one last time. She felt their warmth.

"Everything is packed in the car. Are you ready to leave?" Jack asked.

"Yes." Marka said. "Now, I can leave Ridley with a peaceful heart."

AUTHOR'S NOTE

The Germans from Russia have a compelling history.

Catherine the Great of Russia, lured thousands of German people with her Manifesto of 1763, a document that granted freedom of religion, release from all taxes for 30 years, and assurance that they would not have to serve in the Russian military for 100 years. An estimated 26,000 German people made their way to the steppes of Russia between the years 1764-1767. They held to their traditions and beliefs.

In 1876, Czar Alexander II revoked the exemption from military duty, prompting immigration to the United States, Canada, Argentina, and Brazil. Those who remained in Russia suffered. Severe famines struck in the years 1891-92, 1921-22, and in 1931-32.

When Hitler invaded Russia in 1941, there were 605,500 ethnic Germans living in the Volga area of Russia. Stalin proclaimed these people to be enemies of the state; loaded them into cattle cars and shipped them to Siberia and Kazakhstan. They were sent to the Gulag, work camps. The Volga colonies disappeared.

The Germans from Russia have been subjected to harassment on two fronts since their immigration to the United States. First, during World War II for being German, the FBI was looking for fascist sympathizers. Second, during the McCarthy era, for being Russian, anyone suspected of being a member of any socialist type of group was arrested and charged with being a communist.

Since 1990, with the collapse of the Soviet Union, over four million emigrants have been allowed to leave and resettle in Germany. They are called Aussiedler. It has been estimated that there are six million descendants in the United States and Canada.

READERS GUIDE

1. During the course of the story, Marka struggles with life and herself. Does understanding her German Russian roots help her? Does living in the small town she grew up in help her or hinder her?

2. Marka finds herself attracted to an old high school classmate. Does she make the same mistake she made in Denver? Is she trying to get even with Stella?

3. Were Anna's fears about Senator McCarthy's witch hunt valid?

4. Why do Marka and Millie both have a problem with men?

5. What does the novel say about children who have issues with their parents? Why is forgiveness important to moving on with your life?

6. Why does Marka strike up a friendship with Ruby even though Anna warns her that Ruby is a Gypsy and cannot be trusted? Is it because she feels safe with Ruby? That she can share her feelings, be heard, and validated? How does learning to forgive help Marka?

7. What are some of the challenges of living in a small town? Do all small towns have gossip mills and competition?

8.   There are similarities between Anna and Ruby. How are they similar in the way they regard their culture? What guilt do they carry?

9.   Freedom is one of the themes in the story. Those who left Russia before the Revolution are "free" to live their lives in America. Why then is Marka not free to be her own person? Why doesn't she know herself very well?

10.   In the novel, what draws Marka and Jack together? If Jack had received Marka's letter, how might things have been different?

11.   In your opinion, what is the main lesson the novel showed you?

12.   Why does Judy end the story the way she does?

Judy Frothinger, the daughter of German Russian immigrants, was born and raised in western South Dakota. Judy's father was born in Omsk, Siberia, Russia, where her grandfather was a schoolteacher. Judy's mother was born in Canada, after the family emigrated from the Volga region of Russia.

Judy has a degree in Psychology from Sonoma State University in California. She has pursued writing with a goal of preserving the history of her people. She is a three-time winner of Storytelling Contests of the American Historical Society of Germans from Russia. She lives in Santa Rosa, California, with her husband, Mike.

Contact Judy at: jfrothinger@gmail.com

Web site http://www.judyfrothinger.com

Made in the USA
Charleston, SC
12 August 2011